The
Astronomer

ALSO BY
LAWRENCE GOLDSTONE

NONFICTION

Birdmen

Drive

Going Deep

Dark Bargain

The Activist

Inherently Unequal

FICTION

Anatomy of Deception

Deadly Cure

The Astronomer

LAWRENCE GOLDSTONE

PEGASUS BOOKS
NEW YORK LONDON

THE ASTRONOMER

Pegasus Books Ltd
148 West 37th Street, 13th Floor
New York, NY 10018

Copyright © 2017 by Lawrence Goldstone

First Pegasus Books hardcover edition November 2017

ISBN: 978-1-68177-551-7

10 9 8 7 6 5 4 3 2 1

Printed in the United States of America
Distributed by W. W. Norton & Company, Inc.

Historical Note

February 1, 1534

Seventeen years have passed since an obscure German monk named Martin Luther posted his Ninety-five Theses on the door of a Wittenberg church. His denunciation of Catholic excess has spawned a new religion, which has spread across Europe, challenging the old order. Theology has spilled over into politics, with wars of territory fought in the name of Catholics or Reformers. François I, king of France, is pivotal in the struggle for the soul of Europe but dallies in his religious commitment, more concerned with defeating his nemesis, the Holy Roman Emperor Charles V. England's Henry VIII, while capturing the popular imagination with his marital intrigues, is but a secondary player in the overall drama.

In science, new learning on all fronts threatens to overwhelm dogma. Traditional, Church-approved theories of geography, anatomy, medicine, chemistry, and especially astronomy are all under intense pressure from men who insist that human knowledge is separate from the Church.

Inevitably, science, politics, and religion will clash. The result will change the world.

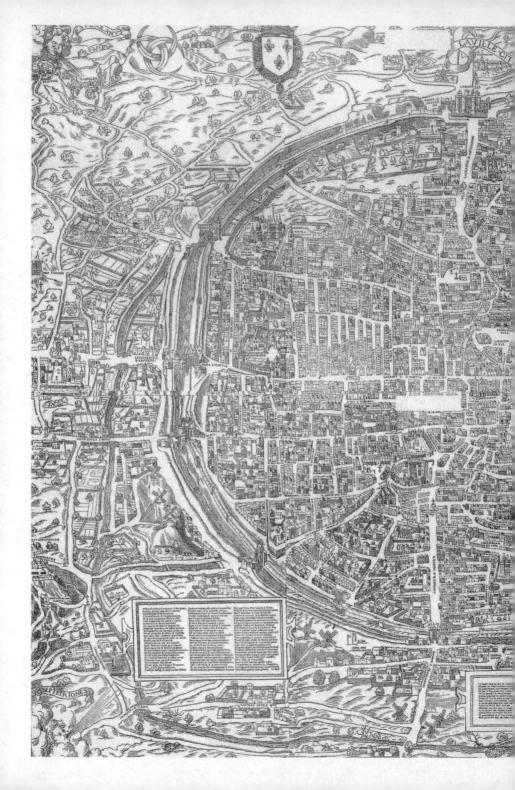

Paris, 1534

I

Paris, La Ville. February 19, 1534

THE GAUNT MAN in the gray robes of a Franciscan friar walked the chill streets for most of the day, the coarse wool of his cloak bristling against his legs and his sandals echoing a soft clack-clack on the stone. He certainly looked the mendicant, all hollow cheeks, stubble, and deep-set eyes, and thus experienced little difficulty in arousing the guilt of the many stylish Parisians who passed him by. As the late-winter sun dipped below the towers of the Louvre, Frère Jean-Marie, as he called himself, had taken in the princely sum of ten silver francs. He deposited the munificence in the *boîte des pauvres*, the poor box, in église des Celestins. The needy, after all, were the needy, even if they were Catholic.

When the last traces of daylight had vanished, the *Franciscain* ventured to rue des Bales to choose the most strategic location for his vigil. He had hoped to scrutinize the comings and goings from the safety of shadows, but the moon was full in a cloudless sky. At last he settled on a niche next to the doorway of a tavern at the bend of the street on the southern side. He was visible, but at least his features would remain indistinct in the reflected moonlight.

The *Franciscain* squatted, his back against the cold stone of the wall,

1

and extended his begging bowl in front of him. The paving stones inclined downward from the buildings to form a crude drain at the center of the street. The smell of waste, both animal and human, permeated the air. After a few moments, his thighs began to burn. A lance of pain shot through his knees each time he shifted his weight. Five years before, when Frère Jean-Marie was not simply a *nom de guerre*, he had often remained in this position, without relief, for as long as eight hours. Such a fool he had been, he thought, begging for alms while the elders grew fat.

By reflex, his hand started to the tingling bare spot at the crown of his skull, the tonsure he had shaved the previous day. He quickly jerked it back. Followers of Saint Francis were inured to the tonsure. Rubbing might be a small thing, but small things were noticed. Even here, he might be the observed as well as the observer. Any misstep could mean betrayal to the Inquisition, and then imprisonment, torture, and slow roasting at the stake.

But he had chosen well. A steady flow of traffic to and from the tavern camouflaged what appeared to be just another of the Lord's beggars attempting to capitalize on the shame of Christians about to break the Commandments. In less than an hour, he noted with irony, four more coins had been dropped into his bowl.

Finally, on the opposite side of the street, the door to the shop opened. The boy who emerged appeared slight, fragile, as if he might be carried away by a gust of wind. The hose, short doublet, cape, and soft cap he was wearing hung on him, as though borrowed and not his own. The friar ran a hand across his cheek. He had not been told he would be following a child.

As the door closed, the boy glanced nervously up and down the street. After a moment, he stepped out gingerly, and then, gathering himself, turned left, away from where the friar had established his post.

The *Franciscain* left the coins from his bowl on the street lest they jingle in his cloak, then forced himself stiffly to his feet, taking care not to appear hurried. Measuring the distance between himself and the youth, he set off in the same direction, remaining on the opposite side of the street.

The boy proceeded apace but then stopped abruptly at the corner. He felt at his sides, seeming to have forgotten something. This gave him the excuse to turn about and check behind. The friar continued to walk up the road, his empty bowl extended to three revelers who were at that moment fortuitously heading for the tavern. Feeling the boy's eyes on him, Frère Jean-Marie stepped in front of the three and pushed the bowl aggressively at the man in the middle. The man was thickset and bearded, in the manner of King François, who was famous throughout France for his beard.

"For God's grace," the friar brayed, his bowl practically under the man's chin.

"God's grace, indeed," the bearded man replied angrily. His breath smelled of sausage and cheap wine. "A body cannot walk four paces in this city without one of you offering God's grace. As long as it's paid for, of course." The *Franciscain* did not move. "Oh, all right," the man sniffed, "here . . ." He pulled a tiny coin from his purse. "God's grace will be cheap tonight," he grunted. He dropped the coin in the bowl and maneuvered around the friar as his friends did likewise.

Only after they had passed him did Frère Jean-Marie look up. The boy in the cape was gone.

The friar was certain he would have noticed had the boy crossed the road to go left. Frère Jean-Marie hurried to the corner and looked to the right. Candlelight seeped from the windows, illuminating his quarry scurrying away in small, quick steps. The friar followed at a distance, staying close to the buildings to remain in shadow. The boy at first made a number of twists and turns onto side streets, glancing over his shoulder. But soon he straightened his route and ceased to look back.

It occurred to Frère Jean-Marie that the boy was feeling the same dread, the same intensity to have the episode done with as was he. The boy, he decided, had spent so much time exercising total vigilance that now, with completion so close at hand, he was desperate for these last few moments to pass. Desperation bred a need for speed. Speed bred carelessness.

The friar was thus able to close the distance between them as they neared le Monastère des Religieuses de Zion. He exploded in perspiration.

His cloak clung to him, the cold, bristly wool prickling in a thousand places against his skin.

The boy picked up his pace. When he reached the corner of the ancient monastery, he spun on his heel and turned right on grand rue Saint-Denis.

The friar turned into an alley that would lead him to where he might intercept the boy. Just short of breaking into a run, Frère Jean-Marie reached the wide boulevard just before his quarry emerged from the shadows. He took a position that would require the boy to pass in front of him and extended his begging bowl.

The friar waited until the youth was almost upon him, and then said in Latin, softly but in a manner that would command attention, "*Subsiste, frater!* Halt, brother!" The youth froze. "Go no further, if you value your life." Then, in a louder voice, in French: "Sir, for God's grace . . ." Frère Jean-Marie shoved his bowl under the boy's chin.

The youth remained rigid. He was dark haired, with just a sparse frill of whiskers; handsome but unformed, like a sculpture not quite finished. His eyes fixed on the figure of the friar before him. A quiver appeared on his upper lip.

Frère Jean-Marie kept his bowl extended, staring into the boy's eyes. The boy nodded finally and fumbled in his purse for some coins. When he leaned forward to place them in the bowl, the friar whispered sharply, again in Latin, "*Tu proditus es*": "You have been betrayed."

The boy's eyes flitted from side to side. His breathing was audible in the night air.

"I have been sent to help," Frère Jean-Marie whispered. "You will not reach your destination alive unless you come with me."

"Betrayed by whom?" The boy's voice squeaked, high-pitched.

"Philippe Sévrier," Frère Jean-Marie replied, blurting out the first name that came into his head. "A spy at the college."

"I don't know any Philippe Sévrier," the boy protested. He was frightened of heeding the friar and frightened of ignoring him.

"But he knows you," said the friar, getting quickly to his feet. "The meeting has been changed. I'm Frère Jean-Marie. I'm to take you by a safe route. You can give your communication then. You have it, yes?"

The boy patted his doublet. Frère Jean-Marie took one step back to the north. The boy did not move. This was the moment—would the boy give in to authority and follow or, because of suspicion, fear, or just ordinary stubbornness, refuse and continue along his original route? The youth teetered on the possibilities as the friar stood, his hand outstretched, as if offered to a drowning man.

I've lost him, the friar thought. But then, no. The boy strode after him.

"We must hurry," whispered Frère Jean-Marie as they moved east, away from the foot traffic. "Our enemies are near."

They passed into darkened streets. The friar felt a tug on his cloak.

"Where are we going?" the boy asked. "This is the wrong way."

"We are going to enclos du Temple," the friar said sharply, cocking his head in the direction of the complex that held the great fortress of the Knights Templar. Without waiting for a reply, the friar resumed walking. "Magister Ory himself awaits you."

"Magister Ory? At the Temple? Why?" The boy, having ceded prerogative, hustled along, whispering, as if to cement the conspiracy. "How did he find out?"

Frère Jean-Marie did not break stride. "The heretic dog Sévrier was persuaded to confess. It is lucky for you that he did." They had come to a small, narrow street. The friar turned in. "Quickly," he said, "in here. It leads directly to our destination."

The boy hesitated only a fraction of a second before following. Frère Jean-Marie had steeled himself for what had to come next, but nonetheless felt his heart beating so rapidly that it felt as though it would explode from his chest. I must do it, he thought. Now.

The friar spun. Before the boy could see the dagger that had been concealed in the sleeve of his cloak, Frère Jean-Marie had plunged it into his abdomen, just below the breastbone. The friar withdrew and struck again, in almost the same spot.

Blood, warm and syrupy, spread over the friar's hand and wrist. The boy, his eyes wide and uncomprehending, reeled back against the wall. He opened his mouth to cry out, but all that came forth was a soft gurgle.

The boy shook his head feebly once or twice, then slid slowly to the ground. Within seconds, he was dead.

Frère Jean-Marie stared, partly in horror, partly in wonder, at what he had done. Then he glanced up and down the alley. There was no one, but exposure could come at any second. He reached frantically into the boy's doublet. There were the two sheaves wrapped in oilcloth. The smaller had been given to the boy at the shop. The larger contained the great secret, the discovery that would change Christianity forever.

The friar removed both packets. Blood covered the wrappers. They were sticky to the touch. The friar jammed the parcels into his sleeve where the dagger had been. He stood and checked once more to the left and right. Still no one. No sound. He had the vague feeling of having forgotten something, but could not think what. The friar stuffed his gore-soaked right hand into his left sleeve and walked quickly from the alley in the opposite direction from the way he had entered. If he could make it to the street, he would be safe.

At the end of the alley, he peered out. God was with him. The road was deserted. He stepped out and made his way north. A huge breath escaped him as he passed into Saint-Antoine. He could leave this filthy city in safety. He had passed his mission unobserved.

Or so he thought.

II

Université de Paris, Collège de Montaigu, February 20, 1534

AMAURY DE FAVERGES grasped the icy metal door handle and then leaned gently against the cracked, pitted wood. A squeal of rusted hinges could betray him as quickly as a sentry. Flogging and a month in isolation on prayer, bread, and water in a bleak, airless, unheated cell would follow. But God was with him and the door gave way. Slowly and silently, Amaury pushed it open just wide enough to squeeze through. He had been dubious when Bernard, by all appearances nothing more than an amiable half-wit, had been recommended as an utterly reliable accomplice. But Giles had been correct. If Bernard was paid to see that a lock was disengaged at two hours after midnight, disengaged it would be. Four months and Bernard had not failed him once.

Amaury stepped inside and peered about. No one. He swung the door shut, set the bolt, then padded to the archway that led to the sleeping quarters. Amaury opened the sixth door on the right, again unlocked, with hinges he had greased himself. Only when the door closed behind him did he breathe easy.

He surveyed the cubicle that had been his home for nine years, sighed, and flopped down on the straw bed, poked and prodded by errant shafts.

There would be scant time to sleep before he was required at morning prayers.

To put himself in such peril, he thought. Simply to read a book.

Two hours later, Amaury stood in the same dank archway. This time he held a hooded candle in front of him. His empty belly roiled and his eyelids throbbed. But there would be no food for seven hours and no sleep for fifteen. He would spend this day like every other day, in prayer and endless disputation. If his eyelids drooped, even for a few seconds, the leather straps would crack across his back.

The moon had vanished, replaced by a cold late-winter rain—*pleut de Paris*. Students abhorred the *demi-saison*—too warm for the ground to freeze, but sufficiently cold for the mud to feel like ice when it oozed over the soles of their sandals. The chapel was easily reached through the passageways, but the college doctors, the magisters, had decreed that inclement weather was God's will. Students were therefore required to walk across the open courtyard. The magisters, of course, kept under shelter.

Amaury suddenly felt a wave of dizziness and grasped the wall for support. Oh, God. To be back outside these walls, in his tiny rented room, exploring the wonders of the heavens—Aristotle's logical formulations and Ptolemy's inspired description of the Lord's astral creations moving around the Earth, embedded in imperceptible spheres. Or pondering the German physician Paracelsus's notion that disease was caused not by imbalance in the humors but by outside agents. Perhaps even to be able to observe a dissection at the school of medicine, where a new theory of human anatomy seemed poised to overthrow a millennium of ignorance.

But instead, Amaury de Faverges languished at Collège de Montaigu. Where learning was beaten in. How could anyone suppose that true education was attained through pain, deprivation, and forced devotion? That intimidation and abuse brought one closer to God? Yet that was most certainly what the Church fathers did believe. For they had chosen Montaigu, one of the smallest of the forty-two colleges that comprised the University of Paris, to be perhaps the most important center of ecclesiastical education in the Christian world.

Amaury gazed about. The very setting doused illusions of learning. Montaigu was housed in a squalid, centuries-old, three-story stone quadrangle erected around a miasmic courtyard. Green moss covered the roof, giving the configuration the feel of some great bog. The entrance was on rue Saint-Symphorien, a narrow, refuse-strewn thoroughfare also called rue des Chiens—the Street of Dogs. When Amaury arrived to begin his studies nine years before, he had been forced to pick his way along this open sewer to reach the main gate. Once inside, the stink of rot and human waste that covered the college like a shroud hit him full on, but the students scurrying in their hooded robes between the chapel, their bare stone rooms, and the grim classrooms seemed impervious. Amaury had learned to wear the same mask, but was never unaware of his misery.

But while dismal sobriety was prerequisite within the walls, outside they snickered. The great wit and scholar Erasmus, who had fled after a single year as a student here, described Montaigu as a "filthy, bleak barrack, clotted with dirt and reeking of the foulest smells." Rabelais called it *Collège de pouillerie*—college of filth. But for once, neither Erasmus nor Rabelais had been able to outdo ordinary Parisians. On the streets of the city, Montaigu was commonly known as "the very cleft between the buttocks of Mother Theology."

Crushed in that cleft, Amaury toiled, enduring beatings, feculence, lice, deprivation of sleep, terrible food, and trivial disputations. All to attain a position of "honor." To become one of the doctors himself, a *magister in theologia*. To wipe away the stain of his birth.

And there were still six years to go.

Amaury could put the moment off no longer. He was about to step out into the muck when he felt fingers digging into his shoulder. He flinched, then spun about. Magister Ravenau stood before him, expressionless and forbidding.

Had Amaury's absence been noticed after all? Perhaps it was nothing more than the few seconds of idleness in the archway. Ravenau reveled in dispensing discipline, either in God's name or his own. So severe were his ministrations that, during his last beating, Amaury had almost cried out. The first time in five years. He had bit down on the side of his cheek,

determined to deny Ravenau the satisfaction. When Ravenau had finished, Amaury swallowed the blood that filled his mouth.

Amaury stood stolidly in the cold and awaited the sentence. He hated
the beatings. Not so much for the pain but for the humiliation of sub-
mitting to abominations like Ravenau. Of abdicating his will.

But there was to be no sentence. At least not yet. Ravenau had come
with a summons. Amaury was to report to the syndic's rooms immediately. Le Clerc. The head of the college.

Amaury slogged across the courtyard, the frigid droplets stinging his
skin. The syndic's chambers were on the top floor. Hunger and lack of
sleep made the exertion of two flights of stairs near exhausting. He
paused at the top, his temples pulsing in a dull, regular drumbeat. To
the left of the hallway, a series of open vaults overlooked the courtyard.
The entrances to the living quarters of the doctors were on the street side
to the right. Three candles set in sconces along the right wall crackled,
burned to their last bits of tallow, providing only bursts of illumination
as they sizzled to extinction in the coming dawn.

At least this summons had not come three months earlier. If it had,
Amaury would not be facing the ineffectual Le Clerc, but rather Noël
Beda. Ascetic, unyielding, ever-righteous, soul-flaying Beda. A law unto
himself. Beda, who had ordered men burned at the stake without consult-
ing pope or king. But Beda, thank the Lord, had derided François' authority once too often. After more than a decade of devout autocracy,
Beda was finally gone. Probably dead. Le Clerc was mean and vindictive,
it was true, but also pompous, vain, and fat. No half-herring, rotting-egg,
stale-bread dinners for him. The new syndic was a man on whom no student feared foisting a whispered jibe. No one had ever made light of Beda.

Amaury blew out his own candle to preserve the remaining tallow.
The sound of his breathing echoed softly off the stone. Even with one
side open, the smell of mildew hung in the walkway. The heavy door was
closed when Amaury arrived. He placed his candle on the small table
next to the door, then rapped on the thick, darkened oak, as austere as
the magisters whose privacy it ensured. His knuckles felt the scrape of
hewn wood. He heard a metallic grate as the catch bolt was disengaged,

then the door swung open to reveal Guillaume, Beda's—now Le Clerc's—ancient servant. Guillaume had likely been tall as a younger man but was now stooped and haggard, unshaven, virtually toothless, but with quick rat's eyes and, it was suspected among the students, ears to match. More than once during Amaury's tenure, the masters had acquired knowledge of whispered conversations held in the deepest secrecy.

Guillaume shuffled to one side. Amaury had never before entered these rooms. Inside were polished stone floors unadorned by carpets, and unpainted vaulted roof beams, oak like the door. The stone walls were largely bare, save for a case of books on the right. The books were old, folios, penned by scribes. No printed works here. The syndics lived for the past. A lectern for reading stood at the far end of the room under two small, plain windows. A pair of hard wooden chairs without cushions was set opposite the fireplace on the right, and a doorway on the left led to the master's private chambers. Two candles, one on each wall, these freshly changed, provided muted light.

The room was empty aside from Guillaume. Amaury took two steps in and waited. No fire burned in the grate. A chill even more penetrating than that in the courtyard had settled in the room. He heard the door close behind him. Guillaume, who ordinarily was privy to every confidence, had not remained. Amaury waited. Finally, he heard shuffling in the other room, and then the sound of sandals on stone. Seconds later, the door creaked open and a figure emerged.

Passing through the doorway was not the fleshy Le Clerc, but rather, his face frozen in piety and perpetual accusation, the glowering figure of Noël Beda.

III

Beda! He was back. How was it possible? He had been arrested and exiled by the king himself. A sentence of death was said to have been applied by royal edict. And yet here he was, standing in his old rooms, the very personification of a wrathful God. Had he returned with François' permission or in violation of the king's order?

Tall and cadaverous, with a long, hooked nose and thin, bloodless lips, Beda moved slowly across the room, his arms buried to the elbow in the opposite sleeves of a maroon robe pulled in at the waist with a knotted ocher sash. He stopped at the near side of the lectern and turned to face Amaury straight on. His hair was white under a black peaked skullcap, his skin pallid, almost translucent, but his eyes—those eyes, which students said could peer into one's very soul—appeared almost black in the flickering candlelight. At first he made no movement or sound. Amaury found it impossible to detect his breathing. The effect was awe inspiring, supernatural.

A second man entered from the private chambers, his robe black, tied with a black sash. He was younger than Beda, shorter, fuller without being thickset. He had even, almost handsome features, his face placid,

12

unlined. The face of a man who discharged his duty without compunction or guilt. His mien might have been pleasing, even soothing, if not for the fact that his duty was often to order men and women to imprisonment, torture, or agonizing death.

Ory. The Inquisitor. Amaury knew him from the sermons he had preached at Montaigu. Sermons warning of the perils of flouting orthodoxy. Tales of branding, of hacked-out tongues, of slow burning at the stake.

Beda began to speak. "You are surprised to see me," he said, his voice grown even more raspy since his exile. His lips moved only slightly, yet his words were clear and seemed to fill the room. "Perhaps you thought a mere king could overrule the will of God?" He paused and drew in a breath. "I have been charged with the stewardship of this faculty for thirteen years, a time when the Church has come under its greatest threat since our Lord Jesus Christ died to establish the True Religion. To protect our Catholic Church from those who would destroy it is a task that requires constant vigilance and my every energy. I work to neither king nor pope, but to God alone. Perhaps you think me extreme?"

"No, Magister, the Church needs you," Amaury said firmly. Students had died from Beda-ordered floggings.

"There exists a disease in the world of Man," Beda rumbled, as if from the pulpit or a mountaintop. "A cancer that seduces the people, does injury to the doctors, detracts from the power of the Church, overtly creates schism, contravenes and distorts Scripture, and blasphemes against the Holy Spirit. It was sown by the Antichrist, Luther, the besotted German who pretends that he alone has more knowledge than all the others in the Church, past or present. He dares to prefer his own judgment to that of the ancients and the doctors of the Church. To add to the sum of impiety, he means to invalidate the decrees of the sacred councils as if God had reserved for him alone the role of discerning what is necessary for the salvation of the faithful.

"We declare," Beda went on, his voice rising, bitter in condemnation, "and commit our very beings that this wickedness, being destructive of the Christian commonwealth, must be wholly and publicly consigned to the flames." The muscles at the corners of Beda's jaw twitched and knotted, but he did not move his eyes off Amaury, not even to blink. "*Wherever* it is found."

His imprecation done, Beda began breathing shallowly, a faint wheeze audible at the end of each breath. He reached out and placed a hand on the side of the lectern for support. Amaury was suddenly looking at an old man. How? Beda must have become ill during his exile. Was the titan close to death? Was Amaury to be somehow a part of his valediction?

"I am going to leave you now." Beda's voice had become a grating whisper. "But everything that Magister Ory is about to tell you is with my approval and is to be held in the strictest confidence. If that confidence is violated, there is no penalty that will be deemed too severe. None. Do you understand?"

Amaury nodded.

Then, in a morning of strange happenings, came the strangest of all. Noël Beda moved slowly from the lectern and placed a hand on Amaury's shoulder. His steps had become unsteady, but his grip remained powerful. Amaury felt as if he were clutched in a hawk's talons. "Don't forget, my boy," the old man said. "You are to have a great charge. The heretics must be exterminated. Exterminated without compunction or pity, as one would exterminate vermin. You are fighting for the soul of France, perhaps for all of Christendom."

Beda removed his hand from Amaury's shoulder, turned, and shuffled softly from the room. Just before the door of his private chamber clanked shut, Amaury heard a dry cough.

Ory's demeanor, deferential in Beda's presence, hardened once they were alone. He extended his fingers, palm up, toward one of the chairs. The wood was as hard as the stone floor, but Amaury found the curved, slatted bottom surprisingly agreeable. Ory settled into the other chair.

"As Magister Beda implied, we have a task for you. One that will require an absence from the college. Does that displease you?"

"I am here to do God's will," Amaury replied.

"Very deft," Ory said with a small, stiff smile. Amaury began to protest, but Ory silenced him with a raised finger. "Deftness will not work against you here, Faverges. Quite the contrary. But, for the moment, a modicum of honesty is required. You do not like Montaigu, yes?"

Amaury considered his alternatives. If Ory or Beda wished to condemn him, they could have done so at their whim. No meeting would have been necessary. His father's position would not have mattered one whit.

"Perhaps not," Amaury conceded. "But I cannot see why those sentiments matter so long as I discharge my obligations."

"And you feel you do?"

"I attempt to."

"Hardly, Faverges. You are intelligent and a fine scholar. One of our best, I suspect. So why do you not excel? Why do you remain baccalarius? You should have long since achieved baccalarius formatus. You seem to find canon law and theological disputation unworthy of your efforts. Your interests apparently lie elsewhere."

"My only interest is to be a worthy student."

"Theology is a calling," Ory continued, ignoring him. "And you have a secular bent. But in secular scholarship—arts and science—you would simply have ended up as a clerk. Or an arts master." Ory used the term with derision. "Even illegitimate, however—like you—doctors of theology are positions of enormous stature. You might even gain a seat on a *parlement.* That is why your father insisted you matriculate here. Completion of the course was his price, was it not? If you leave Montaigu, the pope will receive no petition of legitimacy, and you will live out your days as an outcast, a royal bastard of the Duke of Savoy."

"My father had only my welfare in mind," Amaury lied.

"Of course," Ory lied in return. "A fine and pious man. And you have been dutiful in acceding to his wishes." Ory reached across and tapped his index finger on Amaury's knee. "Or perchance your desire for legitimacy overwhelmed your loathing." Ory shrugged, exaggerated and artificial. "But no matter. Despite what you may think, your feelings do not concern me in the least. What does interest me is that, in your desire to continue your scientific studies, you have bribed a servant to aid you in sneaking out during the day to purchase forbidden tracts, which you have secreted in a rented room, and then you slipped away in the dead of night to read them. You have read heterodox interpretations of the structure of the human body, of the cause of illness, of the origin of tides, and even the configuration of the heavens themselves."

"How do you know that?" Amaury was stunned. "You have been in my room?"

"Of course. And to the bookseller from whom you purchased most of your library. You have no secrets from me." Ory shrugged again. "But, as it happens, your malfeasance coincides nicely with the requirements Magister Beda and I have for the mission I am about to propose. You will be rewarded for sin. Because you are secular, you will not betray yourself among our enemies at the first heretical statement, as would your more pious classmates. This is your opportunity to achieve what you sought by coming here, only at a far greater level. You are not, I take it, averse to opportunity."

"Only a fool is averse to opportunity."

"Precisely." The Inquisitor clasped his fingers under his chin, as if making a final decision on his offer. After a moment, he put his hands back in his lap and leaned forward. "The rewards of a grateful Church for the successful completion of this mission will be as great as the challenge. No man who expresses his faithfulness in so crucial a task should then be forced to go through life penalized by an accident of birth. The Holy Father himself supports our aims and will, upon your return, sign a decree of legitimacy." Ory nodded, three slow bobs of the head, as if to digest the magnitude of the favor himself. "You will be free to attain high office in the Church and perhaps even inherit your father's title and his lands." He paused. "That is better than waiting six years to achieve the same end here, is it not?"

No reply was necessary.

"Your duties," Ory said, adopting an inquisitor's monotone to make even plainer that he was speaking with an inferior, "will consist of helping us ensure a steady flow of information from elements of the Lutheran cabal. We must know not only what our enemies are doing but what they plan to do."

"You want me to be a spy."

"No!" Ory snapped with a determined shake of the head. "Not a spy. Spies undermine the righteous for the sake of the evil. You will be an agent of God."

On which side of that equation one fell depended on one's definition, Amaury thought, but he remained silent.

"I warn you, however," Ory added, "we deal with a committed and ruthless enemy, and in order to save the Church we must show equal commitment . . . and, when necessary, equal ruthlessness. Are you prepared for such dedication?"

"I would not accept a charge that I was unprepared to execute faithfully."

"We shall see. Your task is specific." Ory lowered his voice. "There is a conspiracy among the Lutherans. A conspiracy so great that few are even aware of its existence. It has come to us that these conspirators plan to unveil some great revelation, something of such significance and import that, as they put it, 'The old ways will be torn down forever.' "

"What sort of revelation?" Amaury asked. "The notion sounds preposterous."

"I assure you it is not. These foul heretics claim to be able to disprove the Holy Scriptures . . . at least the Holy Scriptures as they are now accepted by all of the True Faith. It concerns the Book of Genesis."

"What? That isn't possible. Genesis is the word of God himself. No one can disprove it." The proposition would be laughable if it were not emanating from the Inquisitor of France, a man who had likely never uttered a laughable sentence in his life. "And further, why would the Lutherans wish to disprove Genesis? It is part of their creed as much as it is ours."

"I agree," Ory replied. "Nonetheless, that is precisely what the Lutherans intend to do."

"I don't mean to question you, Magister, but are you certain this is not simply a grand hoax?"

"Quite sure. One of the faithful ingratiated himself with the Lutherans and assured us that the conspiracy is genuine."

"Why is he not able to discover its nature then?"

"Bad luck. Or betrayal. He was murdered in the streets last night. Stabbed in an alley near porte de Temple. It had the look of a simple robbery. Perhaps it was. A dozen men each night meet such an end in Paris. I hope for your sake it was a random act. But whatever the case, someone must now continue in his stead. Does the danger give you pause?"

Amaury thought for a moment. How much worse was death than to be crushed for six more years in the cleft of the buttocks of Mother Theology?

"I am not dissuaded," he said simply.

"I thought not. We will take extraordinary steps to shield you from discovery. No one will know of your mission save Magister Beda and myself. You will leave Montaigu, expelled from the college after forbidden tracts are found in your room. You may retrieve your science texts. Do so tonight using your customary means. You will not return to your rented room after that. We have other plans for your living arrangements.

"We will give you some Lutheran material as well. Word will go out that you were only saved from execution because of the position of your father. Your expulsion will include a beating, I'm afraid. Magister Ravenau will be unaware of the deceit, but his... enthusiasm... will help convince any who might be suspicious. We will not meet again. You will report regularly to a member of the faithful, whose identity you will only learn at the appropriate moment. He will watch over you." Ory smiled slightly. "Others may watch over you as well."

Spies for the spy.

"Have you any questions?"

"Who was the murdered man?"

Ory tilted his head to the side. "Ah, yes," he said after a moment. "Another student. Only in his first year. Giles Fabrizy. I believe you knew him."

Amaury, by a sheer act of will, did not change expression. "Only slightly," Amaury said. "He seemed like a fine student."

"Yes."

"I would like to see the body."

"An odd request."

"You are asking me to risk my life, Magister. I would like to understand fully what has gone before."

The Inquisitor considered this, but could not seem to detect any nefarious motive. "Very well. Someone must arrange for Fabrizy to be returned here for burial. You will be assigned the chore."

"Thank you, Magister."

"There is one last thing," Ory noted, as if he were remembering something that had slipped his mind. "A formality. We will need you to take an oath."

IV

AS A CORNERSTONE OF HIS LEGACY, King François was determined to transform Paris into the most magnificent city in the world, and thereby banish the specter of Italian social superiority once and for all. As part of his beautification campaign, he had decreed that murder victims were no longer to be left in the streets until the dead cart happened by, but rather were to be hauled off by gendarmes to one of the most storied buildings in all Paris, the Conciergerie, on Île de la Cité.

In the thirteenth century, the Conciergerie had been the royal palace of Saint Louis, an elegant, sprawling walled compound dominated by the Royal Gardens, the Jardins du Roi, to the east, and the tower of the magnificent Sainte-Chapelle to the west. In the fourteenth century, it was the center of royal administration and the meeting hall for the *parlement*, and then in the fifteenth it was converted to a prison, grandeur replaced with decrepitude. At the turn of the sixteenth century, Louis XII commissioned a garrison to the building. Cité, in the middle of the Seine and possessed of the only five bridges by which Parisians could make their way from La Ville on the right bank to l'Université on the left, afforded quick access to wherever trouble might arise within the city's walls.

The Conciergerie was as every place of incarceration in France. The rich lived on the top floor in minimal inconvenience. Most had a suite of cells, a bed brought from home, a writing desk, books, and good food. Some had servants living on the premises. With a well-placed bribe, they were even allowed out of their cells during the day to stroll freely through the grounds.

The semiwealthy occupied the floor immediately below, living in comfort if not luxury. Those of lesser resources might still afford a single cell with a window. Even those of minimal means could share accommodations aboveground. For the wretched poor, the pailleux, however, there were only the oubliettes—dank, vermin-ridden, belowground cells, where prisoners could await nothing but disease, madness, and miserable death. The corpses from the streets were also deposited in these cellars, the dead thrown in with the near dead, until they were either claimed, sold to the medical school to be used in dissections, or hauled off to be dumped in an anonymous grave outside the city.

Despair permeates a prison. As Amaury strode through the entryway, misery seemed to cling to the walls. A sentry box stood on the right, just inside the massive oak doors. Two bored soldiers in filthy tunics emblazoned with the lily crest of the Valois kings slouched inside. Gendarmerie was a detested detail for fighting men. Policing civilian rabble afforded neither honor nor loot. At first, the soldiers would not even deign to reply to the man in the university garb who stood before them. Finally, the older of the two, a reedy, unshaven lout with moist lips and few teeth, turned and spit; a huge glob struck the wall behind him and slithered to the ground like some giant slug. He turned back, sneered, then directed Amaury to a staircase past the balustrade to the right.

Within the walls was a feeling of perpetual twilight. Amaury reached the opening and gazed upon a stairwell that seemed to descend into the very bowels of the earth. What must it be like to be doomed to such a hell?

With each step, the stones on the walls and the surface of the steps became clammier. Halfway down, moss appeared along the sides of the stairs. At the bottom was a door, once sturdy and thick, now rotting and split. Dim light shone through the cracks. At first, the door, swollen at the ends from centuries of absorbing moisture, would not budge. Amaury gave a shove with his shoulder. The aged wood groaned and the door swung open.

Amaury was stunned by the scene before him. He stepped across the threshold into a long, wide corridor covered with filthy hay. The only light was from short candles that flickered in the damp. Even these were set sufficiently apart to render the scene dim and dreamlike. During Saint Louis' time, this vault had been used for the storage of produce, the combination of cold and moisture from the river perfect for maintaining freshness. What was ideal for vegetables, Amaury thought, was far less so for human beings.

A series of doors was set on either side, leading to the cells. Sounds more animal than human echoed through the chamber; mostly moans, but occasionally streams of jabbering from the mad.

Amaury forced himself to move forward. In the center of the corridor stood a pallet, on which six corpses were laid out. The nearest, thrown on its back, right arm at an odd angle next to its chest, mouth agape, eyes staring sightlessly at the blackened stones of the ceiling, was Giles.

Glorious Giles. Even in death, to be in this terrible place. Amaury felt as if his chest was constricting, forcing his heart up into his throat, as if the center of God's creation would be vomited forth. He became so frightened that for a moment he clamped his hand on his mouth to prevent the loss of his soul.

A piercing scream from one of the cells cut through the murk. A guard appeared, a large shambling figure carrying a pike. The guard favored Amaury with merely a glance, then shuffled to where the poor devil had screamed. There seemed to be small grates set high in each door. The guard rammed the pike through and growled, "Any more howling and it's the dungeon for you."

My God, Amaury thought. There was someplace worse than *this*?

The guard succeeded in silencing the wretch, for whom terror had overwhelmed even madness. He then turned his attention to Amaury. "You here for *him*?" the guard asked, moving forward, gesturing with his pike at the figure of Giles on the pallet.

Amaury was too transfixed to reply.

"Couldn't be no one else," the guard muttered. "Whenever we see a tonsure, we call you people." That the university was a law unto itself was a source of resentment among the gendarmerie. "Student fetched by his master," he added with a sneer. The guard assumed Amaury was a magister, not merely a student.

Amaury moved tentatively to the pallet. He had seen cadavers before, of course. Given the omnipresence of disease and violence, it was impossible not to. But not since his mother had he been forced to view the dead body of one whom he held so dear. Although his skin was ashen, Giles appeared more stunned than dead. Amaury met Giles' unwavering eyes hoping they might move, flicker, and this nightmare would be at an end.

The guard had sidled next to him. "So?" he asked. "You going to take him, or what?" He turned the pike point down and poked Giles in the chest.

Before either of them knew what had happened, Amaury had his hands at the man's throat. The guard dropped the pike and grabbed Amaury by the wrists, trying to pull them apart. The guard was strong, still a soldier after all, but Amaury's grip possessed the iron of madness.

The guard's eyes went wide. Amaury squeezed harder. The guard's jaw moved open and shut as he sucked desperately for air. Amaury felt the pressure on his wrists weaken. He realized finally that, if he did not release the man, he would die. He took his hands from the guard's throat. The guard fell to his knees, gasping.

"You crazy?" the guard croaked once he began to recover. "I should kill you for that." But he made no move to retrieve the pike. If a common soldier attacked a university doctor, even in self-defense, he'd have to appear before the *parlement*. That could mean a flogging or worse.

"Get up," Amaury said curtly. The guard pushed himself to his feet.

"You'll treat him like the dauphin, is that clear? If I find he's been sent to the medical school, you'll see me again. He is not going to be cut open and disemboweled before a roomful of strangers."

The guard rubbed at his throat. "What's he, your brother or something?"

"Yes," Amaury muttered. "My brother."

"*Merde*. Sorry. I didn't know."

Amaury gestured for the guard to move away. Ory's words came back. Bad luck or betrayal. Which of those two accounted for Giles' death could determine whether Amaury ended up on a pallet as well. Perhaps a clue to the killer's identity had been overlooked by these peasants of gendarmes.

Amaury leaned down on one knee. He must forget this was Giles. Reduce the problem to logic. He noticed first that a middle button on the doublet was missing. Although the possibility that the button had come off innocently in the course of the evening could not be completely discounted, far more likely was that it had come off when he was killed.

He spread the shirt open. Two wounds, one about six inches above the other, both now clotted with dried blood. The wounds were clean, indicating that poor Giles had been taken by surprise. Other signs of struggle were absent. No bruising anywhere. The missing button, then, pointed most likely to the search for Giles' purse. Nothing remarkable there.

Still, something was not right. One thrust, then another. Both directly from the front. That meant Giles had seen his attacker before him in the alley, then stood as the robber had plunged a knife into him not once but twice. Why had Giles not tried to flee? At least turned away? One of the wounds should have been to the side or back. He obviously had been so stunned at receiving the first wound that he had merely stood still for the second. And why had he entered the alley in the first place? Had Giles known his attacker?

Out of the corner of his eye, Amaury saw that the guard had returned and was standing over him. "What are you looking for?" the guard asked. "Was a robbery, like they told you."

There was a catch in the guard's voice. Fear of offending the man who had just throttled him, to be sure, but something else as well. The man was lying. Amaury made to examine the wounds even more carefully, to draw out the encounter. Under pressure, liars oversell. Soon the guard began to shift from one foot to another. Amaury turned and stared at the man as if he had made a discovery.

"It *was* a robbery," the guard bleated. "We didn't take nothing."

Amaury stood slowly. Aware that he had blundered, the guard retreated, his hands in front of him for defense.

"How much?" Amaury asked, taking a menacing step forward.

"Nothing," insisted the guard, shaking his head so fiercely that his helmet dislodged. The stink of fear had overwhelmed that of rancid breath, filthy clothes, and unwashed flesh. "It's against the law to steal from the dead."

"Listen to me well," Amaury said evenly. "My father is the Duke of Savoy. If you tell me what I want to know, I won't tell anyone else. If you don't, I will use my influence—which is considerable—to see that you get to join your friend in there." Amaury gestured with his head toward the cell from which the scream had come.

The guard nodded. He seemed to have deflated before Amaury's eyes.

"Where is the purse?" Amaury asked.

"Tossed it in the back," the guard moaned miserably.

"Get it."

"But it's empty. And he's dead." Greed then stiffened the man's resolve. "I ain't giving the money back. You'll have to kill me first."

"Get the purse," Amaury repeated.

The guard slunk off toward the rear of the chamber, disappearing into the dark. Amaury realized that the row of cells stretched much farther back, and the most desolate of the prisoners lived in a world almost wholly without light. The guard reappeared moments later. He handed Amaury a purse made of soft leather. Giles' father was a tanner, but Amaury was certain he had never had a purse like this. It was not the one he used at the school.

"Are you sure this is his?"

"I'm sure."

"This is expensive. Why didn't you keep it for yourself?"

"It's a dead man's." The guard crossed himself. "What do you take me for?"

Amaury let that pass.

"How much was in there?"

"Five silver francs when I got it. There was more when he was found. Probably a lot more. Those that brought him helped themselves to most of it."

"How did they claim robbery when the purse had not been taken?"

"They said they found it next to the body."

"With five silver francs still in it?"

The guard shook his head. "I suppose. Guess they figured leaving some money would look like the robber had to get away fast. I don't know."

Amaury nodded. "All right." The guard exhaled in relief. "You can keep the money," Amaury added. The guard's relief turned to tentative delight. "But I want some things in return."

"Like what?"

"I want him—my brother—removed from this pallet and laid out and covered. I'm going to send a burial party. Do you understand?"

The guard nodded, dumbfounded. For five silver francs, he had expected to be asked to perform an act far more infamous.

"Next," Amaury continued, "and most important, I want no mention of anything that passed between us to leave this room."

The guard nodded gratefully. "Don't worry," he said.

Amaury knelt down once more. He felt tears come but willed them back. Good-bye, Giles, he thought. He reached out and touched the cold flesh of Giles' cheek. I will avenge you if I can.

Then he stood and turned quickly to leave. As he reached the door, however, he stopped. The guard was already preparing to move Giles to a less offensive spot.

"One more thing," Amaury said. "When it arrived, was the body precisely as I see it now?"

The guard looked perplexed. "What do you mean?"

"You didn't rip his clothes when you moved him, did you?"

The guard shook his head. "We don't haul 'em by the clothes. We grab arms and legs. Heads sometimes."

"Would the gendarmes who found him have done it?"

The guard considered this for a moment, rubbing his leathery fingers on the stubble of his beard. "Ripped the shirt? You mean to make it look more like a robbery? Anything's possible. Don't see why, though. Nobody would have asked."

"Thank you," Amaury said.

But the guard had not finished. "Maybe it was torn already. Your brother was a student, right? I mean, you'd know better than anyone how they dress."

"Yes, perhaps you are correct," Amaury replied, seeming to give the idea due consideration. But the guard was not correct. The button had been very much attached late yesterday afternoon, when Giles had announced he intended to slip out for the evening. "Now that I think about it," Amaury added with a nod, "I believe he was missing a button earlier. Very good, sergeant. A mystery solved."

"Not a sergeant," the guard replied mournfully, but nonetheless grateful for the praise.

"Well, you will be if you continue to be so observant." The seas would part first, Amaury thought.

The guard brightened, transformed from adversary to ally. When Amaury looked upon him now, a poor fool, as young as he but looking much older, whose lot was only marginally better than those in the cages, he felt only pity. He could not be sure on whom God had played the worse trick—the jailed or the jailer.

Then, leaving the guard with visions of promotion that would never come, Amaury mercifully took his leave of the oubliettes. Before he left the building, however, he stopped once more at the sentry box. "I want to see the men who brought in the body."

The reedy soldier paused, as if deciding whether to turn and spit again. Instead he smiled, shrugged, and replied, "But they're asleep."

"Wake them."

V

TWENTY MINUTES LATER, Amaury stood at the edge of the Seine, watching the river undulate past, part majesty, part sewer. The rain had ended and the sun shone translucent behind a thin layer of clouds. As the sun began its march toward the western horizon, Amaury finally disengaged himself from his reverie and crossed pont au Muniers. Amaury walked north toward porte de Temple, almost as far from the university as one could go and still remain within the city walls.

The streets had grown cold. Amaury pulled his cloak tighter. He glanced upward at the gray sky and wondered suddenly why most forms of light seemed to generate heat as a by-product. But some minerals produced light without heat. Was that light somehow different? Or was it, perhaps, that heat generated light? How could one devise an experiment to determine which was which? Giles could have done it. This was precisely the sort of problem at which he excelled.

The gendarmes at the Conciergerie, after the obligatory grousing, had informed him that Giles had been found near rue Pastourelle, two streets south of the enclos du Temple, the huge walled quadrangle that held the towering fortress and an opulent church. Amaury had no trouble locating the correct spot. Although the buildings in the enclos were among the most well-appointed in all Paris, the surrounding area, once swamp, was downtrodden, home to the poor, beggars, and the unemployed. The streets were without paving stones, and grime adhered to the flimsy wooden walls of unending lines of ramshackle buildings. Soot hung in the air and a rancid odor of fat and gristle attacked the nostrils. Whores dotted the street corners and thieves the alleys. Few with money in their purses ventured on these streets after dark.

What was Giles doing in such a neighborhood? An errand for the Lutherans? For Ory? How could someone Amaury knew so well, whose very soul seemed aligned with his, have been leading a parallel existence of which he had neither known nor suspected?

The alley ran north to south between rue Pastourelle and the next street, rue Portefoin. The way through was narrow, camouflaged by piles of refuse. On first blush, as the gendarmes had said, the ideal venue for an ambusher to lie in wait. But gendarmes knew nothing of the heavens. For most of last night, no one hoping for the element of surprise would have chosen that alley as a place of concealment.

A large stain, almost certainly dried blood, lay at the base of the north wall only a few steps from where Amaury stood at the rue Pastourelle entrance. Another problem of inquiry, as at the prison. Three possibilities presented themselves: Giles had been stabbed on the street and dragged to where he was found; he had been waylaid on the street, but not stabbed until he had been pulled into the alley; or he had entered the alley willingly. The first could be dismissed: There was no blood on the street or leading from the street, and, besides, no one would stab a victim on the main road unless there was no other choice. The second could be equally dispensed with. The frontal wounds were such that they could not have been administered during a struggle. That left the third alternative—that Giles had entered the alley willingly. But had Giles done so alone, to meet with someone he knew would be waiting, or had he entered the alley *with* the man who subsequently murdered him? Had Giles, in fact, come here, to this seedy section of the city, with that man? Would the killer, then, have been someone whom Giles knew and trusted?

Information would not be easy to obtain. Citizens of Paris kept their mouths shut. They particularly did not speak to either gendarmes or snobs from the university. Still, someone might have seen something. The backs of houses sat on either side of the alley, the entryways of which were on the larger streets that abutted it. Eight to ten windows opened out, each shuttered. But had they all been shuttered last night? Citizens of Paris were also notorious snoops.

Amaury stood, hands on hips, surveying the walls. Then he heard a soft scrape. He pressed himself against the wall from where the sound had come, opposite the bloodstain, and waited. But there was no further noise and, after two minutes, Amaury was about to give up. Before he moved, however, he heard the scrape again. He looked up and saw a small hand and then a thin wrist very slowly, very quietly, pushing open a set of shutters directly over his head. Soon he was staring at the gullet and underside of the chin of an old woman who had stuck her head out the window. The woman glanced up and down the alley. Only after she had determined there was no one in either place did she look beneath her.

"*Sacre Dieu*," she gasped. A second later, the shutters slammed shut.

It was a simple matter for Amaury to circle back to the street and find the building, then the room, in which the woman resided. He rapped on the door. When there was no response, he pounded harder. Eventually the woman appreciated that whoever was outside had no intention of leaving, so she opened the door a crack.

A stale odor escaped the room. The smell of the aged. The woman looked past Amaury, surprised that he had no companions. Then she seemed to comprehend that he was not of the authorities, but rather, from his dress and bearing, a man of position.

"You will do well to speak with me and tell me what you know, woman," Amaury said curtly. "I would not like to return with soldiers, but I will if you need persuasion."

The door opened full.

The old woman lived in one decaying room. She wore a much-mended dress of threadbare green wool and a bonnet that had faded from yellow to almost white. But she had not surrendered to poverty as much as it had overwhelmed her. The room was clean and tidy, and vestiges of earlier, more prosperous days sat moldering on tables and shelves. An iron pot hung on a frame in the hearth, although, judging from the chill, a fire was surely a luxury. A thin counterpane was laid over a straw mattress on the woman's bed. Next to the bed hung a medal on a ribbon, a presentation by the king to the families of those who had fallen in battle.

Once she had agreed to let Amaury inside, the old woman felt obliged to ask him to sit and to offer him a glass of wine. Amaury lowered himself carefully into one of the two hard chairs at a rickety table but politely refused the wine. The woman sat in the chair opposite.

"Your husband was a soldier, madame?" he asked.

She shook her head. "A weaver. He was a conscript. He died at Pavia."

Pavia was a blight on the reign of King François and the honor of France. Nine years before, during François' misadventure in Italy, the French army had been routed by the Holy Roman Emperor Charles V, and François himself had been taken prisoner. The country had been forced to agree to an enormous ransom, raised, as such sums inevitably were, by taxes levied on those who bore no responsibility for the disgrace. François sent his young sons to prison in his place in order to guarantee payment and, as he set foot once more in France, exulted, "I am king again!" The boys were not released for two years. As one of the first acts upon his return, François had raised taxes once more, this time to pay for the beautification of Paris. The widow Chinot, for that was her name, now survived on the tiny pension granted by the crown.

"I would like you to tell me about last night, madame," Amaury said. He spoke softly. Having seen the woman's circumstances, he could no longer consider bullying her.

"You mean the boy who was killed downstairs? Terrible. A terrible thing."

"Yes," Amaury agreed, "it was. I'd like to know what you saw."

"Nothing," the woman replied, shifting her gaze from his.

"I think you did see something, madame," Amaury continued gently. "You won't get in any trouble for telling me."

A tiny smile appeared in the corners of Veuve Chinot's mouth. Everything she did caused her trouble.

"I'm not from the law," Amaury said. "And nothing you say will go any further than this room."

"I'm telling you, I couldn't see. It was too dark."

"Pardon me, madame, but there was a bright moon last night and, if my calculations are correct, at the time the incident seemed to have occurred, the moon would have been shining into the alley. You would have seen quite clearly."

The widow gaped at Amaury as if he were a sorcerer. "Your calculations? Astrology is against the law."

"I don't compute the position of the heavens to predict the future, madame. Only to understand the present. Now please tell me what you saw."

Veuve Chinot cocked her head. "He was a friend of yours, wasn't he?"

"An acquaintance."

She shook her head. "More than that, I think. I know the look, you see. When someone important goes away and never comes back. I've worn it long enough myself."

"Very well," Amaury said softly. "He was more than that." Paris, it seemed, was a city of the lonely.

The woman sighed and then reached across the table and patted Amaury's hand. "You have to bear it. They tell you that time makes it better, but it doesn't. You miss them so much, no matter how much time has passed."

Amaury nodded. "I know."

"What do you want to know, monsieur?"

"You saw him killed, didn't you?"

"No. I didn't see the poor boy killed. Just what happened afterward." Veuve Chinot then described a thin man in a Franciscan cloak.

"A friar?" Amaury asked. "Are you sure?"

"I didn't say he was a Franciscan. Just that he was dressed as a Franciscan."

"You think he wasn't?"

Veuve Chinot smiled. "I'm sure he wasn't. Just the way he walked was enough."

Amaury was not sure if a Franciscan could be judged by the way he walked. But there was another possibility. "If he was dressed as a friar, then he had a tonsure. Could he have been a student in disguise?"

Veuve Chinot shook her head. "Too old. But he wasn't a professional assassin."

"How can you possibly know that?"

"He stared at the body for a long time. Not to make sure he was dead. More that he couldn't believe he had done such a thing. Anyone used to killing would have gotten away as quickly as he could to avoid being seen, right?"

"Yes. That's correct. You are very clever, madame."

"Of course, it's correct." Veuve Chinot leaned forward. Her eyes had lit up. "Then, after a few moments, he finally seemed to realize he had to hurry and began ripping at the boy's clothes. Pulled out two packets. He was looking for them, I'm sure. He was not as interested in the first one, but very careful with the second. He turned it over in his hands to make sure it was what he wanted. Then he stuffed both parcels in his cloak and hurried away by the rue Portefoin side. He left the money. The boy's purse was still on him when he ran off."

"Yes," Amaury said. "I know. You are very observant as well, madame." Perhaps she could tell a Franciscan by his walk after all.

"Observing is what I can do. I'm not a busybody, you know. Or at least I didn't use to be. These days, though, there's not much else left for me."

"Did you see who reported the body?"

"A priest. He came from the rue Pastourelle side. He walked down the alley, looked down at the poor boy, shook his head, and went to fetch the soldiers. Strange that he never bent over to check, but I suppose it was obvious that he was dead. When the soldiers came, they found the purse. Must have been heavy, by the way they looked at each other. They tried to shoo the priest away, but the priest had seen the purse, so they couldn't just empty it and throw it in the alley. And neither of the soldiers was going to risk being caught with it. Bet it was still on the body when they delivered it, but a lot lighter."

Amaury smiled. "You should be an investigator, madame."

But Veuve Chinot shook her head. She was not finished. "But there was someone else first. A girl."

"Girl? What girl?"

"Small. She seemed young by the way she moved. I couldn't see her features. The hood of her cloak was up. She arrived about ten minutes after the boy was killed. Ran into the alley as if she'd been looking for him. She was very upset. Leaned down and looked for something. I couldn't be sure if she was checking to see if he was alive or if she was searching to see if he still had the packets on him. Then she stood up, put her hand to her mouth for a second, and hurried off the way she had come."

"How long afterward did the priest arrive?"

"Quite a while. Much longer than if she'd fetched him from the church, if that's what you mean. Église de Temple is only two minutes away."

"Thank you, madame," Amaury said. "You have been a great help." He reached into his purse and withdrew a silver coin, then placed it on the table.

The woman considered the offering. Pride dictated that she refuse, but deprivation ordered a different course. She swept the money across the table and let it drop into her apron.

When Amaury stood to leave, she looked up at him and smiled briefly. "Perhaps, when you gather more information, you will come and talk again."

"Perhaps," he replied.

The old man paused at the base of the dark staircase. His hips and knees had so stiffened that he now more hauled himself up than walked, grasping the stone railing and pulling with each step. He could measure the passage of his life by this staircase. When he had first arrived here . . . what was it, thirty years ago now . . . he had fairly bounded up. And now he almost crawled. The Lord might be merciful, but He could sometimes play terrible tricks.

Yes, the end was near. That was certain. And still he was no closer to a decision now than ever. The decision that had almost been made for him twenty years ago, when he stood before the pope. Leo, that sad creature. Forced to follow Julius. What a fate. It might easily be said that Leo had brought on the turmoil that now beset Christianity. In his zeal to rebuild Saint Peter's, to have some achievement of his own that was not dwarfed by his towering predecessor, Leo had precipitated the crisis by commissioning the avalanche of indulgences that had so incensed the German monk. Others decried Luther, but the old man understood him. The farther one is from Rome, the simpler and more pious one's upbringing, the more the corruption offends. The Church might easily have saved itself from this cataclysm with a few simple reforms, but who reforms after centuries of doing precisely what one wants? Now the crevice had widened into an abyss and reconciliation seemed impossible.

But the old man had stood before Leo on a practical matter, not a theological one. How to bring the ecclesiastical calendar more in line with the seasons it was supposed to represent. Lent should not come in midsummer, nor the day of Christ's birth in autumn. He had hinted to Leo what the problem might be, and Leo—indolent, perhaps, but no fool—had expressed interest. The Holy Father had even asked for a paper on the subject. But Leo had become occupied with weightier issues—or so it seemed at the time— and ultimately nothing had come of it. The old man, not so old then, had returned home to his castle on the bay to continue his work.

He was nearing the top now. His bony forearms ached along with his legs. One of the servants could help him, he knew, but the old man had been *toiling in solitude for so long, he feared the presence of another might disturb the calculations that simply must be done correctly.*

Tonight he was particularly eager. A missive had arrived from Capua, from Cardinal Schönburg. An encouraging letter. Warm. Urging him to go forward. Schönburg was a voice in the wilderness, certainly, but the old man thought that this time perhaps he might just prevail.

Two years before, when he began to feel death's fingers brush his cheek in the night, he had taken some tentative steps. For the first time, he sent an abstract to friends. Without the full proof, of course. Enough to test the waters, but not enough to roil them. The response, the old man had been gratified to note, was heartening.

But to present the entire formulation now. When so much was at stake. When the very definitions of Christianity were under assault and might tilt on his findings. At the very least, he would overturn dogma that had been accepted for almost three centuries—and promulgated by a saint. That was too much to consider. For the moment, in any case. And besides, the proof was still not quite perfect.

The old man finally reached the battlements. A wind came in off the bay, adding crispness to a beautiful, clear, almost moonless night. No mist. No fog. The heavens were as accessible as if they had been painted on his ceiling. Deo gratias. He had not made the effort for nothing. The castle was on a hill, rendering the view to the water below as if from the stars. The ships in the bay, no longer icebound, were just visible, like ghosts, from the parapet on which he stood. He could hear the waves crack against the shore. The old man had spent so much time here that the bay had almost become his bay; each small stretch of rocky coastline, the river inlet with its moored fishing boats, almost family.

The old man sighed. This was no time to bask in the comfort of his surroundings. This was time to work.

VI

Paris, Saint-Antoine, February 25, 1534

IN A PRACTICED INSTANT, Madame La Framboise took the measure of the bedraggled man in the worn tunic and threadbare cloak standing at her door.

Stubble where a tonsure had once been shaved—she knew *that* lot well enough. Disgraced, expelled from some order or another, he had likely come to Saint-Antoine, the Lutheran section of Paris, to try to find redemption. He would undoubtedly alternate bouts of drinking and tears. Madame La Framboise had been letting rooms long enough to have lost all interest in being either confessor or surrogate mother to the defrocked. To say nothing of cleaning up vomit in the early morning. A widow presiding over a rooming house in the shadow of the Bastille could not afford to be all that choosy, it was true, but certainly she could be choosy enough to avoid some fallen Catholic who would barely have two coins to his name.

No, she told him with some gusto, she did not have rooms available to let, despite anything he might have heard at the café.

After the rebuff, Madame La Framboise had been about to close the door in the man's face when the most exceptional thing occurred. Never taking his eyes from hers, the man raised his right hand, turned it over, and opened his fist. Inside was a coin. A gold coin. Not large, but positively, without question, gold. Gold was by law reserved for the nobility; silver was the currency of commoners. Ordinary people caught trafficking in gold were flogged, although the authorities exempted persons of importance. The prohibition, however, as prohibitions are wont to do, only made gold more coveted.

Madame La Framboise looked from the hand to the face. Perhaps she had been hasty. This was a pleasing face, she decided. An educated face. A face exuding bearing and breeding. So what if he had been booted out of an order? They were all fanatics anyway.

As quickly as the English winds blew away French clouds, Madame La Framboise's frown turned sunny. With great ceremony, or at least with what she considered great ceremony, she stood aside and, with a sweep of her arm, invited the gentleman to enter. When the door had closed behind him, landlady and prospective tenant stood face-to-face.

"You come highly recommended, madame," the man said, although he did not specify by whom. He was younger than he had first appeared, not yet thirty, but spoke with authority. "You are known as a woman who provides both hospitality and privacy."

"I am that," she agreed, pleased with the reference despite its anonymity. "I make an excellent stew and only open my mouth when I'm eating it."

"Highly desirable on both counts."

"I have a room that opens on the back—quite comfortable. You will be able to get air without worrying who's watching from the street . . . if that's the sort of privacy you had in mind, of course."

"It sounds delightful," said the man. He offered the coin. Madame La Framboise opened her thick hand to receive it and then deposited it in her apron.

"Dinner's at six," she said.

"Stew?"

"Not tonight." Madame La Framboise cocked an eyebrow. "Unless you want to pay for the sausage and the duck."

Amaury smiled. "I might be willing, if you cook well enough. Anything not to eat herring. A good wine would be appreciated as well."

Madame La Framboise held out her hand a second time. "Leave it to me," she said.

Amaury was pleasantly surprised when he saw the room. Madame La Framboise's accommodations were agreeable and commodious. The room was on the second floor, airy. The window faced the city's west wall, two streets away, and, as promised, let in a profusion of sunshine in the afternoon but not prying eyes from the street. There was a clean smell of vinegar about the place, so Madame La Framboise was a conscientious housekeeper as well. Perhaps she would prove to be as good a cook as she boasted. Best of all, in the northeast corner, was a bed, a real bed, with a rag-stuffed mattress and pillow, covered with a quilt, puffed with feathers. Amaury gazed upon the remarkable appurtenance and, for a moment, thought himself on holiday.

He dropped the sack containing his belongings onto the floor, lowered himself slowly to the bed, swung up his legs, and laid back gingerly. The welts from Ravenau's parting gift were still tender. When he had settled in, Amaury clasped his hands behind his head. After some moments of simply staring at the ceiling beams and breathing deeply, he unfolded his arms and stretched them out in front of him, splaying his fingers as wide as they would go. Freedom. Glorious freedom. The feeling washed over him, settling gently, like falling leaves.

Suddenly he was back in Savoy, sitting next to his mother in a carriage, rumbling over rutted mountain roads. February had turned to April. The laurel was in bloom; splotches of pink and white dotted the landscape. Mama was staring out the window and had not spoken since the man in the tunic emblazoned with the duke's coat of arms had come for them. Amaury, only seven, had grown fearful in the silence. Mama had always been so caring and open. But somehow he had known to remain silent as well.

Finally he could endure it no longer. He asked, "Where are we going, Mama?"

"To see your father."

"But I thought my father was dead. A captain of the guard, killed at Forenza."

"No."

The carriage passed through the gate of a huge château. Amaury's eyes went wide at the splendor. How different from the simple houses in Faverges. Once inside the gate, the carriage had gone straight toward the magnificent palace in the center of the courtyard. Instead of pulling up in front, however, the driver turned right and went around to the side. The coachman got down, opened the door, and gestured for Amaury and his mother to alight. She held his hand as the coachman led them to a small, heavy wooden door. The door was opened immediately by an ancient, stern-looking chamberlain who glowered at Mama and looked with curiosity down at him.

The old servant led them to a small antechamber. Mama squeezed Amaury's hand and then released it. "You've got to go with this gentleman," she said. "He will take you to your father."

"Aren't you coming with me, Mama?"

"I am not allowed," she said softly. She reached down and tousled his hair. "You will be fine." Then the glowering servant had placed a hand at the back of his head and led him away. As he walked through the cavernous palace—the walls hung with immense tapestries, lit by a thousand candles even in daylight—a sprite suddenly appeared. Small, golden haired, and quick as a cat. She darted across the hall in front of him and disappeared behind a pillar. Amaury looked up, but the servant either hadn't noticed her or was pretending not to have. As Amaury passed the pillar, he turned his head to see, but the girl was no longer there. Maybe she wasn't real after all. But, as he crossed the great hall to enter his father's chambers, she appeared again in the far doorway and again was gone in an instant. This time, however, Amaury noticed her eyes, blue like the autumn sky. He didn't see her again during his visit, but decided she had been sent to protect him from the terrifying spirits that haunted that huge and forbidding palace. He thought about her every day afterward.

When his mother died three years later, the same attendant brought him to the château to live with the servants. Would she still be there? But she was not. All day he looked—in the halls, in alcoves, behind every pillar—but the golden sprite was not there. Finally, after he had been fed in the great kitchen, he trudged miserably to his tiny room to sleep. Just before he reached the door, she darted from a dark corner. She leaned to him and whispered in his ear.

"I've been waiting for you."

A strange voice interrupted. Not hers. Not from Savoy. Amaury became aware of Madame La Framboise calling him for dinner, her voice indistinct, seeming to come through liquid. Amaury blinked at the sunlight pouring into the room, although the sun itself was about to be obscured by the building across the street. How long had he been asleep?

When he arrived downstairs, the table was set for three. The two other boarders were already seated. One was a Swabian named Hoess. A wine seller. He was tall, about fifty, affable, with small eyes, hanging jowls, and a bulbous, outsized nose. The other was a short, dour lawyer from Brittany named Turvette. Amaury introduced himself. As he took his seat, Hoess thanked Amaury for funding the feast.

"You will soon find out what a wise decision you made," Hoess added. "You are in the presence of culinary artistry unmatched even in the Louvre."

"Yes," Turvette agreed. "We are fortunate to have someone so obviously prosperous share our table. What brings you to Paris?"

"I have been in Paris," Amaury replied.

"Where?"

"At Collège de Montaigu." He became conscious of a sumptuous aroma wafting in from the kitchen.

"Montaigu?" asked Turvette, raising his eyebrows in surprise. The lawyer was a horse-faced fellow with narrow, pinched lips that seemed perpetually moist, lending him an air of morbid anticipation. To Amaury, he conjured up the image of a man happy to sign warrants of execution all the while avoiding responsibility for actually carrying out the sentence.

"Yes," Amaury muttered. "Nine years."

"Bon appétit!" Madame La Framboise trilled as she led fat Sylvie, the kitchen maid, to the table. Sylvie carried a large metal pot by the handle, protecting her hand from the heat with a thrice-folded piece of sackcloth. After Sylvie placed the pot on a large tile, Madame La Framboise shooed her out and ladled the bowls of stew herself. She placed the first bowl before Amaury. The instant she did so, he felt his jaws begin to work. The perfume of the sauce, rich, flavorful, and hearty, settled into his nostrils, all but overpowering him. He reached for his double-tined fork but at first could not bring himself to lift it, so long had it been since he had tasted such food. He found himself afraid to do so now. Finally, he succeeded in getting his hands and arms to move. What to try first? He chose the morsel of duck breast against the side of the bowl. He speared it and placed it in his mouth.

Amaury had studied the nature of Heaven for nine long years, but never had one of the magisters described Paradise in terms of a small piece of duck. But what did they know? He washed it down with a sip of excellent red wine, donated for the occasion by Hoess. Amaury heard himself almost purr. Suddenly, he looked up and saw that both Hoess and Turvette were staring at him.

"Sorry," he mumbled, "but it's been quite a while since I've tasted anything so good."

Madame La Framboise beamed. Hoess nodded and cocked an eyebrow, as if to say, "I told you." Then Turvette said, "The rigors of Montaigu are sufficient to drive many away, I'm told."

"More than sufficient," Amaury agreed curtly. He returned to his dinner, switching to his spoon for a taste of beans and thick sauce.

"And you left by choice?" the lawyer continued, before Amaury could swallow.

"Not by choice, no." Amaury tried once again to busy himself with his food. If Turvette asked one more question and ruined his meal, Amaury swore to himself that he would leap across the table and implant his fork in the man's forehead.

Mercifully, Hoess changed the subject. "Did you hear the latest from Amboise?" The king was then in residence at his château on the Loire. "It seems that our François took a new mistress, the Countess Caron-Roussillon." Hoess chuckled, his jowls flapping like a hound's. "Unfortunately, he could not bring himself to part with Angeline de Bec, his old mistress. Angeline was supposed to be in Aups, visiting her mother, so François felt free to play his game of *boules* with the countess."

Amaury settled in, slowly and luxuriantly ingesting the magnificent dinner. Hoess seemed a natural storyteller and this had the makings of an amusing tale.

"But Angeline returned unexpectedly," Hoess went on. "Very late at night. She decided to surprise her lover by slipping into his bed. Au naturel." He made to trace a woman's figure with his hands. "The king's guard, who was supposed to warn His Majesty of just such an eventuality, had fallen asleep outside the bedroom door. Angeline tiptoed past the poor wretch, removed her garments, crept over to the bed, lifted the covers, and got in. Imagine her surprise when, instead of the royal instrument, she encountered the somewhat more malleable form of the Countess Caron-Roussillon, who was attired as was she."

"No!" gasped Madame La Framboise, raising a hand to a gaping mouth.

"Yes," chortled Hoess. "Evidently, there was a scream. Followed by a second scream. The guard awakened and burst in, only to find two naked woman wrestling and pulling each other's hair on top of the bed."

"What was the king doing?" asked Madame La Framboise breathlessly.

"He was *laughing*!" Hoess replied. "He let them fight for a good five minutes before he had the servants break it up."

"How did you hear of this?" asked Madame La Framboise.

"I sell to the steward," Hoess replied. "We wine merchants have excellent sources of information."

Amaury had a morsel of sausage on his fork but put it back. The stew had begun to settle in his belly, evolving from a feeling of blissful fullness to bloated discomfort. He took some wine to aid his digestion.

"What happened?" he asked.

Hoess smiled at him. "Both women left Amboise before morning. The guard is gone as well. Lucky François enjoyed the spectacle, or the guard would not be alive. The king, I am told, is currently being consoled for their absence by Marie-Ange Montbrison, a beauty and the daughter of Eugenie Montbrison, a previous mistress." He took a swig of wine, his nose rising like a promontory. "You don't hear stories like that at Montaigu, I'll warrant."

"True enough," Amaury admitted. Other than an occasional trip to a brothel, he had had no contact with women, naked or otherwise, in longer than he could remember.

"I have never met a Montaigu student before," Turvette interjected. "How does one enroll in such a place?"

"Leave the man alone," Hoess said before Amaury could reply. "The last thing a newly freed man needs is to be reminded of his captivity." He turned to Amaury. "You seem like a fine fellow. I'm sure we are going to be friends."

VII

THE NEXT MORNING, Amaury visited Fournière, the bookseller on rue des Bales. From the outside, Fournière's was an unprepossessing establishment, a plain stone storefront on a small, grimy, narrow street at the rear of église Saint-Antoine, about a ten-minute walk from Madame La Framboise's rooms on rue de la Cerise. But, as bibliophiles from across Europe were aware, behind the shabby exterior lay one of the finest establishments of its kind to be found anywhere on the continent. Many of Fournière's wares—incunabula, rare manuscripts, works of early printers like Fust and Schoeffer, even a *Catholicon* from the great Gutenberg— were of such rarity and value that the shop could rightly have been called a museum.

Fournière himself was over sixty although no one seemed certain just how far over. He had a fringe of white hair, skin almost as pale, and was so bent that, without the stick that he used to lead him from place to place, he would certainly have pitched forward and lain helpless, commalike, on the floor. Although he lived only one floor above, Fournière spent little time in the shop, clunking through with a scowl two or three times a day to peruse the stock, muttering to himself as he went. He occasionally paused over a volume to check for dust or to ensure that the vellum or morocco covers had been polished with the special oil that prevented cracking or shrinkage. For the remainder of the time, Fournière remained invisible. Day-to-day operation was entrusted to Broussard, his assistant.

Broussard had persuaded the old man to hire him three years before, appealing to Fournière's dual loves of indolence and loot. While preserving the antiquaria for which the establishment was known, Broussard brought a contemporary feel to the shop, adding the newest translations of Plato, Aristotle, and Thucydides from the printer Estienne, Fuchs's herbals, agronomy texts, and the latest edition of Dürer's *Apocalypse*. Broussard had cleared an entire section at the front of the shop to display the satires of Erasmus and Rabelais, the bestselling authors in Europe.

As a result, the shop now attracted a younger, more vigorous clientele, members of a well-heeled bourgeois class who had benefited from François' obsession to build a younger, more vigorous Paris. Fournière grumbled even more than usual whenever he meandered through the sections of the shop that Broussard had modernized, but not so much as to eschew the additional revenues that his ambitious young assistant deposited in his coffers.

Broussard was near the front when Amaury walked in. He noticed the change at once. "Much more suitable," he said, gesturing toward Amaury's doublet, tights, and shoes. "An aberration or permanent?"

"Permanent. I have left. Finally."

"Congratulations. Took you long enough. I always wondered why you went to such pains to please a father who wouldn't even deign to acknowledge your existence. I never did."

"You never had the opportunity. But you're quite correct. It was, it seems, a fool's errand run by a fool. When a father is displeased at the very birth of a son, there seems little that son can do to alter the feeling." Broussard was one of the few to whom Amaury had confessed his lineage. Or rather the lack of it.

Broussard's given name was Geoffrey. He was, in theory, the son of a French linen merchant and an English lady-in-waiting to Mary Tudor, Henry of England's younger sister. A quarter century earlier, Mary, renowned as the most beautiful woman in Europe, had been married off to François' predecessor, Louis XII, in order to provide a male heir. An odious chore, as Louis was thirty years her senior, bent, dyspeptic, and covered with scabies. But if Mary was successful, Henry would have a direct line to the French throne. She apparently discharged her responsibilities faithfully—Louis died two years later, succumbing, it was widely speculated, to sexual excess, but without producing a son. Mary immediately absconded with jewelry and gold, sneaking back across the channel with her true love, the Duke of Norfolk. Broussard's mother had been left behind and tossed into a cell in the basement of the Louvre.

The new king, François, ever sensitive to a woman in distress, released her on the condition that she marry a Frenchman and remain in the country. Rumors abounded that François had exacted other conditions as well, rumors considerably enhanced by Geoffrey's height, long nose, and prominent chin. Amaury had thus found a level of comfort with Broussard that was almost filial. All bastards were, in effect, only children.

"Come to the back," Broussard said, taking Amaury by the elbow. "Now that you're a free man, there's something I want to show you." He released his grip, but only to clap Amaury on the back. "Actually, I would have shown you anyway, but it's more fun now. We can drink some of the old man's ghastly wine to celebrate your release."

Amaury followed Broussard to the back room. The walls were floor-to-ceiling bookshelves. A heavy wooden table and chairs sat in the center. In here, Fournière kept his most prized possessions. Amaury and Broussard had often passed time poring over a prized volume. Amaury had always been forced to cut short the visits so as not to be missed at Montaigu. Until now.

Broussard poured two cups of wine and delicately removed a thick folio, finely bound in white vellum, from a middle shelf. He placed it on the table, in front of Amaury.

"Go ahead. Look through it. I was holding it for you before I put it out. It's Colines' edition of Ruel's *De Natura Stirpium*. If you want it, it's yours. I'll even give you the famous Fournière's discount."

"Nothing?"

Broussard shrugged. "A man must earn a living."

Simon de Colines was one of the first of the French printers to produce works in the sciences. Amaury opened to the title page, an intricate arbor spun with grape vines over a fountain filled with flowering plants, designed by the great astronomer and mathematician Oronce Finé. Botany was not his field, but who could resist a work both beautiful and encyclopedic? The author, Jean Ruel, was physician to François, and this volume contained descriptions of six hundred plants, the most complete treatise of its kind ever produced in France.

"This is glorious," Amaury said. Broussard stood over him, arms crossed, as proud as if he had printed the folio himself. "Is it the original?"

"No," Broussard sighed. "Only a second edition. The first sold out instantly and is almost impossible to come by. This edition is quite difficult to acquire as well."

"And therefore expensive?"

"What is good in life that does not come with a price?"

"And that is?"

"A quarter *écu d'or* will do nicely."

"Nicely for you, perhaps. But very well. Keep it here for the time being. I'm staying temporarily in a room on rue de la Cerise. I'll let you know when I make permanent arrangements." Amaury looked about as Broussard returned the volume to the shelves. "You know, Geoffrey," he said finally, "I have often noticed that, in an establishment of such extensive stock, there seemed a paucity of a certain variety of book."

"And what type of book is that?"

"Theology seems to be vastly underrepresented."

"Not at all," Geoffrey demurred. "Why, just yesterday we received a shipment of Froben's new edition of the works of Saint Augustine."

"*Meum testimonium subtile,*" said Amaury. "My point exactly. Augustine is fourth century and will have little companionship on your shelves among farmers, physicians, and astrologers."

Broussard stroked his long Valois chin, then took a drink of wine. "Are you certain you're not spying for Montaigu?"

"Actually, I'm spying for the Inquisition. Ory himself recruited me. I insisted on a particularly energetic beating to defray suspicion."

"Quite. But in times such as these, one must take care. It's best to avoid flaunting one's true beliefs." Broussard rolled his eyes toward the ceiling that was the floor of Fournière's bedchamber. "He is not in agreement, of course. He would have every one of the saints memorialized on the wall and a shrine to the pope in the doorway."

"And you would have the works of . . . more recent religious philosophers?"

"Perhaps," Broussard replied. "Although I have nothing against the Church. It is, however, difficult sometimes to see past the excesses. Your experiences at Montaigu, which you have so eloquently described, are but one extreme. The living standards of Church fathers in Rome are quite another."

"Certainly true," Amaury said. "I heard that one of the cardinals recently hosted a dinner of sixty-five courses, at the end of which a naked boy of thirteen leapt out of a cake."

Broussard emitted a snort. "I'm no student of Scripture, but I'll wager naked boys and cakes are not to be found in any biblical text, or perhaps I've been reading the wrong translation."

"You *are* with the Reformers then?"

"One does not have to be with the Reformers to believe in reform."

"Indeed," Amaury said.

"Have *you* gone with the Reformers? After nine years in the theology faculty?"

Amaury laughed. "Nine years. Yes. Sufficient to either guarantee one's allegiance or his antipathy."

"And in your case it was the latter?"

"I am finished with the Church," Amaury answered, "if that's what you are asking. But that doesn't necessarily mean that I'm ready to throw my lot in with a group that may be no better."

Broussard mused for a moment, his large brow furrowed. It looked like hedgerows. "Oh, but they are," he said finally. "A good deal better."

Broussard placed his hand on Amaury's shoulder. "Reform is a revelation, my friend. I would never have believed I could be so fervent about anything. Except money, of course."

"Are you certain you are not simply rejecting your own past? Choosing a path only because it runs counter to what you were taught?"

"Quite certain. Reform is new. It's young. It has swept away the stultification and corruption of centuries. We are the true religion, Amaury. The religion that Christ died for."

"Perhaps," Amaury allowed grudgingly. "But I have read some of the 'new religion' . . . was beaten for it . . . but I am, I confess, still dubious that the Lutherans have any more to say than the pope."

"Anyone has more to say than the pope. Why don't you come with me to listen? There is a meeting tomorrow. One of the new leaders of the movement will be speaking. Quite clever. Like you. You'll find him stimulating if nothing else."

"Perhaps. Just who is this exciting new leader?"

"His name is Jean Chauvin. He was forced to flee after running afoul of the Inquisition but has sneaked back into Paris just to address our group."

"All right, Geoffrey. I'll allow you to corrupt me. Where is this meeting of yours to take place?"

"The location is secret. Even I won't know until tomorrow. Meet me here one hour after sundown, and I'll take you. You'll need me to vouch for you in any case. Come to the back door."

"Conspiracy and Scripture. What better way to spend an evening?"

"Broussard will be your entrée into the Lutheran conspiracy," Ory had said. "It seems that not only were you purchasing heretical literature, but you were doing so from a heretic. Now you know why you are so perfect for this assignment. Besides," Ory had added, "we are almost certain Fabrizy came to the attention of the Lutherans through Broussard himself. Fabrizy visited the shop regularly. As did you."

Amaury made to stand, but then stopped. "Oh, yes. I had almost forgotten. A mutual acquaintance of ours was killed. Stabbed. In a foolish street robbery, of all things."

"*Mon Dieu.* One cannot take three steps in Paris these days without risking death. Who was it?"

"Giles Fabrizy. Another student. Young, but a wonderful scholar."

Broussard pursed his lips, then placed an index finger on the point of his chin. "Fabrizy, you say?" He thought for a moment more, then shrugged and shook his head. "No. I don't think I know him."

VIII

AMAURY HAD LEARNED by necessity how to travel at night un-observed. Many a journey to either gaze at the heavens or read about them had been spent with senses honed to detect if he was being followed.

And he was being followed now.

He had left Madame La Framboise's after dinner and walked along rue de la Cerise toward the Seine. When he turned right at the wall that abutted the river, someone had materialized behind him.

Amaury continued west toward pont Notre Dame, walking casually. He must lose the pursuer, but without the man being aware it had been done intentionally. Announcing that he was on guard against surveil-lance would mark him as much as if he allowed himself to be followed to his destination.

Amaury made his way slowly along the wall, clicking the wood heels of his shoes against the pavement stones, occasionally humming loudly. As the towers of Notre Dame came into view, Amaury increased his pace. He ceased to hum. By the time he reached the bridge to Cité, Amaury was walking briskly, but taking his steps smoothly to disguise their speed. He made no sound. He could not yet hear anyone behind him, although he was certain that his pursuer was now hurrying to keep up.

Amaury turned sharply to the left on pont Notre Dame, keeping close to the buildings on the eastern side. As he passed into the broad plaza, the facade of the magnificent cathedral came into view. After three centuries, the Gothic beauty of Notre Dame never failed to inspire awe. With all its treasures, Paris would cease to be Paris without this greatest of monuments to God and Church. How starkly different was Cité than when he visited the Conciergerie. Candles burned in both towers in sufficient numbers to cast a glow on Sainte-Chapelle and create a false daylight below.

He turned in to the plaza and hurried to a spot in the shadows. There he waited, just another Parisian taking the air on a late winter night. A steady stream of pedestrians entered the plaza: a young man with a scraggly beard in a red jerkin, an *ancien* in a green cloak, two heavyset women laughing at some unheard joke. Then Hoess.

The wine merchant, affability vanished, hurried across, light on his feet for a man of his girth. His head swiveled to and fro as he searched the plaza for his lost quarry, jowls flapping like folds of cloth. For a moment, Amaury was tempted to stroll out and greet him, just to see Hoess attempt to stammer an explanation for being there.

The Swabian stopped, hands going to his hips. When he concluded Amaury could not have made it all the way across into Quartier Latin, he turned and walked quickly toward Notre Dame. Amaury, he reasoned, must have entered the cathedral. The interior was so vast, and the stream of worshippers, even at this hour, so steady that Hoess would need some moments to check the nave and side aisles.

Amaury waited a moment or two after the wine merchant entered the great doors to be certain the Swabian would not change his mind and pop out again. Then he emerged from the shadows and proceeded quickly across the bridge.

At the far side, he entered grand rue Saint-Jacques. Montaigu was a mere ten-minute walk south from here. His appointment, however, took him east, to a basement on a small residential street, rue Alexandre Langlois, the third building in from grand rue Saint-Victor. After looking up and down the street one last time, he descended the small staircase and rapped softly on the door.

There was no response. Had he mistaken the date or the time? After a few more moments, Amaury turned to remount the steps. Just then, he heard the click of a lock being turned. Soon afterward, the door swung open.

He started inside but he could not see where to walk. The interior was completely dark. What scant illumination from the street penetrated the blackness seemed arrested at the threshold. Amaury leaned forward, trying to make out something or someone, perhaps just an object of reference, but could not.

"Come in," said a voice, soft but somehow strained. "Your eyes will become accustomed."

Amaury moved forward in tiny steps, his right arm extended to warn him of any obstacles. Why was there no light? Was his go-between with Ory blind? Amaury moved completely into the gloom before he noticed the softest glow coming from a room ahead and to the left. As the voice promised, his eyes were becoming accustomed to the surroundings, and he was able to make his way down the hall until the turn without stumbling. Ahead of him was a room with a table and chairs. A tiny candle sat in a cylindrical holder with high sides, shielding the flame so that only the most feeble gleam escaped. He made for the table and sat in the nearest of the chairs. There was a soft crunching behind him. A figure passed. All Amaury could see was the back of a cloak, its hood pulled up. The figure inside seemed to waddle more than walk, its feet not leaving the floor sufficiently to avoid scraping. The figure paused at the other side of the table before turning to sit in the opposite chair.

When he did so, Amaury could not stifle a gasp. Opposite him sat the most astonishingly ugly man he had ever seen. Not even a man, really; more like a flayed animal. The creature had leathery skin, alternately dark and pasty white, which seemed to be flaking off like the bark of a plane tree. Two elliptical holes were set in the center of the shriveled face in place of a nose. Below the oblongs were dry, pale lips.

The man smiled ever so slightly, the skin around his mouth bunching grotesquely like a child's horror mask. "You can understand why I am averse to an excess of light," he said in the same strained manner, as if speech itself was an unnatural act. He removed his arms from his cloak to slide the candle to the side. The hands were gnarled and misshapen. Claws. He was forced to place one on either side of the candleholder to slide it even a short distance. Finally, Amaury understood that he was in the presence of a man who had been horribly burned.

"That is less offensive, is it not?" the man asked, laboriously replacing his arms in his sleeves. In fact, the small distance the candle had moved had not changed the vision at all.

Amaury was too stunned to respond. He simply continued to stare across the table. As he became inured to the man's deformity, revulsion began to turn to wonder. Only then did he notice the man's eyes. They were pale green; intelligent and intense. They dominated the face, as if all the ugliness was artificial, camouflage for an indomitable and forbidding spirit underneath. Once Amaury gazed into them, he could not look away.

"Would you care for some wine? I have found that it aids those who must remain in my presence." The voice did not waver, had no inflection. With the unvaried cadence, Amaury could not be certain if the remark was jest or fact.

"No, thank you," he replied. "I do not find being in your presence taxing."

The crinkle of skin over the man's eyes rose. Where his eyebrows had once been. "Do you not? I thank you for saying so, even if it is untrue."

"It is true," Amaury insisted, and realized, to his surprise, that it was.

"*Tu egisti bene in mea sententia*," the man said in Latin. "You have done well, I believe."

"Have I?"

"Yes," the man replied. "You have advanced your friendship with Broussard. Have you learned anything?"

"Only to confirm what I had already been told. Geoffrey claimed not to know Giles Fabrizy, but I could tell he was lying."

"Indeed?" the man replied. "Do you think Broussard had a hand in Fabrizy's death?"

"There is some distance between denying knowing someone and being complicit in his death."

"You like Broussard?"

"Of course."

"He is a friend?"

"Of a sort."

"But you would betray him to . . . us?"

"If he is responsible for Fabrizy's death . . . yes, I would."

"You cared for Fabrizy then?"

Amaury remained silent.

The man nodded. "Yes. Perhaps, then, you would tell us," he allowed. "Perhaps not." The man paused, looking down at the top of the table. "Perhaps you have grown to like Broussard too much. He is, after all, a bright and charming young man. Perhaps you will grow to find his heresies appealing as well. All that nonsense about bringing Man closer to God. Allow me, then, to enlighten you, to tell you a story about your Lutheran friends."

Amaury began to protest, but the man raised one of those shriveled claws to stop him. "You do not need to protest your innocence. I, as you, thought them simply men of good will misguided by a desire to initiate reforms to a Church that, as we all can see, is greatly in need of them. I, as you, met some quite amiable people among the Lutherans. But unlike you, my young friend, I have experienced Lutherans not merely as agents of change, but as rulers." He reached once again to grasp the candle, this time to move it closer so that his hideous skin was fully illuminated. "The thing you see before you is the result."

The man replaced the candle with a dry chuckle. "I no longer fear fire," he said. "I have so little skin left to burn." He raised his eyes to Amaury and began his tale. "My name is Johann Liebfreund. I came to Paris from Basel three years ago. My emigration from Switzerland was not by choice.

"I am—was—a tutor by trade. I spent my days trying to stuff the classics down the gullets of spoiled offspring of the merchant class who aspired to be taken for something better. I was what has been termed a 'humanist.' I had scant interest in theology, although, of course, I attended church and participated in the sacraments. As I am sure you know, Basel was perhaps the most cultured city in Europe . . . including this one. Scholars from across the continent came to study at the university and participate in the interchange of ideas. It was the most tolerant city as well, orthodox and reformers living side by side, worshipping freely. Erasmus himself chose Basel after he left Paris. When he arrived, he was assigned an assistant, a minor clergyman named Hausschein. Hausschein was a sour, foul-tempered man of mediocre ability, and Erasmus often teased him unmercifully.

"Although Catholics still dominated the upper classes, Lutherans had begun to make inroads so that, five years ago, after Erasmus was long gone, power teetered between the two. To maintain its reputation for tolerance, the city council passed an edict guaranteeing freedom of worship, the first of its kind in Christendom. That was too much for the Lutherans. They had effected their gains by stoking the resentment of the lower classes to what they howled were excesses by the Church, including the hoarding of riches. The uneducated are particularly susceptible to demagoguery.

"In response to the new law, a Lutheran minister organized a mob. He had Latinized his name to Oecolampadius. In German, of course, it would have been *Hausschein*, 'house light,' but Oecolampadius sounded a good deal more impressive to Erasmus's old assistant. In any event, Oecolampadius organized a mob. Eight hundred met at dawn in the town square. After stoking their rage with a speech in which he assured them that the Catholics would steal their money and their souls, he demanded an end to Mass and the expulsion of Catholics from the government. When they had reached the appropriate level of fury, he turned his rabble loose on the city. By evening they had taken over the center of town, and by the next day their ranks had grown to thousands. The mob ran through the streets, ransacking churches, smashing idols and artifacts, murdering priests, and burning down whatever buildings they decided were harboring Catholics. In some sections of gentle, tolerant Basel, the streets literally ran red with blood.

"Finally, they arrived at the home of my employer, a silk merchant from Italy named Frondizi. A quite decent man, said to be Catholic, even an agent of the pope. His two sons were quick and eager, and I had come to be treated as a member of the family. A rumor had gotten started that Signor Frondizi kept large sums of gold and silver in the house, a rumor that was unfortunately incorrect. When he refused to produce that which was not there, the leader of these God-fearing apostles of reform and true religion ordered the mob to fire the house. I was on my way down from my room in the atelier when the torches struck.

"There had been little rain for weeks. The wood and paper in the house, including a magnificent library, caught fire almost instantly. The house became an inferno so quickly that by the time I had reached the second floor, the staircase was impassable. I turned back to try to find a window to leap from, but the first two rooms I entered were too filled with smoke and flame to get through. By the time I reached the third room, I realized that I must make my way across to the window or die. I began to rush through, but was immediately enveloped in flames. The pain was so great that at first I was conscious of nothing—I heard horrible screams and only afterward realized that they were mine. I began to sink to my knees when, incredibly, there was a hand on my shoulder, pulling me out. I was told later that a handful of broiled skin came off in that hand. Signor Frondizi had come up a back stairway. He dragged me back down the same way and pitched me into the street. I immediately fainted. I found out later that, in the attempt, Frondizi himself had been horribly burned and died two days afterward.

"In the entire household, only a maid and a charwoman escaped unscathed. Of the family, all but Signora Frondizi perished, and she had been blinded and crippled. I was taken to a local physician, where I lay for six months, oils applied to my burns. Mercifully, I remember almost nothing of my convalescence. I was told later that for the first weeks, I shrieked in agony almost constantly. For the remainder, every time I slept, the fire came back to me. I avoid sleep whenever possible to this day, lest I wake screaming, the pain of the burns as fresh as—" Liebfreund paused and made to smile. "But enough of my misfortune. Suffice to say that only after two years was I well enough to get about on my own . . . if you can call this getting about." Liebfreund paused. "A terrible story, is it not?"

There was little Amaury could do but nod in agreement.

"Actually, that was not the terrible part. The terrible part came later. Only after the incident did the mob learn that Signor Frondizi was not an agent of the pope after all. He was not even anymore a Catholic. Although he did not make a spectacle of it, he had become a convert to the teachings of Luther. He had even sheltered other Lutherans fleeing persecution from his native country. Do you know what Oecolampadius said when he found out about this ghastly mistake, these murders that he had incited? He said, 'To die in such a fashion proves that Frondizi was, in truth, an agent of the pope after all.'"

Amaury merely sat by the flicker of the small candle, staring across at a man who, in effect, had been burned at the stake and lived.

"There is some justice, I suppose," Liebfreund sighed. His breath had become labored from the exertion of recounting his tale. "Oecolampadius died two years later. A particularly painful cancer, I am told. I suspect that whether God is as the Lutherans describe Him or the Catholics, someone of those . . . sensibilities . . . will not be welcomed in Heaven. Or, at least, that is what I need to believe."

"I'm certain you're correct," Amaury offered.

Liebfreund looked for a moment into Amaury's eyes, then returned to the subject at hand. "Tell me of your fellows at the rooming house."

"They are all Lutherans, as I am certain you already know. Turvette seems to be the more suspicious, but Hoess, the wine merchant, attempted to follow me here."

"Do you suspect *them* of complicity?"

"In the murder?"

"In anything."

"Perhaps. I am still not convinced that a conspiracy exists."

"Skepticism is a healthy attitude . . . have you ever been to Nérac?" Liebfreund asked suddenly.

Amaury said he had not.

"You know why I ask?"

"I assume you are referring to Queen Marguerite," Amaury replied. That King François' elder sister, Queen Marguerite of Navarre, sheltered and encouraged Lutherans at her palace in the south was common knowledge.

"Yes." Liebfreund's tone was venomous. "Queen Marguerite. The vile heretic adulteress. King François, for all his fecklessness, in his heart fears God and respects orthodoxy. But, with deceit, that unclean harpy has swayed and twisted him. With misplaced affection, he is reluctant to displease her. She claims to have remained within the Church, but, unbeknownst to the king, she has set her sights on no less than claiming France for the Lutherans. Without the intercession of those of the True Faith, she might well succeed. It has come to us that Nérac is where the conspiracy is centered. There has been increasingly frequent travel between here and there. Quite well organized by Lutheran standards. They have even established way stations along the route, so that they pass their nights without fear of exposure or betrayal. Communications of great interest to us—and to you—pass regularly. We would all benefit greatly to be able to learn of the contents."

"What is it you wish me to do?"

"Contrive a reason to travel to Nérac. To be *asked* to travel to Nérac. The conspirators are, at least for the moment, extremely small in number. They have lost an important courier. They will be anxious to recruit another. You will merely have to convince them that you are a likely convert. Can you do that?"

"I believe so," Amaury replied.

"I suspect that in the process you might well find out who murdered your predecessor. That would please you?"

"Of course."

"There is to be a meeting tomorrow night. Supposedly secret at a location outside the city walls. You will have little difficulty gaining an invitation from Broussard."

"I am already invited."

Liebfreund raised his eyes and stared across the table, a living death's head. "Good," he said, but Amaury was unsure if the compliment was genuine or if the Swiss was instead curious as to why Amaury hadn't mentioned the invitation earlier. "Go just as you had planned. Don't look about or give a sign that anything is amiss. As far as anyone is concerned, you are simply a man who has become disillusioned with orthodoxy and have become curious about reform. We will do the rest."

"What is 'the rest'?"

"We will simply observe," Liebfreund assured him. "Gather information. That's all."

"They are not all like Oecolampadius," Amaury said.

"Of course not," Liebfreund replied easily. "I know that."

IX

AFTER HE LEFT Liebfreund's grotto, Amaury stopped at a tavern and downed three cups of wine, spilling some of the final portion on his sleeves. He waited until an appropriately late hour, then made his way back to rue de la Cerise. When he arrived, he pounded on the door until Sylvie came out from her room behind the kitchen to admit him. He barged in, apologizing for the hour in slurred speech. Brushing past her closely, he made sure Sylvie smelled the drink on his clothes. Amaury then walked noisily and unsteadily to the stairs and hauled himself up. When he entered his room, he slammed the door loudly behind him.

Amaury knew within moments that his room had been searched. He would have been surprised had it not been. Anticipating the likelihood, he had placed his sack precisely four finger widths from the wall under the window. When he checked, the space was slightly wider. Inside the sack, everything had been replaced in the order he had left it but, once more, just a bit shifted from its original position. He removed the book he had taken with him and checked the letter to his father he had placed inside. Yes, whoever had gone through his things had read the letter. The letter that foreswore Montaigu and the interpretation of canon law that the school represented, that announced his disgust with the state of the Church and his need to seek a new path for himself, away from the false piety into which Catholicism had sunk. He begged his father's forgiveness but asserted he had no choice but to make this decision.

Amaury refolded the letter and replaced it in his sack. Perhaps one day he might actually post it.

The next morning at breakfast, Amaury stared at the bread, sausage, and cheese and mumbled a string of apologies for his behavior. Madame La Framboise wagged a finger at him and informed him that such conduct was unacceptable in her house. Amaury swore he would not do it again. He asked absolution for one indiscretion, caused only by nine years' confinement in the prison that was Montaigu. Madame La Framboise considered the question briefly before deigning to forgive him. Through it all, Hoess sat at the table, effusive in his amusement at Amaury's transgression, at one point chastising Madame La Framboise for her lack of understanding. It would have been more shocking if the poor lad had *not* needed to go out at least once, he said. Not for an instant did the wine merchant betray himself. When Amaury rose unsteadily from the table, claiming *mal d'estomac*, Hoess called after him. "Next time, take me with you."

Grateful for the excuse of illness, Amaury passed the day in his room reading his book, *Epytoma in almagesti Ptolemei*, "The Epitome of Ptolemy's Almagest," by the German Regiomontanus, perhaps the most important astronomical text of the past hundred years. Regiomontanus was a great trigonometer as well, and was thus able to clarify the positions and movements of the sun, stars, and planets in the spheres that radiated out from the Earth.

To spend hours with a great astronomer without fear of discovery and punishment was a joy he had not experienced in almost a decade. Regiomontanus had employed new theorems of triangular behavior to bring clarity to Ptolemy's circular orbits. Amaury marveled at how science was springing forward in almost every discipline. Some thought it blasphemous for Man to seek knowledge of the wonder of God's creation, but how could it be blasphemy to use the tools that the Lord himself had provided? The greater blasphemy, Amaury was certain, lay in the perpetuation of ignorance.

He begged off dinner, claiming that his head still felt as if it had been used to batter down a door. He told Madame La Framboise that he was again going out, this time to spend the evening in penitence. When he left the rooming house, Amaury made directly for église Saint-Antoine. He did not think Hoess would be so obvious as to follow him again, but it would not do to take any risk that might be avoided.

After sundown, Amaury left the church by a side door. An English wind had blown a thick layer of clouds from the west. Amaury waited in a cul-de-sac, but no one had followed.

At rue des Bales, he knocked lightly on Fournière's back door. Broussard opened it quickly and motioned him inside with two flicks of the wrist.

The shutters were closed tight across the single window. The back room was lit only by a single small candle that sent flickering shadows across the bookcases that lined the walls. The mood was reminiscent of Liebfreund's dungeonlike dwelling the night before. Also like Liebfreund, Broussard was dressed in a long black hooded cloak that covered all but his face. Framed thus, his large head and distinctive features looked even more François-like. When he took note of Amaury's ocher doublet, brown breeches, yellow nether hose, and tan cape, Broussard shook his head reproachfully, then ducked into another room and emerged with a second black cloak.

"Wear this," he said. "You can't just go strolling about, you know. The Inquisition has agents everywhere. Everyone is at risk. Chauvin will be burned if he is caught. By the way, are you armed?"

"A dagger."

"You're an optimist." Broussard pulled back his cloak to reveal the hilt of a sword.

The two men stepped into the alley. Broussard closed the door behind him slowly so that it emitted only the most innocuous creak. He turned left, heading north.

Amaury was treading much the same path as had Giles the night he was murdered. Could Broussard be leading him into the same sort of trap? Broussard hadn't wielded the knife. He was hardly the thin *Franciscain* Veuve Chinot had described. Another might lie in wait, however. Two days before, Amaury would never have considered such a possibility. But now he could hardly afford not to.

Amaury fingered the dagger in his waistband. He allowed Broussard to walk a bit ahead of him and on his right. They passed rue Pastourelle. Amaury glanced up, wondering if the old lady was sitting at her window, watching two cloaked figures slink past.

Broussard skirted the Temple fortress to the city wall, then followed it west to porte de Temple. The guards at the city gate issued no challenge but simply waved the two men in black cloaks through, thinking them, Amaury realized, to be Dominican friars. As they passed over the deep dry ditch that surrounded Paris, the wind suddenly blew away the clouds and they were bathed in moonlight. They walked north to an open field, then turned east when a line of windmills lay between them and the guard towers on the battlements. Broussard turned to Amaury and grinned.

"There. That wasn't so hard. I confess I sort of enjoy skulking about. You?"

"Yes, Geoffrey. It's thrilling being in your company. Might you now tell me where we're going? Is this meeting to be with cows?"

Broussard patted him on the back. "Hardly. Well, perhaps one or two. We are headed to La Croix Faubin, my friend. The town is just north of porte Saint-Antoine, but that gate is next to the Bastille, so the guards think they have to challenge everyone. Porte de Temple is easier to pass."

They followed the paths through the fields before eventually turning back south, Amaury continuing to trail Broussard just in case. Soon, however, they arrived at La Croix Faubin, a small, walled hamlet with gates at the north and south. The north gate, which Broussard chose, was unlocked and unmanned, and so the two black-cloaked figures walked through unchallenged. Amaury surmised, correctly, as he later learned, that the sentries had been paid to absent themselves.

The village consisted of one main road, rue Saint-Denis, which ran through the center, with smaller streets spurring off in either direction. About halfway, Broussard took a narrow street to the right and made for a large house at the end. Two younger men were just going in the door.

"We try not to all arrive at the same time," Broussard told him. "It takes longer to convene and adjourn a meeting, but it's worth the effort."

When they reached the entrance, Amaury was astonished to be greeted by a large woman of about forty, wearing an incongruous wig of yellow ringlets and a plethora of face paint. Her huge bosom squeezed out of an orange crinoline dress that was many sizes too small. She favored them with a large smile filled with stained teeth. She gave off an overpowering smell of roses.

"Welcome," she crooned in a voice somewhere between girlish and graveled.

Broussard returned the greeting, referring to the woman as Madame Chouchou.

After she took their cloaks, Madame Chouchou checked Amaury up and down. "I haven't seen you before, *mon beau fils*. Maybe you can stay after the meeting."

Amaury replied with a noncommittal grunt. In truth, he was sorely tempted. It had been eight months. No, nine. The broken-down old whore in rue Dupin. In principle, he was as contemptuous of prostitutes as every other God-fearing person. Women who pandered to human weakness with false flattery and the pretense of mutual pleasure, who provided only a moment of release followed by hours of regret, and who then charged for the privilege. From a practical standpoint, however, there was little alternative. And without the availability of such women, the murder rate among students would be even higher than it was.

Amaury and Broussard walked through the front hall, perused by Madame Chouchou's charges, who were congregated near the staircase that led to the rooms on the second floor. They ranged drastically in age. Girls who seemed little more than thirteen intermixed with hags older than Madame Chouchou herself. The heavy scent of women was in the air. Broussard leaned close to Amaury and whispered.

"See? As I told you. One or two cows."

Amaury nodded absently. His eyes had fixed on one of the younger women. She was not more than eighteen, small, with large mournful eyes, brown hair, and full lips. She wore neither wig nor face paint nor suggestive clothing. But her ease and obvious confidence bespoke her experience with men. She was quite beautiful, and Amaury felt himself stir. The girl smiled.

They passed through to a large common room at the back of the first floor. The furniture was arranged to face a lectern against the back wall. Wooden crates had been dragged in to supplement the chairs. The shutters were closed and heavy drapery covered the windows. As soon as they were through the door, Broussard laughed. "Surprised?"

"I wasn't expecting to listen to scriptural analysis in a brothel."

Broussard turned his hands palms up. "What could be better? Madame Chouchou knows everything and everyone. She seeks God's grace like the rest of us. There isn't a better location to ensure privacy in all France. You should be more open-minded, my friend."

About twenty men were in attendance, speaking in small groups. Like the women outside, their ages were disparate, some older, most young. Amaury looked from one to another, trying to discern if any of the attendees were thin with either a tonsure or closely cropped hair. But no.

Broussard gestured across the room toward a tall, painfully thin man with a wispy goatee. "That's Jean Chauvin." Chauvin was speaking to a group of five men who seemed to be taking in his words with reverence. "He's Latinized his name to Johannes Calvinus. A bit pretentious, but I suppose we must allow him that. It's Jean Calvin in the vernacular. Come. Let me introduce you."

Calvin was in his twenties, younger likely than Amaury. Up close, however, he appeared older. Dark blotches rimmed his eyes. His skin resembled parchment. A pinched, even pained, expression seemed stamped on his face. But Calvin's eyes, light blue, shone fierce and attentive. Amaury thought immediately of Beda.

"This is Amaury de Faverges," Broussard told Calvin. "Amaury is a fine fellow, late of nine years at Montaigu. But instead of dogma, he acquired good judgment. He has finally decided to seek a new path in life."

"Montaigu?" Calvin asked, his French heavy with a northern country accent. Picardy perhaps, or Brittany. His voice was high and nasal, like that of a much older man. "I studied there myself, although almost a decade ago. But my father was urging me to become a lawyer. After two years, I decided that if Montaigu epitomized theology, the law would certainly be preferable."

Amaury agreed that he also found it difficult to reconcile Montaigu with the word of God.

"I understand Beda has been resurrected," Calvin said, seemingly as an afterthought. "Is the Old Satan his usual self?"

Amaury began to reply that Noël Beda, although near the end, had lost none of his fire, but he seized back the words before they could pass his lips. Beda's return had not been announced publicly until after Amaury had left Montaigu, and thus Amaury should have no way of knowing the state of the old man's health. "I have heard of Magister Beda's return as well," he responded instead. "I pity the students. Le Clerc, for all his faults, was not nearly so extreme."

"Few could be," Calvin agreed. Suddenly he grimaced and bent double, his hands clutching at his stomach. He remained in that position for several seconds. Finally he took some deep breaths and straightened up. His face was ashen but he no longer seemed in distress.

"A vestige of Montaigu," he said. "The food and miasma caused agony in my bowels that no ameliorant seems able to lessen. They burn as if Satan himself were present within me. I suppose I should be grateful, however, since pain helps one to see God."

"Quite true," Amaury agreed, although he thought the notion ludicrous.

They were interrupted by a man in his mid-thirties, bald, with a fringe of black hair surrounding his pate. The stubble of a thick black beard covered his cheeks and chin. He would have appeared Moorish, save for small, deep-set eyes and thin lips. By the ease with which he approached Calvin, he was clearly someone of influence. He told Calvin in Swiss-accented Latin that someone he referred to sneeringly as "the Italian" could not be located in Paris.

"Has he been apprehended?" Calvin asked in French.

The swarthy man said he had not. News of an arrest would have been reported. "He is rumored to have never even arrived in the city. Still in the south, I was told."

"I should have known better than to risk my freedom on his account," Calvin snapped. He turned to Amaury. "He is a scoundrel, this man. A scoundrel and a poseur, who would tear down the Church, not simply repair its flaws."

"Surely no Christian wishes such a sinful act," Amaury replied. Would irritation inhibit Calvin's reserve?

"This man does. He dares postulate that God is so common as to exist in all men. Not simply that. God exists in rocks and trees, in the very floor beneath our feet. Thus, when we trod from one end of the room to the other, we are walking over God. Walking on God! What blasphemy! Now he avers that science is part of God's glory as well, and must be incorporated into dogma. He claims to be privy to a revelation that will disprove the common interpretation of Genesis itself. Absurd!"

So Ory had been correct. Incredible. Amaury wanted to pursue the inquiry, to ask for details, but Calvin turned to the swarthy man, whom he now addressed as Henri. "I suppose we should begin then. The rogue has left us no other choice."

Amaury moved to the rear and sat on a long maple chest with a clasp on the front that was likely used for clothes or bedding. A conspiracy to disprove Genesis. Using science. But how? Science proved Scripture, not the other way around.

He became aware that someone had quietly sat next to him.

"You're new," said the young prostitute with the mournful eyes.

Amaury nodded perfunctorily. The girl was indeed quite beautiful. Her teeth were white and her skin clear, with a tinge of olive. Her eyes were chestnut flecked with gold. Under the plain woolen dress lay a high full bosom.

"I'm Vivienne," said the girl.

Amaury gave his own name in reply. He shifted in his seat, feeling another rush of lust. Before he could think what to say next, Calvin stepped to the front of the room.

From a distance, Calvin seemed even more of a wisp. But as he grasped both sides of the lectern with his bony fingers and leaned forward, the power of his presence rendered his physical appearance inconsequential. He surveyed the group for a few moments, then began.

"We, my brothers—and sisters—have been accused of perverting the word of Christ. Of denying dogma. That is rubbish, mere propaganda issued by the dying and corrupt. It is the Catholic Church that perverts dogma. Show me a passage in Scripture that appoints a priest as intermediary between Man and God. Show me where it commands one man to confess to another as a way to speak to God. Show me where it allows one man to grant absolution to another. Show me where it commands that services be held in Latin, a language that few common people can understand, and which further distances parishioners from understanding the dictates of God . . ."

Calvin raised a bony forefinger. A pinch of red showed on each cheek. "True repentance, repentance of the soul, cannot come without understanding. We who believe in reform try to bring man and God closer together, not keep them apart just so that a cabal of priests and bishops may grow rich and fat by interpreting God's word. The Catholic Church has stultified. Priests reciting prayer by rote; sacraments administered by sleepwalkers. How can a parishioner hope to gain true salvation guided by such men?

"I have come to discuss a Trinity, but not the Holy Trinity. A Trinity of Salvation. I have studied this question at some length and have arrived at certain conclusions that may be a revelation."

Calvin spent the next hour explaining that he had come to believe three things: first, that Man, because of Sin, was damned; second, that those few who were saved were granted that rare and undeserved gift through God's mercy alone; and, third, that God was too powerful a force to leave the identity of those who would be saved to chance. He had thus come to believe that God knew, before Man was even created, who was to be saved and who would be damned. There was no way, of course, for Man to determine that which God had preordained. Good works in pursuit of salvation was, therefore, pointless. Whomever was saved would learn of salvation only upon death.

Amaury sat stunned. The notion that free will had no role in salvation ran counter even to the teachings of Luther. How hopeless, if true. What would then be the point of existence? The quest for salvation, the struggle to overcome one's basest instincts—surely these were why God placed Man on Earth. Not to be part of some great lottery.

Amaury seemed alone in his shock. Many in the audience moved to the front, anxious to hear more of Calvin's theory. Amaury decided he should do so as well, so as not to betray his feelings, when he felt a tap on his arm.

"I don't understand," the girl, Vivienne, said. "Is he saying that it doesn't matter what you do in life?"

"That is how I understood him."

"That you may sin and still go to heaven?"

"So it seems."

Vivienne smiled. She was graceful rather than obvious, alluring rather than prurient. "Very appealing for those of us here," she observed drily.

Amaury felt himself grin. "Yes. I suppose." What was this girl doing here? She was nothing like the whores who populated l'Université.

"In fact," she continued, "it would seem foolish *not* to sin, since it makes no difference to God."

"That is logical."

She placed her hand on his. Amaury felt the breath go right out of him. "Perhaps we should test this theory," she said softly. She smiled once more, but this time it was different. "Would you like to stay and have a cup of wine?"

Amaury looked to the front of the room. Calvin was already gone. Whatever he sought to learn about murder and conspiracy would hold until morning.

"Yes," he told the girl. "I'd like that very much."

X

EXTRAORDINARY. Amaury had come to La Croix Faubin prepared for many things, but not this.

He paid a smiling Madame Chouchou, then retired to an upstairs room with Vivienne. As he anticipated, her body was beautiful: smooth, young, rounded. She gave off an intoxicating, musky scent. Amaury desired her so completely, so profoundly, that he coupled with her instantly. It was all he could do not to complete the act in seconds. Even so, thrusting against her, hearing her breathe, smelling her, he could control himself for only a few moments. The release was heaven itself, but, the instant he was done, his disappointment was overpowering. For it to be over so quickly.

Then Vivienne had done the most exceptional thing.

"There is no rush for you to leave," she said. "Lay here with me for a bit. You may find the second time even more pleasing."

He had.

An hour later, Amaury was awash in a deep sense of peaceful satisfaction. He would fairly float his way back to the city. When Amaury had told him that he intended to stay, Broussard had laughed. "When I told you to be more open-minded, I didn't think you would take my words quite so much to heart."

When Amaury returned to the first floor, however, a familiar figure stood before him. "Not in church after all, then?"

"No, Monsieur Hoess. As you see, I have sought stimulation of a different sort."

"I do indeed. I'm pleased not to have been forced to wait all night."

Amaury had not seen Hoess at the meeting. Had the Swabian been secreted, or had he arrived only recently? "Where's Geoffrey?" he asked.

"I sent Geoffrey on ahead." Hoess extended his hand. "Come inside with me, Faverges. There is someone who wishes to meet you." He led Amaury back into the room in which Calvin had spoken. The furniture had been returned to its standard arrangement. Inside was Henri, the swarthy Swiss who had spoken with Calvin. The wine merchant ushered Amaury in, then took his leave.

The Swiss wasted no time on introductions. "Brother Broussard describes you in glowing terms and assures us that you would make a valued member of our group. Brother Hoess doesn't trust you. Brother Turvette is certain you are a spy."

"I seek neither membership nor trust," Amaury replied, although in fact he sought both. "And you must decide for yourself if you think me a spy."

"What did you think of Brother Calvin?" Henri asked.

"Obviously an excellent mind. Beautiful logic. His rejection of the Mass and priestly intervention seems quite correct to me, although the notion that one may be damned even before birth is not altogether appealing."

"Interpretation of the word of God is not undertaken to appeal," Henri retorted. "But perhaps we can discuss this further on the way back to Paris. That is, if you don't mind my company."

"Not at all." Amaury retrieved his cloak, but noticed that Henri wore only the dark blue doublet and black hose he had worn inside. Instead of heading north, they made directly for porte Saint-Antoine. "I thought this route was too dangerous."

Henri sighed. "Geoffrey came by porte de Temple? He always does that. Porte Saint-Antoine is safe enough."

After they had walked a bit, Henri said, "I understand from Geoffrey that Giles Fabrizy was your friend. His death was a great loss. Brilliant young man."

"But I thought Geoffrey said he didn't know Giles."

"Don't be foolish, Faverges. Of course he did. As you well deduced. Lying is not one of Geoffrey's best developed skills."

Amaury did not reply.

"I seek the day when such mindless violence will no longer stain Man's path on Earth," Henri continued, raising his voice slightly in an attempt to make the platitude sound more sincere.

"But every act is God's will, is it not?"

"Is it? I'm not certain." Henri had returned to the offhand manner that suited him better.

"But why do you bring up Giles?"

"What I wanted to tell you was that Brother Calvin found you quite impressive," Henri replied, ignoring the question. "Uncommon for him."

"Brother Calvin is too kind."

Henri laughed once more. "He would blanch at that description. But you are obviously an intelligent and resourceful fellow. And I suspect you are ready to throw off the corrupt ways and seek your own path . . ."

Almost precisely what Amaury had written in the sham letter to his father. He was pleased with himself for having thought to produce it.

"We would be honored," Henri went on, "to have you join us. Would you consider it? Assuming you find our ideas worthwhile, of course. There are many streams of thought in the Reform movement. Not just Brother Calvin's."

"Like disproving Genesis?"

Henri waved off the notion. "I actually find that rumor preposterous. I am undertaking a journey soon. I will be gone about two weeks. When I return, there are some people I would like you to meet. If you are willing."

"Where are you going?"

"Out of Paris," Henri replied. He whispered a caution as they approached porte Saint-Antoine but, after a perfunctory challenge by two sleepy soldiers, the two were permitted entry, the Bastille looming above them on the left.

Henri cocked his head toward the huge fortress as they passed. "It was built to be impregnable," he said. "Two centuries ago. Walls eighty feet high, two feet thick. Yet la Bastille has been besieged seven times and surrendered on all but one of those occasions. Obviously, what was invulnerable in the planning turned out to be less so in practice. The Catholic Church was built to be impregnable as well. I suspect it will suffer the same fate."

"The Catholics may prove to be more resilient than you imagine," Amaury replied.

"Resilient? Perhaps. But also top-heavy, with a rotten foundation. A bad combination in a strong wind and, let me assure you, Monsieur Faverges, our wind is strong indeed."

"Winds are unpredictable," Amaury observed. "They blow back in your face when you least expect them."

"You do not curry favor. I'll say that for you."

Inside the city walls, Amaury was about to turn left toward rue de la Cerise and home, but Henri bade him continue on. "Come to my lodgings," he said. "We can share some wine and talk some more. There are some matters on which I would like your opinion."

By reflex, Amaury's hand went to his dagger. Being trapped in Henri's room had not been part of his plan, but there was little choice. To say no might well close off Henri permanently as a source of information.

They walked quite a distance together saying little until Henri gestured and turned left at pont Notre Dame, the same bridge that Amaury had used the previous night to visit Liebfreund. Instead of turning east off grand rue Saint-Jacques, however, as he had done last night, Henri turned west just before the Sorbonne. They entered a warren of small streets, most of which held cheap residences for students or foreign visitors.

All at once they heard footsteps behind them, noisy footsteps, matching theirs. Two men, it seemed, perhaps three, making no effort at concealment. At first, Amaury thought this might be an ambush of Henri's making, but one look at the man's wide eyes told Amaury the threat was from a different source. Henri stopped and threw an arm across Amaury's chest, then spun around and listened. The footsteps ceased as well.

"We must hurry," Henri whispered, as he motioned for Amaury to start up again. He turned in at the small street to their left. The footsteps began again, growing louder, more distinct. At the next corner, Henri turned left. "We must make it to my lodgings," he gasped. "Before they cut us off."

They turned right down a narrow street, little more than an alley. They were walking more quickly, heading toward the Sorbonne. If they could make it, there would be more foot traffic, even so late at night.

Henri continued along a serpentine path, but the footsteps never left them. He and Amaury began to walk faster, but the sound was relentless. They were moving away from the Sorbonne now, heading for Henri's lodgings. "Two more streets," Henri gasped. Together, they broke into a run. Their pursuers began running as well.

The footsteps seemed now to be just behind them. Amaury glanced back but saw no one. He pulled out his dagger. Henri made a quick turn down a narrow street to the left. Amaury followed, looking back again just before the turn to see if the men were gaining.

Amaury was still looking over his shoulder when the strangled cry came. He spun and saw Henri in the grasp of a large, coarse ruffian who held the hapless Swiss across the chest with his other hand over Henri's mouth. Henri attempted to kick his way free or cry out, but his captor was far too strong. Henri appeared as a child's marionette, kicking comically into the air.

Amaury took a step forward, leveling his dagger. The thug holding Henri made no move to draw a weapon of his own, but simply kept his victim between himself and Amaury. Amaury took a step to the side, to gain a better angle of attack, when he suddenly felt a numbing blow on his wrist. The dagger went skittering away. Amaury found himself in the grasp of another of the hooligans. His adversary, while not large, was strong and practiced. He grabbed Amaury by the upper arms, then pinned him with a powerful arm across his chest. Amaury felt a hand clamp over his mouth.

Henri and Amaury were held facing one another, each helpless. Another man, a ferretlike creature, unshaven and in a filthy brown jerkin, emerged from the gloom. He looked from Amaury to Henri, and then, after a moment, as Amaury watched helplessly, walked to the Swiss, removed a long knife from his belt, and calmly slit Henri's throat.

Henri's captor released him as a geyser of blood exploded from the gaping wound. Henri's mouth opened and shut quickly, as if he were trying to speak. Only a horrible, soft gurgle emerged. Henri took two drunken steps forward. Amaury recoiled, pushing his back into his assailant as the torrent of blood splashed on the ground near his feet.

Henri, his eyes fixed, seemed to stare at Amaury for a moment. There was a twitching at the corners of his mouth. Then, abruptly, he reeled backward, smashing against the wall of a building. The poor Swiss was suspended for a second, then sank to the stone pavement. His eyes remained open and unblinking. His clothing, down to his shoes, was drenched with blood. And there, Henri died.

The man holding Amaury released his grip. The man with the knife took a step in his direction. Amaury's head spun, as if on a swivel, as he desperately sought an avenue of escape. But they were all around him. He was about to run in whatever direction he faced, when he saw everyone's attention turn to a darkened doorway. A figure shuffled out, a misshapen creature encased in a cloak, only his deformed face visible in the dim light.

Liebfreund glanced briefly at the figure on the ground. "It is fortunate that I came along," he said. "The thugs one is forced to employ are easily confused. It might have been you over there instead of that scum."

Amaury stared at the dead man. He had seen men killed during brawls on the streets of Paris in his time at the Sorbonne, but a knife thrust was clean and neat. Nothing compared to this. Slowly, he regained control and, as he did so, shock was supplanted by fury. "You cannot murder innocents in the name of God," he shouted at Liebfreund. "You become everything your enemies say you are."

"Keep your voice down," Liebfreund snapped. Then, he added softly, "And he was not an innocent."

"Why?" insisted Amaury. "Because he did not believe as you do?"

Liebfreund stared at the body of the dead Lutheran for some moments, then raised his hideously charred face to Amaury. "His name is Henri Routbourg. I know him. He was at Basel."

XI

THE NEXT MORNING, Amaury stuffed his belongings into his sack. His clothes stuck to him from the previous night, and he hadn't slept. God rot Paris and religious cabals and plots against Genesis. He would leave this city to the fanatics and murderers. What a fool he had been to believe the path to honor could be shortened by acts of dishonor. Now, as reward for his stupidity, the monstrous vision of Henri Routbourg slumped against a wall bathed in his own blood would remain his companion.

But where would he go? Savoy? Never. Perhaps across to England and Oxford, where the study of science was treated more nobly than in Paris. But King Henry was tearing through the countryside, burning monasteries and destroying countless records. Germany? Science thrived in the German states, true, but chiefly in the Lutheran provinces. In any event, a decision to be made once he was outside the walls of this hellish place. Ory had told Amaury that if he refused the assignment, he would live out his days as a royal bastard. That prospect no longer seemed so onerous.

Amaury pulled the drawstrings of his sack so hard the thongs cut into his hands. Liebfreund. Good Lord! To have pitied him. At first, Amaury had not believed that Henri Routbourg had been a leader of the mob that had torn through the streets of Basel. He thought the gruesomely deformed Swiss had fabricated the tale, just a facile excuse to justify unprovoked murder. But Liebfreund had not been lying. He knew too many details. His hatred was too caustic, too genuine.

"Was this not God's justice?" the repulsive creature had asked. "Didn't Routbourg deserve to die for the horrible crimes he perpetrated? Not just my disfigurement, but for Frondizi, his wife, and four children, all of whom were innocent of any crime at all?"

But what of it? Who was Liebfreund to act for God? Or Ory? Or any of them? Amaury might have struck a whole man.

And what was more, even *that* was a lie. Liebfreund could have had Routbourg killed anytime he chose. Killing the Lutheran was not retribution but strategy, a ploy to clear the way for Amaury to make Routbourg's journey in his place. Well, Amaury would indeed make a journey, but he would no longer let anyone choose his destinations. Not Liebfreund. Not Ory. Not his father.

Just as Amaury was hefting the sack to leave, there was a knock at the door. Probably his landlady on some transparent pretext to pry another coin out of him. When he coldly asked who was there, Madame La Framboise's trill penetrated through the wood.

"Monsieur," she called, "a surprise."

Amaury jerked the door open. Madame La Framboise stood coyly before him, hands clasped in front of her, an expression of maternal satisfaction on her face. "A visitor," she cooed, ignoring his scowl. She allowed a discreet smile to play across her narrow lips, then glanced to her left and made a quick gesture with her head. A small, delicate figure in a large hooded brown cloak moved sidelong into the doorway.

"Vivienne?"

The girl nodded shyly.

Amaury glared from one of the women to the other. Angry as he was, however, the memory of his hour with Vivienne had remained intoxicating. Still, it was in that hour that Geoffrey had been dismissed back to Paris and his meeting with Routbourg had been arranged by Hoess.

"I need to see you," Vivienne said softly, not waiting for Amaury to speak. "It's very urgent. Otherwise I never would have . . ."

"Very well." As much as Amaury tried to remain stolid, the swell of her breasts made his heart rush and the scent of her skin was in his nostrils. The words came out stiffly rather than curt.

As he moved aside to allow the girl to enter, Madame La Framboise blinked twice in rapid succession to acknowledge the dispensation she was providing in permitting a boarder to entertain a woman in her rooms. Amaury swung the door shut, leaving his landlady to scuttle away.

"I'm so relieved you're safe." Vivienne spoke just above a whisper. "We heard about Monsieur Routbourg at Madame Chouchou's. The news is all over Paris. I knew that you had left with him."

"Yes, I heard as well," Amaury lied. He lifted his sack off the floor, a man in a hurry. "We had split up before he was attacked," he lied.

"Oh. I didn't know." Vivienne made to move toward him, but then stopped.

"And how did you know where to find me?" Amaury demanded. He wanted to be closer to her, but would not be played for the fool twice.

"Madame Chouchou knew where you were staying. I don't know how. Perhaps from Monsieur Hoess. When she saw how upset I was, she sent me to check to see that you were all right."

"Madame Chouchou sent you?" She lies no better than I do, he thought.

Vivienne nodded, her eyes not leaving Amaury's.

"Thank you. I'm fine."

"I'm so pleased," she said, a small, rueful smile making a brief appearance, then disappearing. "But there is another reason I came. I need to speak to you. As I said, a matter of great urgency. But I see you are on your way out." Still she did not move to the door herself.

So, Amaury knew, here was the choice. He should leave and not wait to hear what fabrication she had been put up to by Hoess or Madame Chouchou. But Vivienne had the fascination of a sorceress.

"All right," he grunted, "what is it?"

As she hesitated, Amaury suddenly knew what she was about to say. And it was not what he had been expecting.

"It concerns Giles," she said.

Of course. It all fit now. "So it *was* you in the alley the night he died. You came upon the body then ran away."

She stiffened. "How did you know?"

"Unimportant." He was pleased to have surprised her. "What matters is that you were there. Did you see the man who stabbed him?"

"No. I arrived too late."

"How did you know where he would be?"

"I didn't. Not precisely. He told me that he was going to the bookshop, then afterward for a rendezvous nearby."

"He was at the bookshop the day he died?"

"I can't say for certain. Only that he intended to go there."

"Do you know *why* he was killed?"

She shook her head.

"Then why were you looking for him?"

"I thought he might be in danger. He took such chances. I told him to be more careful, but he refused to listen."

"Why did you think he would be in danger that night?"

"He told me he was running an errand. Something very important. For Monsieur Routbourg, I think. I had a . . . feeling. I'm not sure. But I knew something terrible might happen. I was trying to find Giles. To stop him. But I arrived too late. Now Monsieur Routbourg is dead as well. Almost certainly by the same hand."

"Yes. Almost certainly. And last night, you were asked to . . . occupy me . . . to contrive to allow me to leave with Routbourg."

"I'm sorry," she said.

"Why?"

"I don't know. They only told me to . . ." She looked away, appearing genuinely abashed. An abashed whore? Perhaps she lied better than he had thought.

"And who sent you here now? Hoess? And for what purpose?"

She shook her head. "Monsieur Hoess was as surprised to see me downstairs as you are now."

"Why then?"

"Giles told me to contact you if anything happened to him."

Amaury stiffened. Was it true?

"Giles died over a week ago. Why did you wait?"

"I wasn't sure who to trust. I was afraid to expose myself, even to someone Giles told me was a friend. Then, last night, before the meeting, I overheard Monsieur Hoess giving your name to Monsieur Routbourg . . . that you would be arriving with Geoffrey Broussard."

"Then why didn't you tell me last night? When we were . . . alone?"

"Giles spoke of you all the time, you know," she replied, instead of answering the question. "He said you were the wisest man he had ever known."

"He overstated."

She shook her head. "No. I'm sure he was correct. I know a good deal about people. Men. I felt . . . feel . . . very safe with you."

"Safe from what?"

"Giles was killed because of his activities for the Brotherhood. I will be risking the same fate."

"You? How?"

"Henri Routbourg was to journey to Nérac."

"He will be going to Nérac," Liebfreund had said. "You will now go in his place. It will be child's play to arrange."

"I go nowhere for you."

Liebfreund had emitted a raspy sigh. In profile, his noseless face appeared even more grotesque. "And the murder of your friend? Does it not to you matter that the man lying in the street had likely ordered it?"

"The only one I know of who has ordered a murder is you."

Liebfreund had become so calm as to be almost casual. "All the same, he is almost certainly responsible."

"I don't believe you. How can you possibly know that? Where is your proof?"

"The proof is in Nérac. You need only to travel there."

"Routbourg told me he was taking a trip," Amaury said to Vivienne, "although he didn't mention the destination."

"It was Nérac. He had urgent business there."

"But how would this put you at risk?"

"I was to go as well. Posing as his wife."

"His wife?"

"Monsieur Routbourg told me that the Inquisition would stop at nothing to apprehend a member of the Brotherhood. He said they had found a couple was less likely to arouse suspicion than a man traveling alone."

"Why would you volunteer for such a task?"

She smiled. "It's my opportunity."

"For what?"

"A better life. To leave my current . . . profession. Forever. Did you think I became a whore for the joy of it?"

"No. Of course not." In truth, Amaury had never considered why someone would choose such an iniquitous calling. He had always simply assumed it was a combination of greed and weak virtue.

"Will you help me then?"

Amaury toyed with the thongs of his sack, which still lay in his hand.

"It's not just that," Vivienne pressed. "I believe we could learn about Giles' murder there."

"Why?"

"Giles told me he had come upon some rogue Lutheran sect. He said it was centered in Nérac. When I told him I had volunteered to accompany Monsieur Routbourg there, he asked me to observe closely when we arrived. When I asked what he wanted me to observe, he said I'd know when I encountered it. Whatever Giles hoped I would find, I'm certain you would be more fit to assess its import than I."

"Even so, why would Routbourg's cohorts trust me to go in his place?"

"Monsieur Routbourg was not going by choice. There was no one else in their group who could undertake the journey without being recognized. I think his friends would be eager to accept an offer from someone unknown to their enemies."

Liebfreund and the girl telling exactly the same story. And Giles seemed to have been the source for both. Still, something was not right. Amaury felt at the edge of a vortex from which, if he did not escape now, there would be no further opportunity.

"I'm sorry, Vivienne. I would like to help you . . ."

Vivienne reached into her cloak and withdrew a small packet. "Giles gave me this for you. In case something happened to him."

Amaury opened the packet. Inside was a single piece of paper. On it was drawn a diagram.

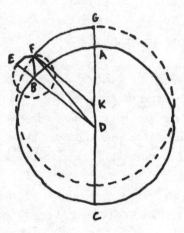

On the back was a brief message. Two short sentences, written with a reverse slant in small, perfectly formed letters. Unmistakably from Giles.

Amaury stared at the remarkable drawing for some moments, then folded the paper and deposited it in his sack.

"Very well, Vivienne. I'll go."

The old man sat at his desk, the sun streaming through the window, lighting the cluster of papers in front of him. He stared at the problem that had vexed him for years. It was almost a Greek paradox. How can a thing move backward and forward at the same time? Others had explained the anomaly, of course, but only through contrivance. He would do so with geometry and mathematical calculation.

Today he was especially frustrated. One needs continuity, and he could not retrieve his inspiration. Last week, at the moment he had felt himself on the verge of a breakthrough, a summons had arrived from Count Stefan. A physician was needed at Stefan's home. His niece had taken ill. Shortness of breath and an intolerable pain in the bowel. The old man had been terribly fatigued—on clear nights, he got almost no sleep at all—but there was little choice but to accompany the servant who had arrived with Stefan's message.

He arrived at the count's castle after a day's ride and was ushered immediately into the young girl's bedroom. She was a tiny thing, about fifteen, obviously in pain, but even more in fear. The old man had suspected immediately what was the cause of her malady, so he shooed everyone but the girl's maid from the room.

In moments, he knew he had been correct. The illness was not an illness at all. The girl's corset had been laced extremely tight and, as soon as the maid loosened the bindings, the truth made itself apparent. The girl, who could now breathe easily, burst into tears.

She begged the old man not to tell her uncle. The count's fury would be boundless, and he would stop at nothing to uncover the name of the culprit and then have the hapless lad executed most unpleasantly. The girl confided to the old man that her tutor, a young man of just twenty, was the father and, further, that they were very much in love. All she needed was time, the girl assured him, and she would find some way to persuade her uncle to allow them to marry.

The old man agreed not to tell the count. He told her not to lace her corset quite so tight, that no one would notice for some weeks yet.

But he did not have high hopes for the outcome. Affairs such as this always ended badly. The girl's condition was certain to become known and it would render her unfit for the marriage of state that the count most certainly had in mind for her.

The old man had wanted to return immediately, but the count, still believing his niece's condition to be an illness, insisted that the old man remain for three days. Now, after another day's journey, the inspiration he had felt before his departure was lost. The problem once again seemed as insoluble as ever. How could something move forward and backward at the same time?

XII

Faubourg Saint-Germain, March 1, 1534

ONE HOUR BEFORE DAWN, a wagon filled with the wares of an iron-monger, pulled by a gray-muzzled dray horse, passed out of Paris at porte Saint-Germain. Amaury leaned forward, elbows on knees, loosely holding the reins. He was dressed in a worn jerkin, splattered hose, and torn shoes. Next to him, in a bonnet and flimsy shawl, sat Vivienne. Their journey to Nérac would take nine days.

As both Vivienne and Liebfreund had predicted, Amaury's suggestion that he might be available to replace Routbourg had been greeted with eagerness. Perhaps too much eagerness. As he left the table after breakfast, Amaury remarked to Hoess that Routbourg's murder appalled him. Purged him of any remaining loyalty he might have felt to Catholicism. Left him wondering what he might do to avenge the man's death. "Wait, my friend," Hoess had called after him. "Do you mean that?"

Now the wagon bounced over the rutted streets of Faubourg Saint-Germain, passing the walled market town of Saint-Germain-des-Prés. In the bottom of the sack that held Amaury's change of clothing was a packet of correspondence, wrapped in an innocuous-looking soiled oilcloth tied with a leather thong. Inside, Amaury was certain, was a communication the contents of which Ory, Liebfreund, and now he were desperate to know. The packet itself was secured on all sides with a ribbon set in a Bartholomew's knot. The order in which the various ties and internal loops were fashioned was known only to the respondent and the recipient. If the packet was opened and then retied in any manner different from the original, detection would be simple and immediate.

Amaury rocked back and forth to the beat of the horse's hooves. The old rough-stone abbey that gave the town its name loomed up as a shadow on his right. Already the air was clearer, scents of the coming spring replacing the musty cloud that seemed to hang perpetually over Paris.

Amaury removed Giles' diagram from his tunic. He had recognized it instantly, of course, but this version was different. Why the circle with the dotted line? When he had asked Vivienne if Giles had explained what it was, she had replied, "A riddle." Indeed it was. An irresistible riddle. Amaury had no doubt whatever that the dotted circle was tied to Giles' murder. And the key to the puzzle was in Nérac.

As the sun rose, the wagon passed the series of towns that ringed Paris to the south and west before open country. The road was in excellent repair. Rutted perhaps, capable of turning into a stream of mud in a heavy rain, but clear, straight, and punctuated with stone bridges rather than those of flimsy wood. The king often took this route on his way to his château on the Loire, so a series of guardhouses had been placed just off the roadside.

As the sun began its trek across the sky, dew was transformed into a blanket of mist. Soon the mist vanished as well, and Amaury felt the early March sun warm his face and the fragrance of turned soil fill his nostrils. Cows roamed the fields, and dabs of crocus, purple and yellow, stretched off into the distance. There was some foot traffic on the road, but for the most part they rode in solitude. He looked to Vivienne, sitting to his left, but she seemed lost in thought, content to bounce along to the rhythm of the road.

As they rode on, Amaury drifted back to the day in the field. Lying next to her. He fourteen, she twelve. Hélène. Hélène d'Artigny. His golden sprite growing into golden woman.

They were lying on their sides, facing each other, their heads resting on outstretched arms. "I have decided that we shall always be together," she had mused idly, toying with the petals of a wildflower that grew from the ground between them. "Hélène and Amaury. Like Heloise and Abelard. Even the initials match."

He reached out and twirled a bit of her hair around his finger. "Abelard was murdered."

She giggled. Amaury's heart beat faster at the sound. "We won't do that part."

"Your father will never approve," he said. "Nor mine. I'm not even allowed through the front gate."

"Oh, Amaury, don't be so glum. You were sent here for me. I knew it the moment I saw you. I am telling you that I will make us always be together."

"And you were waiting for me. You told me."

"Yes. I remember. So do not doubt me now."

"But you're only a girl."

She had shaken her head. "No matter. You will find, my dear Amaury, that in the end I always get what I want." Then she had leaned over and kissed him, her lips on his. "Always."

He had sworn to himself to love her forever. To have her with him every day of his life. Hélène. Hélène. She had become a part of him, as much as his hands, his heart, his brain. Love. More glorious than life itself.

Her betrothal had been announced the following year. Promised to an imbecile because a bastard would not do. The walks in the hills stopped after that. He sent her notes that were never acknowledged. She refused to see him alone, even to speak to him. He never touched her again. He had loved her so. Did he still? The ache from such a love might fade over time, but, like a scar from a great wound, never vanishes.

He tried to remember how it felt to be . . . happy. But he couldn't. It was like reaching for a fish in a stream. When you put your hand in the water, the fish was somewhere else.

Where was she now? Beautiful, vain, clever Hélène. Living in a grand château, no doubt. Surrounded by finery.

To love. To be able to love. Oh, Lord, what must that be like?

As morning ripened, Amaury grew sore from the bouncing of the wagon. And the godforsaken horse was moving slower than a snail. He flicked the reins at the beast's rump, but the creature ignored both the leather and the driver's unpleasant thoughts.

Vivienne continued to ride in silence. She had been subdued since they had met at the stables inside the Saint-Germain gate. Odd, considering how forceful she had been in his room. How grateful when he agreed to accompany her.

"By nightfall, we must reach Pithiviers," he said finally, to fill the silence.

Vivienne merely nodded.

"We are to stay in a manor just outside of the city," Amaury went on. "Care must be taken, as Pithiviers is fiercely Catholic. The lord who will put us up is a Lutheran in secret. In fact, he's a member of the local *parlement*. Something of a difficulty for him, I suppose, being forced to pass judgment on heresy when he is regularly committing it himself."

The statement, strangely, seemed to arouse her interest. "You still consider the teachings of Luther heretical?" she asked him.

"I did, but now I'm not sure," Amaury replied. "But I assure you, this lord's fellows on the *parlement* share no such doubts."

They rode for a bit, then she spoke again. "It must be glorious to be able to learn. To be smart."

"You are smart. And you can learn whenever you want."

Vivienne pulled herself up straight. "Madame Chouchou is teaching me to read. Then I'll be able to learn."

"You can learn now."

She turned slowly. Even under the threadbare shawl and grimy bonnet, her beauty struck Amaury. "No. You need to read to learn."

"Vivienne, I spent nine years among some of the most ignorant people I know. And they read all the time. Wisdom does not come from words printed on a page. It comes from . . . a person's heart."

"Surely a person's head as well."

"Yes. That too. You do not seem deficient in either capacity."

She looped her arm through his. Amaury felt a smile spread across his face.

"Will you teach me?"

"What do you want to learn?"

"Everything."

"I'm not sure I can teach you everything."

"Well, then, can you teach me about the heavens?"

"That perhaps I can manage a little."

"Tonight?"

"If we can."

"Thank you, Amaury."

"Vivienne . . ."

"Yes?"

"Nothing."

"Ah," she said, "I understand. You want to know how I could have fallen so far as to be a common whore."

"No," Amaury protested. "That's not what—"

"It's quite simple, actually. I come from a peasant family near Arras. Six girls, no boys. My parents had no option but to try to marry us all off as soon as possible. My choice then was to spend the rest of my life with a sweaty, foul-breathed farmer, prematurely age, and die before I was forty, or fornicate with a variety of sweaty, foul-breathed men, save a bit of money, and wait for an opportunity to try to live a more decent life. Tell me. Which would you have chosen?"

"I can't say, Vivienne. One cannot choose for another."

"Yet you spent nine years at Montaigu to please a father who would not acknowledge you."

"How—"

"Giles told me. We all make our pacts, Amaury. But we need to know when to break them."

"Yes. I suppose we do."

They lapsed once more into silence. While the horse continued to resist an increase in pace, the beast proved indefatigable. He plodded along for hours without seeming to need rest. Inexorably, he chewed up mile after mile of road. They arrived on the outskirts of Pithiviers as the sun began to reach for the western horizon. Amaury had put on the broad-brimmed straw hat that had been placed with his ironmonger's garb, but Vivienne was forced to raise a hand to keep the sun from her eyes. Their instructions were to search for a road on the right between two stone pillars topped by owls.

The sun descended further. The brim of Amaury's hat could no longer block it. They traveled on, the old horse now finally fatigued after a full day on the road. Amaury wondered if the poor creature would hold up all the way to Nérac. He looked carefully as they clomped on, but could see no pillars. He even looked left, in case he had heard his instructions incorrectly.

The wagon entered a wood, which gave relief from the sun but exacerbated the feeling that he and Vivienne were lost. As the forest grew thicker, the road bent to the left, and soon there was no sight of open land before or behind them. The wagon plunged deeper and deeper into the wood, the canopy of leaves creating an artificial twilight. The road narrowed. Amaury felt as if the tree branches were about to reach out and pluck him from his seat. Another bend to the right was just ahead of them. On the other side lay the unknown. Suddenly, the vision of Henri Routbourg sinking to the ground forced its way into Amaury's thoughts. And Giles, lying among the oubliettes, gaping sightlessly at the ceiling. The eyes of the dead.

Amaury pulled sharply at the reins. The horse was pleased to stop. Amaury felt his heart pounding in his chest. His stomach went taut. He leaned forward. Strained his ears. Yet no sound came from around the bend, not even a squirrel foraging in the underbrush. But murderers would wait in silence. The reins were moist in his hands.

"We passed it," he said. His voice was raspy. Parched. "We must have missed the pillars in the glare."

"No," Vivienne said. "I was watching."

"You're wrong." Amaury did not take his eyes from the turn. "It's behind us."

"No," Vivienne insisted. "We must keep on."

"I tell you it's behind us," Amaury repeated, half yelling, half whispering. "Either that or, God forbid, we've taken the wrong road."

"This is the right road and we have not passed it," Vivienne said, calmly and with total assurance. "We will come to the pillars very soon."

Amaury pulled on the reins once more, this time to turn the wagon around, but Vivienne placed her hand on his to stop him. Her small fingers felt cool against the perspiration on his skin. "God will protect us," she said.

He felt himself nod and urge the horse forward. The wagon started up and was soon at the same plodding speed as before. Amaury bit at his lip as the road began to turn.

The bend was longer than he thought and for a time he could see only a short distance ahead or behind. No sound, no movement. Just menacing trees and low, overhanging branches. Amaury leaned forward, his chin almost between his knees, holding the reins, his eyes fixed ahead. The horse clomped on.

Finally, the road straightened and grew wider. The trees parted sufficiently overhead to allow in light from the fading day. After a small stretch, the road jogged to the left. As soon as the wagon reached the crest of the turn, the wood abruptly ended. The sun was about to reach the horizon on their right and the open fields that lay ahead had turned the muted ocher and dull green of sunset. Just after the break from the wood, also on the right, was a side road, guarded by two pillars, each topped by a stone owl.

Amaury glanced at Vivienne, mortified by his weakness. There had been nothing to fear. Vivienne smiled back without judgment. Amaury thought of their masquerade. If he had been what he pretended to be, a simple tradesman traveling with his wife, he would not have thought life had treated him cruelly to have been given such a woman for a spouse.

The wagon drew up to the pillars. Fields extended on either side. A small caretaker's house lay just inside the entrance. The road disappeared over a rise in the distance and no other building was in sight. A gray-haired man in stained breeches and a leather doublet was raking the soil next to the entrance; when Amaury began to turn in, the man waved for them to stop. He strolled to the wagon, swiveling his head to look in either direction even though there was no one else in eyeshot.

"Meaning to stay here tonight?" the man asked, leaning on his rake and looking past them to the road, backlit by the setting sun. His hands were thick, his face dark and wizened from decades of work outdoors.

"We are expected," Amaury replied.

The man shook his head. "Not anymore. The bishop decided to come for dinner." Pithiviers was famous for its charity hospital, l'Hôtel-Dieu de Pithiviers, administered by the local bishop rather than a specific religious order, a rarity in France. The post was prestigious, as the king had visited the hospital on more than one occasion, and thus the bishop wielded great power.

"Not just that," the man confided. "The bishop's ordered a crackdown on Lutherans and my lord can't chance having you on the grounds. You're to go into the town to a rooming house just off place du Martroi. The proprietor is named St. Jean. You are expected."

"What sort of crackdown?" Amaury was not afraid for himself. He was confident that, if arrested, he had merely to have his captors contact Ory. But Vivienne enjoyed no such immunity.

"Not so bad," the man said. "We've certainly seen worse. A ban on preaching. Some arrests. Inquisition trials maybe. No burnings though. A few floggings and short prison sentences will be the sum of it. Mostly warnings to return to the faith. Seems pretty much for show. The bishop must want something from the pope."

Amaury expressed his relief, but the man shook his head. "You two will need to be careful, though. Being not from here. If the bishop needs to make an example, a couple from Paris would suit him perfectly. My lord couldn't help you in the *parlement* either. He'd have to go along with whatever sentence was passed. But just keep your mouths shut, be on your way tomorrow as soon as you can, and you should be all right." The man cocked his head to the side. "Which way are you headed?"

Amaury shrugged.

"Well, stay away from Amboise if you can. The king's there."

Amaury thanked him for the information. Their route would indeed take them down the Loire. No need to cross the river at Amboise. They could keep to the north bank until Tours.

"One more thing," the workman added. "The innkeeper isn't one of us. As far as he knows, you're just a tradesman who's done some work for my lord. Got all that?"

Amaury assured him that the instructions were not too complicated, then he and Vivienne set off. The light was beginning to fade and Pithiviers was still a half hour away.

"I was hoping to avoid the town," Amaury grumbled. "Its walls and moat are not yet fifty years old. If we are trapped inside, there will be no escape."

"Then we must not be trapped. Who would want to accost an honest and pious ironmonger and his wife? When we get to the rooming house, the first thing to do is ask this St. Jean the location of the nearest church."

Amaury was once again surprised at Vivienne's resourcefulness. She seemed a good deal better at this business than he. No matter what transpired, he would find a way to protect her from Liebfreund, Ory, or anyone else. Betrayal of Vivienne had become a price he was unwilling to pay.

The road was straight, easy, and smooth. Candles flickering in the windows of Pithiviers illuminated their destination. The walls of the town were indeed new and impressive, although the moat was simply a dry ditch about fifteen yards across. On the crest of a hill in the center, rising above all else, was an enormous steeple.

Amaury expected to pass the bishop's caravan en route, but they encountered no one. Was there another road or had the caretaker been lying about the bishop's dinner visit? Had they been betrayed? There was no choice but to push forward.

When they arrived at the gate, a guard emerged with a candle lantern to ask them their business. He was a filthy, unshaven man in a soiled tunic. When Amaury told him of their destination, he nodded brusquely and walked to the other side of the wagon. He moved his lantern close to Vivienne's face and held it there for some time. He began to leer, exposing a set of yellowed, rotting teeth. Vivienne did not flinch, which seemed to arouse the guard all the more. He began to reach out to touch her face, but Amaury snapped the ends of the reins at him.

The guard pulled back, and his hand went to his scabbard.

"We must pass now," Amaury said with irritation. "I have been engaged for important repair work at the hospital. The bishop will be displeased if we are delayed."

The guard held his hand at the scabbard but did not grasp the hilt of his sword. He considered his options for a moment, and then, with a jerk of his head, commanded them to proceed.

"Now it is I who am in your debt," Vivienne whispered when they were clear.

"Not at all," Amaury replied. But he was proud all the same. "But I think tomorrow we should leave by a different gate."

Place du Martroi was in the center of town, on the crest of the hill they had seen from the road. The steeple belonged to l'église Saint Salomon–Saint Grégoire, a beautiful Gothic church just across the square. The rooming house was easy to find.

St. Jean was indeed expecting them. He was much younger than Amaury expected, not yet twenty-five, with sandy hair and a large mole on his left cheek.

"Surprised?" he said, although Amaury had said nothing. "I took over for my father when he died three years ago." St. Jean called a boy to see to the horse and wagon, and then offered them wine, bread, sausage, and cheese.

They had not eaten since midday and so accepted gratefully. There seemed to be no need to inquire about a church, since St. Jean had accepted them with such alacrity. And the question would also have been a bit silly with the massive Saint Salomon–Saint Grégoire less than a minute away.

"I'm sorry there's nothing else," St. Jean apologized with an outsized shrug when they had finished. "If you had only arrived earlier, I could have had something better prepared."

Amaury assured the young innkeeper that he had provided for them amply. Vivienne agreed.

"Do you really think so?" St. Jean replied happily. "You are probably just being kind, but I appreciate it all the same."

Amaury did, in truth, feel quite sated, the food, and especially the wine, providing a warm feeling of well-being.

After still more pleasantries back and forth, St. Jean called for the table to be cleared and led Amaury and Vivienne up the stairs to their room. He threw open the first door off the landing. The room was large, furnished sparely but with taste.

"How long will you be staying with me?" he asked.

"Only overnight."

The innkeeper looked crestfallen. "I was hoping to have you with me longer. I noticed your tools. I thought you might have business in the town."

"I'm sorry, no," Amaury said. His answer felt stiff, perfunctory, but it would be a mistake to elaborate.

"Ah, well," St. Jean replied with a shrug. "One night is better than none at all. Please call me if you need anything. If not, I'll see you at breakfast. You want to be on your way early, I suppose."

"Yes, thank you."

"Until breakfast then." St. Jean left them, closing the door behind him.

XIII

AMAURY DROPPED THE LATCH on the door and drummed his fingers on the wood. "That was too many questions. I don't know why, but he suspects us. There is a reward for turning in Lutherans."

"I don't trust him either," Vivienne said. "We should leave as soon as possible in the morning." She stood in the center of the room for a moment, looking at the bed. "I will sleep on the floor."

"The floor? But why? After all, we have already . . ."

"That was different, Amaury. I was . . . you know. Now we are traveling as . . . something else."

"But I thought you . . . cared for me."

"I do care for you. But I told you. I'm finished with all that. If you didn't know you were with a whore, would you still expect to simply fornicate with someone you had just met?"

"No, of course not. It's just . . ."

"Then you cannot simply fornicate with me now." She reached up and touched him on the cheek. "I'm sorry, Amaury. Truly."

She was completely correct, of course, but Amaury had no use for logic at that moment. After nine years of studying and disputing the nature of temptation, he was at last experiencing it in full flower. He wanted her, wanted her desperately. His ache to have her was so strong that it caused actual pain in his stomach. He felt as if demons had possessed him and would propel him across the room at her. At Montaigu, the doctors claimed prayer could deter such feelings, but now, in the grip of desire, Amaury knew that was absurd.

Vivienne had been in her profession long enough to recognize a man possessed by lust. "Please, Amaury. Respect my wishes."

Not having her was unendurable. But taking her against her will would be as enormous a sin as he could imagine. He merely nodded, in miserable acquiescence. But nor would he allow her to sleep on the floor. He promised they would share a bed but nothing else. Sometimes, Amaury thought glumly, free will was a heavy burden indeed.

"You will still teach me, won't you?" she asked when they were next to one another, almost rigid in their mutual avoidance. "About the stars? Even though I won't . . ."

"Of course. But not tonight. I think we'd best stay indoors."

He lay awake for hours. He did not touch her, but he luxuriated in her smell, the heat off her body, the sound of her rhythmic breathing. He began once to pray for strength, but then stopped, knowing God would want him to find strength on his own. More than once he sensed that Vivienne was awake as well, but neither of them spoke. They awoke side by side just after dawn. It had been among the most blissful and most agonizing nights of his life.

They arose silently and made their way downstairs. The maid, a halting, stuttering half-wit, offered them breakfast. The innkeeper was nowhere to be seen. She returned from the kitchen and placed a plate of bread and pork sausage in front of them. She glanced to the door, then turned to leave immediately, as if she were frightened to be in their presence.

"*Merci, mademoiselle,*" Amaury said effusively, to keep her there. "Monsieur St. Jean says you are an excellent cook."

"*Merci, monsieur,*" the maid replied, but was unable to meet his gaze. She looked toward the door once more.

"And where is Monsieur St. Jean on this lovely morning?"

"*Je ne sais pas, monsieur,*" the maid replied, shifting from one foot to the other.

When Amaury did not immediately reply, the maid spun and hurried through the door to the kitchen.

"We should leave now," Vivienne whispered. "We are betrayed."

"No," Amaury whispered back. "It would be an announcement of guilt. And we would never reach the gate before the alarm was up."

"What then?" she asked.

"Wait here," he replied.

Amaury went out into the courtyard to look for the innkeeper.

He walked around to the back, quickly but not obviously so. Amaury's wagon and horse were there, but the old beast was hardly the medium with which to beat a frantic retreat. Amaury was just about to give up and return to fetch Vivienne when he noticed the innkeeper down the street, deep in conversation with an older man. St. Jean was turned slightly away from him, gesturing as he spoke, exhibiting none of the adolescent good cheer of the previous evening. The man he was addressing was a priest.

Amaury slowed his pace and walked to where the two were speaking. At the sight of him, the priest raised his hand. St. Jean stopped talking and whirled to face him.

"*Excusez-moi,* Monsieur St. Jean," Amaury said after coughing softly to apologize for interrupting. He addressed the priest. "My wife and I have a long journey ahead, Father, but we do not wish to miss Mass. Would you recommend Saint Salomon–Saint Grégoire or perhaps a smaller church?" After nine years of false piety at Montaigu, Amaury had no trouble donning a suitable mask here.

St. Jean seemed nonplussed at the question. The priest stared at Amaury for a moment.

"You wish a Catholic service, monsieur?" he asked, with a glance at St. Jean.

Amaury cocked his head sideways. "I don't understand, Father. What other variety of Mass is there?"

The priest nodded slowly. "Indeed. And what is your name, my son?"

"Amaury La Framboise," Amaury replied. "An ironmonger from Picardy. I am traveling with my wife."

"To what destination, my son?" The priest was smiling, but St. Jean remained sour.

"I was to repair some grillwork at the manor house, but the commission was postponed. My wife and I will go on to Amboise in the interim. I am told that His Majesty, King François, often rides among the people and one may see him pass."

"Yes," the priest agreed. "I am told that as well." He placed his hand on Amaury's shoulder. "As it happens, my son, I also must go to Amboise. Perhaps we might travel together."

Amaury broke into a wide grin. "*Gloire à Dieu*," he exulted. "Now our pilgrimage will be truly blessed!"

"Excellent!" the priest said. "Now as to Mass, Saint Salomon–Saint Grégoire is breathtaking, but I have always preferred a more intimate setting. Might I recommend Saint Lucien de Beauvais? Armand will be pleased to direct you." The priest shot St. Jean a glance. "Won't you, Armand? Two pious believers such as these."

"Of course, Père Marcel." St. Jean appeared quite morose. The innkeeper had obviously been already counting his reward money.

"I shall meet you afterward," the priest said to Amaury. He turned to go, but then stopped. "Ah," he said, raising his hand to his forehead. "I am such a goose. I have an appointment with the bishop this afternoon, and cannot leave until tomorrow. You will be forced to go on your own after all."

"*Desolé*, Père Marcel," Amaury said. "Are you certain?"

"Yes. I'm afraid so." With that, the priest turned and left.

Saint Lucien de Beauvais was, in fact, a lovely church, and Amaury quite enjoyed Mass. Vivienne played her part perfectly, not demonstrating the slightest hesitation. After Mass, they returned to the inn, retrieved the wagon, thanked a still gloomy St. Jean, and set off for Orléans.

As the walls and spires of Pithiviers disappeared behind the rise of a hill, Vivienne put her hand on Amaury's, much as she had done yesterday in the wood. This time, however, she gave his hand a squeeze. And then, seemingly in recognition, she quickly removed it.

XIV

THEY REACHED THE LOIRE late in the afternoon. The Pithiviers-Orléans roads were obviously not favored by the aristocracy. Four times he and Vivienne had been forced to help push the wagon to ford streams, and another to remount a wheel that had come almost completely disengaged in a deep rut. Amaury was exhausted. His arms ached, his hands burned, and his rump felt as sore as after a beating at Montaigu.

He came away from these labors even more admiring of his companions. Vivienne had helped with every crisis, brushing away his protests that such work was for men alone. And the horse. He never complained, never broke stride. Even when it was necessary for Amaury and Vivienne to push from behind, he could feel the beast strain to make the humans' job as easy as possible.

Orléans was on the north side of the Loire. For all that it was but a day's ride on horseback from Amboise, the city had been growing as a center of Lutheranism. Perhaps it was because of the legacy of the heroism and stoicism of Jeanne d'Arc, perhaps it was simply due to chance, but Orléans was the one stop on their journey where Amaury and Vivienne could feel safe in their roles.

They passed through the gate without challenge and easily found their destination, another bookseller's. They were welcomed, given a fine dinner of chicken and vegetables in white wine. Amaury was escorted to a tiny room in the attic while Vivienne slept with the children. An unbroken blanket of clouds lay over the city, so Amaury was once again forced to postpone stargazing with Vivienne. He was, in truth, relieved for the respite. He had another task in mind.

As soon as he closed his door, he reached into the sack that held his belongings and removed the packet of letters he was to deliver in Nérac. He turned the packet over in his hands. If he attempted to read the correspondence and was found out, his mission would be at an end; his life might be as well. Still, he could remove the thong from the oilcloth without difficulty.

Amaury studied the simple ties on the strip of leather. He laid the packet on a table and undid the knot, memorizing the order in which the thong had been opened, to be repeated later in reverse. Lifting the folds of the oilcloth off in the same manner, he was faced with the packet of letters and the cipher of the Bartholomew's knot. The knot appeared simple: a ball of red ribbon fastened with a floret tie on the top. But any attempt to open it without perceiving precisely how the ribbon had been looped and folded internally would render retying the knot without later detection impossible.

If science taught him anything, it was that any enigma could be deciphered with method and care. Giles' murder, Routbourg's, the corruption of Genesis, Giles' chimerical diagram of astronomical movement: The solution to any or all of those riddles might well lie within the sheaf of papers that lay inches from his fingertips, protected by only a thin wrapper and a length of ribbon.

Amaury wiped his hands on his clothes. The ribbon could show no stain of perspiration or soil. He studied the floret: six loops and two ends. Three folds altogether. Amaury grasped the loose ends of the ribbon and tugged ever so slightly. They gave easily, shrinking the loops that had been fashioned last. No traps. Carefully, Amaury pulled on the ribbon ends until the floret was almost undone. He tried to study the ribbon balled underneath to determine whether he needed to place a finger on the top when he undid the floret entirely. No way to tell.

He pulled the ribbon the last bit. As the floret disappeared, the ribbon immediately underneath sprung open. It had been folded. But how many times? Two? No, three. Amaury studied the ribbon carefully to see where the fold marks were. There were none. But three folds for certain.

Another, smaller, floret lay underneath: two loops, two ends. He leaned down to look more closely. Shadows fell on the tied ribbon in candlelight. A twist. Under the floret. He could just make it out. He undid the ribbon once more, this time keeping a finger on the ties to discern which way the ribbon had been twisted before it sprung open and left him helpless. To the left.

It took thirty minutes for Amaury to work his way through the knot. Perhaps longer. He committed every fold, every twist, every order to memory. But eventually he was done. Could he retie the knot precisely as it had been done the first time? He would only know later. If he was still alive in a week, the answer was likely yes.

The contents were before him. The secret correspondence. The contents of these pages had already cost two lives. He wiped his hands one more time, then looked.

The pages were blank.

There were twelve in all. Not a single word on any of them. Nor had they been written on with invisible ink. Amaury held each page to the candle, shifting the angle. No depressions. No indication that any pointed object had ever touched even one of the pages.

What a fool he had been. No wonder Hoess had been so willing to trust him with their secrets. There were no secrets. At least in these pages. These pages had simply been a test to see if their bearer could be trusted. But Routbourg had been scheduled to go to Nérac before his murder. That much was uncontestable. Perhaps the real secrets were in the city itself. Or perhaps for the return trip. Nothing to do but complete the journey and watch and wait.

Amaury took at least twice as long to redo what he had undone. When he finally finished, he stared at the six-loop floret with which he had begun. He had painstakingly retraced each step. But whether his measurements were slightly off, like his sack in Madame La Framboise's room, would only be known after the packet was delivered.

He refolded the oilcloth and tied the thong, returned the packet to the sack. He then lay down on the pallet tucked under the roofline, overtaken by a wave of profound loneliness.

Loneliness. A regular companion but no friend.

The next day they set out early, now traveling the road that ran along the north bank of the Loire. Two days later, they arrived in Tours. After spending the night at the home of a glassblower named Stéphane, they planned to set out early, just after Mass at Saint Gratian, the famed cathedral that had been called the most beautiful in Christendom.

When Amaury led Vivienne from the church, soldiers were waiting at the bottom of the steps, accosting and questioning parishioners as they headed into the square. Most were being herded off toward a road on the left. Amaury took Vivienne by the elbow and started off to the side, but three of the soldiers broke off from the group and stepped into their path.

"You two come with us," barked the one in the middle. He was small and squat, with a livid scar that ran from the side of his forehead to the bottom of his jaw.

"Why?" Amaury asked. "We've done nothing."

"Don't ask questions," the soldier snarled menacingly.

"But, sir," Vivienne replied, as sweet as the soldier was gruff, "we must be on our way. We are on a pilgrimage to view the relics at Toulouse."

"Relics can wait," the soldier said, but in a decidedly more courteous tone. "The king has decided to visit his subjects in Tours. The royal procession is due. You get to see our liege, François I."

"Why didn't you say so?" Amaury exclaimed, a broad, excited smile bursting onto his face. "The king! God bless him and God bless you for allowing us the opportunity." He turned to Vivienne, who was beaming as well. "The king, my dear." Amaury returned his gaze to the soldiers. "Tell me, good man. Where is the route? I want to be there quickly to be sure of a good view."

But the middle soldier was not as easily gulled as the priest in Pith-iviers. "We shall escort you," he said, with a smile for Vivienne. "We will even secure a place at the front."

"How exciting," she said. "Thank you, Captain."

"Just a soldier, madame."

As the soldiers led them to la grande rue, Amaury and Vivienne chattered on about the rare opportunity they had been afforded. But, to himself, Amaury cursed their bad luck. They would lose half a day at least.

The crowd was already four deep on the boulevard when they arrived. The entire city had been turned out, required to line the parade route and express devotion as François and his endless retinue passed. The wait would be hours.

The short soldier with the scar pushed people aside and secured places for Amaury and Vivienne at the front. Then he leaned in close. "Remember, you are to wave and cheer for the king. Failure to do so is grounds for arrest." He straightened up, touched his hand to his forehead, bid farewell to Vivienne, then pushed back through the crowd to snare more unfortunates.

After they were gone, Amaury briefly considered trying to slip away, but soldiers and constabulary were everywhere, ensuring that not a single citizen would choose not to avail himself of the opportunity to view the royal person. He shared a glance with Vivienne and ventured a small shrug. Here they would stay.

XV

THE LOVE OF THE PEOPLE.

François I surveyed the adoring crowds on either side of the road: men, women, and even small children, waving, smiling, cheering. Each of his subjects willing to put aside the work of the day to stand in the sun, sometimes in the rain, to wait for hours, just to catch a glimpse of *him*. All the rigors, all the hardships of rule, became a willing price to pay.

Royal processions were tedious affairs, and the council members were constantly urging him to limit the practice. His ministers whined that processions were taxing on his subjects, unwilling to admit that it was *they* who disliked the people. How ludicrous. The populace lived for these events. If not, why were they here? Each of them would remember for the remainder of their lives the day they saw the king.

And the king would remember them—their love, their devotion. That was why, unlike that malformed troll Emperor Charles, François always rode on an open horse, not in a closed carriage. This was the figure of the man a people would want as their monarch—tall, powerful, virile, with fine, well-shaped calves.

They would turn out just to see his clothes. François took pride in the knowledge that he had totally altered the way a gentleman would appear. No longer could Italians mock the French for slovenly form or brutish garb. He had confounded the devious Italians by first borrowing from their manner of dress, and then improving on it. Doublets, until recently mere vests, were cut to fit tightly across the chest and were emblazoned with embroidery of brilliant color, then finished with slashed silk sleeves. Tights were now of silk—to accentuate those calves—and fitted with balloon shorts in contrasting color. The king, even in warm weather, wore a velvet plumed hat and a silk, fur-trimmed cloak draped insouciantly across his broad shoulders. So much had this manner of dress been copied in court and by gentlemen across France that François had instituted laws restricting by rank the amount of silk with which a lady or gentleman could be adorned. Thus François was assured that only when the king was in view could the people see elegance in its full flower.

Of course, although he rarely mentioned it, he knew it was the women who stared at that flower the most intently, each of them allowing herself the fantasy of sharing the royal bed. And François did occasionally pick a particularly comely maid out of the crowd, then sent a trusted servant to fetch her after the royal procession had passed. He would have to go behind the back of his mistress, of course—mistresses, actually—but an assignation with a commoner held sufficient satisfaction to be worth an occasional snit.

François also enjoyed these rides because, through all the waving and smiling, they afforded him a rare opportunity to think; a time when he could not be hounded by ministers, council members, or an army of supplicants. Today, as always, he was thinking about Charles. The Belgian turd. About Charles and about religion.

Catholic or Lutheran, he wondered. Which would the people prefer? Or, more accurately, against which would they rebel? As for himself, he saw little to choose between them. The Lutherans were appealing because they had no established order to overcome. But that very established order made the Catholics attractive for keeping a restive populace in line. If he went with the Lutherans, he could count on the support of the German princes, but he then ceded the pope to Charles. Something of a waste after taking the trouble to marry off his son Henri to that Medici runt, Catherine. But if he went with the Catholics, he might be betting against the future.

There was always England and Henry to consider, of course. With that bastardized religion he seemed to be promulgating, Henry would, as always, try to dance in between, although the image of the boarlike king of England dancing was difficult to conjure up without mirth. But England grew increasingly weak under Henry's incompetent rule and, as Charles would never forgive him for divorcing his cousin, Catherine of Aragon, Henry seemed to have little choice but to curry favor with France.

So for the moment, François concluded, let the Catholics and Lutherans hurl brickbats at each other. The competition served him well—the mere act of hurling weakened them both, made each eager, even frantic, for a royal ally. Beda, that old fool, had come to him before he left Paris with the silly notion that the Lutherans were hatching a plot to bring down Christianity itself. Something about Genesis. What nonsense. Such desperation. Bring me proof, syndic, he had said, and Beda had claimed to be gathering that proof.

Bring down Christianity. Why would the Lutherans want to do that? They were Christianity too, or at least they were the last time he looked. Still, he had let Ory ride behind him in the royal procession, demonstrating a commitment to the Inquisition the king did not feel. But he would stop short of a commitment to Ory, just as he would stop short of a commitment to Marguerite.

Ah, his, sweet, beloved, hopelessly naïve sister. He did adore her. It was unfair to Marguerite to make her a pawn in this game, but, after all, what were women for? She had even entered into not one but two marriages to help her brother, the king, consolidate power. If he ultimately allowed both religions to coexist, she would be happy; if he chose one over the other, he would find a way to make it up to her.

Yes, let them play off one another, each offering more and more in turn, bidding up the price for the favor of the king. He could—and would—swing this way and that, relying on his reputation as a capricious child to render his vacillation convincing. François laughed softly to himself, realizing that the crowds would think he was pleased with *them*. But François was laughing at the irony—not ten men in Europe would have thought the French king a master of diplomacy. He might be able to play this game indefinitely.

François' attention was suddenly drawn away from royal virtue to the other of his great interests. She was just ahead to his right, small and olive skinned, with large eyes. Quite lovely. Virginal almost. Well, perhaps not completely virginal, as she was standing with a man who seemed to be her husband. The king gave the young wench his most alluring gaze.

What? Was she looking back? Usually, the women he ogled on the route dropped their gaze out of modesty or intimidation. Looking the king in the eye was, after all, technically a crime. But this one met his eyes straight on. There was nothing sexual in her response. Or was there? Her look was even, without fear. Unafraid of the king? François felt a response in his loins.

Then François noticed the husband noticing the king's attention. Oh, he was trying not to let on that he noticed, trying not to let his anger show. But François was far too experienced with men whose women were about to share his bed not to know the look. This one was a tradesman, some sort of laborer perhaps. It would be an easy matter to have the soldiers slit his throat and deliver the girl to him in Amboise. Yes. The thought gained appeal. Let her try to stare him down in the royal bedchamber, stripped of her rags and thrown across his bed.

François was about to signal to the captain of the guard, but then stopped. He felt himself sigh. Perhaps not. The king was feeling generous today. What's more, the scene after his last dalliance three days ago had been particularly energetic. He had barely had time to move his head out of the way of the flying vase.

Ah, well. Let the laborer have her. She would be quite something for a tradesman to satisfy. François rode on. In ten years she would be a hag anyway.

Chance. Accident of birth. One man capricious, juvenile, yet omnipotent on Earth; another pious, questing, and an outcast. What had the magisters to say about *that*? About blind fortune? Where was luck covered in Scripture? Only in admonitions to bear any injustice, to accept that bad luck was not luck at all but part of God's plan. Like Job. Yet whom did that interpretation serve? Only the powerful. The powerful did not need to question luck, only revel in it.

Amaury had stood at the front of the crowd and watched as the king approached. He had never seen François before, although images of the king graced coins, buildings, and churches all over Paris. The king was as large as his legend, more than six feet high, and thick of chest. Although he was now past forty, François had not in the least gone to fat. The beard for which he was famous was flecked with gray, but his small, darting eyes, the set of his large jaw, and even the protracted, Valois nose exuded the energy of youth. He was Broussard expanded by an order of magnitude.

The first line of foot soldiers passed and François had almost come even to where he and Vivienne stood. He and his putative wife were cheering and waving with the rest as the king surveyed his subjects, basking in affection he did not seem to know was coerced. Amaury noticed when the king's gaze settled on Vivienne. He kept cheering but felt a rush of anger and possessiveness, as if Vivienne really *was* his wife. The king kept his eyes on her, his brow slightly furrowed, as if trying to decide something. Finally, François seemed to smile to himself and his gaze left Vivienne, which infuriated Amaury all the more.

Amaury wanted to grab her by the wrist, turn, and force his way back through the crowd. But that, he knew, was not possible until the remainder of the procession had passed. And there would be two miles of it.

Once François had moved on, the soldiers lining the route relaxed. The cheering also stopped and, in turn, participants in the procession felt neither the need nor the inclination to glance toward the crowd. Members of the retinue would pass in order of protocol: first the king's guard, then barons, then minor nobles, then churchmen—all Catholic, of course—and finally, bourgeoisie who served the royal household. Trailing the luminaries were foot soldiers and an immense train of wagons and carts.

As the endless parade trudged along, Amaury peered at the sky, trying to estimate how much of the day would remain when he and Vivienne could finally leave. He had become almost totally distracted until, glimpsing the churchmen, he noticed a familiar face. Amaury was noticed as well.

Ory held his glance for only a second, but Amaury knew, even in that brief time, that the Inquisitor wanted something. He either had information to transmit or a question to ask. But how could Ory have known Amaury would be here? He had sent no reports to the Inquisitor.

Amaury turned to Vivienne to discern if the eye contact had been noticed. She was looking at him, her face placid. She seemed oblivious to the exchange. "How much longer do we have to remain?" she asked.

"When the wagons appear, we can probably slip away," he replied.

Eventually, the wagons approached. Amaury glanced about at the soldiers guarding the route. They seemed to have begun to drift away as well. Amaury decided they could now safely make their escape. But, just he turned to lead Vivienne through the crowd, he bumped into a soldier.

Amaury began to blurt out an excuse for their early departure, a claim that his wife was ill, but the soldier tottered into him before he could speak. The man was drunk.

"Pardon, monsieur," he muttered, grasping Amaury by the arms for support. Trying to right himself, his hands slipped down.

But the soldier was not drunk. As his hand reached Amaury's side, he quickly passed a fragment of paper. When Amaury had secured it in his hand, the soldier, still tottering, plunged on through the crowd.

The message was from Ory—that was certain. And, judging from the size of the paper in his hand, it was also brief. He must read it quickly and Vivienne could not know. Once they had passed through the crowd, there would be scant opportunity to be unobserved.

Vivienne was behind him, so Amaury chanced unfolding the note and, placing his hand in front of him, shielded by his body, he looked down.

The message was indeed brief. On the paper was simply the notation "1:1." Amaury quickly crumpled it and let it fall at his feet to be trod over by the spectators. When he and Vivienne emerged from the throng, they walked quickly to retrieve their wagon and leave Tours.

Ory's message may have been brief, but it was hardly cryptic. The Inquisitor was telling him that the object of whatever conspiracy the radical Lutherans were hatching had been narrowed down from the book of Genesis to its first passage, 1:1, "In the beginning, God created the heavens and the earth."

How, Amaury wondered, astounded, could anyone disprove that?

XVI

Amaury and Vivienne did not clear the city walls until mid-afternoon. No possibility of reaching their appointed destination in Poitiers.

They traveled south, moving deeper into spring. Even just five days from Paris, a caressing warmth was in the air that had been absent from the capital. Rabbits scurried across the road and deer stood vigil in the fields as they passed. Amaury and Vivienne came upon a number of hamlets early in the journey, but they agreed it foolish to stop so soon after they had begun. As the sun plunged to the horizon, however, they found themselves journeying through an unbroken series of open fields, with only an occasional farmhouse dotting the landscape. They considered asking for shelter at one of them, but the risk of exposure, small though it might have been, made the notion untenable.

Wooded areas were a likely refuge for highwaymen. They decided to sleep in the open, perhaps behind a hillock or haystack. Eventually, Vivienne noticed a small barn, away from the road. Amaury guided the horse to the entrance, two unfastened swinging doors.

A storage area for tools lined one wall, and two stalls were along the other. The back wall contained bridles and a plow. A ladder at the rear led to a hayloft. The area in the center was insufficient for the horse and wagon, so Amaury, after situating the wagon on the far side of the shed from the road, released the beast from his bindings and led him inside. There was ample hay and a bucket filled with water for an evening meal.

Vivienne removed some bread, cheese, and wine from the back of the wagon, and she and Amaury sat on the grass. Color drained from the landscape. Vivienne took on a ghostly hue.

Neither spoke, but rather allowed night to come upon them in silence, the ever-brightening stars forming a heavenly canopy over their heads. This was what God had created in the beginning. No one would ever dissuade Amaury of that.

"Can you teach me now?" Vivienne asked suddenly.

"What?"

"About the heavens. You promised you would."

"Oh, yes. Of course." He looked up at the sky. How to describe Ptolemy's Celestial Pearl to a farm girl who could not read?

"The heavens are wondrous, Vivienne. All the stars you see before you . . . a long time ago a Greek named Aristotle said they were fixed in the heavens. We know now that not only do they move, but that they move in regular patterns as they circle the Earth. We know because a man named Ptolemy, an Egyptian who lived two centuries after the birth of Our Lord Jesus Christ, ventured out, night after night, year after year, to observe the stars and measure where they were in the sky. The movements were so tiny from night to night that he was forced to invent a special instrument to measure the changes. That instrument—it is called a triquetrum—is still in use today. I have used one often."

"How does it work?" Vivienne had sat up, arms pulled around her knees. She was listening to every word with wide, unblinking eyes.

"It's very simple. And very ingenious. Ptolemy took three lengths of wood. He placed one end of the shortest piece on a support, standing straight up. The other two, he attached to the standing piece, one at the top, the other at the bottom. The two longer pieces moved and could cross. Do you understand?"

"I think so. So the two attached pieces made a triangle?"

"Yes. Exactly. By sighting along the top piece to a star and measuring the angles, Ptolemy could use something called geometry to decipher exactly where it was. Each night that measurement changed, and, over time, he deduced how the stars moved in the sky."

Vivienne was agog. "And he did this for *every star*?"

"Almost. Quite a task. Others have come along and refined some of the measurements, but no one has shaken the basic theory. Ptolemy described the entire universe, multiple spheres that circle the Earth. The stars are only one of the spheres. He called the whole construction a Celestial Pearl."

"Celestial Pearl. What a wonderful name." Still holding her knees, Vivienne rocked back and forth on the ground, never taking her eyes from the sky. "Thank you so much, Amaury. You're a wonderful teacher."

"Nonsense. It is you who are the wonderful student."

She shook her head, but her pleasure at hearing the words was palpable.

"How did you meet Giles?" he asked.

She turned to look off into the distance. "The way I met you. At a meeting. About six months ago. He arrived with Monsieur Routbourg."

"Did you know Routbourg well?"

"I saw him infrequently. Usually with Monsieur Hoess. But Giles didn't like him. He didn't like Monsieur Hoess either. He called them . . . unctuous. But he seemed to cultivate their society. I was never certain why."

"Did he feel the same way about Geoffrey Broussard?"

"Oh, no. He liked Geoffrey a great deal. He told me once that he could not understand why Geoffrey would associate with such men. 'He will come to no good end because of it,' he told me."

A thought struck Amaury. "Vivienne, did you ever talk like this with Giles? About the heavens?"

"Only about how much he loved looking at the stars and how we could never understand ourselves unless we understood the glories around us."

"And the diagram you showed me . . . he never discussed it with you? Told you what it meant?"

She shook her head. "No. Will you tell me? Does it have something to do with the Celestial Pearl?"

"Yes. It explains the eccentric orbits of some of the bodies in the heavens."

She shifted closer to him. "I don't understand. Please tell me."

"Some stars and planets appear on occasion to be moving backward in the sky. It's called retrograde motion. It's an illusion, of course. Planets don't move backward. Ptolemy figured out the explanation. They're called epicycles." Amaury leaned forward and traced a large circle on the ground. "Imagine this is an orbit . . ."

"The way a planet moves around the Earth?"

"Yes. Exactly. Except the planet is not directly on the orbit." He traced a smaller circle on the circumference of the large one. "The planet's orbit is the small circle, riding on the large one. So you see, some of the time the planet will appear to us to be moving backward when it is merely following its orbit. That's an epicycle."

"I think I understand." The exultation in her voice made Amaury grin widely. "Is that what Giles' diagram showed?"

"Not exactly. Giles' diagram was similar to the way Ptolemy described epicycles, but Giles had added a second layer of data. I can't decide why."

"What is 'a layer of data'?"

"Another piece of information. I'll explain it to you next time. I promise. But Giles said nothing about Genesis?"

"Genesis? No, nothing at all." She paused. "You loved Giles, didn't you?"

"Yes. One does not often meet another who is a reflection of one's soul. Giles reflected mine."

Amaury thought back to all those days, drowning at Montaigu, when he had been sustained by knowing that at least one other person in that place believed as he did, had passion for learning that wasn't shoveled down one's gullet, the way one would feed a goose.

"I was at Montaigu to try to claim a birthright," he continued, looking up at the stars, partly in memory, partly in tribute. "Giles was there to create one. His father is a tanner, you know. Tanners have been pariahs for centuries. The odor of rotting animal flesh and the human wastes used to loosen the hair on the hides is so powerful that, by royal decree, they are required to live outside the city walls.

"Giles was the oldest of six. Ordinarily, he would have been compelled to follow his father into the profession. But when he was but five, he came to the attention of a local priest who was stunned by his intellect. The priest took him in, allowed him to live in the rectory, and tutored him until Giles was old enough to be sent to university. He did brilliantly, of course, particularly in science. When he was offered a place at Montaigu, a chance to become a theology doctor, how could he say no? But he never lost his love of science. As I never lost mine. He was nine years my junior, but we found each other instantly. He was my oasis as, I hope, I was his."

"You were, Amaury. He told me so."

"Really? I'm so pleased to know it was true . . . although I suppose it doesn't really matter anymore."

"Of course it does." Her voice dropped to a whisper. "I want to tell you something."

"What?"

"I wasn't telling the truth when I told you why I became a prostitute. I was forced to choose this path because I was rendered unfit for any other by my uncle. When I was twelve, I stayed with him because my father had no room for me. He began to visit my bedroom. Forced himself on me. I can still feel his hand pressing on my mouth and the filthy smell of him. When my father learned of his brother's perfidy, he was furious. But his fury was with me, not his brother. No man would marry me, soiled as I then was, so he accepted money from others to allow me to be used similarly. After two years of horror, I escaped. Eventually, I found my way to Madame Chouchou. She is a kind and decent woman also forced by circumstance into a life of sin. I hope you can understand why I would risk even death to be free of such a miserable existence."

They sat for some moments. A chill had begun to settle in the air.

"We should take shelter now," Amaury said.

They slipped into the barn, trod softly past their sleeping horse, and made their way up the ladder to the loft. They each cleared a spot in the hay. They lay still for some moments. Even the horse was completely silent in the stall below. Finally, an owl hooted in the distance.

"Good night, Amaury," Vivienne said softly.

"Good night, Vivienne."

XVII

AMAURY'S EYES OPENED. He could not place where he was. Only that he could not breathe. A hand. A hand was over his mouth and nose. He began to struggle, when he realized it was her. Vivienne. Of course. The barn.

His senses began to focus. When he ceased to squirm, she bent and placed her mouth near his ear. He felt her warm breath against him.

"I hear noise outside," she whispered.

Amaury was still not fully awake. "Animals?" he whispered in return.

"No. Men."

"How many? Can you tell?"

"Two, I think. They've only been there for a minute or two. I was awake when I heard them."

Amaury tried to shake out the haze and decide what to do. Confronting two men was out of the question. His dagger would be of little use. If left alone, they would likely simply make off with some of the goods that could be easily carried. They would wish to avoid a confrontation as much as he. If they wanted an ironmonger's goods, they could have them.

Then he remembered. The sack! He had left it in the wagon. No matter that the pages were blank. He was not supposed to know that. He must defend them as if they held the secrets of the ages. He cursed his stupidity as he pushed himself to a sitting position.

"The letters are in the wagon," he whispered. "I must try to save them."

"I'm going, too," Vivienne whispered in return.

Amaury began to protest, but, from her tone, he knew it would be fruitless. Besides, there was no time. He moved silently to the ladder and descended to the floor. Seconds later, Vivienne was next to him. The horse remained still. He could hear definite sounds of scraping and voices outside. Two men? Yes, two.

Weapons? What could they use? The two men might be thrown off guard if he and Vivienne burst out of the barn holding... what?

Pitchforks. There was hay, so there must be pitchforks. When they had arrived, he had seen tools along a side wall. Morning must have been near at hand, because sufficient light penetrated the shed from a small, high window on the road side to allow Amaury to make his way about. He soon located four pitchforks, two long-handled, two short. He grabbed the former and handed one to Vivienne. He whispered that, on his sign, they should throw the doors open as quickly and loudly as they could, then rush out and confront the robbers before they could react.

They padded to the front of the barn, Amaury at the left door, closest to the wagon side, and Vivienne at the right. She was looking across, waiting for his signal, ready, even eager, to begin.

Amaury listened. The robbers outside were still at their work. He heard a short, muffled chuckle. He threw open his door, Vivienne following. In an instant they had rushed to the side of the barn, their weapons leveled. "Be gone!" Amaury yelled.

The men jumped back from the wagon. Both were small and rodent-like. Neither was young. The iron goods were scattered at their feet, but Amaury could not see the sack. Instead of running, however, each pulled a long club. But they did not move forward.

The four faced off. The man on the right tried to look menacing. "You two just leave this to us, and you can go on your way," he said with an exaggerated sneer. "We don't want to hurt nobody, do we, Jacques?"

Jacques did not speak, but raised his club higher. "G'wan," the first man said. "Or we'll kill you sure."

Instead of retreating, Amaury took a step forward, jabbing with his pitchfork. "I think you're wrong about who is going to die, my friend."

Vivienne advanced as well, brandishing her pitchfork at Jacques. "You two picked the wrong wagon. We're used to the likes of you." Her voice was a growl, menacing, without a hint of fear. "If *you* don't turn and leave, we'll skewer you. We done it to better."

The first man glanced to Jacques, trying to urge his partner forward, but Jacques was staring at Vivienne's weapon and did not budge. Amaury moved up another step. "You heard her. Stay here one more minute and you'll each have two holes to show for it."

The men at first remained rooted in their tracks, but disinclination to advance was the same as retreat. Vivienne made another jab. Jacques took one step back. That was all the first man needed. Soon they were both drawing away. "All right then," said the first man. "No harm done. We didn't take nothing." Within minutes the robbers had disappeared into the early-morning gloom.

When the men had gone, Amaury stepped forward to see the inside the cart. The sack was still undisturbed under the seat. Amaury placed the pointed end of the pitchfork into the ground and stood with his hand on the top of the shaft until he was sure they weren't coming back. When he looked to Vivienne, she had also placed the pitchfork in the ground. Her hand was high up on the handle and she wore a look of triumph. Then she laughed.

"Well, those two won't be bragging to their friends in the tavern about *this* night, I'll tell you."

"No," Amaury replied. "I suppose not."

"Oh, Amaury. Such an adventure. What fun!"

"Fun?" But her laughter was infectious. "Well, perhaps in the way it turned out."

Suddenly she rushed to him and grabbed him about the waist. He hugged her in return. At first the feeling was simply shared relief, but soon Amaury became aware of the press of Vivienne's breasts against him. He must have betrayed the change, because Vivienne stiffened and pushed herself away.

"It will be dawn soon," she said, and began returning the items on the ground to the wagon.

Three days later, they reached Nérac.

XVIII

NÉRAC. A hotbed of lies, deceit, and intrigue, if Liebfreund and Ory were to be believed. What would such a place be like? A dark, shadowy warren with conspirators behind every post? Lutherans and Catholics each plotting the other's destruction? Where one must always keep weapons at the ready to ward off assassins?

The truth, as truth often is, could not have been more different than expectation.

Nérac itself was a small, bright city situated on the east bank of the river Baïse. Across the narrow waterway lay the grand palace of Queen Marguerite and her husband, Henri d'Albret. The walls were limestone, shining almost white. The roof was of terra-cotta tiles, Mediterranean, rather than the gray slate of the north. The outside barricade was low, only two stories high, more suited to discouraging unwanted guests than to repelling invaders. Cylindrical towers, which appeared to have been a recent addition, occupied each corner.

Amaury pulled the wagon up to the front gate, a large wooden door rather than a portcullis. A sergeant at arms stepped from the barred guardhouse and asked them their business. Amaury, as he had been instructed, replied that he had come from Paris to hear the sermon on the hillside. The sergeant returned inside, then, some minutes later, the door was unlocked and swung open. The sergeant was waiting inside. He signaled to a groom to lead the horse, and Amaury and Vivienne were directed to the left, toward the stables.

The center court was not as expansive as the Louvre, perhaps, but was similar in size and scale to his father's palace in Savoy. Marguerite's husband, Henri d'Albret, was, after all, an independent monarch, king of Navarre, although in practice the Duke of Savoy wielded a good deal more power than King Henri.

As the horse ambled across the courtyard, however, similarity to Savoy ceased. Any number of gaily dressed young men, and even a few unescorted women, walked about. Others sat in open-air chairs. A woman sat playing a lute. Animated conversation abounded, not at all conspiratorial. Some of the courtiers chose to remain alone, either taking the air or reading, while others listened to the music. The palace far more resembled a sanctuary than a den of vipers.

When Amaury and Vivienne arrived at the stables, a jolly-looking man, florid-faced and round, wearing a brilliant red jerkin and blue plumed hat, bade them dismount. He took the reins from Amaury and gave them to a waiting groom.

"Welcome to Nérac," he said in accented French. "I'm Castell'buono. I serve Queen Marguerite."

"An Italian?" Amaury asked before he could stop himself.

The man made to frown. "You are shocked? Cannot an Italian serve a Navarrese queen? I assure you, I hold no prejudice."

"Nor, obviously, does she," Amaury replied with a small bow. *The Italian had failed to come to Paris, Routbourg had told Calvin. He remained in the south.* Amaury introduced himself and Vivienne, whom he called Mademoiselle d'Arras. He had never, he realized, learned her proper surname. Vivienne gave no sign that the appellation was incorrect.

Castell'buono's smile vanished for just an instant. "Routbourg could not come?"

"Routbourg is dead."

"An accident? He fell into the Seine, perhaps?"

"His throat was cut."

Castell'buono heaved a sigh but exhibited no other sign of surprise. "Those responsible were arrested?"

"No. And Monsieur Hoess . . . you know him?" Castell'buono nodded. "Monsieur Hoess assumes they will not be."

"I understand," the Italian said. "And you, Monsieur Faverges, volunteered to take his place? A brave thing to do. We are in your debt." He gestured toward Vivienne. "I'm sure the opportunity to spend a week with such a beautiful creature played no small part in your decision." He smiled at her, somewhere between broad and lascivious. "It certainly would have for me."

"I was fortunate in my companion," Amaury replied simply.

"But Faverges . . . Faverges," the Italian went on, tapping a finger to his lips. "I do not believe I have heard your name before. You are new to the brethren?"

"Quite new. And not, at least as yet, of the brethren at all." Amaury recounted briefly his banishment from Montaigu, his encounter with Broussard in Paris, and his attendance at the meeting in La Croix Faubin. Once again, he noted that he had been with Routbourg until minutes before his death.

"In that case, Monsieur Faverges, our debt to you is that much greater. A risk borne not of conviction, but simply because of one's sense of right and wrong . . ."

"Right and wrong is conviction enough, is it not?"

"Indeed." Castell'buono put his hand to his cheek, as if to recognize a faux pas of etiquette. "But you must be fatigued after your journey. Your quarters will be in the guest wing. Queen Marguerite is expecting you in one hour. She has many questions about Paris." He turned his attention to Vivienne, removing his hat with a flourish and bowing deeply. "And you, mademoiselle . . ." Castell'buono dropped a sensuous flourish into his voice. "Those who undertake these arduous journeys in the name of tolerance and freedom are highly valued, no matter what their station.

You will have a room with the queen's ladies in the royal apartments. I shall escort you myself."

Vivienne at first looked stunned, and then a deep blush began at her chest and rushed up her neck to her face. The royal apartments. For her. Amaury realized that she was unable to speak.

"*Merci mille fois*, Monsieur Castell'buono," he said, trying unsuccessfully to match the Italian's unction. "Mademoiselle and I are most grateful."

Castell'buono nodded but kept his eyes on Vivienne. "You will find suitable clothing in your rooms," he said. "Any difficulty, or if the accommodations are not to your taste, mademoiselle, please report to me. Directly." He favored Vivienne with another smile. "I would be honored to see to any situation personally."

Amaury moved between the Italian and Vivienne. "You are very kind, monsieur. Now, perhaps we can be taken to our rooms? We are quite fatigued."

"Of course," crooned Castell'buono. He swept his hat broadly through the air. "Please follow me."

Amaury asked him to wait a moment. He walked to the front of the wagon and placed his hand on the horse's snout. The beast raised his head against Amaury's palm.

"Well, we have certainly gotten to be friends," Amaury said softly, stroking along the animal's nose. "I have learned from you and will always remember our time together. I expect our paths will not cross again, so I wanted to wish you long life."

Amaury removed his hand and turned to leave, but the horse nudged him with its nose. Amaury turned back for a second, smiled, and then left the stables. As he walked across the courtyard with Vivienne, Castell'buono met another man, somber and emaciated, with piercing eyes and hair cut to the skull. The Italian introduced him as Philippe and said he had been assigned to show Amaury to his rooms and see to his needs. Castell'buono, as promised, was to escort Vivienne to the queen's apartments. Before he left with her, however, he took Amaury aside and spoke to him so that the other two could not hear.

"What were you told of your mission?"

"Nothing beyond delivery of the correspondence."

"The correspondence, of course. Nothing of the return?"

"No. Are there instructions for the return?"

"There might be. In the meantime, when you have your audience with Queen Marguerite, respond to her questions, but relate nothing of the correspondence you carry, nor any details of our activities in Paris." Castell'buono smiled and shrugged. "The queen, glorious as she may be, is still a Catholic, after all ... as are you."

"Of course."

"Where is the correspondence, by the way?"

Amaury patted his sack, which he had removed from the wagon. "Do you wish it now?"

"No. Leave it on the shelf of the armoire in your room when you go to meet Queen Marguerite. It will be well cared for. You and I will speak later. I also have many questions about the goings-on in Paris, although they will be different from the queen's."

Castell'buono then returned to Vivienne. Amaury watched them walk across the courtyard, the Italian gesturing theatrically as he spoke.

After Vivienne and Castell'buono disappeared around the corner, the servant Philippe led Amaury to the north wing and up a set of stairs to the second floor. Philippe made no pretense of pleasantries, not even turning to see if Amaury was behind him. He was like a wraith, his sandals making no sound as he walked. Veuve Chinot had described such a man in the alley, standing over Giles, but Philippe was not the only thin man in France with cropped hair. Still, not someone to turn his back on.

The floors in the corridors were tile, with mosaic inlays depicting scenes of farming and rural life. The walls were scrubbed and the candle sconces were of blown glass. Philippe opened a door halfway down the corridor, but did not move to enter.

"Queen Marguerite is of the modern fashion," he noted, "and does not favor grime or foul odors. She herself bathes as often as twice per week." The man spoke in a dull monotone, emotionless, as if neither the content of his speech nor the identity of his correspondent was of consequence.

Amaury reluctantly agreed to a bath, although rinsing of the hands and face would have done just as well. He stepped inside and closed the door, leaving Philippe to wait. The room was wide and open, with a large bed. The armoire Castell'buono had mentioned was filled with clothing. A washbasin and pitcher lay on a wide table next to a line of eaus de toilette. A small cup to rinse one's mouth sat there as well. A chamber pot was parked discreetly at the foot of the bed. Amaury placed the packet of correspondence on the shelf of the armoire, as he had been instructed, whispering a prayer that he had retied the knot correctly.

When he stepped back outside, Philippe informed him that a room at the end of the hall had been set aside for bathing. "I took the liberty of warming the water," he intoned. "Her Majesty always insists on warm water. She has said that it benefits the health as well as providing comfort." Amaury was instructed to leave his ironmonger's clothes in the bathing room to be taken away and given to the poor.

The chamber they entered was at the far end of the corridor with a window that looked out over the hills. A large copper tub had been placed in the center of a blue-tiled floor. A cistern heated by a low flame was situated against the far wall. Amaury removed his clothes and left them in a pile by the door. Then, feeling rather foolish in his nakedness, he climbed into the tub. Philippe transferred large pails of water from the cistern, pausing when the tub was about one quarter full to add some perfumed crystals. He performed these activities with studied dispassion.

Amaury was relieved when the water was high enough to cover his genitalia, although Philippe gave no sign that these activities were anything but the most common of occurrences. They might have been in ancient Rome. Once Amaury relaxed, he slid down a bit and let the warmth soak into him. Philippe continued to add water from the cistern. For just a moment, Amaury had the sensation that Philippe intended to drown him, but the man continued his duties without hesitation, and Amaury dismissed the thought as ridiculous. The ambience as he settled into the bath was, in fact, intensely soothing. He wondered if, in the royal apartments, Vivienne was, at this moment, lying naked in a tub of her own.

Clearly, he was supposed to wash as well as luxuriate, so, after a bit, Amaury rubbed the soap that Philippe had supplied over his body. He had evidently behaved correctly because, just afterward, Philippe asked if he was ready to dry. When Amaury said that he was, Philippe fetched a large blue velvet robe, which he held open at the side of the tub. Amaury stood, turned his back—although again a feeling of disquiet ran through him—and slipped his arms into the sleeves. He noticed that the water had turned dark as mud. Had he really been covered with that much filth?

Philippe led him back to his room, Amaury leaving wet footprints on the tile in the corridor. Had he been supposed to dry himself in the bathing room? The manners of the palace were completely foreign to him. In Savoy, which considered itself enlightened due to its proximity to Italy, even his father's mistress had bathed only once per month. Perfume did the rest.

Philippe remained outside the room, leaving Amaury to dress himself. When Amaury swung the door of the armoire open, the packet of correspondence was gone.

XIX

THE ARMOIRE CONTAINED a large variety of clothing. No crimson velour, of course—that was reserved for nobility—but brocaded doublets with silk sleeves, and many pairs of silk tights and balloon shorts in contrasting colors. Amaury had a difficult time choosing. Each of the garments was substantially more ostentatious than anything he had worn in the past.

Amaury finally chose a deep green doublet punctuated with gold sequins placed in rectangles, gray stockings, deep violet shorts, and a plain black hat and shoes. They were the most understated choices before him. He eschewed a cape, although he nonetheless felt singularly ridiculous when he examined himself in the glass. When he decided that he could put off the moment no longer, he heaved a sigh and opened the door.

When he appeared in the hall, Philippe looked him up and down but said nothing. On the walk across to the palace, Amaury asked their destination. Philippe informed him that Queen Marguerite was in the receiving room, where she customarily sat in the presence of her guests until well after dark, when dinner was served. When Amaury commented on the lateness of the dinner hour, Philippe told him that five meals were customarily taken each day, the fourth of which had been completed while Amaury took his toilette.

The guard at the palace door nodded as Amaury and Philippe walked through. The interior of the palace wing had been recently renovated and showed even more of a southern influence than the exterior. The halls employed a liberal use of arches, and the tile work on the floor seemed almost Moorish. Nérac had been conquered by the Arabs in the eighth century on their march north, before Charles Martel won his great victory in the fields between Tours and Poitiers. When they constructed their palace, King Henri's forebears had apparently chosen to celebrate the vanquished rather than the victor.

Two guards stood at the receiving room's set of lacquered wood double doors wearing the Albret coat of arms, a remarkable polyglot of Navarrese gold ropes, Valois fleurs-de-lis, and English lions. Amaury looked to his left, but Philippe had vanished like a phantom. The guards reached for the door handles, preparing to swing them open.

Amaury's eyes became fixed on the doors. Thirteen years. The last time he had been at court. Why had his father done it? To elevate him? To humiliate him? Everyone knew. He had realized that instantly. The snickers and sidelong glances. Placed at a side table where he could watch his half siblings be fawned upon whilst he was treated with disdain, even by the servants. No one spoke to him. Even Hélène seemed embarrassed by his presence. His father glanced his way every so often, but he could read nothing in the old man's face. As the meat was served, Amaury saw Charles, the duke's oldest true son, fourteen but with the malevolence of an adult, huddled with his friend János, a Hungarian prince. They were looking Amaury's way and guffawing. Finally, János stood and strolled over to where Amaury was seated. Amaury refused to look up. "Ah," János had said with mock curiosity, "you're the son of the whore, yes?" Without a second's hesitation, Amaury had stood and, in one motion, lifted the leg of mutton on his plate and smashed it across János's jaw. The boy went down in a heap. The duke rose from the table and in a thundering voice ordered Amaury from the room. Amaury tried to meet Hélène's eyes as he stormed out but, as had become her custom, she deliberately turned away. Three weeks later he was on his way to Paris, to the university. As he rode through the gates, he swore he would never return unless he sat at the same table as his father. Acknowledged as a true son. Amaury de Savoie.

He blinked and realized the guards were waiting for him to take a step forward. Amaury nodded and they swung the doors open. He stepped into a large, sumptuously furnished room, different in every way from his father's raucous, martial court in Savoy. The ceilings were at least fifteen feet high. Scrollwork adorned the crossbeams, and the ceiling in between was inlaid in fleurs-de-lis. The floor was inlaid as well, in a diamond pattern of dark and light wood. Two enormous windows dominated the north wall, hung with deep-purple velvet drapes opening onto manicured gardens below. Tapestries depicting pastoral scenes adorned the side walls, but there were none of hunting or other violent pursuits. Two enormous gilt mirrors flanked the walls on either side of the entrance.

At least twenty people were present, in remarkable variety even by Valois standards. Even more remarkable was that the room held no throne. Queen Marguerite sat in a large cushioned chair, only slightly more opulent than those of her guests.

The queen both resembled her brother and at the same time was completely different. She was large like François, but delicate where he was burly. She featured the Valois nose, long chin, and small eyes, but the angles had somehow softened, rendering the queen, if not beautiful, certainly pleasing to look at. She exuded the same aura of authority but was inviting rather than commanding. Well past forty, her face seemed unlined, with a placidity almost ethereal. Her courtiers did not seem like courtiers at all, but rather friends who had gathered for an afternoon of pleasant society. Even the servants standing against the wall seemed relaxed. Many of those in the room were speaking among themselves, some enthusiastically so, but Amaury had never been in a room that exuded such a sense of peace.

Queen Marguerite wore no frills or other finery, but rather a plain black silk dress with a thin black scarf as head covering. She raised her gaze to him and smiled—a shy smile, yet totally welcoming—and then bade him, with the smallest curl of her fingers, to enter and approach. Amaury bowed and walked lightly across the floor.

As he neared her, Amaury attracted the notice of a pinched, malignant-looking man of about forty clad in a worn and grimy cloak, hatless, and slouched in a cushioned chair, his torn shoes resting on a marble-topped table. Obviously, this man had chosen to ignore the queen's admonitions pertaining to personal hygiene.

"Now there is a pious young lad," the man intoned, but with obvious sarcasm. "How could he be otherwise in such understated dress?"

Amaury stopped in his tracks.

"Don't mind Rabelais," smiled an older man wearing a simple cloak, sitting close to the queen. "He is always misanthropic late in the day."

"Nonsense. I am misanthropic all of the time."

So this was the infamous Rabelais.

"Piety is as a boil, my dear Roussel," continued the author of the sensational *Pantagruel*, which had scandalized half of France and left the other half helpless with laughter. "Full, throbbing, and likely to burst forth at any moment with pus and corruption."

"You are confusing piety with your own personality, François," Roussel noted calmly. Gérard Roussel had preached a Lutheran sermon to five thousand in the courtyard of the Louvre during François' absence, then had been forced to flee Paris when the king returned. "Piety is a trait, no better or no worse than the person in whom it resides."

"As is wit, François," the queen interjected.

Rabelais did not retreat, even before the queen. "Better sharp wit in a cad than dull wit in a saint," he said.

The queen allowed a small smile. "There is truth in that," she agreed. "But we have not greeted our guest. Monsieur Faverges, is it not?"

Amaury dropped to one knee. "Yes, Your Majesty."

"Arise. Faverges is in Savoy. Are you from there?"

When Amaury confirmed that he was, the queen looked at him more closely. She lingered on Amaury's square jaw and hazel eyes. Amaury met her gaze, praying she would not pursue the subject. But the queen merely smiled and moved to a different topic.

"You bring news of Paris, Monsieur Faverges, do you not?"

"Yes, Your Majesty," Amaury replied, relieved at the queen's discretion but still anxious. Others in the group must know his father. Had anyone else guessed?

"The city is at peace?"

"For the moment, Your Majesty."

"It is my hope that Catholics and Lutherans in France may soon learn to live side by side in harmony. Do you see any progress in that direction?"

"I cannot be certain, Your Majesty. Lutherans and Catholics remain separated and view each other, I'm sorry to say, with antipathy. But there is little outright violence or open persecution."

"A positive development, as I'm sure you would agree," Marguerite observed. "I am told that you are late of Montaigu," she said suddenly. "A rigorous education, is it not?"

"Yes, Your Majesty. Rigorous indeed."

"The king was persuaded to allow Magister Beda to return to his post as a gesture of goodwill. I advised him against it. Magister Beda is hardly the voice of tolerance that France needs to allow her to access the talents of all her subjects."

"Magister Beda is old and, I am told, quite ill," Amaury offered. "Perhaps as he nears death, he will seek reconciliation."

"Not him," the queen said tersely. She seemed about to say more when a side door opened and four young women entered.

Amaury felt himself turn to stone. Second into the room was Vivienne. She was arresting, clad in a lace dress of deep blue, a buff silk scarf draped over her head. Her hands were clasped in front of her as she walked, her eyes cast down as if she had just entered a cathedral. She was trying her best to move with ease, but her terror was apparent.

But Vivienne was not the cause of Amaury's astonishment. Just behind her was another woman, tall and golden haired. Her skin was without blemish and the color of fine linen, her eyes the blue of an autumn sky. She wore an ocher dress and pale green scarf. She appeared to float rather than walk.

Hélène.

"I am told that the two of you know each other," the queen interjected.

Vivienne looked up, her eyes darting reflexively from Amaury to the queen, but he knew to whom Marguerite was referring.

"One of my very good friends," Marguerite continued. "She sought the peace of my court two years ago and has been here ever since."

"Hello, Amaury," Hélène said softly, stepping around Vivienne. Her diction was perfect and she had the same lilt to her voice that he remembered. Like water in a brook after a spring rain. Vivienne had frozen in place.

Amaury's head spun from one to the other as if he was at a tennis match. Vivienne, doomed by an accident of birth but righteous and good, and Hélène, who did little with her life except cultivate her beauty. If there were any justice, Vivienne's nobility would diminish Hélène's vanity. But the world is unjust and Hélène's ease among the aristocracy made Vivienne appear as out of place as the poor girl surely felt. A whore in good clothing.

But allure is not determined by virtue. In those few seconds Amaury knew, knew beyond any doubt, that he loved Hélène as much now as he ever had, as much as he had that day in the field. A love that had burned in him, brought him misery. But he would not allow her to know. He would not.

"Hélène," he said, with a small bow. "You look splendid, although that is hardly a surprise."

"Thank you, Amaury." She tilted her head sideways to take him in. "As do you, albeit more than a little uncomfortable in those clothes."

He lowered his gaze to examine himself once more. "Yes. I feel more as if I should be participating in a *tableau vivant* than warding off the ripostes of Monsieur Rabelais here."

"Ah!" interjected Rabelais. "I was mistaken. Not pious at all. He is using me to try and bed her! Ha! Don't forget *droit d'auteur*, young man."

"That is *droit de seigneur*, Monsieur Rabelais," Hélène replied in an instant. "And since I was married, it is hardly applicable."

"Married or not, madame, you are a jewel of Europe. I generally eschew jewels—they don't suit my idiom—but in your case . . ."

"In any event," Hélène interjected, "the custom is reserved for lords, which you, God be praised, are not."

"If I were, madame, there would not be a virgin left in France, unless she be scabrous or smell like a cow."

"Speaking of those who smell like cows . . ." Roussel observed.

"I don't believe your protection is required, Gérard," interjected the queen. "My dear Hélène seems to have sufficient sting in her tongue to fend for herself."

"A jewel with the tongue of a scorpion," sighed Rabelais. "I may swoon."

"We should all be so fortunate," Roussel muttered.

"Calm yourselves," the queen commanded, but with a smile. "Can we not let Monsieur Faverges renew his acquaintance in peace?"

"'Was married'?" The words were out of Amaury's mouth before he could stop them. Vivienne looked briefly from him to Hélène, then averted her eyes. Amaury felt like a scoundrel. But he wanted the answer all the same.

"My husband is dead," Hélène replied. "He died three years ago in a shipwreck in the Aegean." She did not exhibit remorse at her widowhood.

"My condolences," Amaury said, although his insincerity felt transparent.

"I am now free to pass my days with Her Majesty, who was sufficiently gracious to offer me sanctuary."

"Sanctuary from what?"

Hélène gave him a small smile. Tiny crinkles formed at either corner of her mouth, as they had when she and Amaury were children. "Shall we walk in the gardens and recount our mutual tales?"

"Perhaps later," Amaury replied. "We have had a long journey and are somewhat fatigued."

"Bravo!" exulted Rabelais from the side. "Never appear too eager." He lowered his voice. "That was always my problem."

"Your problem, François," rejoined the queen, "is that the only women who can bear you are paid for their endurance."

By reflex, Amaury glanced to Vivienne. Her expression remained as before, but he knew she must have been using all her strength to keep from running from the room. He felt for her, but his eyes immediately returned to Hélène.

"Later, then," she said with a small, grave smile. "I'm eager to hear of the years since we last met."

"Of course," Amaury replied, bowing once more. "Although there is little of interest to tell. I fear you would be bored."

XX

AMAURY REMAINED for another hour. Conversation swirled about him. He should have been listening, he knew, trying to pick up some snippet of conversation that would help him proceed, but he heard almost nothing. Instead he participated mechanically, his eyes always returning to the same spot, a divan against the far wall.

Hélène. Like a sorceress. Brought to Nérac to unnerve and destroy him. Amaury resolved with all his strength that he would not allow her to do it again.

Eventually, Castell'buono entered. He was obviously well-known and well regarded. Even Rabelais greeted him warmly. As he made his way across the room, he stopped to greet Hélène. The Italian spoke with his back turned to him, but Amaury was certain that he was the subject. Before moving on, Castell'buono glanced briefly his way, smiled, and gave one small nod.

Amaury ignored some question or other about Paris as he watched Castell'buono move to Vivienne. She was surrounded by three young courtiers, but the Italian squeezed his way in to sit next to her. He spoke with his usual animation, eliciting smiles and laughter from all. Amaury felt himself redden as he watched Vivienne take in the Italian's chatter with obvious enjoyment. After a few moments, Amaury felt eyes on him. He turned to see Hélène staring from across the room. When their eyes met, she excused herself from those with whom she was sitting, rose, and made her exit. She did not look at him again.

Amaury left soon afterward. He looked toward Vivienne, but she seemed to be at ease speaking with the courtiers. The Italian had vanished. When Amaury returned to his room to dress for dinner, however, Castell'buono was waiting just outside the door. He motioned that they should speak inside.

"Well, Faverges," he began, effusive as always, "beautiful women seem irresistibly drawn to you. Perhaps you might share your secret."

"My lady and I are old friends," Amaury mumbled. "We knew each other as children in Savoy."

"I was told she seemed to give you quite a jolt."

Had he been that obvious? "I was surprised to see her. That's all."

"And the other one. Vivienne . . . d'Arras?"

"She was remarkable on the journey. I would not have made it here without her."

"You have feelings for her then?"

"Of course. How could I not?"

Castell'buono sighed. "That means no. Just as well. She would complicate your life terribly."

"I appreciate your concern, but I'm sure you have more pressing issues on your mind."

"Yes. That's true. I wanted first to thank you once more for the enormous service you did us. The risks you undertook were not in vain. The correspondence you brought held some invaluable information."

"I'm gratified to have been of service."

"Aren't you curious what it contained?"

"Of course. But the essence of secrets is that they are not shared."

"Well, I'll share this much with you. Our brothers in Paris have concluded that Henri Routbourg's assassination is proof that the Inquisition has succeeded in planting a spy among us. Do you agree?"

"I'm hardly in a position to agree or disagree," Amaury replied. "Although Giles Fabrizy's killing would certainly indicate that some mischief is afoot."

"You do not believe the murder of Fabrizy was the by-product of a robbery?"

"No."

"Nor do I. He was killed for his political activities. Of that I am certain. Perhaps you would be kind enough to share with me in more detail what you know of both deaths? Also a fuller explanation of how you came to be here."

Amaury again recounted the tale of his dismissal from Montaigu, Routbourg's murder, and its aftermath. He was certain to make the second narration factually identical to the first. Castell'buono would be listening for inconsistencies. But he took equal care not to use the same phrasing, so it did not appear as if he were giving a recitation. Amaury claimed no real knowledge of the circumstances of Giles' murder, except to repeat that it could hardly have been a coincidence. Through it all, Castell'buono listened carefully, occasionally wrinkling his brow, but not otherwise giving any indication whether or not he believed the account. When Amaury had finished, the Italian reached out and patted him on the shoulder.

"You were indeed fortunate to have been too fatigued to see Henri home. If you had been more energetic, we likely would not have met."

Amaury didn't reply.

"Faverges," the Italian went on, "you seem to be a smart fellow. Where would you look for Ory's agent?"

"Among your hierarchy."

"I agree. Here?"

"There is no way for me to venture an opinion on that."

"True enough. In my position, would you suspect yourself?"

"I would certainly suspect anyone whose activities could not be fully accounted for."

"My sentiments precisely. And you were *never* curious as to the contents of the packet you were risking your life to transport?"

"I was always curious. Do you wish to show them to me now?"

"I'm afraid not. You're an odd fellow, Faverges. You risk your life to help us, but yet you seem to lack allegiance to anything."

Amaury began to deny the accusation, then stopped. "Perhaps I'm seeking something to have an allegiance to," he said instead.

"Certainly true. More so than you think."

"And you have some deeper insight?"

"Yes, I do. You're a doubter."

"A doubter? What do I doubt?"

"Everything."

"I do not doubt God."

"Not His existence, perhaps, but certainly you doubt His nature, or at least what you have been told of His nature by the doctors at Montaigu, or even the fanatics of Lutheranism."

"Are you not a fanatic of Lutheranism?"

"That is a determination you must make for yourself."

I will, Amaury thought. Aloud, he offered, "But is not doubting the only path to enlightenment?"

"It is one path, certainly," Castell'buono admitted, "but tortured. For you, my dear Faverges, I suspect life is a continual search for meaning. After all, how can a doubter ever be sure of anything? I am fascinated by doubters. I, myself, have few doubts. Many questions, perhaps, but few doubts."

"Questions. Doubts." Amaury gave a backhand wave. "There is no difference. This is rhetoric without substance."

"Oh, no," Castell'buono said with a single shake of his head. "There is a very great difference. Those who question—like me—seek solutions. And as such—in wanting to find truth—we can then recognize it when we see it. Doubters—like you—can never find truth, because . . ."

"We doubt its existence."

"Precisely. As a questioner, I have found a set of beliefs in which I find complete comfort, to which I can pledge both my life and my soul. Have *you* ever found such comfort?"

"And if you are not a fanatic of Lutheranism, what is it that you believe in so strongly?" Amaury asked, rather than admit to Castell'buono that he was correct.

"God, of course. But also nature. Science. What greater evidence of God's glory exists than the wonders of the world around us? What makes wheat grow? How do currents appear in the sea? How do the stars remain in the heavens? Misguided zealots would have us believe that the answers are found in some agonized construction of Scripture. I do not. I believe that they are mysteries that God created for Man to solve."

Amaury might have used those precise words to Giles. "And why does God take such pains?" he asked.

"To give life meaning, of course! To give Man a reason to exist other than simply to spend his years in worship. Performing ridiculous rituals that mean nothing. Superstition. My word, Faverges, is that the sort of God you believe in?"

Of course he didn't, but Amaury was not about to cede the Italian the advantage.

"You seem to know everything, Monsieur Castell'buono. Then I suppose you know why Giles Fabrizy and Henri Routbourg were killed."

"As a matter of fact, I do. Precisely why."

"But you will not tell me."

"Not quite yet."

"Would it have anything to do with why you didn't show up for your meeting with Monsieur Calvin?"

Castell'buono allowed a slow smile to cross his face. "Very *good*, Faverges. You show depth. I'm relieved not to be wasting my time with you. But to answer your question . . . no. My absence in no way caused or hastened Henri's death. Although if I had known he was in such peril, I would certainly have attempted to save him."

"Calvin said that you would destroy Christianity altogether."

"Yes. I'm sure he did."

Should he take the risk? Why not? "By denying Genesis."

"How silly," Castell'buono replied with a dismissive wave. "Genesis is the word of God. No believer in Christ would do such a thing."

"How then?"

"You would have to ask Calvin that."

"You speak of Routbourg with affection and Calvin with derision. I thought the two were allies."

"A fair conclusion, but totally incorrect."

"Is it not possible, then, that Calvin's allies were responsible for Routbourg's death and not the Inquisition?"

"Another fair conclusion, but, no, it is not possible."

"So where you do stand in all of this? What *is* your role here?"

"I am . . . a sort of adviser. The queen believes that Lutherans seek merely to worship freely within Catholic France. I am here to help bring that about."

"A noble ambition."

"But hopelessly naïve. What the queen cannot comprehend is that France will never tolerate two religions. One will flourish and the other, inevitably, will be stamped out. If we are on the losing side, we can expect only blood and flames. France will continue Catholic until the king finds some advantage in divorcing himself from the pope. The queen herself will never disavow Catholicism. It thus becomes a matter of endurance. If we can maintain our position, no matter how tenuously, as the tide shifts across Europe, François might one day conclude it suits his purposes to turn France Lutheran. If not . . ." Castell'buono shrugged.

"Why are you so open and honest with me, Monsieur Castell'buono? You have all but announced that you don't trust me."

"I don't. But one has to take risks to attain rewards."

"How do you know I won't simply report everything you've told me to Queen Marguerite? I expect she would be none too pleased at your ideas."

"She would not. That's true. I tell you because I think you're an intelligent man and would be a valuable ally. I tell you because you believed everything I said, even if you are loath to admit it. I tell you because it will change you from doubter to questioner and be your salvation."

"Assuming I am not a spy."

Castell'buono laughed. "A spy? You? For whom? The king? Calvin? The Inquisition? You would be a terrible choice."

Despite himself, Amaury felt distinctly insulted. "Why do you say that?"

"Because you are a doubter. Haven't you been listening? Doubters can never be trusted to maintain loyalty. They are too prone to rejecting one philosophy and moving to another."

"I might have done it for money."

The Italian shrugged. "Wouldn't matter. If you lost your belief in whomever employed you, you would ultimately betray them rather than those whom you had come to embrace."

"Thank you," Amaury muttered. "It's nice to know that I should avoid spying as a profession."

"Don't worry. It's not much of a profession anyway." Castell'buono moved for the door. "It's getting late, Faverges. I have to dress for dinner. We must speak again later."

"Yes. We must. By the way, is Philippe my servant while I'm here? Or yours?"

"He is at your service, if you need him."

Amaury nodded. "He seems rather serious as compared to . . ."

"Me? Yes, I suppose he is. But do not judge Philippe too harshly. He was among the Franciscan order for fifteen years. It has left its mark."

"A Franciscan, you say?"

"Do you find something odd in that?"

"No. Not odd at all."

"After all, you were at Montaigu, as was Fabrizy. Didn't Montaigu leave a mark on you?"

True enough, thought Amaury after the Italian had departed. But neither of us had been seen by Veuve Chinot in an alley wearing a Franciscan cloak, standing over a dead body, holding a bloody knife.

XXI

WHEN HE RETURNED to the queen's wing of the palace, Amaury asked the maître d'hôtel if he could be seated near Vivienne at dinner. The man expressed his regrets but said that the seating could not be altered. When Amaury entered, he discovered that Vivienne had been placed at the far end of the right table, next to Castell'buono. The Italian nodded perfunctorily; Vivienne smiled brightly. She had slipped into the appropriate demeanor with remarkable facility. Amaury realized that, had he not known her origins, he would never have suspected she was anything but a well-born lady at court.

He was escorted to the main table and placed to the left of Queen Marguerite. On the other side of the queen, next to Gérard Roussel, was Hélène. She didn't look up when he entered, although she could not have helped seeing him. Amaury took his seat between a dowager and a plain, empty-headed, marriageable maid from Aragon.

The meal was sumptuous, particularly for people who had eaten only hours before. After days of bread and cheese, Amaury found himself ravenous. The food—roasted lamb, trout from the river, winter vegetables, cheese—was superb. The drinking quotient varied widely. Rabelais, seated at the far end of the queen's table, drank copiously, while Marguerite and her intimates merely sipped.

Conversation was constant and lively, creating a steady hum that drowned out all but the talk in one's immediate vicinity. The women on either side of him chattered incessantly, but Amaury paid almost no attention. His focus was on Castell'buono, oozing bonhomie to Vivienne. The Italian gesticulated, laughed, and made a variety of faces, all while apparently relating one diverting tale after another. Vivienne listened appreciatively, smiling and giggling. At one point, Amaury and the Italian made eye contact and his mask, just for an instant, fell away.

Placed as he was, Amaury could not see Hélène until the dinner was finished and the guests stood to leave. She faced him for a second, her face blank, and then turned to depart with Roussel.

As the dinner guests milled about, Amaury walked to where Castell'buono and Vivienne were standing. The Italian seemed to be making apologies for leaving. When he saw Amaury, he swept out an arm.

"Ah, Vivienne my dear, here is Faverges. Just in time. I'm certain he would be thrilled for your company."

"You're going?" Amaury asked.

"Alas. I have duties to attend to. But I will see you both in the morning. We hold our services on a hillside outside the palace. Very inviting. Roussel will preach tomorrow. Why don't we meet there?"

Then, barely waiting for acquiescence, the Italian hurried out.

Amaury turned quickly to Vivienne. "I'm sorry, but I must go as well."

Amaury peered into the hall just in time to see Castell'buono turn a corner. He followed quickly. If the Italian stopped to check if anyone was behind him, the game was up. A big risk to take, considering Castell'buono's destination might be as nondescript as his own bedroom. But this business demanded good instincts, and Amaury's told him that, from the haste with which the Italian left the room, a bit of surveillance might pay dividends.

When Amaury reached the end of the hall and peeked cautiously around the corner, Castell'buono was no longer in sight. Both a door and a staircase were at the end of the corridor. Amaury hurried to the end.

He could hear no footsteps, so he bet on the door. He carefully pushed it open, checked to see if anyone was immediately outside, then stepped into the courtyard. Torches placed along the walls lit the yard, but the doorway was in shadow. Amaury looked about and finally saw a short, round figure moving toward the chapel. He waited a moment, pressed up against a wall, obscured by darkness. Castell'buono suddenly whirled to look behind him, then, satisfied he was alone, entered the chapel through a side door. Amaury scurried after him.

He could not enter through the same door as the Italian. For all he knew, his man was just inside. Instead he chose a stairway that led upstairs to the gallery. He blessed his Montaigu experience; he had learned to open a door soundlessly. He slipped inside the chapel and immediately heard the murmur of voices. He padded through the gallery until he was just above the sound. Listening carefully, Amaury could just barely hear Castell'buono talking softly beneath him.

"Well, Philippe, what do you think?"

"He seems genuine enough, I suppose. I wouldn't trust him, though."

Castell'buono chuckled softly. "You don't trust anyone, Philippe. But if we trust no one, our numbers cannot grow. We need clever, talented people. You do think he's clever, don't you?"

"I suppose."

"Cleverness is a sword that cuts both ways, of course. Perhaps he was so clever as to maintain his Catholicism. So clever as to affect disinterest. He is no fool, this Faverges, and whether for personal reasons or something more, he does not tell all that he thinks."

"You don't think he's Ory's man?"

"Anything is possible, Philippe, but Ory has never before chosen someone so unsuitable."

"Unsuitable? He seems perfectly suitable to me."

"That's because you want everything to be the way it seems to be."

"What of the woman he arrived with?"

"A whore from Paris. Henri told me he would use her. She knows nothing."

"Whore or saint, Ory will employ anyone to destroy us."

"She is evidently quite resourceful. She has feelings for Faverges, but might also have seen some evidence of whether or not he can be trusted. As such, she merits some cultivating."

"We should not take chances with either of them."

"What you propose is hardly in God's path, Philippe."

"We cannot afford to be squeamish. We will roast for it."

"Perhaps, Philippe. But we do not murder the innocent no matter what our suspicions. We leave that for our enemies."

Philippe grunted.

"I confess I like him," Castell'buono continued. "This Faverges. He was quite effective in not giving away that he knew that the correspondence he was carrying was blank."

"But less effective in hiding that he had seen it."

"One twist. On the whole, though, he did rather well with the knot."

"While violating his word not to look at what was inside."

"Oh, Philippe, I would have been more concerned had he *not* tried to look."

"What is the point of testing someone if you ignore when they fail?"

"*I* didn't test him. That was Hoess. He is so enamored of intrigue. I prefer to judge the man."

"So you will risk giving him the real papers for the return trip? On your judgment of the man alone? If he betrays us, or even simply fails, and we do not publish what we have, all our efforts will have been for nothing. Everything I have done . . ."

"I haven't decided yet whether to trust him. But you must trust *me*, Philippe. I would never imperil our cause . . . your sacrifices. But this Faverges is worth a bit of time. He would be a valuable ally. His father is the Duke of Savoy. And he *can* be an ally. He believes as we do, Philippe. I'm certain of it. I think we should wait and observe the Savoyard and see what he does."

"I'm against it."

"We can always take action if need be. Where is he going to go?"

"He might not wait for you to decide if he is trustworthy. He might slip away to Paris on his own and betray us all."

"Then you will leave as well, Philippe. Nothing could be simpler. One more thing. Are you certain no one observed you in the alley?"

"Quite certain. Why do you ask?"

"Because Faverges reacted oddly when I mentioned that you had been a Franciscan. I wonder—"

"What?"

"They were both at Montaigu. They might have known each other. Perhaps he is not here for the manuscript at all. Perhaps he is only here for the boy, Giles. For you, Philippe. That would certainly change things."

"In either case . . ."

"No. Not yet. But be ready, my friend."

His life, the old man realized, had been a race. Now the race was nearing the end, although just how much farther the course ran, he could not be sure. What did seem more and more evident, however, was that, whatever time was left to him, he would not reach the finish.

Despite perseverance bordering on obsession, the problem, the paradox that had confounded him for over a decade, remained insoluble. Or, at least, insoluble to him. Another natural philosopher would certainly follow after the old man was dead and see the solution. It would likely turn out to be quite simple. Basic and obvious. The best the old man could hope to do now was to carry the standard.

But, he thought with a sigh, isn't making a contribution what science is? Not individuals filled with pride or hubris, but rather a steady stream of the curious and the dogged, each edging human knowledge ahead, confident—and gratified—that another would always arise to take his place in the vanguard.

How can an object that is moving forward at the same time move backward? If he could have solved that problem, his model would have been elegant and complete. Ptolemy had resorted to the contrivance of epicycles. The Egyptian called the creation his Celestial Pearl. String of pearls was more like it. The old man had been determined to discard that machination, but ultimately could not. He must, then, be content with his basic findings and leave epicycles for another to eliminate.

Of course, the central thesis—he almost chuckled at the pun—was the most vital. His time had hardly been wasted. And, imperfection or no, there could be no doubt that his construction was correct.

And he rejected the notion that its dissemination would overturn Church dogma. Nothing in Scripture ran counter to his findings. The current interpretation was not Divine Word but a theory originally postulated by Aristotle. A brilliant mind, surely, but hardly a Christian one. True, the Blessed Thomas Aquinas had adapted Aristotle to Christianity in order to reconcile science with Scripture. But would the Church really suffer if it had to make

151

accommodations to new knowledge? God's glory remained. And the old man could also not comprehend why Man would lose his uniqueness if Aristotelian—and Ptolemaic—interpretation was supplanted. Ptolemy, after all, was another pagan.

Many in the Church, like Cardinal Schönburg, saw the situation just that way. Even Pope Leo had expressed tolerance for the idea. But Leo was dead and Schönburg was in a tiny minority. Luther was the reason, of course. The cursed German. After Luther, the matter had taken on new import. Any formulation that bore the slightest potential of causing the faithful to question was now seen as a threat. Pope Clement, not the strongest of men to begin with, was increasingly falling under the influence of the reactionaries.

With matters so tenuous, friends and enemies alike had gotten word to the old man that any attempt to publish his findings as fact would bring a charge of heresy and death by fire. His very name would be anathema in the annals of the Church. He had even been told that he risked assassination if he so much as attempted to publish. So he had waited.

Still, no politics, no delay, and no threats could change the truth.

The Earth circled the sun and not the other way around.

XXII

AMAURY LAY IN BED, propped against the headboard. After midnight. He had given up on sleep and opened the drapes to let in the breeze. Half light from the moon penetrated the room and created spectral shadows on the wall.

How confusing this had all become. He had found Giles' assassin. The reason he had come. He should denounce Philippe, make him pay for his crime. Or kill the man himself. But that would expose them all. Expose him. End the charade. And whatever secret Philippe and Castell'buono were protecting, he would forfeit his chance of discovering it. It would be left for Ory. But it might well be a secret that he, Amaury, would also want to protect. That Giles had wanted to protect.

He must have begun to fall asleep without realizing, because all at once he was aware of a scratching in the hall. As he gained focus, he realized the scratching was from a key being placed in the lock of his door.

Philippe. There to assassinate him. The Franciscan was taking no chances, no matter what Castell'buono had said.

Amaury slipped out of bed and retrieved his dagger from his clothes.

Giles' face once more flashed in his mind. Philippe would not find an unarmed innocent this time. He walked quietly across the room and stood behind the door.

Slowly, the door began to open. When it had opened halfway, it stopped. Amaury held the knife steady, ready to strike.

A figure slipped quietly into the room. Not Philippe. A woman. Wearing nightclothes. As soon as she was inside, the pale, beautiful figure was unmistakable. She closed the door behind her and padded on tiptoes across the room. She stopped at the empty bed. Amaury dropped the knife to the floor.

"Hélène."

She spun, wide-eyed as a fawn, glanced down at the dagger at his feet, but didn't speak. Instead she extended her hand. Amaury moved to her. He stood inches away. She smelled of flowers, of dew, of everything sweet and wondrous. He could hear rhythmic breathing but was not sure if it was his, hers, or theirs both. She reached up and placed her fingertips on his cheek. The touch of an angel. She placed her hands on his shoulders and pushed him down to sit on the bed. She took one step backward. Then, never taking her eyes from his, she reached up and grasped the ties of her nightdress. She held the ties for a moment and then pulled them. The nightdress fell to the floor.

Hélène stepped out of the pile of silk but remained at the side of the bed, letting Amaury look at her. Her body was long and full, but without heaviness. He watched her stomach and breasts move in and out as she breathed. Amaury was too transfixed to budge. The two of them remained there, suspended in time and space for some moments, until Hélène moved to join him on the bed.

They made love for hours, a lifetime of release crammed into a single night. Whenever Amaury tried to speak, to breathe her name, she placed a finger on his lips. Finally, the impending dawn began to lighten the sky. Hélène arose, dressed, then slipped out as silently as she had entered. Amaury stared at the door for some moments after she had departed, as if a spectral presence of the woman remained in the wood.

He would love her until the day he died.

XXIII

As THE SUN WARMED the fields on a beautiful spring morning, Amaury made his way out of the palace to attend the Lutheran service. He should have invited Vivienne, he knew, but he could not face her.

Amaury reached a shallow hillside where about thirty worshippers were gathered for the service. Roussel stood at the front. Neither the queen nor any of the luminaries from the palace drawing room were among the crowd. It was true, then. Most of the court had remained Catholic. As he scanned the congregation, Amaury spied Vivienne sitting near the front. So she had not waited for him either. Sitting next to her was, once again, Castell'buono. They were speaking, as at the dinner, in a manner quite animated. Amaury remained at the rear, and soon Roussel moved to address the congregation.

The Lutheran service had retained much from the Mass. Roussel recited the same psalms, followed the same liturgy, and offered the same Communion. The differences, however, were significant. Conducting the service in vernacular French created a more vibrant mood. Those among the worshippers who knew no Latin would feel as much a part of the proceedings as those who did. As a result, the congregation was unified, communal, seemed somehow closer to God.

Music was far more important to the Lutherans than Amaury would have expected. The congregation sang many hymns, including one penned by Luther himself, "A Mighty Fortress Is Our God." Amaury found the heavy German intonations somewhat ponderous and repetitive, but was nonetheless impressed listening to a composition by the very man who had founded the new religion.

Roussel, the orator who had filled the courtyard at the Louvre, possessed a power to preach that had in no way been understated. The sermon was powerful and compelling. The topic was Man's place in the universe. Roussel spoke of Man as being master of the natural world, assigned that role by God, and therefore responsible not simply for his own destiny but for that of all around him. "Man is at the center of God's plan," Roussel said, "unique in the universe, and bears the weight as well as the glory of that role."

When the service ended, the flock, Vivienne among them, moved forward as one to praise the shepherd. Roussel accepted the paeans with a shy smile. At one point, Roussel placed his hand on Vivienne's shoulder and spoke to her directly. Castell'buono stood next to them, beaming but for once letting someone else speak.

Amaury was trying to decide whether or not to join them when he felt a hand on his own shoulder. He turned to find himself face-to-face with a priest.

"Hello, my son," the priest said with a slow nod. He was about thirty, lean and fair, with a hawklike brow. His voice rolled gently from within him. "Amaury, is it not? I am Père Louis-Paul. I am confessor to Her Majesty."

Amaury returned the greeting, uncomfortable with the priest's conspicuous piety. He felt suddenly as if he was back at Montaigu.

"Did you enjoy the service?" Père Louis-Paul asked, demonstrating no rancor in asking about branded heretics. "The Lutherans have been clever in their choices to render Christianity more egalitarian, have they not? I expect our Church will be forced to make some changes to make services more . . . entertaining. Do you agree?"

"I am not qualified to judge such high ecclesiastical matters," Amaury replied.

"After nine years at Montaigu? Oh, you are too modest." The priest shrugged. "Then what of your own reaction? Did you find the service appealing?"

"Appealing? Yes, it certainly was that."

The priest bowed his head slightly, so as to peer at Amaury from the tops of his eyes. "But *you* remain within the True Church yourself, do you not, my son?"

"Yes. Of course, Father."

Père Louis-Paul smiled. Then he switched to Latin. "*Pro moment in ullus vices.*" "For the moment, in any event."

"I have no plans to change."

The priest nodded. "Why don't you come for Confession, then?"

"I will certainly do so," Amaury lied. He had no intention of confessing anything to this nosy priest within the intrigue of Queen Marguerite's court.

"Come today," the priest said softly. "Just after midday meal."

Amaury looked at Père Louis-Paul more closely and saw that the priest was doing the same to him.

"I am interested to learn what you have discerned in your travels."

"*You* are interested?" Amaury asked.

"Yes. As is Magister Ory. He is, in fact, awaiting your communication with great expectation." The priest paused. "You do not wish to disappoint him, do you?"

"No. I will be pleased to share my observations."

"Good, then," said Père Louis-Paul. "I shall see you presently." The priest smiled, although the gesture did not reach his eyes. "Do not fret, my son. You will find the experience cleansing."

XXIV

THE SENSE OF PEACE exuded by Queen Marguerite extended to her church. Calm and serene with superb acoustics, the interior bore a faint trace of her scent. Delicate, almost floral. Also in Marguerite's idiom, the facility served both Catholics and Lutherans, possibly unique for a place of worship in France. Except during services, it was impossible to discern from a glance the liturgy to which any particular supplicant adhered.

The priest was waiting. Père Louis-Paul did not appear either so pious or so kindly as he had in the courtyard. Rather, he had adopted an air of somber impatience.

Each entered their respective doors of the confessional and softly closed them. As Amaury knelt, the curtain pulled open. The outline of Père Louis-Paul was visible through the lattice in the dim light.

Amaury had never before been in a confessional without saying, "Forgive me, Father, for I have sinned," but on this occasion he merely sat and waited for Père Louis-Paul to begin. For some moments, the only sound was the breathing of the two men. Finally, Père Louis-Paul seemed to recognize that no Sacrament of Penance would precede the interrogation.

"Well, my son," he began in his confessor's whisper, "what have you learned?" The sound seemed to float in the tiny enclosed chamber.

"Not very much, I'm afraid," Amaury whispered in return, in Latin. "As Magister Ory suspected, there does seem to be a substratum of the Lutherans who are more radical than their brethren. And there does seem to be talk of some grand conspiracy to disprove Genesis, although I continue to doubt if the effort is serious."

"This is no more than we knew already. Surely you learned *something* more. The Italian, for example. Castell'buono. Is he involved?"

"Certainly," Amaury replied. "But this can hardly be a revelation to you."

"And the girl? The one you traveled with. Has she deduced your true affiliation?"

"No."

The priest was silent for some moments. He surely suspected Amaury was lying to him but was in no position to launch a specific accusation. "Well, my son," he whispered finally, "although you seem to have little to tell us, we have something to tell you. Magister Ory has an assignment that he wishes you to carry out. It is the reason you were brought here. You will, you see, have the opportunity to demonstrate your worth after all."

"I am grateful," Amaury said.

"In Castell'buono's rooms are documents. Very explicit documents, I'm told. They come from a man living in the east and give the details of the Lutheran conspiracy. You are to read them—read them with great care—and report to me on their contents."

"Excuse me, Father," Amaury replied. "How am I to read documents that Castell'buono has secreted in his rooms? Am I to simply ask him to show me material that could have him burnt at the stake? I must also ask, why me specifically? With your position, you would seem more apt to access this information than I."

"You are to read them because they are technical—mathematical. They concern some aspect of natural philosophy that the Lutherans believe will throw into doubt the Church's interpretation of Genesis 1:1. You were chosen for this assignment because Magister Ory believes you to have a brilliant mind for such things."

"Magister Ory flatters me."

"Hardly. He also imparted that your faith and commitment are both questionable. You are under great scrutiny, Faverges. I suggest you do not take this admonition lightly."

"I take nothing from Magister Ory lightly."

"Very wise. It has been observed that you do not seem to be proceeding with the energy Magister Ory expected of you."

"I don't see how I could have exhibited more energy," Amaury protested. "I got myself assigned to come here and have since insinuated myself into Castell'buono's circle. That he has yet to give me his unvarnished trust after one day is not surprising."

"A fine argument for a disputation, Faverges," the priest replied. "And perhaps even valid. Still, your traveling companion has managed to forge a more intimate relationship with Castell'buono, and she is not even of our cause."

"She possesses virtues I do not," Amaury countered.

"True enough," allowed the priest. "As to the 'how,' arrangements have been made. Signore Castell'buono, although he does not know it as yet, is about to go on a journey. He will be asked by Her Majesty to travel to Angoulême to fetch some documents held at an abbey there. He will be gone at least two days. During that time, you can find occasion to visit his rooms and read whatever it is that is secreted. On the floor under your seat, you will find a key. It will allow you entry into the Italian's room."

"So I am to be a thief in the night."

"Do it in the day if you wish," said the priest. "Now, I, as you, fully expect that this material will be some sort of hoax or piece of mysticism and do nothing to bring any of the Holy Scripture into question. In the current environment, however, with the Lutherans undermining faith at every turn, the True Church can take no chances."

"I agree."

"I am heartened. Oh, yes, there is one more thing."

"Yes?"

"You are under suspicion by the heretics. Sévrier watches your every move."

"Sévrier?"

"Your supposed servant Philippe. You must discharge your assignment with an eye to his movements." Père Louis-Paul paused. "We perhaps don't fully trust you, but we would still prefer that you remain alive."

By the time Amaury left the chapel, the sun had vanished. A flat, ominous gray sky, under which dark clouds were gathering, promised rain. How fitting, he thought.

The courtyard was deserted. Amaury was grateful for the privacy. He decided to leave the palace and walk in the fields. Not Savoy, perhaps, but open air provoked clear thought. As he headed for the gate, one man tarried on a small bench against the palace wall, clad in soiled, threadbare clothing, seemingly rapt in the attempt to twist an errant cuticle off his thumb. Amaury began to walk past when the man unaccountably lifted his head.

"My, my, Faverges, don't you look downcast," said Rabelais. He glanced skyward. "And on such a fine day."

Amaury nodded briefly but continued on. Thunder rumbled in the distance.

"No, no. Wait." Rabelais rose and gestured that they should walk together. Amaury's instinct was to avoid him, but somehow Rabelais, because he respected nothing, was the only person in the palace in whose company Amaury felt at ease.

"You have not been successful?" the writer asked.

"Successful? In what way?"

"In bedding the woman, of course. Or even women. To what else would I refer?"

Amaury averted his gaze.

"Then you were successful! Which one? The cold aristocrat or the passionate peasant? I would prefer the latter. But I am an egalitarian."

"May I ask you a question?" Amaury asked instead of replying.

"Of course. About women, I hope."

"Are you what you pretend to be?"

"*Quel dommage*," Rabelais replied with a sigh. "How boring. And,

161

besides, the question is oxymoronic. If I was pretending, then I could not prima facie be genuine. What you want to know is if I am what I *appear* to be. As outlandish."

"Yes. You seem almost as if you had stepped from your writings."

"Perhaps the writings stepped from the man," Rabelais replied. "But the answer to your question is yes. I am precisely as I appear. Shocking as it may be, there is no pretense or artifice in my manner, either personal or social. On the other hand, you, I deduce, feel you are not what *you* appear to be."

Amaury did not reply.

"Therefore, you either do not know how you appear, or do not know who you are. Or, God have mercy, both. But I suspect you know what you appear to be, thus you must not know who you are."

"Yes. That's true."

Rabelais indicated another bench, against the north wall of the palace. "Come sit," he said. Amaury felt a drop of rain and looked up. "Don't worry," Rabelais chided. "If water will not harm one who does not bathe, I feel certain you will be safe."

They strolled through intermittent raindrops. Rabelais' feet scraped along the ground as he walked. Once they were seated, he continued. "Usually, my young friend, when people do not know who they are, it is because they do not wish to be what they *think* they are. Is that the case with you?"

"Yes. Perhaps."

"So let us start with the simpler question. What do you think you are?"

"Castell'buono says I'm a doubter."

Rabelais waved dismissively to the air. "Castell'buono is a dissembler. His opinion would not matter in any case. Only yours is germane."

Amaury considered the question. "I think I am a noble bastard whose ambition is fueled by denial of his birthright. I think I have led a life of dishonesty, trying to attain by good works what I was denied by corruption of lineage."

Rabelais seemed stunned. "My good and merciful Lord. An honest man. I did not think they existed."

"I'm hardly honest," Amaury muttered.

"Why? Because you deceive others? That doesn't matter a tit. You are honest with yourself. A far more difficult proposition. And, because you are honest with yourself, I will be honest with you."

"Thank you."

"I began in the Church. In a monastery, in fact. I was far younger than you are now when I grew disgusted by the hypocrisy. When that German pus ball Luther came along, I read his work and found him little better. I studied medicine—I am rather a fine physician, you know—because I thought earthly matters far more noble a pursuit than competing to be the most pious man in a heaven that may well not exist. And what is piety, anyway? An arbitrary construct created by men who drink, whore, accumulate wealth, and father illegitimate children—excuse me—while denouncing similar behavior in others.

"When I began to write, even I feared the repercussions, so I created an anagram of my name, Alcofribas Nasier. It fooled no one. My work has been banned by the Church, condemned by right-thinking people every-where, and, if not for King François—who enjoyed *Pantegruel* immensely, I'm told—I would likely at this moment be no more than a pile of ashes.

"So the question I am sure you wanted to ask is . . . do I regret my deci-sions? Correct?"

Amaury nodded. The rain had increased to a fine mist, but Rabelais seemed unconcerned.

"No! There is your answer. As Erasmus said—he's also a bastard, you know, although of the priesthood—minor priesthood, not nobility: 'Give light, and the darkness will disappear of itself.' I give light."

"Erasmus also wrote, 'It is the foremost point of happiness that a man is willing to be what he is,' did he not?" Amaury asked.

"Yes," admitted Rabelais, "although I would appreciate if we stopped quoting that Dutchman and began quoting me. *I* wrote, 'One falls to the ground in trying to sit on two stools.' Good, is it not?"

"Indeed," Amaury agreed.

"Better even," Rabelais pressed. "More wit. Less pretension."

"Definitely less pretension."

"Erasmus was always pretentious." Rabelais clapped his hands on his knees and pushed himself to his feet. "Fine, then. Let us continue. You were saying?"

"It was you who was speaking. Telling me of your lack of regret."

"Ah, yes . . . come, let us walk . . . so tell me, my friend, all this fakery you've engaged in . . . has it brought you any closer to what you seek?"

"No. I suppose not."

"But you think the reason is that you have not done enough. If only you were more worthy, tried harder, engaged in even more good works— then your hopes would reach fruition. That's right, isn't it?"

Amaury nodded.

"But what if the problem was not the distance you have traveled but the road you have chosen? If that is true, then the further you go, the deeper into the thicket. The more lost you become. The test is simple. Do you feel more or less lost?"

"I'm not sure."

"That means more."

"I suppose."

"There you have it." Rabelais looked quite satisfied with himself.

"And the alternative?"

"You pick a path, my young friend, not because you think others would choose it for you, or would even approve of your choice, but simply because it is *your* choice."

"And what was your choice?"

"My choice was to put my thumb in the eye of pompous fools. And I have never regretted it for a second."

"What if you lose the king's favor and are imprisoned? Or worse."

"I'm neither fool nor zealot. I will regret being imprisoned. Or worse. But I will not regret the choices that brought me to such an unfortunate end."

The rain had begun falling more heavily. Amaury looked down at the front of his clothes and realized he was soaked. He turned his hands palms up and watched water run off his fingers.

"You are of feeble constitution," Rabelais grunted. "You'd best go back and change."

XXV

AMAURY RETURNED to the palace by a side door, shaking from the chill of his wet clothing. He warmed himself by a fire in the entrance hall and considered what Rabelais had said. More, actually, he considered what Rabelais *was*. Not a buffoon at all. Rather, a man utterly comfortable with his existence. A man who followed his own road, regardless of the opinion, lack of approbation, or even the jeers of others. A man who felt God but rejected the Church's definition of Him. A man with many questions, perhaps, but without doubts. A man to be envied. Perhaps emulated.

After the fire had done its work, Amaury located an alcove in a quiet hall. He sat on the stone seat, gazing for a moment at the rivulets of rain snaking their way down the outside of the small, stained-glass window set high in the alcove's wall. The window had a rose in the center. The movement of the water created the sensation of a flower shimmering in the wind. He leaned out into the hall to ensure that he was alone, then removed the folded paper from his pocket and once more studied the riddle Giles had penned.

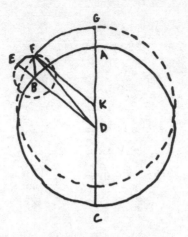

The material in Castell'buono's room was mathematical, Père Louis-Paul had said. Scientific. Amaury had no doubt that it related in some fashion to this diagram. But the diagram was incorrect. Or seemed to be. It contained the extra layer of data he had mentioned to Vivienne. Amaury was as familiar with the concept as he was with the snows of Savoy. He traced his finger over the diagram as it *should* have been drawn. In his mind's eye, he saw:

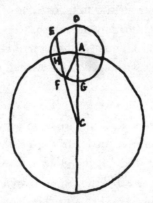

Here was Ptolemy's illustration of an epicycle, the one he had drawn in the dirt for Vivienne. C, to Ptolemy, would be the Earth, stationary at the center of the universe. A was a point on the orbit of a body, Mars, perhaps. Mars rode on the smaller orbit around point A. Thus, during half of its orbit around A, Mars would appear to someone on Earth at point C to be moving backward. But in Giles' diagram, there seemed to be two centers, K and D.

Why the change? Who would question one of the most fundamental and universally accepted precepts of science? And what could this alteration have to do with a reinterpretation of Genesis?

"Monsieur Castell'buono is in the courtyard. He wishes a word."

Amaury jerked his head up, hurriedly folding the paper. Philippe Sévrier was standing over him. Amaury had neither seen nor heard him approach.

"Of course. Could you give me a moment, please?" Had Sévrier seen the paper? How had Sévrier even known where he was?

Sévrier nodded and withdrew. Soon after, Amaury composed himself and made his way outside. The fine rain continued to fall and Amaury was again chilled as soon as the mist settled into his doublet. How spoiled he'd become. At Montaigu, he never would have noticed such a minor inconvenience as cold.

Castell'buono was near the gate, seated astride a large bay, saddle and bunting emblazoned with the crest of Navarre. Two of the queen's soldiers were mounted behind him. Sévrier stood at his side, listening as the Italian leaned over slightly to impart instructions. When Castell'buono observed Amaury's approach, he spoke more quickly, glancing up occasionally to ensure that he finished what he wanted to say before Amaury was in earshot. He straightened himself in the saddle as Amaury arrived.

"You wished to see me?" Amaury asked.

"To say à bientôt. It seems I am to travel to Angoulême for Her Majesty on a matter that cannot wait." Castell'buono's grin was absent.

"A testament to the esteem in which you are held by the queen," Amaury replied.

"No doubt. I am flattered at the attention. Will you be here when I return, or do you intend to leave to reclaim the joys of Paris?"

"I had thought to journey north, but I believe I will remain here for a time. I am drawn to the vibrancy of Queen Marguerite's court."

"Yes," Castell'buono acknowledged. He glanced upward, toward the apartments on the second floor. "I've noticed. In any event, I hope you do remain. In the interim, Philippe can continue to see to your needs." Castell'buono made to begin his ride, then stopped. "Oh, yes. One last thing. I saw you speaking with that priest. Take care. I have suspicions that he serves a master other than God. Or Queen Marguerite."

"Thank you for the warning. *Bon voyage* then."

Castell'buono nodded. "Yes." He snapped the reins and Amaury watched as horse, rider, and the two soldiers moved through the open gate. After the Italian had departed, Amaury turned and observed Philippe Sévrier staring at him, even and unblinking. As Amaury walked across the courtyard toward the palace, he felt Sévrier's eyes like two fingers pressing into his back.

He was going to need help. That was certain. After a number of inquiries, Amaury finally located Vivienne in the chapel. She was knelt in prayer, four rows from the rear.

Amaury scanned the interior for Père Louis-Paul, but the priest was not present. Neither had Sévrier appeared. Amaury moved into the row behind Vivienne so that she might complete her prayers without interruption. Almost immediately, however, she turned and saw him. For an instant she seemed startled.

"Might I speak with you when you are done?" Amaury whispered.

"I've finished," Vivienne said softly. She rose slowly and moved to the aisle, then knelt once more to make the sign of the cross.

Amaury had intended to speak with her outside, in some corner of the courtyard, where prying ears could not reach, but the rain continued to fall. Instead he led her to an alcove at the far end of the nave.

"Vivienne, I have an apology and a request." He spoke softly, just over a whisper.

"An apology, Amaury?" she asked, matching his tone. "What do you have to apologize for?"

"I have deceived you."

"No. The instant I saw the way the two of you looked at each other, I knew. You haven't deceived me."

Amaury had been prepared for any number of responses, but not that one. "But that was long—"

"It's all right. I know you have feelings for me, just not the same feelings you have for her. At one point, I admit I did think what it might be like . . . with you. Traveling as husband and wife as we were."

"So did I."

She touched his hand. "But this way is better for both of us. I'm certain."

"Is that why you have been so . . . friendly . . . with Castell'buono?"

She laughed, clear and girlish.

"Castell'buono is amusing, surely, but I have no affection for him. I was afraid, Amaury. I am still afraid. How do you think I felt, walking into the palace with a woman of noble birth? Your childhood love? Castell'buono wanted me from the first—I have sufficient experience in *that* regard to know—and was willing to guide me through this torture. When I realized you were not, I accepted his attentions."

Amaury felt like a cad, even worse for what he was about to ask. "I'm sorry, Vivienne. Truly. But when I said I had deceived you, I wasn't talking about . . . Hélène. I meant that I have not told you the truth about my mission here."

She waited.

"I was asked by Monsieur Hoess not only to deliver correspondence but also to observe the Italian. There is little question that a spy has been placed among the Lutherans. Routbourg's murder attests to that. Castell'buono's absence at the meeting at which Calvin spoke convinced Hoess that he may well be the traitor."

Vivienne looked stunned. "Castell'buono. I would not have guessed. But I suppose his absence at La Croix Faubin was suspicious."

"Yes. Hoess felt certain that, if Castell'buono was the spy, proof could be found in his rooms. I refused to take on the task, but during our journey here I have become more committed to your cause. If Castell'buono does have incriminating material in his rooms, I think we should find it before other lives are lost."

"We?"

"Yes, Vivienne, that is my request. I need your assistance."

She agreed instantly. "Of course, Amaury. Anything."

Her acquiescence and trust made Amaury feel even worse for the lie. But he was determined to see the materials in the Italian's room. Not to satisfy his commitment to Ory and the Inquisition. In fact, he now had little intention of telling the priest what he discovered. Castell'buono had been correct. He made a terrible spy. He sought truth not for his employer but for himself.

"I need you to distract Castell'buono's man, Philippe, so I may enter the room unobserved," Amaury said.

"Not difficult." She smiled wryly. "This is a task for which I am well suited."

Amaury was relieved when she did not think to ask how he intended to gain entry to a room that would undoubtedly be locked. "But you must take great care, Vivienne," he added. "Please, do not be overconfident. This Philippe is dangerous." Amaury began to say, "He murdered Giles," but stopped when he realized he was not willing to explain how he had come by the knowledge. Instead he said, "One need only to look at him to know that."

"He is a man, is he not?" Vivienne replied.

"I'm not certain what he is. But in any case, you will need to be very much on your guard. Keep him in a public place."

"Just tell me when you wish his absence. I'll do the rest."

"I am worried for you, Vivienne. If anything should happen—"

She turned suddenly serious. "What, Amaury? What are you trying to say?"

"I would not forgive myself," he replied, his voice trailing off.

A cloud appeared on her face, then passed just as quickly. "I will be quite safe."

XXVI

Although entering Castell'buono's rooms in the middle of the night would minimize the chance of anyone stumbling upon Amaury at the Italian's door, such an odd hour would provide no opportunity for Vivienne to convincingly divert Sévrier. Instead, Amaury chose a time late in the evening, just before the final meal of the day. The halls would be largely deserted, but sufficient activity would be available to provide Vivienne her chance. Amaury had cut two candles of equal length. He gave one to Vivienne and told her he would remain in the Italian's room as long as the time required for the candle to burn.

Amaury waited in his room as the hour neared, peeking through the drapes out to the courtyard. Just as Marguerite's courtiers began arriving for dinner, he spotted Vivienne. She was leading Sévrier toward the wing that housed her room, actually holding the man by the wrist, gesticulating broadly. Sévrier appeared a reluctant companion but, from the incongruous look of helplessness on his face, was equally unwilling to pull himself away. Sévrier even glanced up toward Amaury's window as he dolefully tromped across the sand.

As soon as they disappeared, Amaury was out the door, walking quickly down the corridors that would take him to Castell'buono's apartment. There would be no sentries—the priest had seen to that—but stumbling on a late-arriving dinner guest could betray him just as surely. But the Lord was with him and he met no one.

Amaury stopped in front of the Italian's door and once more checked both ends of the hall. No sound. Amaury removed the key from his pocket. Just like sneaking back into Montaigu. Afraid and exhilarated. Heart pounding. Breath coming in short gasps.

One last look. Then the key in the lock. Turn slowly. Hand over the plate to minimize the metallic click of the bolt. Remove the key. Hold the door tight against the hinge to prevent a squeal when he pushed it open. Slip inside. Close the door quietly. Drop the bolt.

Safe.

Amaury pulled the carpet forward and crammed it under the bottom of the door to prevent light from showing in the hall. The door was heavy and tightly fitted to the frame. No light would escape around the sides. He padded across the room and closed the heavy drapes. In the dark, he lit his candle. The process of deterioration of the tallow began. Solid to liquid to gas then gone. Vivienne would have lit hers some moments earlier, so he needed to leave a margin for error. He set to work.

Before he entered, he had assumed his task would involve a careful search of the Italian's room for a false drawer, secret compartment, or loose floorboard within which the materials he sought would be located. He had prepared himself to examine every inch of the Italian's room. But Castell'buono had secreted the material not by hiding it, but by camouflage. There were papers everywhere. Books, sheaves, and bound manuscripts filled the room, in bookcases or in piles on the floor or on tables. Amaury's time would not be spent combing through the room but rather rummaging through documents. And, with each document he examined, a bit more tallow would burn away.

What the Italian could not have known was that, from the diagram, Amaury could narrow his search to the discipline in which the material he sought would lie. Even better, from the principle the diagram enunciated, Amaury would recognize the treasure when he came across it.

Still, there was far too little time available to simply proceed willy-nilly. Amaury had to think like Castell'buono. The hiding place would match the man. Castell'buono would desire the audacious. A casual arrangement rather than a formal one. The floor and the tables, not the bookcases.

As Amaury riffled through stacks of papers, the candle burned.

Much of the material was scientific, and across a spectrum of disciplines. Botany, anatomy, medicine, mathematics, comparative geography. Writers famous and obscure. As he pored through the documents, Amaury found the desire to pause and read some of the material almost overwhelming. The thought of leaving such a trove of riches unexplored was sacrilegious. The Italian had not been untruthful when he claimed that he believed science and God existed as one. But there was no time for a sojourn. The candle continued its inexorable progress.

Of the nugget Amaury sought, however, there was no sign. He searched through pile after pile but found nothing to explicate Giles' drawing. The candle was now one-quarter gone. He turned his attention to the bookcases. Nothing. When he was done, the candle was more than half burned away. Once it was out, the murderous Sévrier might return at any time.

Perhaps he had missed it. Or perhaps the priest had been misinformed and the material was not here. Perhaps there was a hidden cache somewhere in the room.

No. Amaury was certain. Castell'buono was like Rabelais. He would need to thrust his thumb in the eye of his adversary. Castell'buono would hide the item of greatest value in plain sight.

Amaury quickly checked about once more. A small stack on the windowsill. Had he already looked through it? No. New material. Nothing he had seen before. His fingers worked frantically through the stack.

About halfway down, he came upon an unprepossessing bundle of papers, unbound, tied with green ribbon in a simple knot. The cover page lacked an author's name, reading simply, *"De revolutionibus orbium coelestium"*: "On the revolutions of heavenly spheres." Amaury nearly gasped. He wiped his hands on his clothing, staring as if he had just stumbled upon a lost book of Scripture. Perhaps, in a sense, he had. He reached for the manuscript, but his hand jerked away as if God was forbidding him from performing an unholy act. What might he turn loose on the world? Would he be consigned to eternal flames for this heresy? Did not all great knowledge come with a curse?

Nonsense. Such sentiment was Montaigu speaking. God smiled on reason. Castell'buono was correct about that as well.

Amaury pulled the ribbon. The green silk dropped to the side. He reached out slowly, letting his fingertips linger on the page. Finally, he turned it over. On the second page was an author's note:

Dear friends. I have prepared this sample of my work for your comments and criticism. As you know, I have yet to complete the entire body of proof, and therefore will not make these observations and calculations available to a wider audience. The first postulates on the following page will, I know, cause great consternation in some quarters and perhaps place me in personal peril, for my life or even my soul. But I cannot remain silent entirely, so I send this to you in the hopes that you will support the ideas within.

It was signed *Nicolai Copernici. Frauenburg, October, 1533.*

The text began on the page following. From the first, Amaury was awed by the elegant simplicity of the argument. Its obvious truth. The Earth is spherical and maintains, with the other planets, a circular orbit about the Sun. So it was true. He had known in his heart as soon as he had seen Giles' diagram. He leafed through the pages. Yes, there it was in Book Three, about one third of the way through. The diagram Giles had copied and given to Vivienne.

Amaury devoured the information greedily. The geometry was precise, the observations detailed, the arguments explicit. Page after page of exhaustive formulae and calculations, all to prove one incontestable fact—the Earth circled the sun. The Earth, home to Man, God's unique creation, was not the center of the universe.

Amaury heard a crackle and leapt up as if a bolt from a crossbow had been shot into the wall next to his head. But it was only the candle. Almost gone. Amaury had no time to read further. He rebound the manuscript and replaced it in the stack. He extinguished the candle and pulled the rug out from the under the door. He put his ear to the wood to listen. No sound. He swung the door open, stepped out into the hall, closed the door behind him, and locked it. Then, holding in his mind as immense a secret as had ever existed during the reign of the Lord Jesus Christ, Amaury quickly moved down the hall.

XXVII

A REVELATION SO GREAT could not be held in silence. In silence, it might merely be a dream.

By a circuitous route, Amaury made his way to Vivienne's room. Those guests or residents whom Amaury encountered nodded perfunctorily and were on their way. He saw only one sentry, in the main hall, a bored, somnolent, gray-haired man slouched in a chair rather than standing post. Nocturnal comings and goings were apparently sufficiently commonplace in Queen Marguerite's court that the queen had chosen discretion over security.

Vivienne opened her door quickly. She did not seem at all surprised to see him.

"How did you distract Sévrier?" he asked as soon as he was inside and the door was closed behind them.

She laughed. "With ease. I simply told him that I was certain an intruder had been in my room and that I was terrified he would return. Sévrier attempted to put me off, but I insisted Signore Castell'buono assured me that I could call on his good friend Philippe at any time if I was afraid or in need. I dragged him to my room and made certain he remained there until the candle had burned away."

"You were alone with him in your room? But I told you—"

Vivienne giggled. "There was no danger, Amaury. *He* was afraid of *me*. I was sufficiently frantic that Sévrier likely wondered if I had become unhinged. I gave you a bit of extra time, then told the poor fool that I was exhausted and must rest. I thanked him for his invaluable assistance and shooed him out quickly. I thought you might come by."

Amaury began to scold her for being so foolhardy, but she waved him off. "I want to know if your adventure was a success," she said eagerly.

"Immensely so." The instant Amaury began to speak of the wonders he had read, he forgot everything else. "This manuscript will change everything, Vivienne. A heliocentric theory of astronomy. With a precise mathematical proof. By a man named Copernici living in Poland. Astounding. I should have known from the diagram—Giles' riddle—but the idea was too simple, too shocking." Amaury was speaking so quickly, gesturing so emphatically, that he was unaware that only someone steeped in science would be able to follow.

"Amaury, wait," Vivienne demanded, taking him by the wrist. "I want to understand. You know that. What does this have to do with what you told me in the field?"

"I'm sorry. It says that what I told you in the field was wrong."

"Wrong? And you're excited by that?"

"Let me start at the beginning. You know of the Egyptian Ptolemy's observations. I told you when he published the *Almagest*, it confirmed what a Greek named Aristotle had said centuries before. Do you remember?"

She nodded.

"Aristotle wrote on many subjects—rhetoric, politics—there is almost nothing we study today, except Scripture, of course, on which Aristotle did not blaze our pathways to knowledge. Think of it, Vivienne. In astronomy, here were two men, neither Christians, who demonstrated that the universe was just as it had been described in Scripture."

"And this was important? Why did the Church need confirmation of Scripture by pagans?"

"Because until the thirteenth century, no Christian was capable of enunciating the proof. Then the Blessed Thomas Aquinas used Aristotle's system, backed by Ptolemy's observations, to demonstrate that, as an axiom of True Faith, the Earth *must* be at the center of the universe. As Man is unique in the eye of God—at the center of Creation—so must Man's home, Earth, be at the center of the universe. Thus, Aristotle's system with the Earth at the center—it's called geocentric—became not only science but a cornerstone of our Holy Church. The uniqueness of Man is basic to all Christianity, Lutherans as well as Catholics."

"And what you found disproves what Saint Thomas said?"

"Yes. Heliocentric means that the sun is at the center; that the Earth revolves around it. So do the moon and all the other planets. The Earth is not unique in the universe at all. This means that perhaps Man is not unique in God's eyes. He is possibly not even created in God's image."

"I don't understand, Amaury. Of course Man is created in God's image."

"If so, it cannot be deduced from astronomy."

"And Genesis?"

"'In the beginning God created the heavens and the Earth' has been taken to mean that the Earth was created before the Sun. 'Light' is not mentioned until Genesis 1:3, and the creation of the Sun not until 1:14. Placing the Sun in a superior position to the Earth creates doubts as to the accuracy of Scripture for both the Church and for Lutherans. All of the Church's immutable constructs will have to be reexamined. Not doubt about the existence of God, but that only the Church can tell us what knowledge is, or even the nature of God Himself. In today's world, the Church means men like Beda and Ory."

"You disapprove of the Inquisition?"

"I loathe it. Fanatics. Persecutors. Everything Our Lord Jesus Christ would have hated."

"But . . . so what will happen now?"

Amaury sighed and shook his head. "I don't know. Everything will change, I hope for the better. Their kind of religion—and Calvin's—might well be forced to give way, replaced by a new Christianity in which science and empirical knowledge exist side by side with dogma."

"And this pleases you, Amaury?"

"Oh, yes, Vivienne. Freeing Christians from blind adherence to dogma will allow them to be closer to God. With science and worldly knowledge will come a new tolerance bred from the awareness that not all is known. Christianity will become a religion of the present and the future, not just the past. Science will couple with love of God and lead the way to a new world. This discovery will save Christianity, not destroy it."

"Many will disapprove."

"Only the narrow-minded, the ignorant, and the ambitious. With the power to control the mind and soul of Man in the balance, fundamentalists in both sects will stop at nothing to suppress the new knowledge. But we who see the future of the Church must not allow the forces of reaction to prevent dissemination of this great work. We must protect both the science and the man who formulated it."

"Yes," Vivienne agreed. "We must."

XXVIII

NOISE. At his bedroom door. Metallic. Hélène?

Amaury blinked his eyes open to see men burst through the doorway. Soldiers. Four of them. Why? Then, following the uniformed men, Père Louis-Paul.

Before Amaury could gather his wits sufficiently to even sit himself up, the soldiers' hands were on him, grasping him tightly by the upper arms. The priest moved to the bed and stood over him.

"You are under arrest by order of the Inquisition," the priest intoned.

"But—" Amaury tried to stammer a denial, but a gloved hand struck him across the mouth. His head snapped to the side and he could taste his own blood.

"You will speak only when asked," the priest said. Cold, but with a hint of pleasure. "And you will be asked soon enough." The priest sighed. "And don't tire us with denials. We have proof, you see."

The soldiers hauled Amaury to his feet. The hands were so tight on his arms that he began to lose feeling in his fingers. Before they dragged him out the door, the priest spoke again.

"And do not expect help from Her Majesty, Faverges. Queen Marguerite takes none too kindly to guests abusing her hospitality. You are a great disappointment to her. I expect you will find your next accommodations a good deal less comfortable."

The priest nodded and the soldiers marched Amaury out the door.

The cell was completely dark. No window. Tiny. Too low to stand up straight, too narrow to lay flat. The walls were cold stone, the floor dirt. Moisture clung to every surface; a stagnant puddle had collected in one corner. Deposited in another corner was a filthy pile of hay. Either bed or toilet.

Amaury lowered himself to a sitting position, knees drawn up, back against the stone. The moisture immediately soaked through his nightshirt, creating an icy spot on his back. After a few minutes, his eyes began to become accustomed to the gloom. He could make out a barred grate set high in the door, the vaguest light cast on the opening from a candle set somewhere in the hall outside. He raised his hand but could not see it in front of his face save to block out the light in the door.

He remembered the dungeon at the Conciergerie. Was he to become one of the pailleux, those pitiable, howling wretches, lost and abandoned without hope? Or was his lot to be tortured? Branded, limbs broken by iron bars, tongue hacked out, and finally roasted slowly, his bones thrown to the dogs?

Amaury began to shake. Vivienne. If he had been betrayed, so had she. Vivienne, thrown into one of these cells. Oh, Lord! He moaned aloud. The walls were too clammy to create an echo, but the sound caused scurrying somewhere in the dark.

Crawling. On his feet. Tiny movements. Amaury reached down and frantically brushed off the lice. No matter. Off his feet, they were on his nightshirt. An army of the foul creatures, preparing to feast on the banquet that had been deposited in their lair.

The scurrying again. Not lice. Larger. In the walls. Rats. They would not attack immediately, but rather wait for Amaury to sleep, as sleep he inevitably must. Then they would be on him, gnawing.

Suddenly, Amaury heard a loud, piercing scream. He thought at first

he was not alone in the dungeons, but soon after realized that the voice
had been his own.

Madness. In such a hell, does one avoid it or attempt to hasten its
arrival? To be mad is to be immune. No. He would not lose his reason.
He would not.

He swatted at the lice, knowing their assault would be inexorable but
determined to inflict casualties of his own. The rats could be kept at bay
with noise and movement. Amaury stood slowly, feeling with his hands
to avoid striking his head on the ceiling. He could straighten his legs by
keeping his shoulders hunched and his head down, or straighten his
torso by bending his knees.

Time and space. Must keep track of both in a place with no day and
no night. Amaury tried to scuttle from one side of the cell to the other, to
get dimensions, some measure of length and width so that he could at
least perform basic mathematical exercises. Next he counted, trying to
imbed some standard of time on his brain.

After a time—he could not tell if it was long or short—Amaury grew
terribly fatigued. His joints ached. His muscles were leaden. He was shiv-
ering uncontrollably. But worst of all, he could not keep count. He would
reach a number and then forget. And he knew that, once forgotten, his
sense of time was lost forever.

He had lost his guideposts. Was it day or night? Had he been in the
dungeon hours or days? How long since he had eaten? Slept? Exhausted,
he slumped to the floor, once again drawing up his knees and leaning
against the stone wall. The lice were on him instantly, but he had lost the
strength to fight them off. At least the rats . . .

Ahhh! Amaury screamed, shocked awake by pain at his feet. He
kicked wildly, screaming all the while. The rat, interrupted in its meal,
dashed off. To wait.

Time passed. But how much? Amaury could not count. He felt the
beat of his heart. Heard the sound in the silence, echoing in his ears. Too
slow? The lice feasted. Amaury allowed them his body. Too tired to fight.
Lassitude. Madness would surely follow. But how long?

Then, noise. Not the rats. Voices. People. The light outside the bars in the door grew brighter. Amaury tried to pull himself up, but his arms and legs seemed weighted. A key in the lock. The door opened. Brilliant light. Blinding. Amaury threw his hands up before his eyes. But it was only a candle. Held by a soldier. With Père Louis-Paul following inside. Another soldier brought a chair so the priest would not be forced to bend.

Amaury blinked, trying to clear his head. Don't give him satisfaction. Like Ravenau and the beatings at Montaigu.

"Well, Faverges, I see you have settled in. I'm pleased to see you are comfortable. You might be here for some time. Or perhaps a very short time."

Amaury stared up but could make out only the priest's outline. In the candlelight, everything seemed to exist in shadow.

"We are aware of everything, you know," the priest went on. "You might as well confess your sins. An honest confession this time. It might save you a good deal of discomfort."

Vivienne. "You tortured a woman?" Amaury could not recognize the scraping, halting voice as his own. "And you claim to speak for God."

"Torture a woman? I believe you have lost your reason, Faverges. To be honest, I thought you would hold out longer."

"How else could you coerce Vivienne to betray me? You are an abomination, priest."

"Coerce? You think I coerced Vivienne? Oh, Faverges, you *are* a fool."

Then Amaury knew the truth. A fool. Yes. At the least. He turned away. Please, Lord, just let the priest leave him to die.

But Père Louis-Paul had not entered the cell to leave matters half resolved. "Take him!" he ordered.

Each of the soldiers grabbed Amaury by an arm and pulled them back until his face was on the floor next to the priest's sandals. The pain in his shoulders was searing. Amaury felt saliva running from his mouth, but refused to cry out.

"Now, you traitorous heretic, you will hear the truth. Do you agree?"

Amaury made no sound.

A terrible pain suddenly shot through him, beginning from where the soldier kicked him in the genitals, radiating to every spot in his body. For a few moments he was blind. He heard himself moan and cursed the sound.

"I will accept that noise as assent," the priest said. He nodded to one of the soldiers, and Amaury's head was pulled back by the hair until he was forced to look at the priest.

"Good," Père Louis-Paul said. "Now we can speak. I would like to read you this letter. It is from your Vivienne. The handwriting is my own, since, as you know, the young woman lacks the necessary skills. I can assure you, however, that this is an accurate rendering of her words." The priest delicately cleared his throat.

My dear Amaury. We have shared a glorious journey together. I pray you will find it in your heart to forgive what you are about to hear.

How I was chosen I do not know, but one day, under the guise of a summons to ply my profession at the home of a customer, I was taken to a small house in La Ville. Magister Ory was there. He was a kind man, not at all like he is painted by the Lutherans. He told me that those who serve the True Church can be absolved of sin. That the Holy Father himself was prepared to grant such absolution. Magister Ory promised that if I accepted a mission, on its completion he would personally gain me acceptance to the convent of the Sisters of Sainte Clare at Rouen. Admittance to that convent is generally reserved only for those of high birth.

How could I refuse an offer to wipe away the stain of my past, to become one with God? I vowed before God that once I left Madame Chouchou's, I would remain chaste for the remainder of my days.

Even with so much at stake, I had reservations when I met Giles. Betrayal is also a sin. To commit a sin to be absolved of sin. A terrible choice. Then I learned that Giles, too, worked in the name of the True Faith. All that was required was that I not reveal my role to him.

Although I do not know who committed the act itself, Giles was murdered on orders of the wine merchant, Monsieur Hoess. He had stumbled on the very material you found in Monsieur Castell'buono's

room. Monsieur Hoess was certain it would be given to Magister Ory.
I learned of the plot only on the night it was set. I left Madame
Chouchou's, frantic to warn him. I arrived too late.

Magister Ory then informed me that he had secured another to
continue the work poor Giles had begun. But he could not give this
new man his trust. He was too drawn to secular knowledge to be a
reliable servant of God.

After the journey to Nérac, upon the successful completion of my
task, Magister Ory promised that I could return to Paris and thence
to Rouen. I wanted to protect you, but my oath was to tell Père
Louis-Paul anything I might learn. Père Louis-Paul, like Magister
Ory, is a decent man. He has given me his solemn word that you will
not be harmed. After a few days, you will be released to return to
Savoy. I ask you to believe that I would not have cooperated with him
further, regardless of consequences to me, had he not made this promise.

The priest stopped reading. "She does not overstate. You should be
quite flattered, Faverges. You are unworthy of her loyalty." Then he took
up the letter once more.

I do not believe we shall ever see one another again. I asked Père
Louis-Paul to write down what you have read to explain why I was
forced to behave as I did. I once again beg your forgiveness. When I
am safely ensconced with the Sisters, I will pray for you every day.

The priest folded the letter. "I am abashed, Faverges, to have not been
completely truthful with the young woman. I have no intention of allowing you to travel to Savoy or anywhere else."

The priest then brandished a second piece of paper. "But even after all
your duplicity, you might have escaped the harsh treatment you so richly
deserve. Her Majesty is a gentle and peaceful soul. Although she is upset
that you would use the sanctuary of her home to spy, she might well have
eventually weakened and allowed you merely to be banished. Sent on to
Savoy where you could live out your life in a bastard's comfort. But not

now." He waved the second paper under Amaury's nose. "Do you recognize this?"

Amaury didn't move. His head had been pulled back for so long that he could barely breathe.

"It is the oath you signed in Magister Ory's presence. An oath that obviously meant nothing to you. But it does mean something to others. Her Majesty, for example. So there will be no mercy, no weakening. Unless you issue a confession of your sins, you will be left here. For days, or months, or even years. You will never see daylight again. In time—a very short time—you will begin to rave. Or perhaps we will choose to deal with your heresy forthwith. You will confess—we have very persuasive means to assure that you do so—then be taken to a hill outside the palace that is an ideal location to conduct a burning. Your screams will be heard for miles. I leave you here to contemplate which fate would be worse.

"As for your discovery, Magister Ory and I are in your debt. We have now not only identified the basis of the conspiracy to undermine Scripture, you were kind enough to tell us its source. It will be a small matter to dispatch the appropriate agents from Paris to deal with this Pole. Just as it will be a small matter to deal with the conspirators—Hoess, the landlady—we will get them all. Even your friend, the bookseller, though I will tell you he was utterly innocent of the murder of your predecessor. So, Faverges, although I owe you a favor, I am sorry to say that it is a debt I will not repay."

The priest nodded to the soldier. Amaury felt another rush of pain as he was kicked in the genitals once more. The soldiers then threw him on the hay against the wall, took up the chair for the priest, and left the cell. The door slammed shut. The bolt slid into place. The light receded.

Amaury rolled onto his side and pulled his knees up to his chest, his hands between his thighs. The pain lessened just a bit. Suddenly he vomited. He tried to move his head away but lacked the strength. The stench was at first overpowering, but after some time he became accustomed to it.

The lice returned. The rats scratched in the walls. All that was left now was to face the future, either torture or slow death, with as much dignity as possible. To finish his days in this horrible place pure in the eyes of

God. If tortured, his body would be broken; if not, his mind. But God would know that he had attempted to remain true to His word.

Amaury began to pray, but he did not utter a phrase from Scripture. He whispered to God in his own words, a plea for understanding and for mercy. As Rabelais might have done. Amaury reveled in the glory of God's creation, of finding that the full cup of knowledge had not been given to Man at once, but had been left for Man to discover for himself over time. That was, to him, a Christianity worth dying for. Eventually, feeling goodness around him, he drifted off to sleep. Deep, dreamless sleep. The sleep of the dead.

After a time, he had no idea how long, Amaury was awake. Noise. On the steps. So it was to be torture. Amaury prepared himself. He would face it unafraid. The screams, the agony; over those there could be no control. But God would know that his soul remained pure. He would, then, inevitably, be with God.

The light once again grew brighter in the hall and Amaury soon heard voices grow nearer. The bolt slid back and the door opened. Two soldiers bent forward and entered. Amaury rolled onto his back. But following them was not the priest.

It was Hélène.

XXIX

WAS SHE REAL? Amaury blinked. Had he lost his reason already? Hélène, looking in on him from the doorway, put her hand to her mouth and gasped. Only then did Amaury know he wasn't hallucinating.

Amaury recognized the soldiers. They were the same ones who had accompanied the priest earlier. But how much earlier?

One of them spoke. "We haven't much time. Can you stand?"

Amaury leaned forward. Pain again shot through him. He struggled to his knees, then nodded to the soldier. When he attempted to rise, however, his knees buckled. The soldiers grabbed him under the arms, which caused another spasm of agony in his shoulders. Only after a few moments of their support could Amaury stand unaided, although bent and unsteady in the tiny cell.

Hélène retreated into the hall. One of the soldiers stepped out and returned with a bucket and cloth. The second soldier proffered a suit of clothing. "Wash yourself down and then put this on," he told Amaury.

Amaury first drank from the bucket, then removed his nightshirt and washed himself down with the cloth as best he could. The water stung his raw, bitten flesh. The soldiers held him so he did not fall nor strike his head on the stone ceiling.

"We're sorry about before," one of them mumbled. "But if we don't do what the priest tells us, we end up in here." Amaury looked the man in the eye for a moment but did not acknowledge the apology.

Soon the water left him feeling slightly better. At least most of the lice were gone. He would never succeed in ridding himself totally of *les petites bêtes*, but any of his tormentors who had not latched on firmly would be returned to the floor to await another meal.

The soldiers supported him by the elbows as he got into the clothing. Hélène had obtained an understated doublet, leggings, and shorts; the clothing of a gentleman but nothing to arouse undue attention. After he was dressed, he eschewed the soldiers' assistance and moved out the door himself. He could walk in a slow shuffle.

As he emerged, Hélène stepped toward him. She was dressed in a riding outfit, a long coat slit up the back. Tears welled in her eyes.

"Oh, my dear Amaury..." She placed her hand on his cheek. Her touch was cool. "We must get you away from here. Come." She took a step. Amaury made to follow but stumbled, caught by one of the soldiers. Every time he moved, the pain in his genitals froze his knees and turned the muscles in his thighs to pulp. The soldiers held him as he made his way to the stairs, but as he walked, he slowly regained sufficient strength to move unaided.

"We have thirty minutes. These gentlemen—" She nodded toward the soldiers. "These gentlemen have secured a passage through the palace. Horses are waiting and the gates will be opened. Can you ride?"

Amaury nodded, although the thought of bouncing along on a horse was appalling. Not as appalling as remaining in the castle, however. "Is it night?" he asked her.

Hélène nodded. "Yes. After midnight."

Amaury struggled up the circular stairway, its uneven stone covered by a layer of moisture that made every step precarious. One of the soldiers kept a hand at his back to prevent him from toppling backward. Finally, they reached a closed door. Amaury estimated that they had climbed three stories. He had been languishing deeper in the earth than the roots of the largest tree. The soldier in the lead held up his hand. He opened the door slowly and slipped out.

Amaury was grateful for the pause. In addition to the pain, he was gasping from fatigue. He had not eaten since he had been dragged from his room. "How long was I there?" he whispered to Hélène.

"Two days."

"Has Castell'buono returned?"

"No. He is due in the morning. He is to be arrested."

"And Vivienne?"

"She has been sent to Paris by Père Louis-Paul. She was escorted by six soldiers charged with protecting her with their lives. My maid is . . . friendly with one of them. She told me that Père Louis-Paul evidently gave Vivienne a parcel of great importance. It was found in Castell'buono's room."

After I told the priest precisely what to look for, Amaury thought.

The soldier stuck his head back in through the doorway and gestured for them to follow.

"We must make it through the palace silently," Hélène whispered. "The night guard has been bribed, but if someone should awaken, we will be lost."

Amaury nodded and followed Hélène and the soldiers into the corridor. He was still unsteady, but could shuffle along without assistance. The soldiers led them through a maze of corridors and darkened rooms, then through the servants' quarters to the kitchen. They told Amaury and Hélène to wait while they slipped outside to see to the final arrangements. Amaury leaned against a wall for support.

"A few steps more, my darling," Hélène said, "and then it's to the horses and on to Savoy."

Amaury grabbed her by the arm. "Not Savoy. Paris."

Hélène shook her head. "No, Amaury. That isn't possible. You've been condemned by the Inquisition. You'll be arrested and burned at the stake. I begged Queen Marguerite, as one woman to another, to allow you to come with me so I might finally experience love. She agreed only if I promised to take you to Savoy. She will be publicly furious at your escape but will not pursue us in that direction. That priest will never know. But she—and I—will be helpless if you head for Paris."

One of the soldiers motioned for them to proceed. Amaury tottered to the servants' entrance, the door where the kitchen led to the outside. The soldiers waited impatiently. If they were caught with Amaury and Hélène, they would share the same fate.

Three horses were waiting, their hooves muffled with thick cloth. The third wore panniers, which held clothing and provisions. A sword and scabbard were plainly visible. Traveling without servants would arouse curiosity, but not necessarily suspicion. Two aristocrats on a tryst might well choose to avoid engaging anyone who might later relate sordid details.

The soldiers helped Amaury onto his mount, a steed eager to gallop, not like his old friend the dray. As soon as he was in position, he knew the first hours would be agony. Hélène waved the soldiers away and swung herself into the saddle. She had been expert on horseback since she was six.

One of the soldiers ran ahead. The side gate was opened sufficiently for the three horses to squeeze through single file. The small procession moved slowly, the padded hooves making only a soft, dull scrape. Every time his mount took a step, Amaury felt a spasm shoot through him. But even the most extreme pain is dulled by repetition, and within minutes Amaury knew he would be able to bear it. He turned back one last time, but the gate had already been closed behind them. Within moments, they had passed from eyeshot of the palace walls.

They rode on until Hélène felt at a safe distance from the palace. Then she stopped and fetched bread and cheese. "You must eat something. But quickly. We do not have much time."

Amaury remained in the saddle. At the first bite of bread, Amaury realized how hungry he was. He wolfed down the rest and drank water from a goatskin. Then he turned his horse toward the north road, toward Paris.

"Please, Amaury," Hélène pleaded, "Savoy is your only hope of safety."

"I have no choice, Hélène," Amaury said. "There is no time to explain. I am grateful to you beyond words, but I must go to Paris."

Hélène swung herself back into the saddle. "All right, then. We'll go to Paris. You can explain on the way."

"But—"

"I lost you once, Amaury. It will not happen again."

XXX

PHILIPPE SÉVRIER CROUCHED in an alcove near the servants' quarters. Most were off serving the late-afternoon meal, so traffic was minimal. Still, Philippe's ear was attuned to every sound, especially the regular, heavy cadence that would denote soldiers. Had he been betrayed as well? No way to be certain.

Faverges was a traitor. Or a spy. He had known from the first. Castell'buono had refused to listen and now he would pay for his arrogance.

Yes, he was clever, the Savoyard. Castell'buono had been correct about that. Clever enough to use the whore to distract him. Clever enough to find his way into Castell'buono's room. Even clever enough to unearth the gem in a pile of manure. Then his cleverness had seemed to run out. The whore denounced him. An Inquisition plant whose loyalty had turned. But again he had proved himself clever, this Faverges. The Catholics had released him from the dungeon.

Escape? That was the story floating about the castle. A brilliant, audacious maneuver by the d'Artigny woman effected in the early hours of the morning. The queen was outraged; the captain of the guard at a loss. Ha! Philippe did not believe it for a second. Not any of it. All a ruse to throw potential pursuers off the track. Just like the first tale, of expulsion from Montaigu. But this time, not clever enough.

Now the traitor was doubtless on his way to Paris, already with a twelve-hour start. Maybe more. Once in the city, he would broadcast his tale of escape in order to betray those who had trusted him. Hoess. The innkeeper. Even the fool at the bookshop. But worse, he would betray the great secret of the universe. Betray God. This horrible deed must be prevented. Or avenged.

Philippe would have preferred to await Castell'buono's return before setting out. The Italian was clever too. And, for all his arrogance, he should be warned. But word had just arrived that Castell'buono had been arrested in Angoulême. There would be no help for him. And no hope.

If Philippe had not yet been betrayed, it would only be a matter of hours. No man could keep silent with the branding iron scorching his flesh. But betrayal would be of no matter. Within moments he would leave Nérac, never to return. And after he had done what was needed, he would leave France forever.

Philippe sighed. God forgive him, he missed the Confession. Even the illusion of absolution would be a balm to the turmoil in his soul. And at what price? A few simple prayers, mouthed by rote.

He had always been confused by the power of the Sacraments. How can one take comfort in a ritual one knows is a lie? Can Man be so shallow as to crave only the form of faith but not its substance? Perhaps it was true. Yes. Testament to the cunning of the Catholics was that they had grasped this fundament of the nature of Man. In despair, even false ceremony would be accepted, nay, grasped at. Anything to soothe the pain.

And Philippe was most certainly in pain. He had been so since the night in the alley.

He had been fascinated by the act, unable to get the picture out of his mind. The boy's wide, uncomprehending eyes, the dark stain spreading across the tunic, the crimson liquid soaking his hand. It had been decisive, a gesture of power. Of commitment. Of true belief. Such an undertaking in defense of one's ideals was the highest form of worship. But more than all of that, another emotion had crept into his soul, one that, without a confessor, he dared not share with anyone.

He wanted to do it again.

Philippe made for the east gate. A horse would be waiting in the town. And then north, to overtake first Faverges, then the whore. The notion frightened him. Thrilled him. He felt for the knife in his tunic.

God forgive me.

XXXI

AMAURY AND HÉLÈNE rode for hours before Amaury began to feel safe. The water and food, pedestrian as it was, had done wonders. His strength was returning. The pain had abated sufficiently to allow him to realize how much he itched from the lice. Every hour he grew more fit, more able to discharge the task he had set for himself.

Hélène knew as well. She turned to him often now, smiling at what she saw.

"Why did you come, Hélène?" he asked finally. "What do you want?"

"What I have always wanted. What I wanted that day in the field. Do you remember?"

"I have never forgotten." She was beautiful and regal astride the horse. "The years have been kind to you. You are even lovelier than I remember."

Hélène smiled ruefully. "Thank you, Amaury. You always appealed to my vanity. I suppose I demanded it. I've learned, however, how shallow a gratification that can be. The years, you see, have not been at all kind to me."

"Why? What happened?"

"It began soon after you left. As you know, your father had accepted a proposal on my behalf from Duke Joseph of Austria. It was an excellent match for Savoy and it gave Joseph's father a Catholic ally buffering France."

"Yes," Amaury replied. "Your betrothal to that fool was why I left."

"I thought your father banished you."

"Only from court. After the affair with the Hungarian. When you refused to look at me."

"I didn't refuse, Amaury. I was afraid to. Afraid that if I looked at you even for a second, I would have run to you. If that happened . . . a marriageable maid, a political bargaining tool, in love with a—"

"Bastard."

"Yes. Your father would have been furious. And he would have blamed you. I wasn't certain that even your life would not have been at risk."

"Yes," he conceded. "I suppose you were right. Ironic, though. When I told him that I had chosen to attend university in Paris, he was actually pleased with me. For once. He told me that if I completed study at Montaigu, he would petition the pope for a decree of legitimacy. I would finally be Amaury de Savoie. Of course, by that time, Amaury de Savoie would have no opportunity with Hélène d'Artigny. You would be with another."

"But surely you knew I had no say in his decision?"

"You didn't seem displeased by it."

"Whether I was pleased or displeased was of no concern to anyone. I would eventually be betrothed to *someone*. Even legitimate, marriage to you would have been out of the question."

"Awareness that a phenomenon exists and experiencing it are two very different things."

"Perhaps. In any case, I was actually relieved at the match. Vienna is a fine city and Joseph was two years my senior with a reputation for piety and bravery."

"An inane dimwit."

Hélène smiled. "That he was. But, as I learned, there are traits far worse. You see, I never married Joseph. At the last minute, his father sent word that he had withdrawn his approval. He claimed the dowry was insufficient, or some such nonsense, but, in truth, he had turned his attention east and had betrothed Joseph in secret to Princess Elisabeth of Poland."

"Withdrew? One can't simply withdraw from a betrothal. The scandal must have been immense. How is it that I didn't hear of it, even in Paris?"

"There was no scandal. Joseph's father sent five thousand gold florins to your father to ensure that there would be no scandal."

"And my father accepted? He allowed you to be dishonored? He couldn't have. Not even him. There must have been more to it."

"There was no more. Of that I can assure you. But don't judge him harshly on that account. He had no choice. Joseph's father contacted François and agreed to sign a pact pledging mutual support against the Emperor Charles if François would agree to support the Polish union. François thus gained a buffer against Charles in Germany, and Joseph's father achieved the same end as if he'd married his son to me. If your father opposed them, he'd have been squeezed between two new enemies."

"What of you, then?" Amaury asked. "Whom did you marry?"

Hélène scowled. "A monster . . . although no one suspected so at the time. Your father had to find someone for me quickly, you see, and Wilhelm of Mainz, old Frederick's son, was available. A staunch Catholic, of course. After the wedding, I soon found out why he was available."

Amaury waited.

"He didn't prefer me," she said. "He preferred his servant. All of his attendants were young, handsome boys. One was only twelve. After we had consummated the union, except for rare occasions when Wilhelm was too drunk to care that a woman was his bedmate, we had a marriage in name only." A small, sarcastic smile crossed her lips. "He was, however, quite intelligent."

"I'm so sorry, Hélène. I've spent more than a few hours cursing my fate, but yours was so much worse."

"It was glorious to see you, Amaury. When that girl, Vivienne, mentioned the name of her traveling companion, I thought I must be hearing spirits. I've never stopped thinking of you, of what our lives would have been like if we were together."

"And now we are."

"Yes. Now we are. God has finally used circumstance to reward me."

"You really remember that day in the field?"

"Oh, yes. And you see now that I was correct. I always do get what I want in the end. Although it took a bit more time than I anticipated."

"Thank God for your perseverance."

"Yes. Even better, I am now a rich, childless widow. Frederick paid me, quite handsomely, not to discuss his son's . . . proclivities. Wilhelm was good for that, anyway. Since I am no longer suitable as a strategic pawn, I can do as I please."

"And your pleasure is to bribe guards, conduct jailbreaks, and involve yourself in an intrigue that might well cost you your life."

"Precisely. All those are indeed my pleasure. As are some other things when all of this is done."

XXXII

The Royal Château, Amboise, March 10, 1534

USING ONLY THUMB and forefinger, François soundlessly pulled back the duvet. She didn't stir. He had always been proud that, for so large and virile a man, he could move with extreme delicacy if he chose.

Extending the same forefinger, he very softly touched her right nipple. It immediately began to shrivel to erectness. She emitted a soft murmur but did not awaken. François smiled and brushed the golden hair from the side of her face. Marie-Ange. Perfectly named. Innocent and beautiful. Until aroused, that is. Then she became Marie-Tigre. Only the second time he had bedded the daughter of a previous mistress. He had wanted her for years. Only with royal fortitude had he forced himself to wait until she was sixteen.

He touched her nipple again, this time with just a soupçon more pressure. She began to stir. François shifted as the royal member began to make itself felt. With the ends of three fingers, he stroked the pale flesh of her breast, tracing a circle about the now fully erect nipple. Her eyes opened. Still, largely asleep, she nonetheless looked up with adoration at her liege.

She was perhaps the most instinctive lover he had ever had. She knew just what he wanted. After only the briefest touch on the back of her head, she smiled and pushed the duvet below his knees. She placed a hand on his chest, pushing him back against the pillows. Throwing back her hair to keep it out of her face, she slid down on the bed. She grasped his erect penis and gave the smallest squeeze. François felt the breath shoot out of him. Then, without uttering a sound, she leaned down and took him into her mouth.

François lay back and closed his eyes.

How wonderful to be king.

After Marie-Ange had finished and they had lain together for the appropriate time, François rang for the servants. It would not do to loll away the day, and preparations must be made to leave Amboise for Paris two days hence. Marie-Ange would not accompany him. Just as well. He realized with a mixture of wonder and fear that he might actually be falling in love with her. Such a loss of emotional control could cause no shortage of unfortunate complications at court. Better that she be here waiting for his next visit.

The door still had not opened and François began to feel a rush of annoyance. It could not be because of sensitivity to the girl. Marie-Ange occupied the king's bed with brazen pride. Occasionally she had even left the bed naked just to show the servants what the king had and they didn't.

François rang once more. Finally, the door opened slowly. André de Dauphiny stepped in. He was in his seventies, and his presence in the bedchamber meant bad news. How irritating to follow Marie-Ange with unpleasantness.

André stood just inside the door, a look of terror on his face. Was it war? Had Charles invaded? An alliance with Henry? André cocked his head slightly to the side and François noticed that a placard had been nailed to his door. He donned a robe—how extraordinary to dress himself—then got out of bed to see what it was.

At the title alone, François felt his blood boil. *Articles véritables sur les horribles, grands & importables abuz de la Messe papalle.* "True Articles on the Horrible, Great & Insufferable Abuses of the Papal Mass."

What followed was a four-point indictment of the Mass—vile, despicable, and heretical. André and the other servants stood to the side, cringing as François read. The king was so furious that he quaked. Those among the servants who had questioned the king's devotion to the True Church questioned no more.

In truth, while François found the language harsh and offensive, the bulk of his anger was directed in a different direction. Who in the kingdom would have the gall, the temerity, to violate the sanctity of the royal apartments? *His* royal apartments. At the very moment Marie-Ange was providing her service to the sovereign of France, some sniveling coward was skulking about with his vile placard.

François made his decision right there. Standing in his robe. France would remain Catholic. The Lutherans would be exterminated.

He whirled on the servants. Get everything in readiness, he ordered them. The royal procession would leave for Paris in two hours. After the servants had hurried off to try to complete the impossible, François summoned the captain of the guard. Every Lutheran in the château was to be questioned. No measure would be deemed too severe to elicit information on this hideous plot against the royal person. If the culprit was found, he was to be transported to Paris. He would pay for his perfidy there.

On his return, he would summon Ory. Every Lutheran in Paris would pay as well.

XXXIII

AMAURY AND HÉLÈNE reached Bergerac at dawn. He had told her of his discovery and the need to intercept Vivienne. Stopping in Bergerac meant not only risking exposure but the loss of a day. Hélène agreed immediately that they should press ahead.

At the junction just past the town, Amaury started north, to the Angoulême road. Hélène reined in her horse.

"We can't go that way," she said. "It's longer."

"I must intercept Castell'buono," Amaury replied. "We'll make up the time."

But Hélène was adamant. "It isn't possible. Angoulême is the queen's home, and a good deal of commerce passes from there to Nérac. The road is heavily patrolled. You will be a wanted man among Queen Marguerite's supporters as well as by the Inquisition. You will not do Castell'buono any good—or yourself—if you are arrested."

"I've got no choice. I'm responsible for him being denounced."

"That's absurd, Amaury. Castell'buono made his own decisions. You are no more responsible for him being denounced than you are for the sun moving across the sky simply because you stand under it."

"If he returns to the palace, he'll probably be thrown into that same pit you just got me out of."

"He took that risk when he joined his conspiracy. Willingly, I might add. And besides, overtaking that girl's party will be difficult enough without detours. Perhaps his acolyte will find some means to post a warning."

"Sévrier? Perhaps." Amaury brought his horse close to hers. "I had no idea, Hélène, you'd become so . . ." He searched for the correct word.

"Ruthless?" she said. "Heartless?"

"Resourceful," he countered weakly.

"I'm merely practical. I have become so by necessity, as you have. If we choose to try to aid Castell'buono, we will fail, and in doing so, will also fail to prevent the girl from reaching Ory. Castell'buono's mission was to see to the publication of the astronomical work. The best you can do for him is to help bring that goal to fruition."

"So Castell'buono must be left to his fate?"

"And his faith." Hélène reined her horse to the other road at the junction. "This is the way we must go. I know a route. Every minute we remain here is time lost."

Hélène started up the road. Amaury glanced once to the Angoulême road, then followed. He watched Hélène ride ahead, never looking back. The butterfly he had known at his father's court had grown a core of iron.

Soon afterward she turned onto a side road, little more than a path through the woods. They traveled there most of the day, passing through mile after mile of unbroken forest, until finally they emerged near Périgueux in the Dordogne. Périgueux would be a perfect stopover: popular with aristocrats and wealthy bourgeoisie, the town and its outskirts were dotted with large, recently constructed châteaux. Catholics and Lutherans shared the region with the unspoken truce that the wealthy often adopt so that neither politics nor religion intrude on the pleasures of affluence. No one would suspect a well-spoken, well-dressed couple with money to spend who wished a room and no questions.

They arrived in late afternoon and easily found an inn at the north edge of the town. They were given a large room facing the rear. The magnificent

Château de Beynac loomed across the river. Amaury waited in the room while Hélène visited the town apothecary. She returned with a stoppered bottle of bitter lupines boiled in vinegar.

Amaury paid the innkeeper five silver francs to prepare a bath. Périgueux was one of the few towns in France where such a request would arouse no surprise. The innkeeper had prepared a room in an outbuilding for just such extravagances. The cistern was not as large or grand as in Nérac, nor the bath itself as sumptuous, but to Amaury the warm water would be paradise.

Before he stepped in, he rubbed the lupines-vinegar mixture thoroughly through his hair, both at the scalp and, very delicately, the genitals. The soreness there had almost disappeared. He stepped into the bath, lowered himself. The pain in his shoulders too had become only a dull throb. He luxuriated in the water, letting the vestiges of the dungeon wash off him. His foot stung where the rat had attacked, but even that was healing with no sign of sepsis. He lolled in the bath for almost half an hour. When he finally stood and undid the drain, he watched filth and dead insects run down the pipe and into the ditch behind the building. He left the clothing for the innkeeper and donned a change that he had removed from the panniers. He had chosen a more opulent ensemble. With a sword strapped at his side, for the first time in nine years he would appear as a member of the nobility. He had been fairly adept with the weapon as a boy, but what if he actually had to use it now? He would know soon enough. Then, feeling reborn, he returned to Hélène.

She smiled broadly when he entered the room. "A transformation worthy of a conjurer." She motioned for him to drop the bolt on the door. "Dinner isn't for an hour."

Perfection was God's hallmark. Perfection in all things. In His power, in His wisdom, in His mercy. And in His creation of the heavens. How, then, could a faithful servant produce a description of God's wonder that was not itself perfect?

He had received surprising encouragement from the small distribution of his manuscript. He had been gratified to hear that a cardinal said to have the ear of the Holy Father himself had urged that the full dissertation be published. This cardinal had acknowledged with sadness, however, that De revolutionibus could not receive an imprimatur from Rome. Opposition in conservative quarters remained ferocious. Still, he had issued assurances that the treatise would not be officially condemned.

More disturbing was that two copies had, by some skullduggery, the details of which remained unclear, fallen into Lutheran hands. Despite their proclamations of tolerance, these self-styled "reformers" had shown themselves to be far less open-minded than some members of the True Church. Luther himself was rumored to have privately condemned the theory.

Self-delusion was pointless. Publication would create outrage among both sects sufficient to prompt attempts at suppression and murder. But that was one advantage of old age. The threat of death loses intensity when life expectancy grows precipitously short.

But completeness of the theory itself. Its perfection. That was a different matter entirely.

He must continue to work, even as his powers diminished and his energy flagged. God had charged him with elucidating this great truth to Man. Its beauty. Its elegance. Its Divine inspiration. Once the enlightened studied the observations and the calculations as he had, opposition would melt away.

But only if his manuscript was perfect.

Until then, he would publish nothing.

XXXIV

Orsay, March 14, 1534

SIX DAYS IN PURSUIT. Vivienne had come to be an image in the mist, so close as to touch but, when grasped for, always just out of reach. At each stop, Amaury's inquiries had yielded ever more promising information. Yes, the woman with the soldiers had been through, but she had left half a day before. Nine hours before. Six hours. Three.

At one point, riding in a downpour east of Nogent-le-Phaye, near Chartres, Amaury had been certain that he had seen the party on a hill across a river. Just a blur in the rain, but the woman's form was distinct among the men. But when he and Hélène made to follow, they discovered the old wooden bridge had been washed away. The river was running fast in the storm, so they had lost an hour finding a place to ford. When they were finally across, Vivienne had disappeared.

But seeing her had made Amaury wonder. What would he do, even if they ran her down? He might be a match for one soldier, even two if his skills with a sword had not eroded too badly, but certainly not six. Vivienne would be alone at night, however. Perhaps he could enter her room without being detected. But then what? Reason with her? She was convinced serving Ory was her salvation. If she refused to reconsider her betrayal, could he really silence her, no matter how great the cause? Strangle her? Smother her? Plunge his dagger into her flesh? Had he become that "practical"? Simple to convince himself, with Vivienne somewhere ahead of him on the road to Paris, that he would be willing to take any action necessary to prevent her from giving the manuscript to Ory and telling the Inquisitor what she knew. But in truth he would know his true capabilities only at the moment of opportunity.

And if he was to silence her, he would have to perform the act without heat of passion. For, despite the immensity of her crime, Amaury could not feel anger at the poor girl. How could he resent a creature sufficiently credulous to believe she was rendering herself a modern-day saint by causing the horrible death of those who had trusted her? One cannot blame the instrument, only he who wields it.

Nine years at Montaigu inculcated even the most reluctant student with the conviction that a true Christian will die for a cause. But would a true Christian kill for one?

Philippe Sévrier could have answered that question easily. He felt no ambiguity. What he did share with his adversary was frustration. His pursuit of Amaury was as tantalizing as Amaury's pursuit of Vivienne. He had been certain he would have encountered Faverges and the woman long ago, but the couple was traveling at surprising speed. The woman had evidently not been the burden that he expected. Now, with Paris little more than a day's ride away, he was running out of time. Once Faverges was inside Paris, he would go directly to Ory. Betrayal, imprisonment, torture, and death would follow.

Philippe wished to survive; martyrdom was for fools. But there were, after all, things to give one's life for. To stop Faverges, or at least to stop the effects of his treachery—yes, that was one of them.

XXXV

Faubourg Saint-Germain, March 15, 1534

LATE ON THE FOLLOWING DAY, Amaury and Hélène crested a low hill and saw the walls of Paris looming ahead, only ten minutes' ride, lit by the lowering sun in the western sky. The slate roof of the tower of the great abbey, Saint-Germain-des-Prés, burial place of kings, stood sentinel to the city just to its north, the same massive edifice that had marked the beginning of Amaury's journey with Vivienne weeks before. The entire length of road leading to the Saint-Germain gate lay before them, and Vivienne and her escort were nowhere in sight. She was, then, already within the city, out of Amaury's reach, at this moment being shepherded to Ory, soon to betray not only her former friends and comrades, but truth itself.

"I've failed," he muttered in despair.

"We could not have done better," Hélène told him.

Amaury stared ahead to the city walls. But Ory would require time to complete his victory. The Inquisitor would need to muster his resources before he could act on Vivienne's information. Amaury could be more direct. If he could warn Broussard, he could at least save his friend. He had little concern for the fate of the others. Justice for Giles.

"It will not be safe for you in the city," Hélène said, reading his thoughts.

"We won't be long. I must see someone."

"Let me go for you. I will be quite safe. My devotion is unquestioned. I can travel freely. And, if there is any difficulty, I will be protected. My uncle is now a cardinal. I can run your errands and you can wait for me outside the gates."

"Thank you, Hélène, but I must do this myself. Besides, we agreed that we would not be apart again."

Hélène smiled softly, even shyly, a blush creeping up her neck. "Very well, my darling. We shall bear all risks as one."

As Amaury and Hélène drew nearer to the city, they were surprised to see that the gates at porte Saint-Germain were closed. A sentry was standing at the end of the bridge on the far side of the ditch that surrounded Paris, to be flooded from the Seine in case of attack. Amaury had a moment's anxiety that Vivienne's revelations were the cause of the unusual security. But how? There had not been sufficient time. A different reason must be the cause. A criminal on the loose? Had the Emperor Charles declared war on France?

But whatever the reason, it apparently did not concern them. The sentry immediately waved to a companion looking through a grille inside the walls to open the doors in the gate and allow Amaury and Hélène entrance to the city. But as they started across the bridge, the sentry said, "Hope you aren't planning on leaving anytime soon. Order of the king. Anyone can enter. No one can leave."

"The king is here?" Amaury asked.

"Arrived from Amboise yesterday morning."

Hélène shot Amaury a glance. The sentry noticed and regarded them with suspicion. There was no question of turning back now.

"My wife is upset because we were due at a fête in Rouen," Amaury said with a shrug. "But any order of His Majesty shall of course be obeyed."

The sentry cocked his head to the side for a moment, then nodded perfunctorily and waved them through.

"By the way," Amaury added. "Have you been told the reason for the order?"

The soldier nodded, a smirk forming in the corner of his mouth. "Heretic hunt."

"Can this be about you?" Hélène asked, just above a whisper, once they had passed through the gate.

"I don't see how," Amaury replied softly. "The sentry said the order was from the king, not the Inquisition. I'm not certain why François is back in Paris, but I doubt it concerns me. Still . . . heretic hunt . . . we'll have to be very alert."

"I'm afraid for you, Amaury."

"For me? I should be the one afraid for you. A woman in a situation like this."

"Yes," she replied, reaching over and patting his hand. "I've been so fragile up to now." They had paused at the hub of four roads that led to different sections of the city. Except for a gendarme slouched against a wall, the small plaza was quiet. The sun had dropped below the level of the buildings, and flickers of candlelight had begun to appear in some of the windows. The city smelled of tallow and cooking pots. "Where are we headed?"

"La Ville. Near porte Saint-Antoine. The other end of the city, I'm afraid."

"Why? What's there?"

"A friend. A bookseller."

"What does he have to do with the manuscript?"

"Nothing. But he will be condemned, although he's innocent of any complicity in Giles' murder. The priest told me. I must try to save him if I can."

"But it puts you at greater risk."

"I heeded you about Castell'buono, Hélène. But this is something I must do."

"Very well, Amaury. Let's hurry then."

But instead of heading up rue Serpente, which led to the river, Amaury turned east on rue des Cordeliers.

"Then why this way?" Hélène asked. "Isn't it longer?"

"Yes. But this road leads to the Sorbonne. There might be fewer soldiers near the university. The king is wary of intruding on the rights of the magisters, even to pursue heretics. We can move more freely and then make our way to Cité through the colleges." Amaury cast a rueful smile. "As long as I don't encounter anyone I know."

They had gotten no more than twenty yards up the street, however, before Amaury questioned the wisdom of his decision. Just ahead of them a door flew open, followed by an old man who been hurled from the inside. The man, whose face was swollen and bruised, crashed to the pavement and could not make it to his feet before a gendarme had burst through the door and grabbed him rudely about the shoulders. The soldier drew back his arm and backhanded the old man across the face, his thick gauntlet cracking like a whip on the man's cheek. Hélène gasped as a glob of blood and spittle sailed from the man's mouth.

"So, you want to end the Mass, do you?" the soldier sneered. "Turn France into a nation of the damned?"

A small crowd was quickly gathering, murmuring in anticipation. The prospect of watching a heretic beaten within an inch of his life, or perhaps beyond, was too alluring to ignore. The old man tried to shake his head, to deny the terrible accusation, when the gendarme landed another backhanded blow. Hélène looked to Amaury. The soldier had become aware of being scrutinized from horseback and raised his eyes, glaring at the well-dressed couple, challenging them to question his authority.

Amaury dismounted. "You have proof of this man's heresy, I suppose." He spoke with the studied ease of the aristocrat, a manner he had learned watching his father's courtiers cringe at a whisper in Savoy. His hand rested easily on the handle of his sword.

The soldier straightened up, prepared for a confrontation. "And who are you to interfere with the king's order?"

"Amaury de Savoie. Son of the duke and defender of the True Faith at Collège de Montaigu. And who are you to be dispensing the king's justice on your own authority?"

"I do as ordered," the solider replied. He spoke with the growl of a bully but the uncertainty of a lackey. "The edict was to stamp out heresy. This man was denounced by his own landlord."

Amaury nodded as if to take in the situation. He would be as slow and deliberate as the soldier was instinctive and violent. "Did he owe money to this landlord?" he asked finally.

The soldier's brow wrinkled. Rather than reply to Amaury, he addressed the old wretch. The man was crumpled at his feet, wheezing, still held by the collar.

The old man nodded weakly. "A month's rent," he croaked, almost inaudibly.

The crowd fell silent. Their allegiance began to shift to the pathetic creature on the pavement. Not one of them, Amaury surmised, had not once owed money to his landlord. The soldier sensed the change as well.

"Perhaps further investigation is in order," he said, glancing to the crowd. Drawn to the bit of theater in the streets, the citizenry had continued to pour forth.

"I agree," Amaury said. "And if the man is guilty, I suggest you take him to the proper authority and not mete out justice yourself, no matter how tempting."

The gendarme looked confused. "Has the order been changed? We were told that heretics were to be dealt with on the spot."

"Of course," Amaury replied. Could it be true? Could even François have issued such an order? "But only in the case of irrefutable proof."

The soldier considered the question. Nuanced instructions were a new experience for him. Then a voice came from the crowd. "Let the old man go. It's the landlord you should be arresting." A hum of assent rumbled through the crowd.

The gendarme glanced once more at the growing throng, then leaned down and helped the old man to his feet. "All right then, *grand-père*," he said affably, patting the man softly on the shoulder, "no harm done." The old man stared at the paving stones, afraid to look up lest it jinx his good fortune.

"I'll talk to your landlord," the soldier went on. He smiled, more for the crowd than for the victim. "False accusations of heresy aren't viewed favorably by His Majesty."

Amaury had stood solemnly while the scene played out, never cracking the veneer of authoritarian judgment. He paused a few seconds, as if considering the soldier's performance. Finally, he pursed his lips and nodded off-handedly. The gendarme was relieved and the onlookers grateful. Amaury remounted his horse. The crowd cleared a path and he and Hélène rode through.

"Thank you, Amaury," she said when they had cleared the crowd.

"I didn't do it for you, Hélène."

"All the better then," she replied.

Philippe Sévrier arrived at porte Saint-Germain thirty minutes after Amaury and Hélène had passed through. Unlike them, he aroused no suspicion from the sentry. In fact, for Philippe, the doors were opened with a flourish. That was because he arrived not as himself but as Frère Jean-Marie.

He had known to adopt the Franciscan facade purely by chance; fortuitous in one sense, regrettable in another. He had sensed the previous day that he was finally about to overtake Faverges and the woman. Just a feeling, but powerful and compelling. He rode hard, stopping in a hay field to sleep only when he feared he would fall from the saddle. At any moment, he was convinced the two would come into view.

Philippe was not aware that he actually *had* overtaken them. He had chosen a parallel road to that on which Amaury and Hélène were traveling and, in his frantic pursuit, was, in fact, closer to the city than those he sought. Had he simply continued, he would have entered Paris first and been able to lie in wait for his prey. Instead, at a stop at a hosteller's to water his horse, Philippe chanced to overhear a conversation between two men who had just left Paris. He listened as they talked of the placard tacked to the king's bedroom door: one of hundreds, as it turned out, nailed to walls, doors, and posts across France. The two men then spoke of the order of the king to exterminate Lutherans, to render France

Catholic. Philippe joined the conversation, eventually revealing himself as a reformer. The two men, he learned, were also Lutheran. One was a preacher. Both had been fortunate to escape the city just as the order to close the gates had reached the gendarmerie.

Philippe was left with competing priorities: to pursue the traitors without delay, or to take steps to ensure his ability to move freely within the city. Perhaps, he surmised, he would not overtake Faverges and the woman until they were inside the walls. As a stranger, he would be constantly at risk of being accused of Lutheranism. He would be forced to restrict his movements, avoiding soldiers or crowds. So, eschewing immediate pursuit, Philippe found a greedy tavern owner in Faubourg Saint-Germain to whom to sell his horse, then repaired to a second tavern to shave a tonsure and don the Franciscan cloak that he had taken the precaution of packing.

Once more the pious friar, above suspicion by the detested Catholics, Philippe Sévrier walked to the Saint-Germain gate. As on the night he had followed the courier, Fabrizy, a knife was nestled in the sleeve of his cloak. Assuming his quarry would want to spend as little time inside the walls as possible, Philippe took rue Serpente, the most direct route to the bridges across the Seine. The bookseller's was the place to begin. There he might at least warn the brethren of the coming betrayal. And if, by some chance, Faverges chose to return to the scene of his treachery, Philippe would be waiting.

XXXVI

FRANÇOIS PLACED THE DRUMSTICK on his plate, raised his right hand to examine his fingers—long and thin—and then carefully sucked each one clean. Not the best capon he had ever tasted, but serviceable under the circumstances. He couldn't complain in any event. Not tonight. Tonight was for humility before God. To demonstrate that the catharsis being undertaken in the streets outside these very windows in the Louvre was not for revenge or, even worse, personal pique, but rather to do service to the Lord against those who would defile His Word and His commandments.

The day after tomorrow, just after dawn, he would lead a procession. He would go bareheaded, wearing only a simple black friar's cloak. He had drawn the line at Beda's suggestion that he go barefoot as well. It was still winter, after all. Nonetheless, the ridiculous hour and the ludicrous outfit should be sufficient to convince the citizenry of Paris of his sincerity.

He would begin here, at the gates of the palace, then pace solemnly and silently across to Cité and into the vaults of Sainte-Chapelle. There, he would command that the sacred relics be produced—the true Crown of Thorns, a fragment of the Cross, and a piece of Jesus's robe stained with the Lord's blood. All purchased three centuries before by his predecessor, Louis IX. Saint Louis. Then flaunted by his beatified predecessor to atone for that disastrous crusade. Knights slaughtered by the thousands, headless bodies left to bleach and dry in the desert. Louis himself had been taken captive; his queen, Marguerite, forced to raise a huge ransom to secure his release. François, from the moment he had become king, was determined never to preside over such a debacle.

Then, at Pavia, in 1525, a mere decade after he had taken the throne, François himself had been taken prisoner. By Charles. A debacle at least as immense as Louis'. Forced also to promise a huge ransom. Then compelled by the detestable Habsburg to offer up his own sons as hostages to assure the ransom was paid. Lord, how he loathed that man. How could an absurdly pious dwarf with the lower jaw of an ape continually outwit him?

Well, no more. What had begun as an act of rage outside his bedroom at Amboise had ripened into a brilliant bit of strategy. The placard that had so fortuitously appeared on his door would now be the instrument to finally best his nemesis.

François would take the relics from Sainte-Chapelle and walk with them through the streets of Paris. Praising God with every step. The king abasing himself before the power of the Lord. Heretics would be burned, drowned, branded, and impaled throughout the city as he walked. Merciless retribution meted out to a heretical sect. Finally, François would return to Cité and sit for a Holy Mass in Notre Dame. An example of piety unsurpassed. A show of devotion to dwarf . . . the dwarf.

What could the pope do then? The Medici hypocrite. He would be forced to acknowledge François as the epitome of the faith. To favor France and its king. To begin to be pried away from Charles. At least brought to neutrality. François would then assist Henry of England in his never-ending marital difficulties, and Charles, finally, would be outthought and outflanked.

When he had seen that abominable placard on the door of his bedroom, François had sworn to himself to have its author roasted over a slow fire. No longer. Now the king wished only to embrace him.

XXXVII

AT NIGHT, from a distance, the sights and sounds of horror are discordantly similar to those of celebration. Clumps of men running through the streets, yelling, sometimes cheering; an occasional shriek from an unseen quarter; sparks from torches wafting into the night. Paris might as easily have been celebrating the birthday of the king as murdering its children. As Amaury and Hélène closed in on the university, however, there was little mistaking the nature of events. The shouts bursting spontaneously from side streets and buildings were of anger, not joy; the shrieks were pleas for mercy, not expressions of ecstasy.

Amaury and Hélène could not ride five minutes without encountering a scene that might have been lifted from a painting by the Nederlander Bosch. At one corner, a man was prostrate in the street, kicked at by soldiers, students, and faculty masters, while his two small sons tried desperately to break through to him. On another street, a woman had been stripped of her clothing and was running in desperation, pursued by three soldiers. She was soon caught and dragged into an alley. Bodies littered the streets. Pools of blood lay everywhere. Flames licked out of the shop windows of merchants who had been denounced for Lutheranism. At one intersection, four students sat by a roaring fire, heating irons that would later be used to brand anyone they decided was not Catholic enough.

At first, with each atrocity, Hélène looked to Amaury, although there was no longer any question of attempting to intercede as Amaury had done with the old man. As the monstrous scenes became more commonplace, Hélène stared straight ahead as if to will away the slaughter before her. Amaury at first tried to warn her that such behavior could draw the very sort of attention they were desperate to avoid. But he soon realized that her manner might just as easily be interpreted as aristocratic disdain.

They finally reached grand rue Saint-Jacques, the route to Cité. Blocking their path to the bridge, however, was a pitched battle between two groups of students and masters. Not all the Lutherans, it seemed, were willing to be dragged into the streets to die. The combatants were using anything at hand for weapons: swords, pikes, lengths of iron or wood, paving stones.

Amaury led Hélène to rue des Noyers to avoid the melee. At place Maubert, as they circled around to attempt to reach the bridge, they came upon a hooting, roaring crowd at the public gallows. The onlookers were mostly students, many not older than fifteen. Soldiers had fashioned additional nooses, and three men had been strung up, kicking and jerking, their eyes bulging out of purpled faces. As each involuntarily loosed his bowels, a cheer went up.

This sight Hélène could not will herself to avoid. She sat stiff in her saddle, her jaw clamped shut, her eyes rigidly on the gallows, almost as wide as the poor devils' who were now hanging limp and lifeless in the center of the square. Even by torchlight, Amaury saw that her pallor had become extreme. He reached over and squeezed her wrist. At first she didn't notice. Eventually she turned to him, uncomprehending. She tried to speak, but no words came out. The whoops of the jubilant crowd pierced the night.

They could not tarry. The mob would soon seek another outlet for its lust. Amaury took the reins of Hélène's horse and began to move around the square.

"Out to see the show?" one boy yelled to them. "The lady bit off more than she bargained for, I see." Laughter followed.

Amaury shrugged at the man, as if in agreement, relieved to be able to join a conspiracy rather than be the object of one. Laughter spread and Amaury was able to maneuver the horses away from the square. He found a quiet niche at the south wall of Les Marins, the seamen's church.

Before he could begin to soothe her, Hélène spoke. Her voice was even, a metallic monotone, but surprisingly resolute. "I'm all right, Amaury," she said. "I am, really. I have now seen Hell. I will not be shocked again. Whatever it takes to achieve what you need to achieve, I will never be a hindrance. You have my promise."

Amaury wasn't sure how to respond. Should he take her at her word, or assume that the shock of what she had seen had unhinged her? The answer might determine whether they lived or died. Still, the course of action in either case would be much the same.

"Very well, Hélène," he replied simply. "I know I can trust you."

"One thing, however," she added. "When this is done, and we are safely away, I will never set foot in Paris again."

"First let us try to get safely away," he said. "Crossing Cité will be perilous in its own right. With no other avenue from Université to La Ville, I'm certain the streets of the island will be thick with gendarmes and Ory's agents, ready to grab up anyone even suspected of Lutheran leanings. We'll use the Petit Pont and head directly across the plaza in front of Notre Dame. Audacious, perhaps, but we have a better chance moving brazenly in a crowd than riding furtively through the streets."

Ten minutes later they were at the entrance to the bridge. As Amaury had anticipated, the plaza in front of Notre Dame was thick with soldiers and churchmen. Everyone passing was scrutinized. At the front was a man in magister's robes. Sometimes he would wave a party by; sometimes he would nod to the soldiers to question or detain the terrified wayfarers. Even from a distance, it was clear the man in the robes was enjoying his role.

"What's the matter, Amaury?"

"I know him. His name is Ravenau."

"Can we turn back?"

Amaury shook his head. "We'd be seen. And besides, there is no other way to get to rue des Bales."

"We can't remain here."

"I know how we can get by. It will involve a good deal of risk for you, I'm afraid."

"Tell me."

When Amaury was done explaining, Hélène nodded. "Yes. That will work."

"Remember, keep riding," he told her. "Hold tight to your bridle."

The horses clomped slowly into the plaza. Ravenau was too occupied with intimidating passersby to yet notice his old charge from Montaigu. Suddenly, Hélène's horse broke. The beast began to gallop across the plaza, scattering the throng. Hélène screamed, appearing to be hanging on for her life.

"Help her," Amaury yelled. "She is the cardinal's niece."

All eyes turned to the woman on the runaway horse. The soldiers made futile grabs for the reins as it ran past, but the horse seemed to know when to swerve to avoid them. Amaury waited for a few seconds, then galloped to follow. No one looked his way. When he passed Ravenau, the malevolent fool was looking, as was everyone else, toward Hélène.

Suddenly, as it reached the end of the plaza, Hélène's horse slowed. A gendarme guarding the bridge to La Ville was able to take the reins and stop the beast. Amaury reached the spot soon after.

"Thank you, soldier," Amaury said. "You have saved the life of Cardinal d'Aubuisson's niece. The cardinal will be grateful. We are on our way to the Louvre to see him at this very moment." Amaury had staked his success on Ravenau's unwillingness to diminish his authority by trekking across the huge plaza to investigate the incident himself. Amaury kept his back to where they had come from. He dared not look behind him to see if Ravenau was behaving as predicted.

"You're welcome, I'm sure," the gendarme replied. He looked to Hélène, who seemed shaken but otherwise none the worse for the experience. The soldier then waved back toward the group in front of Notre Dame to assure them that the lady was unhurt. No one was following then. "I am happy to help a lady and gentleman of the True Faith," the gendarme added.

"What is your name, soldier? I must tell the cardinal of your heroism." The soldier gratefully replied. Amaury had forgotten the name as soon it was uttered.

Once off the bridge, Amaury and Hélène turned west toward the palace, but then looped around, heading toward the Bastille and Fournière's bookshop. Lacking the student population, incidents of violence in La Ville were more sporadic but no less ghastly. Armed men, soldiers and civilians, moved through the streets. Groans from the beaten, punctuated by the occasional scream, filled the night air. Flickers from torches bounced in the distance, like agents of Satan guiding the wicked. The streets smelled of blood. Just east of Saint-Gervais, a bonfire brightened the square. It was only when Amaury and Hélène grew close that they realized that inside the bonfire was the figure of a man. Or rather the charred husk of what had once been a man. Hélène gasped and Amaury steered them away from the horrible sight.

Finally they reached Saint-Antoine, the most Lutheran section of Paris, and yet the streets were oddly quiet. Perhaps the soldiers had come here first and the violence had burned itself out. Had Broussard been caught up in the maelstrom or was he safe?

When they reached rue des Bales, Amaury's heart sank. Three soldiers were perched outside Fournière's, drinking wine from jugs, wearing the look of smug satisfaction that comes from persecuting the helpless.

Amaury gestured to Hélène to remain on her horse, then dismounted and strode to the door. He picked out the soldier who looked a bit less of an idiot, assuming he would be in charge. "Has Monsieur Fournière been arrested? Surely, no one suspects such a pious man of heresy."

"Not Fournière." The soldier lifted his jug and swigged some wine. Overflow ran down his face onto his tunic. "His assistant, Broussard. Seems he was secretly using the shop as a Lutheran meeting place."

"Secretly? But I thought Monsieur Fournière lived upstairs."

"He does. But his hearing is not what it was."

"Really. I never noticed."

"When he discovered his assistant's heresy, he lodged a complaint. Pretty surprised he was, when he finally found out. 'I now know my generosity was betrayed by this heretic,' he said. So grateful was he for our arresting the traitor that he has rewarded us with wine." The soldier took another massive gulp. "As you see."

"I see a bunch of drunken louts whose word is hardly trustworthy."

"And who are you?"

"My name is Ravenau. I come from Collège de Montaigu. I work with Magister Ory. You have heard of him?"

The soldier lowered the jug to his side. "Of course." Mere mention of the Inquisitor's name was sufficient to cause the soldier to forget to question why a Montaigu magister was dressed as a gentleman.

Amaury gestured to Hélène. "I am escorting my sister to the Louvre. There I will report to Magister Ory. He seeks to gather as much information as possible about the Lutheran conspiracy. I was hoping to question this Broussard in advance of my meeting."

The soldier looked to Hélène. His glance lingered. Amaury was considering slapping him when the man turned back. "You'll have to go to the Conciergerie. Best hurry, though. Broussard is condemned. He will be executed tomorrow. King's order."

"I have heard of no such order. Who told you the king is executing heretics before they can be properly questioned?"

"The *lieutenant-criminel* himself told us before we were sent out."

"I must check this out with Magister Ory. He gave specific orders as well."

"As you wish." The gendarme turned to return to the shop, hoisting his jug as he went.

"Soldier!" Hélène had barked an order every bit as forcefully as the man's commander. He turned back to face her. The soldier attempted to leer, but Hélène's glower wiped the smirk off his face.

"Traveling to the Louvre will be dangerous. Please assign one of your men to escort us."

The soldier shifted from one foot to the other. He could not let himself back down to a woman, even a woman of breeding. "Can't spare anyone," he muttered.

"Our business is urgent. If we are delayed, I will be certain to mention your refusal to help us to Magister Ory. Heresy can come in many forms, you know."

The soldier stared angrily at Hélène. What had just moments before been an object of sexual fancy was now an exercise in class confrontation. "All right," he grumbled. "Can't see how it matters." He stuck his head inside the shop and yelled. Soon a young solider appeared. He was too young to grow a beard and had obviously been liberally partaking of Fournière's wine. "I'll give you Faston. He doesn't do anything anyway."

"Faston will do nicely," Hélène said.

After the first soldier disappeared inside with Fournière's jug, Hélène smiled sweetly at the boy. He seemed dumbstruck. Hélène was perhaps the most beautiful woman he had ever seen.

"All right now, Monsieur Faston," she said as if she were cooing at an infant, "I want you to walk ahead of us. If anyone even begins to attempt to impede our progress, I want you to say, 'Make way, by order of the Inquisition.' Can you do that?"

Faston nodded eagerly. He was obviously intoxicated but seemed to be one of those whom drink made more amiable. "Oh, yes, ma'am."

"Good. Then let's get started. When we get to the Louvre, I will see that you are commended for your service and are given a fine meal from the king's kitchen."

"Oh, thank you, ma'am." The boy was wide-eyed with pride. His skin glowed with alcoholic perspiration. "Let's be off, then." He placed himself in front of the horses and began to march in front, all the way repeating, "Make way, by order of the Inquisition," in a loud voice, even though no one had thought to challenge or delay the party.

Philippe Sévrier stepped out from the shadows of the same alcove in which he had stood the night he dispatched the courier.

Minutes. That's all. He had been minutes too late. Philippe was furious with himself. If he had cut off his conversation at Saint-Germain-des-Prés. Or not stopped to drink at the fountain. Or taken the first price he had been offered for the horse. Perhaps if he had simply walked more quickly. Anything.

As it was, he had arrived just as Fournière was ushering in the soldiers to have Broussard hauled off. The poor fool. Philippe was close enough to see the terror in his eyes when he was dragged from the shop. Intrigue was more than a game for him now. Philippe had known to avert his face sufficiently so that the pitiful bookseller would not notice the friar loitering outside. Had he not done so, Broussard would certainly have betrayed him. Not by intention. But any reflexive gesture of recognition was sufficient to destroy a man in times such as these.

After Broussard had been carted away, Philippe was left to wonder. Were they all betrayed? All of them? Arrested, dead, or doomed? Hoess? Turvette? The innkeeper? He should immediately flee the city. By the river as he had been instructed. Then make his way to Zurich where he would be safe. Even celebrated.

But not yet.

An escort. To the Louvre. The treacherous Savoyard had finally thrown off the last vestiges of his duplicity. Philippe had almost hurled himself at the loathsome Judas at the sight of the soldier preceding him down the street. But no. First he must check to see if any of the brethren could be snatched from the Inquisition's jaws.

If, as he suspected, he was the only one left, there was then but one task left to perform before he left France forever.

XXXVIII

"YOU CAN TELL His Eminence anything, Amaury," Hélène assured him. "I trust him as I would God himself."

Cardinal d'Aubuisson shook his head. An old man, short and round, but with gray eyes that twinkled. "A bit too much of a burden, my dear. I do, however, pledge to you, Monsieur Faverges, that once I have given my word, I will respect all confidences . . ." The cardinal smiled. Dimples formed in either cheek. "Even heretical ones."

The cardinal's apartments in the Louvre were as sumptuous as Beda's had been ascetic: Plush furniture filled the room, thick carpets lay on the floor, tapestries and beautiful paintings hung almost to the ceiling. A large bookcase lined one wall. Even a cursory glance revealed the contents to be not only theological texts, but also the very sort of secular scientific works that Amaury had read surreptitiously in his days at Montaigu.

But Amaury was not going to place his life in a man's hands because of a fine library and dimples. "You would protect heresy?"

"Not true heresy. But I suspect that what you have to tell me will not go counter to the word of God, but only some fool's interpretation of it."

"And by fools, you mean . . ."

"I expect, Monsieur Faverges, that I mean precisely the same sort of people as you do. I agreed to see you—and protect you—not simply because I adore my niece—although I do—but because I suspect you are in possession of knowledge that will aid the Church. The True Church. The Lord's Church. Not the Inquisition's." The cardinal frowned. "Or, it pains me to say, the king's."

Whether the cardinal was sincere or dissembling, Amaury had little choice. He was at the mercy of this man's whim. When d'Aubuisson was informed that his niece was at the gates of the Louvre, he had more or less smuggled her and Amaury inside. They were escorted through side passages far from the wing holding the king's apartments or the section frequented by more conservative members of the Church. If the cardinal was not as Hélène had described, or what he heard displeased him, Amaury had no hope of escape. But from the man's excitement as Amaury described his discovery, he knew that Hélène had not been mistaken.

"Heliocentric astronomy," the cardinal mused when Amaury had finished his tale. "I have heard rumors. And you say this Pole has proved the theory? You are competent to judge?"

"I am. I did not have the time, of course, to check the calculations, but the methodology was certainly sound."

"Extraordinary. A boon if true."

"A boon? Excuse me, Your Eminence, but any alteration in the theory of Aristotle and its application by the Blessed Thomas has been deemed heretical. Do you not find it so?"

D'Aubuisson wrinkled his brow. "Why would I? God's glory does not rest on the theories of Aristotle or the interpretations of Saint Thomas. Brilliant men, both, but the brilliance of any one man is invariably superseded by the brilliance of another. That is God's way, is it not? Why should the Church not grow with each great mind who serves it?"

"Few of your brethren share those views."

"There are more than you suppose, although, I agree, not yet in positions of ultimate power. Those are currently reserved, sadly, for either hedonists or fanatics. As a result we have a Church that has replaced devotion with corruption, the teachings of Christ with the pursuit of wealth and power, and true piety with rigor and dogma."

"I would not have believed I would have heard such words from a prince of the Church."

"Ory, the Inquisition, and Montaigu do not speak for everyone, Monsieur Faverges. They certainly do not speak for me."

"So you will help us, Uncle?"

"To leave Paris? Certainly. Monsieur Faverges must make his exit from the city as quickly as possible. You must journey to Poland, my son, and find this man Copernici. He is in great danger, as I'm sure you are aware. Poland has remained Catholic. Ory will surely send word to have him arrested, or worse. Copernici must be warned.

"I suggest you leave before dawn. The king's vengeance has just begun. After tomorrow, I'm afraid many more will be swept up. It will give me some sense of peace if you are not among them. If you don't make yourself conspicuous, you should have little to fear from the Inquisition. Word arrived just this morning by messenger. He had hard-ridden from Nérac, pausing only once a day to eat and sleep. The guard that my dear niece bribed was evidently indiscreet. He was discovered and questioned. He was happy to volunteer that the two of you were on your way to Savoy. No one will be looking for you specifically. Clever of you to employ such a ruse."

"I wish we could accept the compliment, Uncle," Hélène said. "But the misdirection was purely by chance. I planned to take Amaury to safety in Savoy, but he insisted on returning here to attempt to save his friend. The guard had already left us when Amaury told me of his destination."

"And you chose to accompany him?"

"Yes, Uncle. I intend to accompany him wherever he goes for quite some time."

"You will go with him to Poland then?"

"Yes."

D'Aubuisson reached out with his short, chubby fingers and touched her cheek. "Such good fortune must be looked upon as a gift from God," he said. "Your quest is blessed, then."

"I would like to think so, Your Eminence," Amaury replied.

"I can arrange safe passage for both of you out of the city, despite the king's order. I will give you both a letter that will identify you as on a papal assignment. My personal assistant, Père Étienne, will accompany you. He is completely reliable and trustworthy. You will enjoy unquestioned passage through any gate in Paris. I will also make arrangements for your travel, at least from Paris to the border. You should have little difficulty managing the rest on your own."

"That is immensely kind of you, Your Eminence," Amaury said. "And I have every intention of making the journey to Poland. But first I was hoping you might help us in other ways."

"What did you have in mind?"

"Two things. First, before I leave I was hoping to learn more specifically what plans Magister Ory has for the manuscript and, more importantly, for the man who wrote it."

"Of course. Both Beda and Ory are here, within these walls. There is a good deal of conversation between them and the king. Such communication has a way of leaking out. I will find out what I can. What else?"

"I would ask your assistance in saving my friend Broussard from the stake."

The dimples vanished. "He is accused of heresy, Monsieur Faverges. Even I cannot aid someone who has renounced the Faith."

"Heretic or no, Your Eminence, I cannot leave Paris with my friend condemned in prison, particularly since I am responsible for him being there."

"You are not responsible," Hélène said. "How could you have known?"

"I agree," d'Aubuisson said. "You do him no good by staying. All that you will achieve is your own exposure and cause his death to be in vain."

"I don't intend him to die," Amaury said. "Since you are willing to sign a letter granting us passage from the city, Your Eminence, perhaps you can also sign one that demands Geoffrey to be released into my custody. So that he be returned to the Louvre and questioned further, perhaps."

"You can't ask him to do that, Amaury," Hélène protested. "He would be found out."

"That is of no concern," d'Aubuisson said. "I am a prince of the Holy Church. François has not gone to all this trouble to cultivate Rome to risk failure by prosecuting a cardinal. But I won't write the letter because it will cause *you* to be found out. In that case, who will make the journey to Poland? I am sorry for your friend, my son, but we must not lose sight of our preeminent objective."

"Your Eminence," Amaury said, "I will not leave without trying to free my friend. The task will be more difficult if you withhold your assistance, but I must try in any event. If I slink out of Paris and leave Geoffrey to his fate, anything else I do has no value."

D'Aubuisson considered his alternatives. "You will not change your mind. I can see that. Once you have freed your friend, you will leave for Poland?"

"We will be out of porte de Temple within the hour."

D'Aubuisson nodded. "Very well. You will have the letter in the morning. Get some sleep. You will have a long day tomorrow. I will have you awakened at six. Best get to the Conciergerie early to avoid the officers of the watch. But you cannot arrive too early. And do not leave your rooms under any circumstances until Père Étienne comes to fetch you. You don't want to chance a meeting with Ory in the halls." D'Aubuisson raised a cautionary finger; his dimples returned. "And you certainly don't want to run into the king."

Hélène moved forward and kissed the old man on the cheek. "Thank you, Uncle. I am once again in your debt."

"Suborning heresy," the cardinal muttered. "This has turned into quite a unique adventure."

XXXIX

PÈRE ÉTIENNE SHUFFLED toward the Conciergerie. A timid creature, he both loved and feared the cardinal. Loved because he had never known a man within whom the Lord so obviously resided; feared because his superior's goodness came directly from God and so the cardinal often ignored the dictates of lesser forces, sometimes even the Holy Father himself. For fifteen years, Père Étienne had planted himself firmly in the cardinal's shadow: indispensable, omnipresent, and invisible. Père Étienne knew he would never rise above his present position, but lack of advancement mattered to him not one whit. When the Lord called the cardinal to his bosom, Père Étienne would enter a monastery. Carthusian most likely, where he could spend his remaining days in prayer without the necessity of chattering with his fellows. Père Étienne was a man who knew his own soul; he was perfectly suited for quiet, secure servitude. The cardinal knew as well and had never asked his loyal subordinate to perform any task for which he was ill equipped.

Until now.

The priest toyed with the sealed letter he was holding under his cloak. If he didn't shift it in his hands, perspiration from his palms would soak onto the paper. He felt at the raised seal, trying to gain comfort from the cardinal's signet, pretending that the dried wax was an embodiment of the man himself. He breathed a prayer of penitence for his distortion of transubstantiation.

"You must take it, Étienne," the cardinal had told him before dawn. "Faverges cannot. If he is recognized he will be instantly arrested. My niece is also unsuitable. A woman would not be believed as a courier. I would take the letter myself, but the presence of a cardinal at the prison would arouse more suspicion than our little cabal can bear."

"Very well, Your Eminence," Père Étienne had replied. His acquiescence, however, was distinctly without enthusiasm.

D'Aubuisson had patted him gently on the shoulder. "That's a good lad. We are all in your debt." The cardinal always called him "lad" when the task was unpleasant. Étienne was forty. "When the man, Broussard, is released to your custody, you will see him, Faverges, and my niece to église Saint-Martin and then return here. Do you understand?"

"Of course, Your Eminence."

So he had set out, the cardinal's niece and the Savoyard with whom she traveled a discreet distance behind. Père Étienne had spent his life able to discharge any duty without a second thought, secure in the knowledge that the power and majesty of the Church was behind him. On this occasion, however, he felt as if he walked alone. He was unused to the sensation and it frightened him. What would he do if events did not transpire precisely as His Eminence assumed they would? If he had to make a decision on his own? If, the Lord forbid, a creative solution was needed to a problem? Père Étienne could not remember a creative act in his entire life.

Once or twice he had glanced over his shoulder to check if the man and woman were still in eyeshot. Each time he did so, they seemed uncomfortable. Just before the bridge to Cité, he turned and saw that they had vanished. Père Étienne realized this was to discourage him from turning to look. He felt himself blush. To be reproved like a child.

Finally he arrived at the prison. The place de la Pays, across from the building, was already packed with citizens of Paris. Four stakes set in bundles of wood and twigs awaited four of the pitiful condemned, and devotees of such affairs had taken no chances on being deprived a prime view. Louts, misanthropes, and drunks—even at such an hour—packed the square. Those of means as well. Even some families. Festivity was in the air. Bread, cheese, and sausage were shared among the onlookers, washed down with wine from large jugs passed through the crowd.

Père Étienne surveyed the throng, then forced his way to the front gate of the Conciergerie. The foul-smelling gendarmes who usually stood watch at the entrance were nowhere to be seen. Instead, the king's guard stood as sentinels. Père Étienne felt his innards roil. Secular authority terrified him. But, mercifully, he managed to keep the sensation under control and he was able to address one of the guards.

"I have been sent with a communication from Cardinal d'Aubuisson. A matter of the highest urgency. Please fetch whoever is in charge." Père Étienne removed the letter and waved it in front of him. He felt ridiculous. No man was less suited to intrigue. He wanted to peruse the crowd once more, to find Faverges and the woman. Have them take over this foolishness. But the cardinal would hardly have been pleased.

The soldier looked the priest up and down. He was a swarthy, steely-eyed fellow; square-jawed, with the bearing of a man always on the verge of killing another. Without a word, he cocked his head at one of his comrades. The second soldier nodded and walked toward the hall that led to the interior. Père Étienne was left staring at the man he had addressed. The priest was also unused to being in the presence of someone not cowed by the power of the Church. He felt the need to glance to his feet, but knew that, representing the cardinal, he must not back down.

A few minutes later an officer appeared, striding ahead of the soldier who had been sent to fetch him. This man was fair-haired with quick blue eyes and an air of culture. Père Étienne breathed easier. Clearly, here was someone who could be spoken to.

"I'm Captain Beaufort," the man said. He spoke in Latin. Père Étienne beamed. "What is this vital communication from the cardinal?"

Père Étienne handed the captain the letter. The captain broke the seal and removed the paper inside, reading quickly. "This says that the heretic

Broussard is to be transported to the Louvre for interrogation. In your custody."

Père Étienne nodded.

The captain considered the request. "You'll have to clear this inside. The executions were to begin within the hour."

"I must go . . . with you?"

"Of course," the captain said. "Do you expect my superiors to come to you?"

The captain turned and marched toward the interior of the building. Père Étienne hesitated for a moment, then, repressing the urge to turn and run from the vile place, slowly followed.

Twice the captain had to stop and wait for Père Étienne to catch up. By the time they reached a large corridor across the courtyard, the captain was making no effort to hide his impatience. Damn Churchmen. They thought the world must move at their pace. Finally, the captain came to a door. He swung it open and strode inside with the letter. The captain closed the door behind him, leaving Père Étienne standing in the hall.

A few moments later, the captain swung the door open again. "Come in, Father," intoned a smooth voice from inside. "Let us chat."

Père Étienne stepped across the threshold. Behind a desk across the room, under a large cross on the wall, at least eight feet high, sat the black-robed figure of Mathieu Ory, Inquisitor of France. Ory held the cardinal's letter in his hands.

"Close the door, Father," Ory said easily. "Come and sit."

Père Étienne padded across the room and sat in the chair opposite the desk. Ory had not moved. After the priest was settled in his seat, Ory made to read the letter, slowly and methodically, although he had quite clearly read through the contents just moments before. When he had finished, he placed the letter on the desktop, then carefully smoothed the paper with both hands.

"An odd communication from His Eminence, wouldn't you say?" Ory had furrowed his brow, but his eyes betrayed no confusion at all.

"I don't concern myself with such questions, Magister," Père Étienne replied. "I simply do as the cardinal instructs."

"So you are unaware of the reason for this request?"

"As I said . . ."

"A letter signed by a cardinal has the authority of the Holy Father himself behind it," Ory went on. "A surprising amount of prestige to bring to bear for a heretic bookseller."

"As I keep assuring you, Magister . . ."

"Even a man in my position dare not disobey such an order. Still, I do find it curious that His Eminence would wish to add the task of interrogating criminals to his already more than ample duties. Does he suspect that I am not discharging my responsibilities adequately?"

"I am certain that is not the case." Père Étienne felt a rivulet of perspiration from his armpit run down his side.

"Perhaps, then, he seeks to join us in our holy duties. Eliminating heresy is, after all, God's work."

"I do not question His Eminence's motives."

"Of course not."

Ory lifted the letter once more. "I expect that you are waiting for the heretic Broussard to be brought to you, so that you may transport him to the cardinal. You would require an escort, would you not?"

An escort? How could he then take Broussard to the church? But Père Étienne knew better than to refuse. "If you would be so kind as to provide one."

"Actually, Father, that will not be necessary." Quite casually, Ory grasped a corner of the paper in either hand, then tore the letter in half, then in half again, after which he allowed the pieces to drop to the desk.

Père Étienne watched the paper settle on the desktop with astonishment. Never, in almost two decades, had he seen a high Church communication treated with such contempt. He glanced from the paper to Ory, then back to the paper.

Ory observed the scene with obvious amusement. "You are shocked, Father. Appalled. The explanation is simple. I work to king and Church. Cardinal d'Aubuisson, at least in this endeavor, works to neither. The cardinal's liberal proclivities are well known. Why he has identified with this particular heretic I am not aware. Although I intend to find out.

What I do know is that he wishes to undermine a Holy Crusade that seeks to rid France of the Lutheran pestilence. Rome shall know of his actions.

"As for you, Father, I suggest you scuffle on back to your master and inform him that his game has failed. The heretic Broussard will feel God's justice this very morning. If His Eminence wishes to further contest the point, I will be right here."

Ory placed his hands palms down on the desktop. "Now get out."

XL

AMAURY AND HÉLÈNE stood at the far end of the plaza, waiting for Père Étienne to reemerge. Amaury had not been pleased when the cardinal had insisted the priest present the letter to the officers of the Conciergerie instead of allowing him to do it, but the logic had been unshakable. The risk of Amaury being recognized was simply too great.

"Don't worry, my son," d'Aubuisson had assured him, "Père Étienne speaks in my name. Your friend will soon be safe."

As the minutes dragged on, however, Amaury suspected that not only was Geoffrey far from safe, but that the priest had come under threat as well. In the cardinal's sumptuous apartments, on a high floor of the royal palace, surrounded by the trappings of power and wealth, assurances had been persuasive. D'Aubuisson doubtless believed them himself. Here, however, amidst a braying mob of cannibals, d'Aubuisson's pronouncements seemed naïve and ridiculous. But if the cardinal could know no better—he never saw this France—Amaury should have. What had possessed him to think he could snatch Geoffrey away from Ory and the Inquisition with all of Paris screaming for vengeance?

As Amaury thought of the Inquisitor, Ory himself appeared at the doorway. He walked slowly across the square, expression implacable, dressed in his black cloak and black peaked skullcap, precisely as he had appeared in Beda's rooms. He mounted a platform that had been erected near the four stakes and cast his eyes over the crowd. In whichever direction he looked, those under his gaze fell silent, only to begin to speak again once it had passed.

Amaury positioned himself with Hélène so that they were behind a stone column, virtually invisible from Ory's perch. He had wanted her to wait at the Louvre, but d'Aubuisson had told him it would be dangerous for him to return to fetch her. Once Geoffrey was free, the three of them would make directly for église Saint-Martin, and then for the city gates.

But where was the priest?

Ory raised his right hand, palm out, and the entire plaza fell silent.

"Citizens of Paris, believers in the True Faith," he intoned. He spoke sufficiently loud as to be heard, but did not shout. "We are here this morning for a sad task, but a necessary one. We do God's work." Feeling the approbation of the Inquisitor, a hum rose from the citizenry of Paris. One or two even yelled, "Praise God," never taking their eyes from the four pieces of wood looming behind the Inquisitor, like fingers pointing to heaven. Amaury noticed that among the spectators were children, some as young as five or six, perched on their parents' shoulders.

"As you all know, there are those among us who would subvert the True Faith, disrupt Man's relationship with the Lord. Send all of Paris, all of France, all of *Christendom*, on a path to damnation. Our great and wise sovereign, King François, champion of the Lord, has decreed that this cancer must be cut out of the body and soul of Christianity and destroyed.

"So, this morning, four of those who would corrupt our Holy Church and . . ." Ory leveled a finger at the crowd, "endanger *your* souls, will be consigned to the flames, purified, so that *their* souls will once more return to a state of grace."

Ory turned toward the building's entrance and nodded. The hum from the spectators increased. Three soldiers appeared, marching side by side in unison, then three more. The noise level in the square rose still higher. Finally, the condemned were brought forward, each wearing sackcloth, escorted on all sides by the king's guard. A cheer went up from the spectators.

Geoffrey was first, the king's own son. François must have known. How could he allow this? The man must be the devil himself, not worthy of the loyalty foisted on a dog, let alone a king. Even Amaury's father would never countenance such an end for his progeny, illegitimate or not. Or would he?

The bookseller was followed by Hoess, then a man Amaury did not know, and, finally, Madame Chouchou. So Vivienne had betrayed even the woman who was teaching her to read. All four wore expressions of terror; eyes impossibly wide, skin almost white, mouths quivering. When they reached the center of the plaza, another cheer went up, louder than the first. Cries of "Burn them!" and "God's vengeance!" and "Praise the Lord!" filled the air. With each explosion of noise, the four wretches seemed to grow increasingly bestial. Soon the four appeared as cattle, being led toward a fate they neither understood nor thought real.

Amaury felt ill. He wanted to rush forward, to either save them or die with them. What could life mean after what was about to transpire? Suddenly he felt a tug on his sleeve.

"I tried. I did all I could. Magister Ory himself tore up His Eminence's letter. Come. We must leave now. I sent word. His eminence himself is meeting us at église Saint-Martin."

"We can't go," Amaury said to the priest. He suddenly found the toadying little man loathsome. "We'll be seen. We've got to stay. Until the end. Then we'll slip away in the crowd."

"Oh, no, Amaury. We can't." It was Hélène. She was shaking as if with ague and had turned away from the horrible spectacle unfolding before her.

"We have to. If we try to leave and are caught, we may be joining those poor devils." Amaury grabbed Père Étienne by the shoulder. He should not abhor the man, he knew, but he did all the same. "You can leave, however, without suspicion. You're a *priest*."

Père Étienne quaked in Amaury's grasp.

"Go to église Saint-Martin. Tell the cardinal what happened. If we are to leave Paris now, I'm not certain that a letter from him will be sufficient to get us past the guards. We'll meet you there as soon as—" Amaury cocked his head toward the front of the plaza. "We're able."

The priest nodded and slinked off.

Hélène had taken refuge, moving completely behind the pillar. Amaury didn't want to look, but he could not keep his eyes away. He felt compelled, somehow, to bear witness.

Geoffrey and the others had been hauled up to small stands that had been fastened a third of the way up each stake, just above the piles of kindling. A black-robed monk was chaining each of them to the post. Geoffrey had turned resolute, even defiant. Hoess stared at the crowd, still seemingly unable to grasp what was to come. The man Amaury did not know, thirtyish, fair, and fat, was whimpering, saliva dripping uncontrollably down his chin. Occasionally a low moan escaped him, which caused the crowd to hoot and cheer.

Madame Chouchou was the most striking of all. She was without her wig and garish clothes; simply a large, plain, fleshy woman with graying hair. She now neither cringed nor wept. A beatific resignation had come over her; she stood silently, almost placid, perusing the jeering mob. Amaury had never seen anyone display more dignity. When he was preparing for just such a fate in the dungeon at Nérac, he had prayed for God to give him the strength to bear his trial with similar decorum. A brothel owner was demonstrating to all how one who believes in God's mercy and deliverance should face death.

Ory began reading prayers. The crowd was once again silent, but Amaury hardly heard the words. He remained next to the pillar at an angle where the Inquisitor would not be able to pick him out of the crowd. Hélène remained behind it.

Geoffrey continued to stare out at the crowd, his jaw set, refusing to give his tormentors the satisfaction of seeing him afraid. Amaury felt tears on his cheeks. Is this what the Church had become? How could these abhorrent men think they spoke for God?

Amaury could not see from whence it came, but a torch was suddenly in Ory's hand. Never ceasing to mumble prayers, to speak to God, the Inquisitor lit the kindling under Geoffrey's feet. Then he moved to Hoess, then to the unknown man, then to Madame Chouchou. The fires burst full almost immediately. At least the four would have fast deaths and not slow roasting over green wood with leaves still on the branches.

The crowd had hushed as the ceremony was carried out. Suddenly, an animal cry filled the plaza, then a series of shrieks as the flames enveloped the condemned. Geoffrey had held out as long as he could, but his screams had eventually come. Madame Chouchou, however, remained silent. She had raised her eyes to the heavens. Her lips were moving in prayer. Amaury was stunned. Did she not feel pain? Did God truly live within the brothel owner? Madame Chouchou among the elect? Calvin would have sneered.

The crowd had been reawakened by the cries of the dying. Their cheering began and grew louder as the flames rose. Geoffrey's head swung back and forth as the fire grew hotter. Suddenly, his arms seemed to explode in a torrent of blood. The fire had heated liquids within him so that the vessels that held them burst. The screaming from the pyres was no longer human. Geoffrey's eyes began to bulge from their sockets. Amaury finally turned away, able to bear the sight no longer, but from the paroxysm of cheers, realized all too well what had happened.

The smoke, gray when the fire began, had turned black. The wind was blowing from the east, and soon a cloud drifted over the square, bringing with it a sickly sweet odor of cooking meat. Rather than be nauseated by the sensation, the spectators seemed exhilarated. "On their way to damnation, and we can smell it," one zealot yelled, and his fellows let out a shout of piety.

Hélène was still behind the pillar, bent over. Amaury put his arm over her shoulders. As the transformed essence of the four Lutherans permeated the arena, the calls to God continued to rise, soon reaching a crescendo, then, with the clearing of the air, began to subside. Fifteen minutes later, it was over. The wood continued to smolder, but all that was left of Geoffrey and the others was bone and strings of blackened flesh. Soon the spectators, spent after their emotional outpouring, would begin to disperse and Amaury and Hélène could make their escape.

He turned to look one last time. He wanted to remember and he would. What he saw would remain with him, every day, every moment, until the day he died.

Four charred husks, black, smoldering, unrecognizable as human except in outline of form. Save for a vague sensation of length, each of the four was indistinguishable from the others. Amaury stared at what had once been Geoffrey: his friend, a scholar, brave, and true to his beliefs. Now a grotesque relic, a testament to the corruption of God's word by those who were convinced they spoke in the Lord's name.

Castell'buono had been correct, God save his soul. Amaury no longer had doubts. For the first time in his life, he was absolutely certain of what he believed. He made a vow. He would fight them. The zealots. The ignorant. He would oppose the Orys, the Calvins, the Bedas with every breath. He would dedicate his life to a better Christianity.

As his first act, he would journey to Poland and save the astronomer.

The spectators were leaving. Most headed for the three bridges to La Ville, although a fair number of students had also come to enjoy the spectacle and had turned toward l'Université.

Ory remained on his platform as the plaza emptied, surveying the scene, an expression of satisfaction on his face. Amaury took Hélène by the arm. "We must go now. You need to gather yourself. We cannot still be here when everyone else is gone. We will drift out. Don't turn to look."

Hélène nodded. She had given her word just yesterday, when she thought she had seen Hell, but that was before its true manifestation had come before her. Amaury tried gently to raise her to a standing position. The plaza was fast emptying and soon they would become conspicuous.

Hélène straightened up, staring over his shoulder. "Amaury!" she screamed.

By reflex, Amaury spun and threw his arm in front of him. He felt a tingling sensation just above his wrist. He knew he was bleeding.

Before him was Sévrier, dressed as a Franciscan friar, a knife in his hand. He stared at Amaury with loathing.

But Amaury's sudden movement had thrown off Sévrier's aim and prevented the knife from finding its mark. Sévrier seemed unsure of whether to attempt another thrust now that his adversary was aware of his presence.

At Hélène's scream, members of the crowd who had been filing by halted, aghast. Watching from a distance in safety as four helpless Lutherans were burned to death was one thing; a mad, knife-wielding friar close enough to send their own entrails gushing across the square quite another. But blood lust was up as well. They didn't rush Philippe, but neither did they back away. Instead they surrounded the mad friar.

Suddenly, a cry cut through the air.

"Stop that man!"

The crowd as one turned to the Inquisitor's voice. Then, after only a moment of confusion, they fell upon Philippe.

Ory was running their way, fighting through the departing spectators, trying to yell, "No, the other one!" but the crowd either did not hear him or did not understand what he meant.

Amaury grabbed Hélène. His wound was bleeding but not profusely. "Come. Quickly." He led her past the pillar to a small side street in the direction of l'Université. As he ducked away, Amaury saw Ory wending his way to where four men had pinned Philippe to the ground. He was trying to make them understand that they had gotten the wrong man.

He led Hélène through small streets and alleys. Although foot traffic was still sufficient to somewhat mask their movements, Amaury turned often from one street to another so they could not be spotted from a distance. He heard yelling behind him, but it soon became indistinct. His pursuers would be unable to know whether he had sought a place to hide or was making for one of the five bridges.

Eventually, Amaury looped back toward the bridges that led to La Ville. He had been grasping his right forearm tightly with his left hand, trying to stanch the bleeding. He lessened the pressure slightly and was relieved to see that no gush of blood followed. His chemise had stuck to the wound, helping to close it. It would bleed again when he removed the garment, but he would worry about that later. For now, he was aware only of his good luck. Had Hélène not screamed precisely when she did, Amaury would be at this moment either lying near death on the ground or in Ory's clutches.

They made steady progress and neared pont au Change. Once across the bridge, they could disappear into La Ville as they made their way to église Saint-Martin. But if they were stopped, even for a few moments, Ory's pursuit would run them down. A group of raucous revelers appeared from a side street, three men and two women. They were not of the lower classes, but neither were they affluent. Merchants, perhaps, or artisans. Amaury motioned for Hélène to fall in with the group.

"Never seen four at once before," one of the men was saying, a dark, husky fellow with thick, heavily calloused hands. "Quite a show. Ory's a good man for that."

"Unless you're one of those on the posts," his friend observed. "No fun then." The second man was more wiry, but otherwise a match for his companion.

"Not me," replied the first man. "I go to church and observe the sacraments."

"Then you'll be safe, my brother," Amaury chimed in. "Free to watch these shows as long as the king approves."

"At this rate, though," one of the women said, "we'll be out of Lutherans in weeks. What will we do then?" She was large and florid, about thirty, already making an unattractive transition to middle age.

"Perhaps the king will then begin on the Catholics." It was Hélène. How she had managed to get a lilt into her voice, Amaury could not imagine.

"Ha! That's funny," said the second man. "After that, what will be left of Paris? Five Jews?"

Amaury and Hélène had now fully integrated themselves into the group. Hélène was walking between two of the men, to their obvious pleasure and the women's irritation. The woman who had spoken took Amaury's arm in retribution.

"Oooh, love, what happened to you?" she asked when she saw the dried blood.

"There was a lunatic back there. Began slashing at people with a knife. The gendarmes have him now, though."

"A lunatic?" said one of the men gaily. "Sorry I missed it."

They were yards from the bridge. Eight soldiers stood guard, but did not seem to be looking for anyone specifically. They would, however, have general orders to sweep up anyone who appeared to even potentially be a Lutheran.

"Perhaps some wine?" the woman said. Amaury was sufficiently well dressed for her to assume he would pay.

"Of course," Amaury said with gusto. They were at the bridge's entrance. He listened for any sounds of pursuit behind him. A yell now could ruin them. "But let's wait until we get to La Ville. And let's go quickly."

"Never can be too quick for a drink," one of the men chimed in. "If we can't celebrate the purification of Paris, what can we celebrate?"

"Of course." The group of seven moved past the guards, too bored spending their day watching pedestrians cross in front of them to do more than glance up. Once onto the bridge, Amaury made sure to keep up the chatter.

He knew he should not, but when they were halfway across, he glanced over his shoulder. The soldiers were not looking their way. Just a few minutes more.

Suddenly another soldier ran up to the guard. He began talking and gesturing. Hélène noticed Amaury's expression and began to look back as well, but Amaury shook his head. He turned and faced forward. Their five companions continued to natter, but Amaury didn't hear. His senses were directed behind them, attuned to the sound of pursuit.

They were far enough across that the soldiers would only give chase if they made the connection. Amaury could imagine what they were saying. "A man and a woman? Well dressed? The man wounded?" Amaury hoped they would also say, "Traveling alone?" If the guards had not noticed them, they would remain at the bridge with the other soldiers, lying in wait to nab the fugitives who had in fact already passed them.

God was with them once more. There was no pursuit. Amaury and Hélène had successfully camouflaged themselves in the group of revelers. How often people look, Amaury thought, but never see.

Amaury, Hélène, and their companions passed out of pont au Change, only two bored gendarmes standing guard on the bridge's far side. As soon as they had passed into the main section of the city, the woman squeezed close to Amaury. He could feel the press of her large breasts. "Okay, love, now where do we go for the wine?"

Amaury turned up a side street so that they were out of eyeshot of the bridge. "I realize that the hour is later than I thought," he said. The mood of the five instantly darkened. "But," Amaury continued, "I am a man of my word. I promised you wine, and wine you shall have." He withdrew twenty silver francs from his purse. Enough to be persuasive, but not so much as to cause his erstwhile companions to be tempted to rob him. "Here," he said, giving the money to the woman, "please drink with my compliments."

The woman pressed against him once more. He tried not to cringe. Hélène, even after the unspeakable events of the last two days, actually stifled a grin.

"Why, thank you, love," the woman trilled. "Gentlemen are so hard to find these days." She glanced sidelong at her companions. "If you know what I mean."

XLI

ONCE THEIR FIVE COMPANIONS had disappeared, Amaury and Hélène made directly for église Saint-Martin. Père Étienne was waiting just inside the door, breathing heavily as if he had run to get there, although Amaury knew it was simply fear. The priest gestured quickly for Amaury and Hélène to follow him through the nave to the door that led to a vestry, glancing about the church as if phantom inquisitors had seeped in through the cracks.

Inside the room was Cardinal d'Aubuisson. He seemed near tears. No dimples now.

"I have been told. I am embarrassed to be a member of the same Church as that murderer. I will do all I can to help you. I cannot believe that the word of God can remain perverted by such men as Ory for much longer."

Amaury was certain that the word of God could remain perverted as long as there was a word of God, but there was no reason to add to d'Aubuisson's despair. "He will denounce you for trying to interfere," he said instead.

D'Aubuisson dismissed the notion with a wave of his hand. "He will find that his brand of piety does not sit nearly as well in Rome as he assumes. Some in the Curia are, like me, seeking reform, to move the Church to a more enlightened, modern incarnation. Others, quite the other way, do not wish their own earthly pleasures to come under question. In either case, such zealotry is anathema. As for the king . . . he cannot very well court the Holy Father's support against Charles by persecuting princes of the Church. No, my son, I will survive very nicely." He gestured for Hélène to move closer, then held out his hands for her to take. "But you, my dear, are under great threat. I encourage Faverges here to undertake his mission to Poland, but could I not prevail on you to eschew such a dangerous journey?"

"No, uncle. After . . . this . . . how can I stop now? If Amaury should fail, what point would there be to continue living?"

"But a woman, chasing after assassins? Is this what you wish, Faverges?"

"I have learned in these past days, Your Eminence, that attempting to make decisions for your niece is a fruitless exercise. But what assassins do you mean?"

"Ory has dispatched a team of killers to Poland. He did so with great concealment but, as I said, there are no secrets in the Louvre. They have, I have been told, already left the city for Calais. From there they will charter a galley. I suspect they will disembark in Hamburg, rather than traverse the Danish peninsula. Then overland to Lübeck, where they will likely charter another boat."

"Did you learn anything of the assassins' identities, Your Eminence?" The cardinal shook his head. "There are four. That's all I know."

"I believe I know the men."

"You? How?"

"That's unimportant, Your Eminence. But the knowledge will give us at least one small advantage. Still, we cannot hope to overtake them if we merely mimic their route. We must travel overland."

"But land travel is slower still."

"Perhaps. But we will need some luck in any event, and March is a stormy month. Their progress on the water might be slower than they imagine."

"Then they will put in and travel by land."

"No. If I'm correct about the identity of their leader, they will stay on the boat, where he can remain belowdecks during the day."

"I don't understand."

"This man will not travel by daylight in an open coach. And a closed one would attract too much attention, especially as he moves through the German states. No, he will stay on the boat."

D'Aubuisson shrugged. "If you say so. I don't know very much of such things, I'm afraid. In any event, it is no longer safe for you to leave the city openly, even under my auspices. We will have to smuggle you out. It should be a simple matter, however. We will secret you in the back of the cart. Père Étienne will drive. I've already arranged horses and provisions to be waiting for you outside the city. You'll find the clothing suitable for a journey north. I have written a letter that will ensure you safe passage through France. It might have benefit with Church authorities in Poland as well, although Poles are notoriously clannish. They might resent interference by a French cardinal. You'll have to judge for yourself when you arrive there.

"I've assigned servants to travel with you and a guard to see you across France. Two men whose skill and discretion I can personally vouch for. Père Étienne has volunteered to go as well."

Amaury shook his head. "The guards will be welcome. But no servants. And as much as we value Père Étienne and are flattered by his offer, he should remain with you in this perilous time."

The priest made to protest, but his relief was apparent.

"Impossible," the cardinal snapped. "You cannot travel alone with my niece on such a journey. Out of the question. Germany is not France, you know. It's a land of barbarians. I can do nothing. They will murder you for a shoe."

But Amaury would not be moved. "I'm sorry, Your Eminence, but we must go alone. This is not an adventure to be shared with even trusted lips. We will see to our own needs. And as we will be passing through territory where Lutheranism abounds, Père Étienne's presence could prove more bane than advantage. I am as cognizant of the dangers of the journey as are you. I won't expose Hélène where it can be helped. I intend to engage mercenaries at each stage of the journey for protection."

"Mercenaries can be as dangerous as bandits."

"True. But in such a case, servants would be of little assistance. And Père Étienne is a man of peace. No, Your Eminence. We will travel alone. We would welcome your prayers, however. If this journey is to have a successful end, we will need the blessings of God."

The cardinal began to protest further, but then his shoulders sagged. He was in no position to insist. "I shall pray that you have them, then."

"Thank you, Your Eminence. I will return Hélène safely. You have my word. One more thing. A girl brought the material to Ory. Escorted by six soldiers. Do you know what became of her?"

"Yes. She was immediately escorted to a set of rooms with guards posted outside. Only Ory himself spoke with her. After a bit, she was sent to Rouen. To a convent."

Amaury smiled. "I'm pleased to hear that."

"An odd reaction to the person who betrayed you."

"She was completely innocent of spirit. I can't wish her ill, no matter what she's done. She will find peace in the convent."

"More peace than those four she denounced."

Hélène moved forward and placed her hand on the cardinal's cheek. "Thank you, Uncle. For everything. Don't fear for me. I have never felt more that my life had meaning."

D'Aubuisson nodded sadly. "It is unfortunate that so often giving life meaning involves taking an inordinate risk of ending it."

XLII

PHILIPPE HAD REFUSED to speak. He had been beaten by both the onlookers and the gendarmes, then hauled across the plaza in front of the smoldering pyres, the smell of charred flesh filling his nostrils. Ory and some soldiers had set off in pursuit of Faverges. Philippe was puzzled as to why, if Faverges was Ory's man, he had fled, and why Ory had then personally led the pursuit. Perhaps the playlet was a ruse to protect the informer's identity. Perhaps now that the manuscript was in Ory's hands, Faverges did not trust that the Inquisitor would not have him eliminated to protect the secret. But whatever the circumstances, Philippe had reconciled himself to never leaving this building alive. But far worse than the forfeiture of his own life was the knowledge that the cursed Savoyard had been clever yet again. Instead of Faverges lying in the street and Philippe on his way east, it was the other way round.

After some moments on the floor of the Conciergerie, kicked at by guards, Philippe had been dragged across the floor and thrown into a cell. He was expecting the dungeons, and so was surprised to be deposited aboveground in a cell with a pallet of straw on which to sleep. A bucket of clean water was in one corner. The accommodations even included a table with two chairs.

Philippe's ribs ached terribly. Every time he breathed deeply, pain stabbed him in the side—ironic, he thought, for a man who killed with a knife. He had lost two teeth. He knew, however, not to lie down or to drink the water; not to become too comfortable in these lavish surroundings. The shock of torture would be that much worse. Instead he merely rinsed his mouth and sat in a chair to wait.

How had Ory known? The way the Inquisitor had yelled across the plaza, Philippe had no doubt he had been recognized. The priest? That a messenger from the south could have arrived here before him seemed impossible. More likely someone in Paris. Either another informer or a member of the Brotherhood who had been caught and tortured. Poor Broussard, most likely. He had never liked the bookseller, but that anyone should endure so hideous a death was an affront.

Philippe sat completely still, comforted by the throbbing in his ribs and the taste of blood in his mouth. His injuries left him feeling like a martyr. He should pray, he knew, but he felt that somehow prayer would lessen the significance of his sacrifice. He was, he realized, impatient to have his fate decided. If he must burn, let them get to it.

After some time had passed—Philippe could not be sure how much—he heard scuffling in the hall. Then the door opened and Ory walked in.

The Inquisitor entered alone, a soft, soundless walk, motioning for the door to be closed behind him. He stood for a moment opposite his prisoner, his expression placid, his eyes cold. Then he pulled out the other chair and sat across the table from Philippe.

"*Tu es fortis vir*," he said softly, speaking in Latin. "You are a brave man. I admire such courage. I urge you to speak openly. If you answer my questions honestly, no harm will come to you."

Philippe regarded the black-robed man. Torturer, murderer, defiler of the word of Christ. Now trying a new role. Trusted confidant. Philippe had prepared himself for torture; he had prepared himself for the flames;

but flattery from the Inquisitor? He refused, however, to condescend to such foolishness. He merely sat and returned Ory's stare.

"I don't know why you are being so obdurate," Ory went on. "We are, after all, working to the same ends, are we not? Protection of the True Faith from the corruption of the heretics."

Then Philippe understood. He had not been betrayed. Ory had received no notice of a Lutheran assassin masquerading as a Franciscan. In fact, no one even knew Philippe was here. Ory, therefore, thought Philippe to be precisely what he appeared to be. A fanatical friar bent on assassination. Mad perhaps. But madness would only make him more appealing.

Philippe sharpened his gaze to bore into the Inquisitor's eyes. Only a madman would do *that*, he thought. "I work to no one," he grunted. "Only to God."

"Of course," Ory replied, his voice even more soothing. "I appreciate your zeal."

"If you had not interfered, that heretic would already be on his way to Hell."

"My apologies," Ory said, heaving an exaggerated sigh. "Those fools in the crowd misunderstood my meaning. I wanted them to hold the heretic, not you. I could see from across the plaza that you were doing God's work."

Lord knew, Philippe felt grateful for the misunderstanding—if it was a misunderstanding, and not just a ploy to cause him to betray himself—but he was now more confused than ever. He could sort out his confusion later, however. He dared not let it show to Ory.

"And now? Who will do God's work now?" He raised his right arm. "This was to be the instrument of God's justice." He scowled and shook his head.

"God's justice may be delayed," Ory said, "but you and I both know that the Lord is never denied."

Philippe did not reply but rather waited, his eyes never losing their fire, never moving from Ory's.

"I don't see why either of us should be frustrated in our aims, Frère . . ."

"Jean-Marie."

"Frère Jean-Marie. All you need do is explain the circumstances that led you here."

"I work to no man."

"No, no, of course not. I only wish to fully understand the actions of one who so obviously sits in the light of God."

Philippe made to consider the request, to be engaging in internal debate as to whether to confide in even so lofty a personage as the Inquisitor. "Very well," he said finally. "The heretic's name is Amaury de Faverges. I have been following him from Nérac. I nearly overtook him outside the city walls, but he is clever."

"And the woman?"

"Hélène d'Artigny de Mainz. Faverges has either persuaded or coerced her to help him in his plans."

"That explains the cardinal's letter," Ory muttered, more to himself than to Philippe. "And what are his plans?" he asked his captive.

"I'm not certain. The blessed priest in Nérac told me that the heretic intended to perpetrate one of the greatest crimes ever against the True Church. If he succeeded, apocalypse could follow. That Faverges must be stopped at all costs. He entrusted me with the task . . ."

"He chose well. But I heard that the authorities in Nérac believed Faverges and the woman to be headed to Savoy."

So a messenger had arrived. "Initially, yes. That is what everyone believed. I told you Faverges was clever. Fortunately, the priest discovered the truth. I'm not certain how."

Ory considered this. Philippe realized that perhaps a second messenger was on his way.

"This priest's name?" the Inquisitor asked.

"Père Louis-Paul."

"I believe I know him."

"Confessor to Queen Marguerite. A thankless task that he performs with grace."

"Thankless?"

"You of all people must know that her court is a hotbed of traitors and heretics."

"Yes. It must have been a trial for a believer such as yourself to exist there. So what will you do now, Frère Jean-Marie?"

"In prison, you mean?"

"I mean if you were not in prison."

"I would pursue this Faverges to the gates of Hell, but first I would need to find out his destination. I assume the cursed Lutherans will aid him in fleeing the city."

"If I believed what you've told me, Frère Jean-Marie, perhaps God would have smiled on you after all." The Inquisitor pushed back his chair. "But I don't."

XLIII

Elbing, Poland, April 11, 1534

THREE WEEKS. Longer than Amaury had thought. But that was because he had never before been in the east. Never comprehended the terrible roads, lack of bridges, endless stretches of forest; the utter wilderness of eastern Germany and Poland. Bloodthirsty tales of the Teutonic knights made more sense to him now. Anyone reared in such conditions would fight with feral desperation. In truth, he and Hélène had been fortunate to arrive in this walled city in *only* three weeks. From here, only one day to Frauenburg, perhaps two.

The early days had belied what was to come. Through France and the Low Countries, the cardinal's letter had opened every door, ensured them of fine accommodations, appetizing food, and, best of all, discretion. Amaury's arm healed and he felt stronger than he had in months. The two guards who accompanied them had little to do but ride in front and behind and appear stoic.

They left d'Aubuisson's men at the German border but had no trouble obtaining replacements. The innkeeper suggested four rather than a pair of guards, but quoted a price a good deal less than Amaury would have expected for just two. The quartet turned out to be brothers, unkempt, dull-witted, and vulgar, but with a blatant savagery that would intimidate all but the most stouthearted bandit. Barbarians evidently had their advantages, and came cheaply besides.

Although they had entered Germany in the north, whenever Hélène mentioned that she was the widow of Wilhelm of Mainz, they were received with deference. Hélène's knowledge of the language further ensured amicable hospitality wherever they stopped. Germany wasn't France, but for three days they traveled easily and rested comfortably. No one at the inns inquired whether they were Catholic or Lutheran or why they traveled with no servants. To Amaury's surprise, no one looked askance at the brothers who, after their charges were safe for the night, drank copiously until dawn. Amaury wondered if they ever slept at all.

The weather had held, one sunny day after another, allowing for excellent progress. Of course, good weather would favor Liebfreund as well, but the sea was notoriously fickle and perhaps conditions were not so propitious on the water. In any case, after a week Amaury had begun to feel a tentative confidence that they might indeed arrive at Frauenburg before Liebfreund and his killers.

The next day, Amaury's optimism received a jolt.

They had gone down to breakfast to discover that the brothers, who had been retained to guide them through to Dömitz on the Elbe, had abandoned them and returned west. When Amaury asked if they had given any reason for their departure, the innkeeper merely shrugged. Amaury scoured the town and finally engaged three local men of high repute as fighters, only to be warned by the innkeeper that they had even higher repute as thieves. He and Hélène were forced to wait the better part of a day whilst a rider was sent to the local landgrave to request reliable men.

The men arrived in midafternoon, two large, thickset brutes, even more bestial than the four they had replaced. The party set out immediately and, ten minutes outside the town, entered a pine forest so thick that the sky was visible only in sporadic blinks. Much of the next ten days was spent amidst these trees with their thick, enormous trunks that seemed to have filled the landscape since creation.

The landgrave's men were dour and taciturn, but clearly adept. One always rode ahead to scout; the other trailed sufficiently to provide ample warning of any attempt to surprise them from the rear. Their hands were never far from the shafts of their lances or the hilts of their swords.

Sometimes there were roads, sometimes not. Sometimes what seemed like a road ended abruptly, leaving one of the guards to lead them through almost impenetrable underbrush. On each of these occasions, Amaury rode with his hand on his sword, expecting betrayal. Landgrave's men or no, there was no telling when the lure of gold coins might overwhelm feudal loyalty. But each time they eventually emerged to find that the road had picked up as precipitously as it had ended.

Within this part of the forest there were no villages, no inns. They ate the provisions they had packed and slept outdoors under bearskin quilts. The guards took turns at watch. They refused Amaury's offer to stand a watch himself, but still Amaury slept only in starts.

Hélène had changed drastically since Nérac. She spoke rarely and smiled even less. She was unconcerned that her hair had matted and her clothing was soiled. Small lines had sprouted on her forehead and about her eyes. She looked older and resolute. But within her purposefulness lay an odd tranquillity. Amaury thought the changes had made Hélène even more beautiful.

After a few days they came to enjoy the sights and smells of the woods at the end of winter. Freshly thawed soil, rich and dark, soft with newly melted snow, poised to erupt with foliage; trees verged to explode in a canopy of leaves. Even under bare trees, they lived in dappled light. The silence was so regular that any sound—a foraging bear in the distance, a bird, a squirrel moving through the brush—rang as clearly as if it had been produced next to his ear. Amaury scoffed to himself when he remembered being frightened with Vivienne outside Pithiviers in what seemed now to be merely a dot of trees.

Amaury knew, however, that the tranquillity was an illusion that could be shattered at any moment. Toward the end of the third day, it was. As they were riding through a dense copse, a huge boar suddenly charged from the brush directly at Hélène's mount. She pulled the reins to avoid the creature, but the boar was remarkably quick for a beast of such bulk. Amaury drew his sword and tried to maneuver himself between Hélène and the boar, but his horse shied. He was about to jump down and engage the beast on foot when suddenly the boar shrieked, a lance protruding from his left flank. The boar spun and made to charge at his tormenter when a second lance pierced his other flank. Another shriek and the animal began running blindly in circles. Moments later, it dropped.

Amaury looked to Hélène. She was staring at the carcass calmly, dispassionately considering, it seemed, how close the beast had come to bowling over her horse.

The guards calmly removed their weapons. They would stop at the next hut, they said, and inform the family of the dead boar. The meat and hide would be a treasure to a poor family.

They came upon a woodcutter a few miles up the road. The man, grizzled and bent at forty, was, as the guards predicted, overjoyed at the prospect of fresh meat. He dispatched three of his sons and two daughters to clean the animal of everything useful.

At the woodcutter's insistence, Amaury and Hélène spent that night in the family's home, a low, sprawling hut fashioned of logs, mud, and thatch.

The woodcutter's family lived in extreme poverty. They all slept in a common room, sharing the space undercover with their livestock. They subsisted on onions, turnips, other odd roots, and, when such bounty as the boar was not available, whatever meat they could trap, rabbits or badgers.

The woodcutter's wife, drawn and gray, although likely younger than her husband, cooked the boar in a stew that boiled in a cauldron set on a hook in the fireplace. She served Amaury first, then Hélène. One of her daughters brought portions to the guards, who had remained outside. Only after Amaury and Hélène had begun did the family eat.

The meal was surprisingly tasty, thick and rich, with a smoky flavor that was quite satisfying. Hélène thanked the woman in German, evoking a smile that revealed more than a few missing teeth. After the meal, Hélène moved to the corner near the fire, the most comfortable spot in the hut, where the woodcutter had insisted that they sleep. The youngest of the woodcutter's children, a boy less than a year old, stared at her. Hélène screwed up her face. The boy laughed. She made a sad face. He began to gawk. Soon she was passing her hand up and down in front of her face, changing from frown to smile on the way up, and smile to frown on the way down. The boy began to giggle uncontrollably. Soon the other children were laughing as well, and then their parents.

Later, as Amaury and Hélène lay under their bearskin, she whispered, "My father always did that when I was a little girl."

As they neared the Elbe, the forest dropped away and they were once more able to pass the night at inns. At Dömitz, they lost their guards. Amaury and Hélène bade them farewell with genuine affection. Hélène tried to give the two an extra gold piece in appreciation. They refused initially, saying they were honored to serve her, but Hélène forced it on them. They finally accepted, becoming halting and shy in trying to thank her.

They engaged two different guards, bored fellows who did their job without zest or flair, and set off for Poland. It turned out to be the worst part of the journey. For days they rode through a dull drizzle. The forests were thick but not inviting; the towns plentiful, but without charm; the people distrustful, unlearned, and superstitious.

Finally, they passed into Poland with hopes that their circumstances would improve. Instead, they worsened.

In West Pomerania, northeast of Walcz, they encountered local soldiers blocking the road. Ahead, the soldiers informed them, was a plague town. No one was allowed to proceed on the road. But to avoid the town meant a two-day detour. Two days lost while Liebfreund and his band of assassins drew ever nearer to Frauenburg. But to pass through a town infested with plague was considered madness. An enormous risk either way.

Amaury drew Hélène aside. "I can't afford to lose the time. The astronomer will certainly be dead by the time we arrive. I intend to ride through. You can wait for me, or the guards can escort you the long way."

"I go where you go. If you are safe, I will be safe. If you die, I will die as well."

"Very well. This is what we'll do. The rogue physician Paracelsus has insisted that disease isn't caused by an imbalance in the humors, as Aristotle postulated, but rather by impurities in the earth, water, or air. Or perhaps by tiny living creatures too small to be seen by the eye of man. If Paracelsus is correct, you and I can wear scarves over our noses and mouths, so no impurities in the air can pass through. We will touch nothing as we ride, not even brush against a tree. I believe if we do that, we will be protected from the disease."

"We will be safe, Amaury. I'm sure of it. Now go speak to the guards."

Amaury asked the soldiers if they might pass at their own risk. They refused. He took one of them aside and pressed three silver coins into his hand. They were on an errand of great urgency, he told the man. He was a physician and could assure the soldier that he knew how to avoid contracting the disease. The soldier appeared dubious but was loath to refuse the bribe. He pocketed the coins, then looked back to Hélène and asked if Amaury intended to take *her*. My wife goes where I go, Amaury told him. The soldier was appalled. Finally he said that anyone who wished to contract plague was free to do so. Patting his hand on the pocket of his tunic, he told his fellows to let Amaury and Hélène proceed.

Their guards refused to go. No amount of payment or assurances of safety could persuade them to change their minds. Once through the town, Amaury and Hélène would thus be forced to complete the journey to Elbing alone. Fortunately, they were only two days away, and the presence of plague would keep the roads clear for a good bit of the journey. Bandits had no more desire to die of the dreaded disease than anyone else.

Amaury and Hélène fastened scarves tightly over their faces and rode ahead.

The town appeared as if God himself had taken vengeance. Bodies of the dead, animal and human, bloated and blackened, lay in the streets, in the entrances to buildings, and especially in a pond to the left of the main road, which had apparently been employed as an impromptu morgue. No living creatures could be seen, but a cough or a moan occasionally escaped one of the buildings. A number of the structures had been burned out, as if the remaining residents had hoped that fire would purify the dead and save the living.

The smell became so powerful that even the scarves provided little relief. They rode at an even pace, looking forward. If Paracelsus had been wrong, they would be doomed to die horribly. They might even infect others to share their fate. But Paracelsus had not been wrong. Amaury was certain. Aristotle's prevailing theories of disease were as obsolete as his prevailing theories of astronomy. He and Hélène would be safe. Science would save them.

Once through the town, they encountered another party of soldiers on the road. The men drew back, stupefied, at the sight of two riders emerging form the holocaust. More silver coins were required to secure passage, as well as instructions from Amaury on how to avoid infection. The soldiers crossed themselves as Amaury and Hélène rode on.

One day later, a storm struck, violent and powerful, borne on a wind out of the north and east that carried with it a stinging, icy rain.

XLIV

AMAURY AND HÉLÈNE were now sufficiently close to the coast that any storm that had broken on them had also struck on the Ostsee, what in France was known as the *Mer Baltique*. Amaury was therefore exultant to feel the wind and rain pelting his face. The wind would also be in the face of any craft attempting to move east. One night in Elbing, then on to their destination.

Elbing was a star-shaped city, modern by eastern standards, protected by inner and outer walls and a moat fed by the river it straddled. A large cathedral dominated its center. The river, also called the Elbing, fed the *Frisches Haff*—"fresh lake" in German—a virtually enclosed lagoon on which, to the north and east, sat Frauenburg.

Although now within the Polish kingdom, Elbing had been a part of the Order of Teutonic Knights, and thus most of the citizenry still communicated in German. Hélène had no difficulty obtaining directions to an inn *gastfreundlich*—hospitable—that catered to the upper classes. They were greeted at the door by a scowling woman as dirty as they were, almost as pungent as the wet wool of their cloaks. She guided them up a set of stairs to a room that would have been sneeringly dismissed by a vegetable merchant in Paris. The woman stood in the doorway for a moment then started to leave before Amaury stopped her.

"Tell her we each require a bath," he told Hélène.

"*Wir wollen jedem Bad,*" Hélène said to the woman.

The woman stiffened as if she had been told Amaury had horns and a tail. "*Bitte?*" she asked.

Hélène repeated the sentence, enunciating each word carefully.

"*Italiener?*" she asked. "Italians?"

"*Französisch,*" Hélène replied. "French."

The woman shook her head in wonder. There were no facilities for bathing at the inn, she told them, but her husband could arrange to bring buckets of water warmed by the large fire in the kitchen.

"That will have to do, I suppose," Amaury conceded. "Ask her if she has any soap."

The woman didn't, but agreed to fetch some at the apothecary. Amaury thanked her and gave her some coins, which, from the woman's expression, was more than enough for the room, the food, the bath, and even the trip in the rain to the apothecary.

It took more than an hour and nine buckets of warm water before Amaury and Hélène had cleaned themselves. The soap had been coarse and caustic but left the skin tingling. It was not Nérac, but at least most of the grime had been deposited in the buckets and sent out the rear of the inn.

When the last of them had been handed out and hauled away, Amaury and Hélène moved to the fire to dry themselves. They sat on the floor wrapped in bearskin, feeling the heat pour out of the hearth, allowing themselves to be entranced by the flickering light. At the same moment, each turned to face the other.

"I have loved you from the first moment I saw you," Amaury told her.

"And I you."

"I'm more content sleeping in the woods with you than if I were sitting on the throne of Savoy. More than if I were king."

She slid closer to him until their shoulders touched. "I've spent my life trying to find things to make up for being so desperately unhappy. Now I need only you."

"We will come through this, Hélène. I can't believe God has finally brought us together only to tear us apart once more."

"No God would be so cruel." She moved around him so that their faces were inches apart. "I love you, Amaury."

They kissed and fell into each other's arms, then made love in front of the fire, suspended, for those moments, in time and space.

When they finally went downstairs and presented themselves for dinner, everyone—innkeeper, servants, and the six other guests—stared at these French with their foolish obsession with cleanliness. To Amaury and Hélène, their fellow guests were more suited to a barn than an inn. They were surprised, then, to learn that one of the men was a minor noble and another a steward to the local count.

The food, however, was a pleasant surprise, a stew rich with turnips and perfectly cooked pork. The wine was passable. As the only foreigners at the table, a man and woman traveling without escort or servants, they were an object of curiosity.

"We are heading to Frauenburg," Hélène told them finally. She had not wanted to reveal anything of their plans, but the questions would not stop.

"Ah!" said the steward. "To visit the cathedral. A stunning Gothic structure. Three centuries old. Well worth the trip."

"No, no," grunted another, a massive man with an equally massive wart on his forehead. "I'll warrant they're on their way to visit the mad canon." His lifted his rheumy eyes to theirs. "Right?"

Hélène glanced to Amaury who, while unable to understand the man, understood the challenge of the expression. She did not reply to the question but instead returned to her food.

"He seems very popular these days with you people," the man went on.

"You people?" Hélène asked.

"French."

"And why popular?"

"Just yesterday another man was asking about him. Skinny fellow.

Came off a boat. Heading to the *Frisches Haff*. Only spoke French. Had to find someone to translate. Didn't ask for a bath, though." The man chuckled at his wit. "I told him that overland was faster from here, but he insisted on the boat. Didn't seem like the type to visit the crazy old hermit, but you never know."

Hélène translated for Amaury. The noble obviously spoke French as well, because he listened attentively and became even more attentive when Amaury reacted with alarm.

"*Pas un de vos amis?*" the noble asked Amaury. "Not a friend of yours?"

Amaury considered whether or not to reveal the threat to the astronomer's life. If he did, how would it be received? With outrage and offers to help to protect a respected local citizen? Or suspicion and xenophobia, causing Amaury and Hélène to be detained whilst their story was checked? A delay that could result in the very outcome they had traveled three weeks to prevent?

"I cannot claim friendship or enmity with someone I do not know, monsieur," Amaury replied.

He and Hélène tarried a few more minutes at the dinner table, then excused themselves. As soon as they were clear of the room, he whispered to her, "We must leave now."

"Yes," she replied. "I know."

Back in their room, they dressed as warmly as they could, ready for a night ride in rain and wind. At least they would ride unmolested. No bandit would waste his time venturing out on such a night.

When they went downstairs, the innkeeper's wife was puttering about. "You are leaving now? In this storm?"

"Yes, madame," Hélène told her. "We will return in two days." She paid the woman, once again far more than two days' board would require.

The woman stood watching as Amaury and Hélène walked out the door. At the stables, they retrieved their possessions. The wind had picked up. The rain was coming in sheets. Hélène donned her second cloak and wrapped herself tightly.

Then they climbed aboard their mounts and set out.

XLV

THEY REACHED FRAUENBURG BY MIDAFTERNOON. The rain had largely ceased, although the east wind was still sufficient to make their eyes water and their sodden cloaks flap about their legs. Their destination had been visible for miles, a hill atop which sat a large cathedral with an even taller belfry nearby. As they drew nearer, they saw that the cathedral was on the north wall of a fortified complex of buildings and towers. It faced the bay, what the man at the inn had called the *Frisches Haff.* The belfry was at the southwest corner. The entire castle, walls, buildings, cathedral, and belfry were fashioned of red brick with roofs of terracotta tiles. Somewhere inside was either the astronomer or his corpse.

The main entrance was on the south wall, a gate that passed through the center of a four-story building with turrets on either side. There was no portcullis, or even a door, but merely a passage under an archway that led into a large courtyard. Amaury and Hélène rode over the bridge that spanned a deep ditch and requested entrance from an acolyte of perhaps fifteen who was posted at the entrance.

The boy asked their business, speaking in German. Amaury told him in Latin that they had come to see Canon Copernici. The boy told them the canon went by his Latinized name, Copernicus, and asked if they were expected. Amaury replied that they were not but had arrived bearing an urgent message from Paris.

The boy directed them across the courtyard to a three-story tower at the northwest corner of the castle and informed them that the canon lived there. Amaury asked if anyone else had visited the canon in the past day. The boy replied that no one had. Of course, the assassins might have come and gone without alerting anyone to their presence.

They rode across the courtyard, the wind whistling within the enclosed space and sending ripples across the puddles. The oaken door to the tower was old and the metalwork pitted with rust. Forcing the door open with a metal bar would not be difficult.

Amaury rapped twice with the large knocker. At first there was no sign that anyone had heard, but eventually the door was swung partially open by a grizzled old man with a few straggly white hairs growing out of an otherwise bare pate. He looked them up and down and asked what they were doing there. He spoke in Latin. His manner was anything but cordial.

"We have come to see the canon," Amaury replied, hoping desperately that this crusty old curmudgeon was not himself the object of their quest.

"Canon Copernicus sees no one after the dinner hour," the servant grunted and began to close the door.

Amaury shot his hand to the door to hold it open. The *ancien* was not capable of exerting much pressure, and so released his grip. "Our message is quite urgent," Amaury said coldly. "If you don't let us in, you might not much longer have a canon to serve."

The servant considered this for a moment, then told them to wait while he checked. He did not invite them inside to escape the wind. Amaury and Hélène entered anyway. The old man trudged up a stairway set against the wall. He turned back for a moment, then frowned, shrugged, and kept going until he disappeared around a corner. Eventually, there was the sound of a knock at a door, then the creak of metal hinges. A few minutes later, the man reappeared around the corner of the staircase.

Refusing to move any further down the stairs, he bade them come up with one contemptuous flick of his wrist.

Hélène and Amaury looked at one another as they went up the stairs. It had not occurred to either of them that, on an errand to save a man's life, they would be unwelcome when they arrived.

They reached the landing on the second floor, but the old man was already halfway to the third and beckoned them to continue. At the top of the stairs the old man stopped at a partly opened door. Amaury hesitated, but the man nodded and cocked his head toward the room. It seemed only yesterday that Amaury had been similarly poised on the threshold of Beda's rooms at Montaigu. But it was a lifetime ago.

The man pushed the door open and walked in. Amaury and Hélène followed. Rather than the ascetic cavern of the Montaigu syndic, this room was open, inviting, and, from the first glance, utterly thrilling. The workplace of a scientist. An eight-foot triquetrum stood in one corner; an armillary, a series of concentric, graduated spheres used for astronomical calculations, in another. A bookshelf stood against the far wall; Amaury wanted to rush across and examine its contents.

A brightly polished trestle desk sat in front of the bookshelf, facing the door, flanked by two of the windows that ringed the room. Behind the desk sat another old man. He had an elongated face dominated by a large nose and even larger chin. His mouth was taut and straight, his hair gray and uncombed. Bushy white eyebrows overhung tired, deep-set eyes. He slouched in the seat; his breathing was deep and labored. He regarded his two visitors with a mixture of curiosity and irritation.

"To what do I owe this intrusion?" he asked in Latin, without pleasantries, his voice even and cold.

"You are Canon Copernicus?"

The man continued to regard them evenly. "I am Copernicus."

"I have read your work," Amaury said. "Briefly. By candlelight. At the risk of my life. I was stunned and exhilarated."

Copernicus tilted his head sideways, unmoved by the flattery. "You are competent to judge?" It was more an accusation than a question.

"I am."

"And you are?"

Amaury told Copernicus his name. The old man responded with a shrug and a shake of the head.

"And you have come here to praise me, Amaury de Faverges? Challenge me? Bring my work to the world?"

"No. I have come here to ensure that you are not lost to the world." Amaury glanced to the man who had let them in.

"Leave us, Anton," Copernicus said. "Leave me with these two." When the door closed, he said to Amaury, "Don't mind Anton. He sees very well to my needs but has little use for visitors. Nor, I confess, do I."

"I would not have come if it were not necessary."

"I thought you were thrilled by my work. And exhilarated. Not so thrilled and exhilarated to trudge willingly on to Frauenburg, though, eh? I don't blame you."

"I'm honored to meet you," Amaury offered.

Copernicus gestured to Hélène. "And her?"

"Without her, I would already be dead, and you would be as well, within a day."

"All right, young man. I'll hear your tale, melodramatic though it promises to be."

"I will be happy to provide whatever detail you require, but later. For now, suffice to say that a team of assassins has been dispatched from Paris to murder you and destroy your work. They will arrive by boat at any time. I am only grateful that I arrived first."

"Assassins? From Paris? You mean Rome, don't you?"

"No. Paris."

Dispatched by whom?"

"The Inquisition."

"Does the Holy Father know of this supposed plot?"

"No. Mathieu Ory, the French Inquisitor, acted on his own."

Copernicus leaned his elbows on the desk and placed his fingertips together. He spoke patiently, as if addressing a lunatic. "And you came to this information by . . ."

"Cardinal d'Aubuisson. Do you know him?"

"I know the name."

"Canon Copernicus, I realize that this all sounds preposterous—"

"At least you realize it."

"—but we've been traveling three weeks to warn you. Matters are quite urgent, I can assure you."

"Young man, I have been working on my theory for more than twenty years. Our definitions of urgency may well differ."

"At least take steps to protect yourself."

"Very well. I see there is no dissuading you. I'll have Anton ride to Elbing in the morning to fetch someone."

Amaury walked to the window that faced north over the bay. Three men were moving up the hill from the quay. One small and thin, two large and hulking. They walked astride one another, not speaking. A boat was moored at the end of the quay, larger than the fishing boats that dominated the harbor. Inside the boat, in a darkened cabin, awaiting news of the death of the astronomer, most certainly sat the twisted, charred figure of Johan Liebfreund.

"There's no time," Amaury said to Copernicus. "They're here."

XLVI

COPERNICUS PUSHED HIMSELF to his feet. He was strained in the movement. "Are you trying to tell me that the men who intend to murder me are strolling up the hill?"

"Yes. That is exactly what I'm telling you," Amaury replied. Copernicus was still not convinced that Amaury wasn't insane, but it wouldn't do to simply ignore a man who told you that killers were on their way. "Now please, canon, tell me how many ways one can get in here."

"Only the door you entered and the door to the battlements, one story down."

"Is the battlement door locked?"

"There is a drop bolt on the inside, like the one on the door you entered."

In other words, useless, Amaury thought. "And the entrance to the castle?"

"Only from the south. The other doors are kept locked."

"The cathedral?"

"All entry is through the courtyard."

"Is there anyone here who might help us?"

Copernicus shook his head. "Only acolytes and servants. The bishop and the other canons are elsewhere. The town is full of eelers and drunks."

"I want you to send someone to Elbing immediately for help."

"Anton."

"If you must." Amaury returned to the window for another look. The three had almost reached the small plaza in front of the north wall. Copernicus walked to the door and called for his servant. He moved with the leaden arms and legs of the aged and infirm. Anton was only slightly more spry, but listened to the instructions and then left as quickly as he could.

"Canon," Amaury said, "when I leave, I want you to bolt the door." He gestured to Hélène. "Madame will stay with you. Don't open it again for anyone but me."

"Where are you going?"

"I will be in the hall. I'll try to hold them off. If we can keep them outside, your servant may have time to fetch assistance."

"You said there were three. You are only one. You will certainly be killed."

"Perhaps. But they are not expecting anyone except an old man. If I can surprise them, I might shorten the odds."

"You are willing to die for me?"

"No, canon. I'm willing to die for your ideas."

"Then you really did read *De revolutionibus*."

"I told you I did."

"And you believe it is worth dying for?"

"Yes."

Hélène had moved to Amaury's side and was clutching his arm. "Don't, Amaury. There must be another way."

"I wish I could think of one. But if I simply stay in here, we lose the element of surprise and we'll be trapped. If I can kill one of them, maybe even two, you two might be able to barricade yourselves in here until help arrives. If the third man cannot get in easily, he might even flee."

"But what about you? About us?"

"We've come this far, Hélène. Don't lose hope now." He smiled. "I've discovered I'm more difficult to kill than I thought."

Hélène tried to smile in return, but could not. Tears were in her eyes. "If you don't return, I shall throw myself off the battlements."

"You can't. Heloise didn't."

"I believe you said in the field, 'We won't do that part.'"

Despite himself, Amaury smiled. "Hélène, I will come back to you. I don't know how, but I will."

Amaury checked his sword and dagger and stepped into the hall. After he heard the bolt drop behind him, he moved down the staircase. He placed himself against the inside wall just after a turn at a corner, so the invaders would not see him until the last possible moment.

How many would come up the stairs? One, to scout? Two? All three? Amaury waited for some time, candlelight shadows flickering on the staircase walls. Finally he heard a crack and then the door at the bottom creaked open. He braced himself against the inside wall. Soft footsteps could just be heard on the stone stairs. How many sets? Three? Probably. Certainly more than just one.

He listened for whispering but could hear nothing. These men had worked together long enough to communicate by gesture alone. He strained his ears, but could not be certain how close his adversaries had drawn. Footfalls were more distinct now. Yes, definitely more than one.

Amaury gripped the hilt of his sword, the leather feeling full in his sweaty hands. Still the sound of soft footsteps, but no talking. Much closer now. He breathed a prayer of forgiveness for his sins. They were almost upon him. When to jump out? Can't move too soon. They could avoid his first thrust. Or too late. Then they would be on him. He cursed that he had spent nine years in useless disputation when the skills he needed were to be found in the streets.

He could hear breathing echoing softly off the redbrick walls. Now? No. Wait. A few seconds more.

Now! Amaury leapt into the passage, sword out. But he had misjudged. The large man who had held Routbourg was beyond sword range. Amaury lunged but the man, though bearlike, was quick and easily avoided the thrust. His compatriot, the other brute, the one who had grabbed him in the alley, moved next to his mate. Both now had swords drawn. The first of the two advanced one step, keeping Amaury at bay. The other man pulled even with him. They were close together in the tight confines of the staircase, but Amaury knew he was not enough of a swordsman to kill both before they reached him. Maybe one, though. Amaury chose the first man up, closest to the inside wall. The assassins had read his thoughts, however, and shifted position so that any thrust from Amaury could be easily parried by his target.

Suddenly the man on the outside seemed to be wrenched backward. An arm was clearly visible around his throat. His dagger appeared in his left hand. He tried to spin but instead gave off a gurgled cry and fell backward down the stairs, the way he had come.

The first man, by reflex, turned his head to see what had befallen his comrade. Amaury did not hesitate, but immediately drove his sword into the man's midriff. And then again. The man turned back, too strong to fall. Amaury slashed at the man's wrist and sent his enemy's weapon skittering down the stairs. The man took one staggering step forward, his hands extended, trying to reach Amaury's throat. One more thrust stopped him. For a second he seemed suspended, then he turned and crashed down the stairs. The sword remained in his chest, pulling out of Amaury's hand as the man fell.

When Amaury reached the bottom, the man he had stabbed lay on his side, surely dead, Amaury's sword broken in half by the fall. The other attacker lay on the floor, faceup, on top of whoever had flung his arm about his throat. One look told Amaury he too was dead. Had old Anton saved him? It seemed incredible. Then whoever was lying underneath pushed the dead man away.

"You!"

Philippe Sévrier nodded perfunctorily, then looked to his side. Blood had seeped onto his cloak.

"Why . . . what are you doing here?" Amaury tightened his grip on his dagger.

"I came to protect the astronomer." Sévrier's eyes met his. "The same as you, I expect."

Amaury didn't know what to say.

"Ory sent me to kill you. By land, in case the boat was delayed."

"I don't understand," Amaury said, "but we don't have time for explanations. There were three of them."

Sévrier's eyes rolled upward at the same instant as Amaury's. "The battlements."

They both hurried up the stairs, Sévrier holding his side. The assassin had wounded him, but he was determined to keep moving. When they reached the second landing, the door that led to the battlements was open. Amaury bounded to the third floor. Sévrier was moving too slowly now to be of help. The skinny man was prying at the door with a short bar. He whirled, and suddenly his knife was in his hand.

Amaury wished for his sword but had only his dagger. His adversary lowered himself into a crouch, holding his knife loosely in an upturned right hand. He seemed to be inviting Amaury to move first. But he would be quick on the counterattack. This man had been fighting with knives since he was a child.

Suddenly the assassin lashed out, his right hand a blur of flesh and metal. Amaury jumped back just in time and the blade only nicked the sleeve of his tunic. The man smiled. Then he looked down the stairs. Sévrier had struggled halfway up. His knife was drawn as well.

The assassin retreated into a corner, a wall to his back on either side. Sévrier came two steps nearer. The assassin's eyes flicked quickly back and forth between his two adversaries. Choosing the weaker was simple. He flung himself toward the wounded Sévrier. Amaury dove across the landing, just able to get a hand on the assassin's ankle. The man was thrown off-balance. He tried to grab Sévrier for support, but Sévrier was able to avoid his grasp. The man's feet spun in the stairs and he began to fall, his body in an awkward twist. He clawed at the wall, trying for the handhold, but momentum carried him down. He tumbled backward, his head striking a stair with a crack. From there he kept falling until he stopped at a corner of the staircase, his face smacking the brick wall.

When Amaury got there, the man's head was at a 45-degree angle to the side. His neck had snapped. He stared up at Amaury through lifeless eyes, as had Henri Routbourg and Giles.

Giles. The wounded man on the landing had saved Amaury's life and taken the life of his friend. As if matters were not complicated enough. But there would be time to sort that out later. For the moment, there were other priorities.

Amaury knocked on the door of Copernicus's study and told Hélène it was he. She threw the door open and rushed into his arms.

"Oh, Amaury, I prayed from the moment the door closed. God has granted me a miracle."

He returned the hug briefly, but then told Hélène that they must attend to the man who had saved his life. Sévrier was leaning against the wall. When Hélène saw him, she gasped.

"But he's—"

"Yes. From Nérac. Fate, it seems, has thrown us together. We need to fashion something for his wound."

Amaury felt an arm on his shoulder. The astronomer shoved him aside.

"I'll fashion something for his wound, young man. I am a physician, you know."

"I didn't. I thought you were an astronomer. But I would be grateful."

"I'm not an astronomer. I consider myself a philosopher of astronomy. But we can talk about that later." He gestured for Sévrier to come inside and sit. Sévrier pulled back his clothing to reveal an angry wound about four inches long. Blood was flowing down his side.

"Lucky," Copernicus muttered, almost to himself. "No bubbling from the wound. Bloody but not serious." He instructed Hélène where to find cloth to use as a bandage, and told Amaury to fetch water from the well in the courtyard. When Amaury returned, Copernicus had almost stopped the bleeding. Several bloody cloths were on the floor at his feet. Sévrier was holding a folded cloth against the wound. It was red but not sodden.

"Warm water would be better," Copernicus said, "but cold will have to do." He dipped a clean cloth into the bucket and wiped the dried blood and dirt from the area.

"Now we will bandage it and apply a poultice to promote healing and prevent infection." Copernicus shuffled off to another room and eventually returned with another folded cloth, on which was smeared a gummy brown substance that gave off a stench as bad as a festering wound itself.

"What is that?" Amaury asked.

"I'll discuss heliocentrism with you, young man, but not medicine." He placed the cloth against the wound and wrapped another long length around Sévrier's ribs, tying it expertly when he was done.

"Well," he asked Sévrier, "how do you feel?"

Sévrier tentatively raised his arm. "Much better."

Copernicus nodded. "Of course."

"Thank you, canon."

"Do not remove the bandage for at least four days. The wound isn't deep, but air may well cause it to turn septic."

"Have you read the works of Paracelsus?" Amaury asked suddenly.

"That maniac? Why would one bother?"

Amaury considered for a moment telling Copernicus that, following the teachings of the maniac, he and Hélène had not contracted plague, but decided to hold his tongue.

Sévrier stood. He was undeniably improved.

"I have one more chore to attend to," Amaury said. "I've got to pay a visit to the boat in the harbor."

"I'm going with you," Sévrier insisted.

"Nonsense. There will be only one man on board and he's a . . . cripple. With his thugs eliminated, he could not be less of a threat."

"I'm coming all the same."

"Please, Amaury," Hélène said plaintively, "let him go. It cannot hurt to be safe."

Amaury shrugged. "Thank you. Your assistance is welcome."

Before they left, Amaury went to the battlements. Two short, crossed wooden poles that the man with the knife had used as a grappling hook were wedged in an embrasure. Amaury pulled up the rope that the man had used to scale the wall and left it inside. Then he set off with Sévrier to meet Liebfreund.

"Did you hear news of Castell'buono?" Amaury asked as they made their way down the stairs.

"Castell'buono is dead," Sévrier replied. "He died under torture at Angoulême."

Amaury sighed. "I'm truly sorry to hear of it," he said. "I realized too late that we were kindred spirits. I wish I could have saved him."

"You could not have saved him," Sévrier told him. "The priest had sent word ahead. He was arrested as he arrived at the city. He saved you, however. Me as well."

"Saved me? How?"

"I was told he held out for a very long time. Both of his arms and legs were broken and his eyes were put out before he finally capitulated. When he did, he told his inquisitor that you worked for the Lutherans and I was an Inquisition spy who had been sent to Paris by the priest to eliminate you."

"Why would he do that?"

"He assumed *you* were Ory's spy. He was correct, of course, at least then. He knew I would follow you to Paris and he wished me to be able to remain free to eliminate you. As a Lutheran, I would have been pursued. A messenger was immediately dispatched from Angoulême to Paris. He arrived soon after I was arrested. I had told Ory precisely the same tale as the messenger related—that I worked for the priest. What choice did I have? But Ory hadn't believed me. The messenger changed all that. Now Ory thought God had dropped me into his lap. He sent me in pursuit of you. When I realized that Ory truly wanted you dead, I knew that you were attempting to save the astronomer, not murder him. By now, of course, word will have arrived in Paris from Nérac giving my true identity, but I have no intention of returning to France."

"I understand." They had reached the courtyard. "I need to know about Giles Fabrizy."

Sévrier grasped himself about the chest. He flinched when he stretched the wound. "Giles Fabrizy? Why do you need to know about him?"

"He was my friend."

"*Your* friend? You mean from Montaigu?"

"Yes. From Montaigu."

"He worked for Ory as well. You knew that, didn't you? We all assumed that once he was . . . gone, Ory had just gone back to Montaigu for his replacement. You. We never suspected that Ory was going to all that trouble just so no one would suspect the whore."

"But you killed him. Stabbed him to death in an alley."

"Fabrizy would have betrayed us. Betrayed the astronomer up there. He *had* betrayed us. We had no choice. What . . . happened to him . . . was his own doing. You must see that. Do you think I *wanted* that assignment?"

Amaury interrupted. "How would he have betrayed the astronomer?"

"He stole the manuscript. The one you read. Hoess had obtained it—I'm not certain how—from someone in the Church secretly sympathetic to our cause. Then someone stole it. Hoess suspected Fabrizy. He devised a test. Sent him on an errand. Gave him the opportunity to betray us. And he did. He was on his way to Ory when . . . when he was stopped."

Amaury allowed the information to settle. Sévrier could not be blamed. Not really. When someone is under threat of torture or execution, how can he be culpable for an act of self-protection? But to absolve Sévrier completely—that would not do either. He could not allow Giles to have died a traitor's death.

"Giles had no intention of bringing the manuscript to Ory," Amaury told him.

"But of course he was going to Ory. Where else?"

"He was bringing the manuscript to me."

"You?" Sévrier shook his head fiercely. "That isn't possible. How can you know that?"

"He wrote to me, telling me of his intentions, on the back of a diagram taken from the manuscript. He knew of the importance of the discovery. He wanted to share it with me. To ask my advice. Vivienne brought the diagram to me after Giles was dead."

"My God," whispered Sévrier. "I murdered him for nothing." He leaned over and began to moan. Amaury felt a wave of reproach for torturing the poor devil, but Giles demanded retribution.

"You couldn't have known," Amaury said, fully aware that the words were hollow.

"Oh, my God, forgive me."

"Sévrier, you couldn't have known." Amaury spoke more sincerely now. "And let us not forget that without you, I would now be dead. And we saved the work. You saved the work. All that must be worth something. Balances the scales somewhat."

Sévrier nodded dumbly. Tears were on his cheeks. "I suppose."

"Come, Philippe." Amaury took Sévrier's elbow and led him toward the quay. "Let us go and balance the scales further."

XLVII

THE BOAT WAS ROCKING gently on the waters of the lagoon, tied fore and aft to the pier. It was a large, flat-bottomed craft, suitable for navigating the shallow waters of the river tributaries and the bay. With that construction, the cabin could not be belowdecks, but sat in the middle of the craft, windows on either side, with curtains drawn. It was easy to discern that none of the crew was aboard. They had most likely retired to the town to drink and whore. Or perhaps the three assassins had steered the boat themselves, so that no witnesses to their movements would remain after they had completed their task.

Amaury and Sévrier stepped onto the deck quietly, allowing themselves a moment to become accustomed to the movement, then walked silently to the cabin. Amaury pushed the door open. As in Paris, the room was in almost total darkness. The curtains that masked the windows were thick and long. Amaury surmised that Liebfreund had brought them on board himself. A single lantern, set on a shelf near the door, its wick almost fully retracted, provided only the most meager illumination. A table was set in the middle of cabin, behind which, encased in a cloak, sat the deformed Swiss. The gentle rocking of the boat sent the lantern to flickering, causing Liebfreund's grotesque features to take on a demonic air.

Amaury stepped into the cabin. He heard Sévrier gasp as he followed.

"Welcome, gentlemen." Liebfreund's speech had become raspier, more arduous. The journey had obviously been taxing. He evidenced no sign of surprise that Amaury and Sévrier had arrived instead of his henchmen.

Amaury halted just inside the door. Sévrier stood next to him, shaking so violently that Amaury could feel the vibrations. He must have felt he was in the presence of Satan himself.

"Please, Faverges," Liebfreund beckoned, "come and sit. Have some wine." He paused. "Your friend seems to be in need of it."

"No, thank you," Amaury replied.

"Why not? That you have arrived here would indicate that you have nothing more to fear from my associates. And you certainly have nothing to fear from me." Liebfreund placed his arms on the table and pushed himself erect. The effort required to raise himself to a standing position was almost more than the Swiss could muster. Amaury began, by instinct, to reach out to help the poor devil, but Liebfreund succeeded in pulling himself erect unaided.

The Swiss shuffled to the shelf on which the lantern sat and laboriously reached up to remove a carafe.

"If you intend to murder me, you can at least allow me a cup of wine first. As I mentioned, you are welcome to join me."

"I don't intend to murder you, Liebfreund." Liebfreund's movement had caused Amaury and Sévrier to move to the side, so that the table remained between them.

"No? What do you intend, then?" Liebfreund shuffled back to the table and placed the carafe upon it. Amaury and Sévrier continued to shift position so the table remained as a barrier. Liebfreund removed a cup from the shelf and placed it next to the carafe.

"The local count will not take kindly to the attempt on the old man's life. The French Inquisition holds little sway here."

Liebfreund nodded. The lantern was now behind him, leaving his charred face almost wholly in the dark. "I see. You will allow someone else to murder me so that you will not have to soil your own hands."

"What is done to you is not my affair. I had almost convinced myself to forgive you for Routbourg. As you said . . . justice. But now you come to destroy not a Lutheran, but a Catholic. One of your own."

"My own? Oh, Faverges, you know nothing at all. Catholic, Lutheran. It makes no difference. That man would introduce *discord*, more discord, plow the ground so those who walk in the footsteps of Routbourg, of Oecolampadius, might grow and flourish in the manure of his theories. Leaving him alive would be placing a torch in the hands of savages so that they may—" Liebfreund paused for a moment, his eyes drifting off to a place Amaury could never know. "Or perhaps they will decide not to execute me . . ."

Amaury suddenly realized that Liebfreund had maneuvered himself between the door and himself and Sévrier. But what of it?

Liebfreund took a step backward into the doorway, then reached up and pushed back his hood. Amaury and Sévrier stood transfixed. They were staring at a skull covered with what seemed to be only a thin layer of parchment. No hair. Holes where ears should have been. But his eyes, green and piercing, never wavered. He appeared as a creature from Hell.

"I would have allowed you to kill me. Welcomed it. But I cannot allow you *not* to kill me. I'm already dead, you see. My life ended in Basel. I have been only a spirit since, not truly human at all. I have often pondered what, in fact, I am. A phantom? An oddity? A walking corpse? Do you know? If you do, enlighten me. The soul continues to live when the body dies, but does the mind? It is not supposed to, yet it did for me. I had not the luxury of madness or death. Only the agony of awareness." Liebfreund shuffled closer to the shelf on which the lantern sat. The light fell on one side of his face, leaving the other in shadow. "And so I have pretended to exist. Deluded myself into believing that, even in this ghastly state, I had a purpose for remaining on Earth. That I was performing a service for God. But that is ended now. I will be exposed to the world as an object of ridicule. Something to evoke revulsion and derision. Laughter and screams from children. Some enterprising sort might even find a way to profit from public viewings of the creature.

"I believe I will spare myself all of that, gentlemen. I prefer to choose my own destiny. Of course, my choice would shock others." He raised one of his claws. "But I have no fear. Unlike you two, I can no longer feel pain." Then, with a swipe of his arm, he knocked over the lantern.

Man and cabin exploded in flames. Liebfreund must have poured some of the lantern fluid on his cloak and on the decks before they arrived. The Swiss, now fully ablaze, stood before the only door, rendering himself an impassable barrier. Flames filled the compartment. Amaury and Sévrier whirled about, looking for another exit. The heat was already close to unbearable. They ripped down the flaming curtains. The windows were small, but might provide an exit if they could squeeze through.

Sévrier grabbed a chair and broke the window on the right. The air rushing in fed the flames. Sévrier fell back, pushing Amaury into the opposite corner. Amaury thought to rush for the door, but Liebfreund had turned into a human torch. Whether he was still alive could not be discerned. Amaury saw two green eyes through the flames, seemingly lit by the fire, but he couldn't be certain if the vision was real or imagined.

There was no way out of the room. Breaking the other window would only feed the flames further. Liebfreund was to have his ultimate revenge.

Suddenly Amaury felt a hand around either of his arms. He found himself lifted off the ground, being aimed at the open window. In a moment he was halfway through, teetering on the window frame at the waist, a fulcrum between safety and Hell. He grabbed frantically for the outside wall as a lever to push himself through. The wall was horribly hot, but he succeeded in propelling himself out. He sprawled on the deck for only a second, then leapt to his feet. He was at the window, but the flames now filled the cabin and were burning the outside walls.

"Sévrier!" he screamed. "Here! Take my hand!"

There was no reply. Amaury tried to look inside, but the heat was overpowering and drove him back. He tried again but could get no closer. He heard himself screaming Sévrier's name, pointlessly and in despair. Finally he was forced to accept that there was no hope. The deck had begun to burn and would soon engulf him. The plank to the wharf was on the other side of the boat. No chance to reach it now.

Amaury took one last look back to the cabin where the man who had taken Giles' life had just died saving his, and dove from the boat into the bay.

XLVIII

COPERNICUS TIED the last bandage around Amaury's hands. "That should feel better. Milk, egg whites, and honey. You are remarkably fortunate, young man. Your friend saved your life."

"My friend?" Amaury had thought of Sévrier as many things, but not that. But how else to describe one who dies for you? "Yes, he did."

"These dressings should be changed daily. Do you intend to stay here for any length of time?" The tone of the question left no doubt that it was not an invitation.

The sting of the burns was already abating. Copernicus had told him that none had done more than singe the flesh. Seconds more in that inferno and the result would have been far different. If Liebfreund had been granted those seconds in Basel, the course of all their lives would have been altered.

"I hadn't decided how long to stay," Amaury told Copernicus. "I was hoping that you might share some of your work with me."

"Share? An ambiguous word."

"I have traveled quite some distance to learn more of your theories."

Copernicus frowned. "But you came uninvited."

"I know that, canon. But if I had waited for an invitation, you would not still be alive."

"I have worked alone for twenty years, young man. I have shared my work only with a few at selected moments. I have no intention of taking on a partner now."

"I would never presume to be a partner."

"I have no need for an assistant either. Or an acolyte. Or even a cook. I dislike company. I'm sorry to disappoint you, but I am what I am, not what you would have me be."

"I would have you be a brilliant astronomer. You are that."

"No, I'm not. An astronomer could not have chosen a less appropriate spot than this. Nine nights out of ten, clouds or fog obscure the heavens. I take sightings when I can, but for the most part, I have relied on the tables of Ptolemy or King Alphonso."

"Without observation, how was this great work fashioned?"

"Why does one need to observe in order to imagine? Observation is a mechanical act. Anton could do it. Or you. It is what one does with observation that matters most."

"I don't understand."

"Heliocentrism is not new. Ideas seldom are. With perhaps a few rare exceptions, all of us merely extrapolate. Push forward in small increments what has come before. Aristarchus postulated heliocentrism before the birth of our Lord Jesus Christ. Even Christians have put forth the notion. Nicholas of Cusa espoused heliocentrism a century ago, but Regiomontanus insisted geocentrism was correct. Others have considered the question since. But no one applied rigor to disproving Ptolemy's construct, so it was never seriously challenged.

"Twenty years ago, High Pontiff Leo summoned me to Rome. The calendar by which Christendom determined the seasons was becoming ridiculously skewed. If the trend continued, the day of the Resurrection would one day fall in midsummer. The pope asked me to study the problem. I soon realized that the fault lay not in the calendar, but in the astronomical system on which it was based. Studying the problem without preconception, I realized that Ptolemy's Celestial Pearl was merely a hypothesis, an axiom, not a conclusion based on data. He began with Aristotle's notion that the Earth was at the center of the universe, and then fit the data to suit the conclusion. It never occurred to Ptolemy to alter his assumptions and allow the data to speak for itself. I did."

"Your theory will change Christianity forever. Just to witness the events of the past months will attest to that."

"Yes, I fear you are correct. That some have already died because of my work pains me. That others are certain to die is even worse. That is why I intend to hold my theories to my own bosom, at least for the present."

"You do not intend to publish *De revolutionibus*?"

"Not until I am ready. My work is not complete."

"But what I saw was wondrous. It must be shared with the world."

"Why? Because you are impatient to see it? I have been toiling at this problem for more than twenty years. I will not consent to have it produced for public consumption until it is precisely as I wish. And that is not yet."

"But men and women have died to protect you. Philippe Sévrier only an hour ago. To protect your work so that it is not relegated to oblivion. I myself have been near death more than once, as has Madame d'Artigny. We watched four people burned at the stake for it in Paris. How can you now refuse to do what so many have sacrificed for?"

"I appreciate what you have done for me, young man, but I never solicited your aid. Nor anyone else's. I don't see how I can be obligated to publish the results of *my* work before I deem it proper."

"But if others come—"

"I will take steps to better protect myself, certainly. But if it is God's will that my work is destroyed, I can do nothing."

"You are a scientist. How can you speak of God's will as denying the advancement of knowledge?"

"Because I am a scientist, I know that God may will anything He wishes."

Copernicus refused to speak of the matter further. The following morning, Amaury and Hélène prepared to leave. Old Anton, who had returned from his errand, informed them that the canon did not eat breakfast, but he had instructed the cook to prepare them a large meal of eggs, meat, and cheese. They ate in silence, Amaury waiting to see if Copernicus would make an appearance to bid them farewell. He did not.

Amaury and Hélène left the castle to return to Elbing, where they would obtain provisions and an escort for the journey out of Poland. The sky had cleared and they rode through open plains warmed by the spring sun.

For a long time, they did not speak. Finally Amaury broke the silence.

"I killed Sévrier," he said softly. "I told him that Giles Fabrizy, the man he murdered for fear of betrayal to the Inquisition, was not on his way to Ory, but rather to bring Copernicus's work to me. That he had slain a man for nothing. I thought Giles deserved that much vengeance. But now . . . Sévrier died for me, Hélène. Out of despair for his act."

"You did not kill Sévrier," Hélène said firmly. "He murdered a man, Amaury. And he would have murdered you. Probably me as well. He repented for a death by saving a life. God would think that just, I believe."

Amaury considered this. "But even so, it was all for nothing. The knowledge will die here with that stubborn Pole. He has made a discovery that will alter the course of Christianity. Change the way Man views his Church and his world. With so much at stake, how can the man refuse to publish his work?"

"He wants the theory to be perfect. After twenty years, I suppose he has a right to that."

"But he's old. You saw how frail he was. What if he dies?"

"Then you could publish it," Hélène replied. "Now that you know what to look for, you could easily reproduce his work."

"No, I could never do that. Not even in his name."

"But you could take up where he left off. Possibly even improve upon what he did. No man knows everything."

Amaury mulled over the prospect, then remembered his talk in the rain with Rabelais. "Yes. Perhaps I could. Yes. And I know just the place to do it. Someplace with clear nights to take observations. Not like Frauenburg. In the mountains. A beautiful spot."

Hélène reined in her horse. "Do you mean Savoy?"

Amaury stopped next to her. "Yes. We're going home, Hélène."

"But what of your father? You will still be Amaury de Faverges."

"Legitimacy will not make me a better scientist. Or a better man."

"Will you see him?"

"That will be his decision. I won't hide my presence. If he wishes to acknowledge me, I will welcome his overtures. If not, I will live life quite happily with you and our children."

"Our children. To have children with you, Amaury. I hope I'm not too old."

"Too old? Ridiculous. We can have ten children."

Hélène laughed. "Ten?" Then she said, "Amaury, the journey was not wasted. You saved Copernicus's life. That was the most important thing. Who knows? Perhaps he will publish after all."

Amaury considered the nature of the man they had just left. Stubborn perhaps, but proud as well. "Yes," he said finally. "Do you know, in the end, I believe he will."

Author's Note

For some time, I've wanted to do a book on the impact of Copernican astronomy not on science as much as the fundamental assumptions under which Man and Church interacted in post-Renaissance Europe. The changes wrought by heliocentrism, I believe, led directly to the Enlightenment and the rise of democracy. The reason I chose fiction was I thought it a better vehicle to explore the extremely unsettling nature of the events surrounding the coming of the new science and, of course, to try to spin an entertaining yarn.

Amaury de Faverges is fictional, but the travails of a student at Collège de Montaigu are not. The college itself is precisely as described, both physically and in terms of the conditions under which the students toiled in order to complete the fifteen-year course leading to a theology doctorate. Both Erasmus and Calvin studied at Montaigu, neither staying more than two years. Although I wish I had thought up the line, a Parisian wit did indeed refer to the school as "the very cleft between the buttocks of Mother Theology."

Illegitimate sons of high-born fathers were often steered into the Church, and the importance to a noble bastard of receiving a decree of legitimacy from the pope was not overstated—certainly sufficient motive to undertake a dangerous mission for the Inquisition.

Both Mathieu Ory and Noël Beda were real and drawn accurately from records of their activities. All the incidents attributed to both men, beyond those directly related to the plot, actually occurred. Ory was Inquisitor of France during the period that *The Astronomer* takes place and was, as far as can be determined, every bit as ruthless and vindictive as described. His network of spies and informers pervaded Paris. Beda was syndic during the period noted and his imprecation against Luther was taken directly from a letter he penned to the king. Beda quite definitely felt himself superior to François and once, famously, had a Lutheran noble under the king's protection, Louis de Berquin, burned at the stake while François was on a hunting excursion. He was eventually exiled from Paris for his excesses.

François I was as described—man-child as king. The anecdote about him substituting his sons as hostage and exulting, "I am king again!" on his return to France is true, as is his interest in fashion and the beautification of Paris. His dalliance with mistresses was legendary, as was his rivalry with Emperor Charles V. Although I have moved up the Affair of the Placards from October and November 1534 to pace the narrative, the affair did take place and was, in fact, initiated after François found one of the placards tacked to his bedroom door in Amboise. After the affair, France was to remain a Catholic country. In 1572, when Protestantism was rising once more, Charles IX ordered another, even bloodier purge, which became known as the Saint Bartholomew's Day Massacre, in which four thousand Protestants were slaughtered. François' indecision as to which religion to embrace for France is accurate. Not devout, at least by the standards of the day, François saw the Catholic-Lutheran conflict primarily in political terms.

The geography of Paris is taken from period sources, particularly the "Plan de Bâle," a remarkably detailed map of the city in the 1530s, produced in 1552 by Olivier Truschet and Germain Hoyau. Every street was delineated, as was every major building. The Louvre is reproduced with the adjacent tower intact, although François had the tower demolished in 1527. He would demolish the fortress itself later in the decade and replace it with the beginnings of the stunning palace that now houses the Mona Lisa (which François had brought to Paris as a spoil of war, along with Leonardo).

Marguerite of Navarre is also as described, as is her enlightened court at her palace in Nérac. She sheltered Protestants, including Gerard Roussel, and France's greatest writers, artists, and thinkers—including Rabelais—were welcome in her court. After a son died in infancy, she dressed simply and always wore black.

Although Johan Liebfreund is fictional, the riot in Basel was as described, as was the role of Oecolampadius in inciting the mob. Many were killed and houses and churches were burned in the conflagration. Erasmus, although having long since left the city, wrote scathingly both of the incident and his old assistant's role in stoking the ire of the mob.

Jean Calvin is also as described, and in 1534 did sneak back into Paris for a theological debate only to have his opponent, Michael Servetus, not show up. It caused enmity between the two and was a factor in Servetus being burned at the stake in Geneva in 1553.

Copernicus's rooms at the castle at Frauenburg (now Frombork), on the Baltic in northern Poland, were drawn from photographs and descriptions from the Copernicus Museum.

The triquetrum was a commonly used astronomical instrument of the period, although opinion differs as to whether or not one was employed by Copernicus. The two diagrams that give Amaury the clue to the puzzle are taken respectively from *De revolutionibus* and the *Almagest*.

Copernicus, of course, finally did agree to publish *De revolutionibus* in 1543, the year he died. The finished book was brought to his bedside just hours before his death by his assistant, Georg Rheticus, but whether or not Copernicus could appreciate the volume is unknown. By then he was only semiconscious and nearly blind.

The impact of heliocentrism was, of course, both scientifically and theologically immense. Giordano Bruno was burned at the stake for it, and Galileo was forced before the Inquisition for espousing the theory. But in the end science could not be suppressed. As Amaury came to understand, the progression of knowledge is inexorable.